THE DISCIPLES OF APOLLO

THE **DISCIPLES** OF **APOLLO**

THE BEST SHORT STORIES OF ERIC BROWN

ERIC BROWN

THE DISCIPLES OF APOLLO
THE BEST SHORT STORIES OF ERIC BROWN
Copyright © Eric Brown 2019

COVER & ENDPAPER ARTWORK
Copyright © Ben Baldwin 2019

Published in September 2019 by PS Publishing Ltd. by arrangement with the author. All rights reserved by the author. The right of Eric Brown to be identified as Author of this Work has been asserted by him in accordance with the Copyright, Designs and Patents Act 1988.

FIRST EDITION

ISBN
978-1-786363-73-2

Design & Layout by Michael Smith
Printed and bound in England by T. J. International

PS Publishing Ltd
Grosvenor House, 1 New Road
Hornsea, HU18 1PG, England

editor@pspublishing.co.uk
www.pspublishing.co.uk

CONTENTS

Introduction

I'VE BEEN WRITING SHORT STORIES NOW FOR FORTY-FOUR YEARS, AND I've been selling them for thirty-two. During those first twelve years—let's call it my apprenticeship—I wrote a couple of hundred tales which never saw the light of day. They were dreadful. Most of them I didn't even bother to type out (I wrote longhand back then), and those that I did type and send to magazines were rejected pretty quickly, and rightly so. During those dozen years I also wrote about twenty short novels, each in the region of fifty thousand words. I read a lot of Ace Double novels at the time, and thought that this was the required length of *all* novels. I submitted a couple of these novels to various places in the UK and US, and they were rejected, too. I also contacted an editor in London outlining an ambitious plan I had to write a dozen colony novels. The editor was John Jarrold, who many years later was to become my agent. John must have laughed at the naïve presumption of the tyro who thought that any publisher would be in the slightest bit interested in a dozen short novels by a previously unpublished writer. I did write five of the series, before moving on to other things. An idea in one of them was to become the central conceit of my first novel, *Meridian Days*, in 1992. But I jump ahead of myself.

In 1985, I began submitting stories to the British SF magazine *Interzone*. I think I had around half a dozen rejections before I sold them "Krash-Bangg Joe and the Pineal-Zen Equation", quickly followed by a couple of others, in 1987. That year I spent in Greece, running a youth hostel on Crete, and while there I received a letter from an agent (not John) asking if he might represent me. And did I have any novels he might look at? We met on my return to the UK, and I told him that I didn't have a novel I was happy with, but that I could bundle up a collection of short tales. Now this was in the day—long gone, sadly—when a major publisher would risk their neck on a collection by an unknown writer. Pan Macmillan did so, and wanted to see a follow-up novel. *The Time-Lapsed Man and Other Stories* came out in 1990, followed by the novel two years later. From then on I've published an average of five short stories a year, and I still write them—even though the market is shrinking and the rate of payment is on average lower now than what it was back then.

So why do I write short stories?

Because I love doing so. Because from initial idea to completion can be as little as a day. Because it's possible to explicate a single idea, with a character or two, in a few thousand words of exerted effort. Because editors still want them. Because, although I'd earn more working at a "proper" job rather than spending a few days writing a tale that might earn me between zero pounds or a hundred or so, the satisfaction of creation—the release of endorphins within my cranium—is greater than the buzz I get from working at a "proper" job, or even writing novels, which is a laborious slog.

The fifteen stories gathered here were selected from 150 published tales spanning a period of thirty years. I chose these particular stories because they're my favourites—they work for me on an emotional level, and also they are pure "story." They're not just character studies, nor just simple "ideas" stories; they're not vignettes, nor merely mood pieces, and they're not in any way experimental (though I've written all of the above). They have a beginning, a middle, and an end. They're traditional in that they present a character or characters in a certain dramatic situation, with their wanting or needing something, and the story is about the working-out of their desire, or need, or dilemma. There are twists along the way, and reversals of fortune, revelations, and conceptual breakthroughs (science fiction is particularly good at this), and always, I like to think, a satisfying dénouement. Now this doesn't necessarily mean that the characters always get what they want, or that the endings are always happy, but that the finale is a complete emotional and intellectual culmination of the situation set up in the story.

I'm less influenced these days by what I read—I suppose I've been writing long enough to be confident in my own ability—but in the early days I was influenced by the writers I loved: Robert Silverberg, H. G. Wells, early William Gibson, Bob Shaw, and Michael G. Coney. I still reread and love Michael's work. He's sadly neglected now, but he wrote the BSFA award-winning novel *Hello Summer, Goodbye*, which I urge you to read, as well as his other fine novels and dozens of excellent, beautifully crafted, and moving short stories. (And I had the honour of collaborating with him on what would be his last published work, the long story "The Trees of Terpsichore 3", which appeared in *Spectrum SF 8.*)

Over the years I've written homages to and pastiches of my favourite writers, including Wells, Verne, Chesterton, Bukowski, and Simak. These have been technical exercises, the coming together of an idea that was admirably suited to the style or approach of a certain author. I've included one of these—"Life Beyond...", an homage to Simak—in this collection.

So there we are. I'll cease my rambling and let you begin, and hopefully enjoy, the fruits of my thirty years at the keyboard.

Eric Brown
Cockburnspath
May 2019

THE DISCIPLES OF APOLLO

*Dedicated to the
memory of my
Mother and Father,
with love*

THE TIME-LAPSED MAN

The idea for "The Time-Lapsed Man" came while I was walking in the Lake District. Across the valley, about a mile away, I saw the tiny figure of a farmer hammering in a fencepost. A fraction of a second later the sounds of his labour reached me. How about, I thought, a story about someone whose sense of sound is increasingly delayed, so he hears things that occurred in the past? All very well, but a bit weak. Then it occurred to me to extend the idea and have all his senses retarded, and to set it in my Engineman future, and the story was born.

THE TIME-LAPSED MAN

THORN WAS NOT IMMEDIATELY AWARE OF THE SILENCE.
As he lay in the tank and watched the crystal cover lift above him, he was still trying to regain some measure of the unification he had attained during the three months in flux. For that long—though it had seemed a timeless period to Thorn—he had mind-pushed his ship between the stars: for that long he had been one with the vastness of the nada-continuum.

As always when emerging from flux, Thorn sensed the elusive residuum of the union somewhere within him. As always, he tried to regain it and failed; it diminished like a haunting echo in his mind. Only in three months, on his next shift, would he be able to renew his courtship with the infinite. Until then his conscious life would comprise a series of unfulfilled events; a succession of set pieces featuring an actor whose thoughts were forever elsewhere. Occasionally he would be allowed intimations of rapture in his dreams, only to have them snatched away upon awakening.

Some Enginemen he knew—in fact the majority of those from the East—subscribed to the belief that in flux they were granted a foretaste of Nirvana. Thorn's Western pragmatism denied him this explanation. He favoured a more psychological rationale—though in the immediate period following flux he found it difficult to define exactly a materialistic basis for the ecstasy he had experienced.

He eased himself up and crossed the chamber. It was then that he noticed the absence of sound. He should have been able to hear the dull drone of the auxiliary burners; likewise his footsteps, and his laboured breathing after so long without exercise. He rapped on the bulkhead. He stepped into the shower and turned on the water-jet. He made a sound of pleasure as the hot water needled his tired skin. Yet he heard nothing. The silence was more absolute than any he had experienced before.

7

He told himself that it was no doubt some side-effect of the flux. After more than fifty shifts, a lifetime among the stars, this was his first rehabilitation problem, and he was not unduly worried. He would go for a medical if his hearing did not return.

He stepped under the blow-dryer, donned his uniform, and left the chamber. Through the lounge viewscreen he could see the lights of the spaceport. He felt a jarring shudder as the stasis-grid grabbed the ship and brought it down. He missed the familiar diminuendo of the afterburn, the squeal of a hundred tyres on tarmac. The terminal ziggurat hove into sight. The ship eased to a halt. Above the viewscreen a strip-light pulsed red, sanctioning disembarkation. It should have been accompanied by a voice welcoming ship personnel back to Earth, but Thorn heard nothing.

As always he was the first to leave the ship. He passed through checkout, offering his card to a succession of bored port officials. Normally he might have waited for the others and gone for a drink; he preferred to spend his free time with other Enginemen, and pilots and mechanics, as if the company of his colleagues might bring him closer to that which he missed most. This time, though, he left the port and caught a flyer to the city. He would seek the medical aid he needed in his own time, not at the behest of solicitous colleagues.

He told the driver his destination; unable to hear his own voice, he moved his lips again. The driver nodded, accelerated. The flyer banked between towerpiles, lights flickering by in a mesmerising rush.

They came down in the forecourt of his stack. Thorn climbed out and took the upchute to his penthouse suite. This was the first time he had arrived home sober in years. Alcohol helped to ease the pain of loss; sober, he was horribly aware of his material possessions, mocking his mortality and his dependence upon them. His suite might have been described as luxurious, but the blatant utility of the furnishings filled him with nausea.

He poured himself a Scotch and paused by the piano. He fingered the opening notes of Beethoven's "Pathétique", then sat down in his recliner by the wall-window and stared out. In the comforting darkness of the room, with the lights of the city arrayed below him, he could make-believe he was back aboard his ship, coming in for landing.

Of course, if his hearing never returned . . .

He was sweating at the thought of never being able to flux again. He wondered if he would be able to bluff his way through the next shift.

—— · ——

He was on his second drink, twenty minutes later, when a sound startled him. He smiled to himself, raised his glass in a toast to his reflection in the window. He spoke but he could not hear his words.

He heard another sound and his stomach lurched with sickening confusion. He called out in silence. Yet he could hear something.

He heard footsteps, and breathing, and then a resounding *clang*. Then he heard the high-pressure hiss of the hot water and an exclamation of pleasure. His own exclamation. He heard the roar of the blow-dryer, then the rasp of material against his skin; the quick whirr of the sliding door and the diminishing note of the afterburners, cutting out.

Thorn forced himself to say something; to comment and somehow bring an end to this madness. But his voice made no sound. He threw his glass against the wall and it shattered in silence.

Then he was listening to footsteps again; his own footsteps, as they passed down the connecting tube from the ship to the terminal building. He heard tired acknowledgements from the port officials, then the hubbub of the crowded foyer.

He sat rigid, listening to that which by rights he should have heard one hour ago.

He heard the driver's question, then his own voice; he stated his destination in a drunken slur, then repeated himself. He heard the whine of turbos, and later the hatch opening, then more footsteps, the grind of the upchute.

There was a silence then. He thought back one hour and realised he had paused for a time on the threshold, looking into the room he called home and feeling sickened. He could just make out the sound of his own breathing, the distant hum of the city.

Then the gentle notes of Beethoven's "Pathétique".

The rattle of glass on glass.

He remained in the recliner, unable to move, listening to the sound of his time-lapsed breathing, his drinking when he wasn't drinking.

Later he heard his delayed exclamation, the explosion of his glass against the wall.

He pushed himself from the recliner and staggered over to the vidscreen. He hesitated, his hand poised above the keyboard. He intended to contact the company medic, but almost against his will, he found himself tapping out the code he had used so often in the past.

She was a long time answering. He looked at his watch. It was still early, not yet seven. He was about to give up when the screen flared into life. Then he was

9

looking at Caroline Da Silva, older by five years but just as attractive as he remembered. She stared at him in disbelief, pulling a gown to her throat.

Then her lips moved in obvious anger, but Thorn heard nothing—or, rather, he heard the sound of himself chugging Scotch one hour ago.

He feared she might cut the connection. He leaned forward and mouthed what he hoped were the words: *I need you, Carrie. I'm ill. I can't hear. That is—*

He broke off, unsure how to continue.

Her expression of hostility altered; she still looked guarded, but there was an air of concern about her now. Her lips moved, then she remembered herself and used the deaf facility. She typed: Is your hearing delayed, Max?

He nodded.

She typed: Be at my surgery in one hour.

They stared at each other for a long moment, as if to see who might prove the stronger and switch off first.

Thorn shouted: *What the hell's wrong with me, Carrie? Is it something serious?*

She replied, forgetting to type. Her lips moved, answering his question with silent words.

Thorn yelled: *What the hell do you mean?*

But Caroline had cut the connection.

Thorn returned to his recliner. He reflected that there was a certain justice in the way she had cut him off. Five years ago, their final communication had been by vidscreen. Then it had been Thorn who had severed the connection, effectively cutting her out of his life, inferring without exactly saying so that she was no match for what he had found in flux.

Caroline's question about the time-lapse suggested that she knew something about his condition. He wondered—presuming his illness was a side-effect of the flux—if she was aware of the irony of his appeal for help.

One hour later, Thorn boarded a flyer. Drunk and unable to hear his own words, he had taken the precaution of writing the address of the hospital on a card. He passed this to the driver, and as the flyer took off he sank back in his seat.

He closed his eyes.

Aurally, he was in the past now, experiencing the sounds of his life that were already one hour old. He heard himself leave the recliner, cross the room and type the code on the keyboard. After a while he heard the crackle of the screen and Caroline's, "Doctor Da Silva", followed by an indrawn breath of surprise.

"I need you, Carrie. I'm ill. I can't hear. That is..." Thorn felt ashamed at how pathetic he had sounded.

Then he heard Caroline's spoken reply, more to herself, before she bethought herself to use the keyboard and ask him if his hearing was delayed. "Black's Syndrome," she had said.

Now, in the flyer, Thorn's stomach lurched. He had no idea what Black's Syndrome was, but the sound of it scared him.

Then he heard his one-hour-past-self say, "What the hell's wrong with me, Carrie? Is it something serious?" The words came out slurred, but Caroline had understood.

She had answered: "I'm afraid it is serious, Max. Get yourself here in one hour, okay?"

And she had cut the connection.

Caroline Da Silva's surgery was part of a large hospital complex overlooking the bay. Thorn left the flyer in the landing lot and made his way to the west wing. The sound of the city, as heard from his apartment, played in his ears.

He moved carefully down interminable corridors. Had he been less apprehensive about what might be wrong with him, and about meeting Caroline again after so long, he might have enjoyed the strange sensation of seeing one thing and hearing another. It was like watching a film with the wrong soundtrack.

He found the door marked "Dr Da Silva," knocked and stepped inside. Caroline was the first person he saw in the room. For a second, he wondered how the flux had managed to lure him away from her, but only for a second. She was very attractive, with the calm elliptical face of a ballerina, the same graceful poise. She was caring and intelligent, too—but the very fact of her physicality bespoke to Thorn of the manifest impermanence of all things physical. The flux promised, and delivered, periods of blissful disembodiment.

Only then did Thorn notice the other occupants of the room. He recognised the two men behind the desk. One was his medic at the Line, and the other his commanding officer. Their very presence suggested that all was not well. The way they regarded him, with direct stares devoid of emotion, confirmed this.

A combination of drink, shock, and fear eased Thorn into unconsciousness.

He awoke in bed in a white room. To his right a glass door gave onto a balcony, and all he could see beyond was the bright blue sky. On the opposite wall was a rectangular screen, opaque to him but transparent, he surmised, to observers in the next room.

Electrodes covered his head and chest.

He could hear the drone of the turbos as the flier carried him towards the hospital. He sat up and called out what he hoped was: *Caroline! Carrie!*

He sank back, frustrated. He watched an hour tick by on the wall clock, listening to the flyer descend and his own footsteps as the Thorn-of-one-hour-ago approached the hospital. He wondered if he was being watched through the one-way window. He felt caged.

He stared out at the sky. In the distance he could see a big starship climb on a steep gradient. He heard himself open the surgery door, and Caroline's voice. "Ah, Max."

Then—unexpectedly, though he should have been aware of its coming—silence. This was the period during which he was unconscious. He glanced back at the sky, but the starship had phased out and was no longer visible.

Thorn tried not to think about his future.

Caroline arrived thirty minutes later. She carried a sketchpad and a stylus. She sat on a plastic chair beside the bed, the pad on her lap. She tried to cover her concern with smiles, but Thorn was aware of tears recently shed, the evidence of smudged makeup. He had seen it many times before.

How long will I be in here? he asked.

Caroline chewed her lower lip, avoiding his eyes. She began to speak, then stopped herself. Instead, she wrote on the sketchpad and held it up: A week or two, Max. We want to run a few tests.

Thorn smiled to himself. *What exactly is this Black's Syndrome?* he asked, with what he hoped was the right degree of malicious sarcasm.

He was pleased with Caroline's shocked expression.

How do you know that? she scribbled.

You mentioned it over the vidscreen, Thorn told her. *I didn't hear it until I was coming here. What is it, Carrie?*

She paused, then began writing. Thorn read the words upside down: Black—an Engineman on the Taurus Line out of Varanasi. After fifty shifts he developed acute sensory time-lapse. It's a one-in-a-thousand malady. We don't know exactly what causes it, but we suspect it's a malfunction in the tank leads that retards inter-neuron activity.

She paused, then held up the message.

Thorn nodded. *I've read it. So?*

She turned to a blank page, stylus poised.

How long did he last? Thorn asked, bitterly. *When did the poor bastard die?*

Quickly she wrote: He's still alive, Max.

Thorn was surprised, relieved. If the present condition was the extent of Black's Syndrome, then what was to prevent him fluxing again?

He wondered at Caroline's tears. If his disease was only this minor, then why all the emotion?

Then he thought he understood.

When can I leave, Carrie? When can I get back to the flux?

He was watching the pad, waiting for a reply. When he looked up he saw that she was crying, openly this time.

He laughed. *You thought you had me, didn't you? Discharged from the Line, your own little invalid to look after and pamper. You can't stand the thought that I'll recover and flux again, can you?*

Despite her tears she was scribbling, covering page after page with rapid, oversized scrawl.

When she came to the end she stabbed a vicious period, ripped the pages out, and flung them at him. She ran from the room, skittling her chair on the way. Thorn watched her, a sudden sense of guilt excavating a hollow in his chest.

His gaze dropped to the crumpled pages. He picked them up and read:

Acute *sensory* time-lapse. Not just hearing. Everything. In a few days your taste and smell will go the same way. Then your vision. You'll be left only with the sensation of touch in the "present." Everything else will be lapsed.

It went on like this for a few more pages, the handwriting becoming increasingly erratic. Most of it reiterated the few known facts and Caroline's observations of Black's decline. On the last page she had simply written: I loved you, Max.

Thorn smoothed the pages across his lap. He called for Caroline again and again, but if she heard she ignored him. He wanted to apologise, ask what might happen to him. He tried to envisage the sensation of having all his senses time-lapsed save for that of touch, but the task was beyond his powers of perception.

He lay back and closed his eyes. Later he was startled by the sound of his voice, his cruel questions. He heard Caroline's breathless sobs, the squeak of the stylus, a murmured, "I loved you..." to accompany the written assurance. He heard her run crying from the room, the chair tumble, the door slam shut.

Then all he could hear was the sound of his breathing, and the muffled, routine noises of the hospital. For the first time in hours the sounds he heard were synchronised with what he could see.

He slept.

On the morning of his third day in hospital, Thorn's senses of taste and smell went the way of his hearing. This further time-lapse dashed any hope he might have had that Caroline's diagnosis had been mistaken.

He had not seen Caroline since her hurried departure on the first day. He had been examined and tested by medical staff who went about their business in silence, as if they were aware of his outburst at Caroline and were censoring him for it. On the third morning in hospital, a nurse brought him his breakfast.

He began eating, and soon realised that he could neither taste nor smell the bacon and eggs or the coffee, which was black and no doubt strong.

He finished his meal. He watched the nurse return and remove the tray, sank back, and waited.

Two hours later he heard the sound of the trolley being rolled in, the rattle of knife and fork. Then the taste of bacon, then egg yolk, filled his mouth. He inhaled the aroma of the coffee, tasted it on his tongue. He closed his eyes and savoured the sensation. It was the only pleasurable effect of this strange malaise so far.

Then he sat up as something struck him. *Two hours!* The delay between eating the food and tasting it had been two hours! Likewise the sound of the nurse's arrival.

If his hearing, taste and smell became delayed at the rate of two hours every three days—then what would it be like in a week, say, or a month or a year?

And what of his eyesight? How would he cope with seeing something that had occurred hours, days, even weeks ago? He resolved to find out what had happened to Black, how he was coping. He sat up and called for Caroline.

She did not show herself for another three days.

Thorn was attended by an efficient platoon of medics. They seemed to rush through their duties with a casual indifference, as if he had ceased to exist, or as if they assumed that his senses had retarded to such an extent that he existed alone in a bubble of isolation. On more than one occasion he had asked whether he could be cured, how much worse it might become, what had happened to Black?

14

But they used the fact that he could not immediately hear them as an excuse to ignore him, avoiding not only his words but also his eyes.

On the morning of his sixth day in hospital, he awoke to silence and ate his tasteless breakfast. The sound of his waking, of the hospital coming to life around him, the taste of his breakfast—all these things would come to him later. He wondered if he could time it so that he tasted his breakfast at the same time as he ate his lunch?

He waited, and it was four hours later when he heard the sound of his breathing as he awoke, then tasted the toast and marmalade.

Later, a nurse removed the electrodes from his head and chest. She opened the door to the balcony and held up a card which read:

Would you like to go out for some air?

Thorn waited until the nurse had left, shrugged into a dressing gown and stepped on to the balcony. He sat down on a chair in the sunlight and stared across the bay, then into the sky. There was no sign of starship activity today.

He realised that, despite the seriousness of his condition, he still hoped to flux again. Surely the state of his senses would have no detrimental effect on his ability to mind-push? He had already decided that when his condition deteriorated to such an extent that he could no longer function without help, which must surely happen when his sight became effected, he would volunteer for a long shift. He could push a boat to one of the Rim Worlds, spend a year of ecstasy in flux. It would probably kill him, but the prospect of such rapture and a painless end was preferable to the life he could expect here on Earth.

Caroline appeared beside him. She placed a chair next to his and sat down, the sketchpad on her lap. She seemed fresh and composed, the episode of the other day forgotten.

He said, *I've been wanting to apologise for what I said, Carrie. I had hoped you'd visit me before now.* And he cursed himself for making even his apology sound like an accusation.

Caroline wrote: I've been with Black.

Thorn was suddenly aware of his own heartbeat. *How is he?*

She wrote: Only his sense of touch is now in the "present." All his other senses are time-lapsed by nearly a day.

How's he coping?

She paused, then wrote: Not very well. He was never very stable. He's showing signs of psychosis. But you're much stronger, Max—

What happens when his sense of touch retards? he interrupted.

15

Caroline shrugged. Thorn read: It hasn't happened yet. It's difficult to say. In a way, if it does occur, it will be easier for him as then all his senses will be synchronised in the "past." But he'll be unable to mix with people, socialize. How could he? Their presence would be delayed subjectively by hours, days. There would be no way for him to relate.

He could still flux, Thorn said.

Caroline looked away. She scribbled something on the pad:

Is the flux all you think about?

It's my life, Carrie. The only reason I exist.

She shook her head, frustrated by this clumsy means of communication. She wrote out two pages of neat script and passed them to him.

I could understand your infatuation with the flux if you thought that the experience had religious significance, that you were in touch with the afterlife. But you don't even believe that! To you it's just a drug, a mental fix. You're a flux-junky, Max. When you left me you were running away from something you couldn't handle emotionally because you'd never had to in the past. For most of your life, Max, the flux has provided you with a substitute for human emotion, both the giving of it and the taking. And look where it's got you!

Thorn sat without speaking. Some part of him—some distant buried, human part—was stunned by the truth of her insight.

You just feel sorry for yourself because you didn't get me, he said weakly, trying to defend himself.

Caroline just stared at him. She shook her head. With deliberation she wrote one line. She stood up and tore off the top sheet, handed it to him and left the balcony.

I'm not sorry for myself, Max. I'm sorry for you.

Thorn pushed the meeting with Caroline to the back of his mind.

In the days that followed he dwelled on the hope that he might one day be able to flux again. If his sense of touch did retard, then, as Caroline had suggested, all his senses would he synchronised and his condition made considerably easier. He might not be able to socialise, but that would be no great loss. His only desire was to re-join the Line.

On his ninth morning in hospital, Thorn opened his eyes and saw nothing but darkness. He called for the lights to be switched on, but instead someone spoon-fed him breakfast. He was unable to tell if it was Caroline who fed him; he could neither see, hear, nor even smell the person. He asked who it was, but the only response—the only one possible in the circumstances—was a gentle hand on his arm. After his first breakfast in absolute darkness he lay back and waited.

His sensory delay had expanded to six hours now, and it was that long before the darkness lifted and he was able to see the rising sun slanting into the room. He had the disconcerting experience of lying flat on his back while his gaze of six hours ago lifted as the Thorn-of-this-morning sat up and prepared for breakfast. In his vision, the nurse positioned his tray and fed him bacon and eggs. Thorn felt that he could reach out and touch the woman. He tried, and of course his hand encountered nothing.

He had no control over the direction of his gaze; his unseeing eyes of that morning had wandered, and he found himself trying to bring his errant vision back to the nurse, but all he saw was the far wall. His vision was interrupted by frequent, fraction-of-a-second blanks, when he had blinked, and longer stretches of total blackness when he had closed his eyes. The only benefit of this visual delay was that now his sight and hearing, taste and smell were synchronised. He saw the nurse lift a forkful of egg to his mouth, heard the sound of his chewing and tasted the food. The only thing missing was the egg itself; his mouth was empty.

"There we are," the nurse said, proffering Thorn a last corner of toast. He wanted to tell her to stop treating him like a child, but that was the big disadvantage of his present condition: what he experienced now had happened six hours ago. The nurse would be elsewhere in the hospital, the bacon and egg digested, the sounds and aromas dissolved into the ether.

Over the next few days he remained awake into the early hours, watching the happenings of the previous day. At four in the morning, then six, darkness would descend, and Thorn would settle down to sleep. Around noon he would wake, spend several hours in darkness, then watch the sun rise eight hours late. If the delay between occurrence and perception continued to increase by two hours every three days, as it was doing, then Thorn foresaw a time when he would be spending more time in darkness than in light.

He would be able to cope. There had been many a long period in the past, between shifts, when he had locked himself in his darkened apartment, with drink and fleeting memories of flux.

After almost two weeks in hospital, Thorn began to weaken. He passed through periods of physical nausea and mental confusion. He hallucinated once that he was fluxing again, this time without the usual euphoria of the union.

The day following this hallucination he awoke early and felt the warmth of sunlight on his skin. Eight hours later he was aware of the sun coming up over the sea. He would have liked to watch it, but his eyes of eight hours ago were fixed on the foot of his bed. The frequency of his "waking" blinks gave the scene the aspect of an ancient, flickering movie. At least it wasn't silent: he could hear the hospital waking around him, the distant crescendo of a starship's burners.

Later, after someone spoon-fed him a tasteless lunch, he felt a soft hand on his arm. He moved his head, as if by doing so he might see who it was. But all he saw was the same old far wall of eight hours ago; all he heard was his own breathing. He recalled the touch of the nurse, but that had been light, platonic, reassuring him like a child that everything was all right. There was nothing platonic about this touch. As he lay there, helpless, whoever it was pulled back the sheets and divested him of hospital garb. He shouted out in silence, tried to fend her off—"her" because his flailing arm caught the softness of a breast. But he could not see the woman and he was unable to prevent the ludicrous rape. He felt a warm, soft weight straddle him, her breasts loose against his chest, and the sensation was what he imagined it might be like to be taken by a succubus.

Caroline? he said. He moved his arms in the clumsy description of an embrace, touched her familiar slender body. He was aroused now despite himself. She found him and he moaned without a sound, ran his fingers through her black invisible hair. He recognised Caroline's style of lovemaking from the past, went along with it as though they had never parted, and when climax came it was as he remembered it from many years ago—a brief ecstasy soon gone, like a second in flux but nowhere near as satisfying. Even the unusual circumstances of the union, the fact that he could not see Caroline, that the source of his pleasure was as it were disembodied, could only intimate a greater rapture and not fulfil in itself.

The invisible weight of her lay against him now, heavy and sated after orgasm, which Thorn had experienced through the silent contractions of her body. She kissed him, and he felt her tears fall on his face.

Caroline? Why?

Her lips moved against his cheek, her breath hot as she formed words. It was like being kissed by a ghost, bestowed silent prophecy.

In the calm aftermath of the act, Thorn began to feel revulsion. The bizarre nature of their lovemaking sickened him. He felt a return of the old guilt which he thought he had long since banished. It was as if the union was a symbol of their relationship to date; for years Thorn had played at loving someone whose essence was invisible to him, while Caroline for her part had wasted her life chasing someone who was emotionally forever elsewhere.

He cried out now and pushed her from the bed. He felt her fall and almost heard her cry of pain. *Get out, Caroline! Go away!* He faced where he thought she might be, but could not be sure. *I don't want you, for Godsake! All I want—*

She attacked him then. She came at him with painful blows and slaps, and no doubt cries and accusations. Thorn was aware only of the physical violence, the punches that struck from nowhere without warning. And he was aware, too, that he deserved everything he was getting.

He lay on the bed, battered and exhausted. Caroline had ceased her attack. He had no way of knowing whether she was still in the room, but he sensed her continued presence. *I don't know why you came here*, he said. *I don't know what you want from me.*

He half-expected another hail of blows, and flinched in anticipation. But none came.

When he thought he was alone he dragged the bed sheets around him protectively, lay back and recalled Caroline's tears on his cheeks.

There could only be one explanation for her visit.

Thorn felt himself weaken further during the hours that followed.

He waited with mounting apprehension, his body covered in chill sweat. Visually it was four o'clock in the afternoon, but the real time was around midnight. It seemed a lot longer than the delayed eight hours until Caroline entered his line of sight.

She moved out of it quickly as she came to the side of the bed. She reached out and touched his arm, and Thorn expected to feel her now, but of course her touch had startled him eight hours ago. Then, Thorn had turned his head abruptly, and now he saw Caroline full on. She wore only a white gown and nothing beneath, and she was crying.

He watched as she undressed him, and the sight of her doing this brought a hot flush of shame and resentment to his cheeks. The sensation of her touch had passed, but as he watched her slip from her gown and climb onto him, he experienced a resurgence of the desire that had overwhelmed him eight hours earlier.

The Thorn-of-now lay still in his bed. He was making love to Caroline, but with his memories of the physical act already eight-hours old, he felt like a voyeur in the head of his former self. He could see her, frenzied blurs of flesh and hair and tongue; he could smell her, the perfume she used and the sweat of sex that overcame it; and he could hear her small moans of pleasure, her repeated cry of his name as she approached climax.

He heard his slurred question: "Caroline? Why?"

They had finished making love and she lay in his arms. "Because I loved you, Max," she had said. "Because I *still* love you."

He knew what happened next. Again he experienced that overwhelming sense of revulsion, brought about by guilt. He watched helplessly as he pushed her from the bed. "Get out, Caroline!" he heard himself cry. "Get away!" He saw her expression of pain, the acceptance of rejection in her eyes, and had it been possible he would have stopped himself saying what he said next. "I don't want you, for Godsake! All I want—"

She came at him and hit him again and again.

The Thorn-of-now flinched, as if the blows he could see coming might indeed inflict pain upon him; he raised his arms as if to protect himself. Yet he felt nothing.

Caroline backed off and yelled at him.

He heard himself say: "I don't know why you came here. I don't know what you want from me."

Caroline was crying. "I came because I loved you, Max. I came to say goodbye."

She lowered her gaze and murmured, more to herself than to Thorn: "Black died two days ago."

Eight hours later Thorn lay quite still.

He deteriorated rapidly over the next few days.

The knowledge of Black's death robbed him of any will he might have had to fight. In his final hours he experienced a gradual diminution of his senses. His hearing left him first, then his taste and smell, though he hardly noticed their absence. Later his vision dimmed and went out, and he was aware of himself only as a small, blind intelligence afloat in an infinite ocean.

Soon even the awareness of his physical self diminished, and then the last sense of all, the cerebral intuition of his own identity, left him too. A familiar euphoria flooded him and the man who had been Thorn knew, before he died, that he was being absorbed into the vastness of the cosmos he had known until now as the nada-continuum.

THE DISCIPLES OF APOLLO

In my twenties I was convinced that I was dying. I'd dwell morbidly on my impending end and write long, dreadful stories about doomed, romantic characters. When I was thirty, a friend of mine, just a few years my senior, died of cancer. His death, and my immature maunderings on the subject of love and loneliness, inspired the following tale. I think writing it acted as some kind of catharsis, and my eventual death seemed a little less imminent. "The Disciples of Apollo" appeared in Other Edens III, *edited by Chris Evans and Robert Holdstock.*

THE DISCIPLES OF APOLLO

"I'M SORRY."

"How long?"

"At least six months, perhaps even as many as nine."

"How will I know when?"

"For two days beforehand you'll feel drowsy, lethargic."

"And pain?"

"I can assure you that your condition is quite painless."

"I suppose I should be thankful for small mercies."

"There is a retreat for sufferers of the Syndrome. Because of the highly unusual nature of the disease, you are advised to spend your final weeks there. Of course, you can go before then, if you wish. Your family will be able to visit you."

"I have no family."

"In that case, Farrow Island might be perfect."

Between the time of diagnosis and the actual realisation that he was going to die, Maitland passed through a period of disbelief. There is a difference between the intellectual knowledge of one's eventual end, and the sudden sentence of death. Grief came one morning when he awoke and knew that his awakenings were numbered, and as he watched the dawn he realised that soon the sun would rise without his continued presence to witness it; grief filled his chest with suffocating nausea, and he turned like a loner in a crowd for someone on whom he might unburden his anguish and regret. There was no one, and this compounded his pain. At times in the past, Maitland had managed to convince himself that he could do without the usual human involvements that most people took for granted. Yet now, with the imminence of his extinction, he realised that no one could live—or die—without having shared in some experience of affection, even love. He cursed himself for so aloofly denying down the years the inner voice that had cried out for human contact, cursed the coward in him that had shied from the trauma of new experience with the excuse that he had existed for so long without it... It came to him with the intensity of a cerebral scream that now it was too late. He had no chance of finding in six months that which had eluded him for a lifetime. He would die alone, as he had lived, and whereas to live alone was easy, to die alone, with so much guilt and remorse, and yearning for a somehow *altered* past, he knew would be beyond endurance.

Then, however, he passed through this phase of anger and entered a period of passive resignation, and he saw his death as the inevitable consequence of a life lived as he had lived it. He would gain nothing from regret, he told himself; his former self was a stranger whose actions he had no way of changing. He could only accept his fate, and anticipate anything that might lie beyond. He recalled the doctor's recommendation, and made arrangements to leave.

In the following weeks Maitland said goodbye to his colleagues at the university, making the excuse that he was taking a short vacation. He sold his house and all his possessions, his books and his classical record collection. He felt a buoyant sense of relief when at last his house was empty. Since the diagnosis, he had been troubled at the thought of his material possessions remaining *in situ* after his death, mocking him; it was as if the acquisitions of a lifetime somehow circumscribed the parameters of his physical existence, and would bear mute testimony to his non-existence when he died.

Spring came and Maitland left the mainland on the ferry to Farrow Island. On the crossing, he attempted to determine how many of his fellow passengers were also suffering from the Syndrome. As far as he knew there were no outward physical symptoms of the disease—the physiological debilitation was taking place on a sequestered, cellular level. Nevertheless, Maitland convinced himself that at least a dozen other passengers, of the twenty or so aboard the ferry, were making their way to the hospice. Their despondent postures and sapped facial expressions spoke to him of moribund futures, bitter presents, and only guilt and regret in retrospect. He realised, as the ferry approached the island, that they were mirror images of himself.

A car was awaiting him on the cobbled quayside of the small fishing village. He was greeted by Dr Masters, the woman with whom he'd corresponded.

"Aren't we waiting for the others?" he asked as he climbed into the car and she set off.

"Others?" Dr Masters regarded him with a smile. "The other passengers are islanders, Mr Maitland. You are my only new resident this week."

The hospice was a sixteenth-century mansion set in wooded parkland on a cliff-top overlooking the straits. Dr Masters conducted him around the workshops and recreation rooms, the library, and dining hall. She told him that the residents could take their meals in their rooms, if they wished, and that the recreational facilities and group therapy sessions were optional.

Maitland was thus reassured. The thirty or so residents he had seen so far in the mansion had about them a collective air of apathy, as if the fact of their ends had reached back and retroactively killed them in both body and in mind.

In contrast, Maitland had briefly glimpsed a few lone individuals in the grounds, striding out resolutely across the greensward, or posed in isolation on the windy cliff-top. Maitland fancied that he detected something heroic in their lonely defiance in the face of death, and ultimately sad and tragic also.

As the weeks passed and spring turned gradually to summer, Maitland imposed his own routine on the identical days that stretched ahead to the time of his death in the New Year.

He would rise early and breakfast alone in the hall before setting out on a walk around the island that would often take him three or four hours. He would speak to no one, not because he wished to be rude or uncivil, but because no one ever spoke to him. He was a stranger on the island and therefore an "inmate" up at the mansion, and the locals viewed the victims of the Syndrome with suspicion, sometimes even hostility.

He would take lunch in his room and eat it slowly, sometimes taking an hour to finish. Then he would sit by the window and read, or listen to the radio, until the gong announced the evening meal at seven.

This meal he did take with the other residents in the main hall, though he rarely joined in the conversation, which he found inane and self-pitying. There were constant debates as to the reason for the disease, and the only conclusion ever arrived at by the residents was that they were the chosen ones of their God, Apollo. These people, in Maitland's opinion, were as irrational as the madmen who could no longer live with the thought of their deaths, and had to be removed to psychiatric units on the mainland.

One night, over coffee, Maitland decided that he had heard enough. He threw down his napkin and cleared his throat. The dozen residents at the table—the people Maitland considered to be the hard core of the hospice's strange religious movement, until now debating among themselves—fell silent and stared at him. They sensed his long-awaited contribution to the discussion.

"There is," Maitland said, "no *reason* for what we have. It's a freak, an accident, a cellular mutation. We are just as likely to be disciples of the Devil as we are to be the chosen ones of your God. In my opinion we are neither."

Later, as he stood by the French windows and watched the sun fall behind the oaks across the river, he sensed someone beside him. "But how can you continue, Mr Maitland? How do you manage to live from day to day if you believe in nothing?"

Maitland could not reply, and retired to his room. He often wondered the same thing himself.

Summer gave way to autumn, and the sunsets beyond the stand of oak turned the golden leaves molten. Maitland struck up an acquaintance with a fellow resident, a retired major who bored him with stories of his army life. The only reason Maitland tolerated his company was because he played a passable game of chess, and they would spend the long autumn afternoons in the library, intent on the chequered board between them. They rarely spoke; that is, they rarely conversed. Maitland tried to ignore the major's monologues, for he was contemplating—in contrast to the old soldier's full and eventful life—the arid years of his own brief existence to date, his time at university, both as a student and later as a lecturer, and the missed opportunities he told himself he did not regret, but which, of course, he did.

The major's going came about on the third week of their acquaintance. The old man had been complaining of headaches and tiredness for two days, and his concentration had often wandered from the game. Maitland realised what this meant, and he was unable to say whether he was shocked by the fact of the major's approaching death, or by the realisation, for the first time, that his own life too would end like this.

On the third day the major did not arrive, and Maitland sat alone by the window, his white pawn advanced to queen's four in futile anticipation of the challenge.

He took to playing chess against himself in the empty afternoons that followed the major's death. Winter came early that year, impinging on the territory that the calendar claimed still belonged to autumn. Maitland found it too cold to enjoy his walks; the wind from the sea was bitter, and it often rained.

He appeared a lonely figure in the library, bent over the chessboard, apparently concentrating but often, in reality, devising for himself an alternative set of events with which he wished he had filled his life. He repulsed all offers to challenge him, not with harsh or impolite words, but with a silent stare that frightened away would-be opponents with its freight of tragedy and regret.

One afternoon, during a storm that lashed and rattled the windows, Dr Masters joined Maitland in the library and tried to persuade him to take up her offer of group therapy, or at least counselling. They had experts who could help.

He wanted to ask her if they had experts who could revise his past, give him the happiness he should have had long ago, but which had passed him by. He stopped himself before asking this, however. He knew that he had only himself to blame for the emptiness of his life.

Dr Masters said that she thought he should mix more with the other residents. Didn't he know that, even now, nothing was so important or rewarding as human relationships?

And Maitland replied that he needed nothing, and never had, of *human relationships*.

One week later he met Ella.

He noticed her first one Sunday at the evening meal. She was at the far table by the blazing fire, and it was more than just her youth that set her apart from the other diners; she was *alive* in a way that none of the others were. Something in her manner, her movements, told Maitland that she could *not* be dying. Then he experienced a sudden stab of grief as he realised that her dynamism might be just a façade, an act to disguise her despair.

Later it came to him—with a sweeping sense of relief—that she was related to one of the residents and down here on a visit. Relatives came so infrequently— like the islanders they saw the victims of the Syndrome as bizarre and freakish, as if the disease were some kind of curse, or could be transmitted—that it hadn't occurred to him that this was what she was: the daughter or granddaughter of one of the afflicted.

She excused herself from the table and Maitland watched her leave the room. Seconds later he saw her again through the window. She crossed the patio and ran across the greensward towards the cliff-top. She wore moonboots, tight denims, and a chunky red parka, and he guessed that she could be no more than twenty-five. Maitland had almost forgotten what it was like to feel such yearning, and to experience it now served only to remind him of his wasted years and the fact of his premature death.

In the morning, Maitland went for a long walk through the wind and the rain. He returned, showered, and ate lunch in his room and, feeling refreshed and invigorated, went downstairs to the library and played himself at chess.

In the middle of the afternoon he sensed someone beside him. He turned and saw the young woman.

She smiled. She was dressed as she was last night, with the addition of a yellow ski cap pulled down over her ears, and mittens. Evidently she too had just returned from a walk.

"Can I give you a game?" she asked, indicating the board. Despite himself, Maitland smiled and began setting up the pieces.

They played for an hour with only the occasional comment, and then she looked up, directly at him, and said: "You're not like the others. You've not given in."

He wanted to tell her that he had surrendered long ago, that his resolution now in the face of death was nothing more than the cynicism that had fossilised his emotions years before.

Instead he smiled.

"I mean it," she said, as she toppled her king in defeat. "There's something about you." She gestured. "The other fools have given in, one way or another—gone stark staring mad or joined that crackpot cult."

She mistook his cynicism for valour, seeing him through eyes of youthful naivety, and Maitland hated himself for the charlatan he knew himself to be.

He felt a sudden sympathy, then, with the residents who had taken to religion, or madness, as protection against the inevitable. At least they had had full and worthwhile lives against which to measure the futility and horror of their deaths.

"Perhaps if you were in the position of these people, facing death, you might give in, too. Don't belittle them..."

Something in her eyes made him stop.

She began collecting the scattered pieces, placing them in the wrong positions. "But I am a resident here," she said. "Another game?"

They played all day, but Maitland gave little attention to the games. During the hours that followed, he found himself intrigued by the young woman, who introduced herself as Ella. He opened up, talked about himself for the first time in years. He wanted to turn the conversation around, to ask Ella about herself, her life before the hospice but mainly her life since the diagnosis. Most of all, Maitland wanted to know how she could remain so overtly optimistic with the knowledge of what was to come.

But she parried his questions and kept the conversation trivial, and Maitland was happy to join her in the exchange of banalities he would have found intolerable at any other time.

Over the next few weeks Maitland and Ella sought each other's company as often as possible. They went on long walks around the island, and spoke guardedly of their respective pasts. Maitland was attracted to Ella because of her courage, her optimism, and her disregard for the proximity of her death; she perhaps was attracted to Maitland for what she saw as similar qualities. It hurt him to deceive her—he often wanted to tell her that you could not fear death if you had never really lived—but as time went by he became too attached to her to tell her the truth.

Their liaison stopped short of physical intimacy, however, and it was as if this was a tacit agreement between them. For his part, Maitland could hardly conceive that intimacy might be possible, much less how he might react emotionally to something he was yet to experience. Perhaps fear prevented him acceding to the desires of his body, as if to consummate what he felt for Ella would bring home to him the fact of how much he had come to delight in life of late, and consequently how much he had to lose.

They talked all day and often into the early hours, but never about their relationship. Maitland was still in ignorance as to her almost blind, at times even childish optimism.

For days now the wind and the freezing rain had promised worse to come, and then one quiet night, with only two weeks to go before Maitland died, snow fell.

In the morning he awoke to find a pearly radiance filling the room. He dressed and drew aside the curtains and was dazzled by the brilliance of the white mantle.

He pulled on extra clothes with the enthusiasm of a child and met Ella in the hall. They embraced, restricted by the bulkiness of their padding, and hurried outside hand in hand.

For as far as the eye could see, snow had covered the land with a perfect record of passage. They were the first residents abroad this morning, and they set off together away from the mansion. At one point, Maitland looked back at the building—its hard angles softened by a thick, dazzling fleece—and he saw their footprints following them to their present position. He looked ahead at the virgin expanse of snow, and he shivered with what he told himself was nothing more than a sudden chill.

They walked through the woods and came out on the far side of the headland. They stood side by side and stared out across the shipping lanes, at the scimitar-shape of a tanker on the distant grey horizon. Then they moved towards the small pavilion where they often spent their afternoons, talking and staring out to sea.

As they made their way towards the open entrance of the small stone building, Ella pulled away from him, then bent double and screamed into her mittens. Maitland looked from her to the pavilion, and saw with revulsion that during the night a resident had chosen this place in which to die.

They returned to the mansion and for the rest of the day and all through the night they remained in bed and made love. This set the pattern for the following week. They would take a brisk morning walk and then seek the refuge of bed and the bliss of each other's body, as if making up for the weeks of wasted opportunity. Ella said nothing about the obvious fear the sight of the corpse had instilled in her—instead it was as if she were trying to exorcise from her mind the fact of her death with the positive catharsis of sex.

Maitland, at last, found what he knew to be love, and he passed through the fear of the inevitable with the knowledge that he might never have found happiness were it not for the fact of his terminal illness. His only regret was that he had not found such happiness earlier.

One week later he felt himself going.

On the morning of the first day he felt too drowsy to accompany Ella on their ritual stroll through the snow. He made the effort, though, but something about his lethargy as they walked side by side communicated itself to Ella, and she was silent.

In the afternoon they went to bed, but Maitland fell asleep beside her within seconds. In the morning he felt vaguely ill, nauseous. He tried to hide this from Ella, but it was impossible. She dressed him and assisted him downstairs to the library, where they played chess. Often Maitland slipped into sleep, and he would awake with a start to see Ella crying quietly to herself at the far end of the room.

On the morning of his last day, Maitland awoke before Ella and forced himself out of bed. He dressed with difficulty, then kissed her on the cheek and slipped quietly from the room so as not to wake her.

He walked through the woods to the pavilion overlooking the sea. Already he was tired, as if the short walk had exhausted him, and he hoped he would be asleep when it happened.

Ella joined him not long after, as he guessed, and secretly hoped, she would. "You should go back," he told her, but he knew it was a token protest. "You still have months to live."

She ignored him; he sensed that she wanted to speak, to say something, but could not bring herself to do so without tears.

Later, for the first time, she mentioned the Syndrome.

"Years ago we wouldn't have known we were ill," she whispered, her breath visible in the air. "We would have *gone*, suddenly, without all these months of..." And Maitland realised, then, that she was crying. "Why?" she said at last. "Why did they have to tell us?"

Maitland held her, shocked at her sudden capitulation. "Modern medicine," he said. "They can diagnose it now. They know when it's going to happen. Given that knowledge, they have to inform the sufferer. Otherwise we could go at any time, anywhere, endangering others besides ourselves. There are many more of us now. The Syndrome has reached almost epidemic proportions." He drew her to him affectionately. "I thought you were doing rather well," he said, and recalled that first Sunday weeks ago when he had wondered briefly if her vivacity had been nothing but an act.

"I was so scared, the only way I could stay sane was to pretend I wasn't affected. Being seen as unafraid by others gave me strength, confidence. Can you understand that? Then I met you and found someone who wasn't afraid."

Maitland stifled a cry of despair. He convinced himself he could detect, in the frozen morning air, the odour of the resident who had died here before him. He felt grief constrict his chest, fill his throat, and render him speechless.

Ella laughed. "Do you know... Do you know what they call us? The islanders? Everyone else out there? They call us the Disciples of Apollo."

They held each other as the snow began to fall.

Then Maitland ignited and consumed her in his flame, uniting them forever in a mutual, carbonised embrace.

THE DEATH OF CASSANDRA QUEBEC

I love stories about future art and artists' colonies. There's a sub-genre in science fiction of such stories: Ballard's Vermilion Sands, Lee *Killough's* Aventine, *and Michael Coney's* Peninsula *tales to name but a few. I find attractive the enclosed, almost hermetic setting, the decadence, and the emotional resonance of stories about obsessed, often doomed artists. I've written a few other tales about artists (and some others set in the colony of Sapphire Oasis), but I think this one my best. It was my tenth sale, and appeared in David Garnett's* Zenith II *anthology.*

THE DEATH OF
CASSANDRA QUEBEC

I CAME TO SAPPHIRE OASIS IN SEARCH OF EXPERIENCE, OR SO I THOUGHT
at the time. I had made my home on Nova Lyon for almost two decades, the
last few years a repetition of café life, parties, and second-rate exhibitions where
even my best crystals failed to sell. I was getting old and lonely and my work was
suffering, and some vague desperation drove me to Earth to experience that which
I might synthesise, through my skill, into art.

The famous crystal *The Death of Cassandra Quebec* was being exhibited for the
first time in ten years, and I made this my excuse to revisit the planet of my birth.
I took a bigship through the interstellar telemass portal to Timbuktu and caught
the mono-train north to Sapphire Oasis.

I had seen many a lavish illustration of the colony—had even admired Tyrone's
famous hologram of '37—and as a result I was overcome with a sense of déjà vu at
first sight. The oval oasis, perhaps a kilometre from end to end, was surrounded
by a great leaning series of golden scimitars, their hilts planted in the sand of the
desert, their arching blades supporting the pendant globes that comprised living
quarters and spacious studios with views across the artificial lake.

That first night I dined alone in the revolving restaurant on the island at the
centre of the oasis. I ate synthetic gazelle and yam, with chutney and Moroccan
wine. The panorama was magnificent. Beyond the illuminated orbs of the individual
domes, and the fringe of surrounding palm trees, the desert extended in dark and
sultry swathes the size of Europe. Across the dunes to the south stood the telemass
portal. As tall as a mountain, its blank interface was braced in a glowing frame like
a hexagon of colossal fluorescents.

It was through this portal that I and a hundred other tourists had journeyed
today from Nova Lyon, and tomorrow it would be opened to the world of

Henderson's Fall, 61 Cygni B. The talk in the dining room was of nothing else but Nathaniel Maltravers, and his arrival tomorrow evening at Sapphire Oasis.

I ordered a second bottle of wine.

As I drank, I thought about another famous artist, a woman this time. Cassandra Quebec had inspired more women than just myself to seek expression through the medium of fused crystal. She was the artist who had shown the world her soul, who had taken the fledgling form and proved it as a legitimate means of self-expression. At the height of her career she was the world's most celebrated artist. Then she spoiled it all by announcing her betrothal—I was young; I wept when I found out—to the minor laser-sculptor Nathaniel Maltravers. A year later she was dead.

I finished the second bottle and contemplated a third. I had known when I booked the bigship to Earth that Maltravers—who was indirectly responsible for his wife's death, after all—had decided to return to Sapphire Oasis for the twentieth anniversary commemoration of her passing, but I had not let it put me off the idea of making the trip. Tomorrow, I would visit the Museum of Modern Art and request a private viewing of the Maltravers/Quebec crystal.

I retired early and lay on my bed, staring at the stars through the dome. A party was in progress on the lawn beside the lake, one of the interminable soirées that gave the place more the air of a luxury resort than that of an artists' retreat. Artists, their rich patrons and guests, mixed with a social ease I found enviable; snatches of cultured conversation drifted to me through an open vent in the dome.

Unable to sleep, and reluctant to join the gathering below, I took refuge in a memory-zip. I placed the crown—more like a skullcap—on my head and selected a pin. As I shed my own identity and slipped into the programmed persona, I could not help feeling a twinge of guilt at my escape. Memory-zips were a spin-off from a device known as mem-erase, illegal on Earth for almost two decades. Mem-erase—the process of self-selected amnesia to which I had once been addicted—had been proven to have certain adverse psychological side effects. As a result of the ban, the simulated scenarios of memory-zips were viewed in some circles with a certain stigma.

I selected the ersatz memories of a fictitious vid-star, lay back and for the next hour lived a life of success, fame, and love.

I awoke early the following morning, booked some time alone with the crystal, and strolled along the palm-lined boulevard to the museum.

On the few occasions when the crystal had been exhibited in the past, I had been loath to experience it. The mere fact of Cassandra Quebec's death had been painful enough, without subjecting myself to the emotional reality of it. But twenty years had passed since the incident; I was older and perhaps wiser now, and I considered myself ready to have the experience.

Not that I was without misgivings. I held, perhaps irrationally, a fierce dislike for the man who had married Quebec and who was ultimately responsible for the accident that killed her. Added to which, Maltravers's production of the crystal had elevated him from the minor artisan he was to the status of a world celebrity. Perhaps what had prevented me from experiencing the crystal before now, quite apart from the emotional trauma I would have to undergo, was the thought that I would be participating in the metaphorical aggrandisement of man at the expense of woman.

That morning at breakfast in the revolving restaurant I had been invited to the table of a group of Hoppers, rich artisans and their hangers-on, who skipped the globe from one artists' colony to the next. They were shrill and opinionated, and I sought the protection of silence, offering nothing to the debate about Maltravers and the reason for his return. I heard one claim that he was returning to seek artistic rejuvenation from the locale of his wife's horrific death; another, that he intended to end his life here, as befits the artistic temperament.

The truth, I suspected, was neither. It was my guess that Nathaniel Maltravers was staging the spectacle of his return for no other reason than that, in the years since Cassandra Quebec's death, his artistic career had floundered. The dozen or so "major" works he'd released upon the universe had flopped abysmally. His return was probably nothing more than a cheap ruse to gain publicity.

The Death of Cassandra Quebec remained his first and last great work.

The museum, which housed the crystal and a thousand other works of art, was an onyx cathedral raised above the desert on flying cantilevers and approached along a sweep of gently ascending steps. It was cool and hushed within, and I took my time and strolled towards the crystal wing. I paused at the arched entrance, showed my pass to the security guard, and stepped inside.

The chamber was empty; I was quite alone. Before me, in pride of place in the centre of the room, was the crystal—in fact a thousand alien stones fused into one faceted, centimetre-thick disc perhaps two metres across. Visually, it was a mere swirl of colour, a coruscating vortex of argent and indigo. Only to the touch would the crystal discharge the stored emotions of its creators.

I must have heard a hundred different reports about Cassandra Quebec's death, and staged and restaged the tragedy in the theatre of my mind. I was on Nova Lyon when I first read about the accident; the article was in a journal almost two years old, and the shock of the news was compounded by the fact that I had learned about it so late.

Her arrival at Sapphire Oasis, with her husband and new-born baby, made world news. It was her first public appearance since the birth of her daughter; the film of their approach in an open-top vintage Mercedes, smiling parents and babe-in-arms, is famous—a scene imprinted on the collective consciousness by the tragedy of the events that followed. The fact that the instrument of her death was travelling with them makes the short clip all the more grotesque. As a wedding present, Quebec had bought her husband a bird-like alien known as a pterosaur from a newly discovered planet in the Serendipity Cluster. It was an ugly, featherless creature, had a beak like a scythe, and was reputedly empathic—a suitably bizarre pet for the world's most famous couple. It could be seen perched on the backseat, maintaining its balance with edgy adjustments of its vast, leathery wings as the automobile swept through the gates of the colony.

Quebec and Maltravers argued often during their first year of marriage. It was reported that their differences of opinion, because they were artists, were all the more vituperative. Maltravers, the rumour went, was jealous of his wife's talent and success; Quebec, for her part, despaired that her husband's constant envy would prevent him from ever attaining greatness for himself.

The one known truth of their relationship was that, however violent their arguments, their rapprochements were just as intense. They were hailed, in media hyperbole, as the planet's greatest lovers—how jealous I felt when I read this!— and as evidence the news media offered up the fact that, as well as sharing a bed, they also shared a studio.

It was in this studio, three days after her arrival at Sapphire Oasis, that Cassandra Quebec met her end.

They had argued. Quebec was partway through a crystal that would stand as testimony to their love, and as such it had to contain *everything*—their imperfections and flaws of character, as well as their strengths. Maltravers was loath to subject himself to so public a scrutiny, and his protestations which began their final argument were overheard by their daughter's nanny.

They were in the studio, facing each other across the sunlit chamber. The volume of their recriminations was noted by several other artists, who paid no heed, as this was nothing new between the husband and wife. The nanny reported that she'd glimpsed the alien pet, flapping in agitation beside Maltravers, before she departed to attend the crying child in another part of the living quarters.

According to Maltravers, they had reached an impasse in their disagreement, a temporary cease-fire, and Cassandra remained staring at him from across the work-strewn room. Maltravers admitted to feelings of anger, and it was this anger, experts testified at the inquest, that the pterosaur must have picked up.

Before Maltravers could move to stop it, the pterosaur left its perch, swooped across the room, and attacked his wife with claws like sickles. Maltravers fought it off, but so savage was the attack that within seconds Quebec was lacerated beyond recognition. He realised—he said later in sworn testimony—that his wife was dying and that nothing, not even the latest surgical techniques, could save her.

The events that followed were bizarre to say the least.

Beside Quebec was the fused crystal, empty but for touches of her love for Maltravers. What he did then, in his grief and regret and overwhelming sense of loss, was to lift his wife and place her on the slab as if it were a catafalque, and then lay his brow against its faceted surface and impress upon it his turbulent emotions. She died in his arms minutes later, and the crystal recorded the moment for eternity.

For three days the world's media vilified Maltravers as a monster, until the coroner reported at the inquest that nothing could have saved Quebec. Then his agent released the crystal, and over the next year or so public opinion swung in Maltravers's favour—and the vilification turned to sympathy and appreciation.

In the silence of the museum I steeled myself, stepped forward and laid my palms on the crystal's surface. Warmth ran up my arms, the warmth of Quebec's love for her husband, with which she had begun the work. This joy lasted only seconds, though, for as I moved my hands from the edge of the piece towards its centre, pain swamped me, physical pain, the scream of every nerve slit through and through again. Beyond this, on some deeper substratum of the crystal, was Quebec's bewilderment, and then her sudden comprehension as she realised what was happening, that life was ebbing from her, that everything she had ever experienced, the hate and the joy and the everyday miracle of existence, was draining away, becoming faint as she approached the terrible point of total annihilation. Her end was a crescendo scream of terror as oblivion descended.

Then my touch encountered Maltravers's pain at his loss. The howl of desolation that communicated itself from his soul to the crystal, and then to my senses, was almost more unbearable than the pain of Quebec's death—for it continued long after her dying, a lament of grief for his wife, a wail of despair at the realisation of his existence without her.

Unable to take any more, I tore myself away, and the sudden cessation of pain was an exquisite relief. I had no idea how long I had been standing before the crystal, so captivated had I been by the raw human emotions. I realised then that I was in tears.

As I made my way slowly from the museum, I knew that I no longer resented Maltravers. The act of creating the crystal had been instinctive, born of pain and the need to share his grief, and not the opportunistic bid for fame I had assumed for so long.

Within a week of his wife's death, Maltravers took his daughter and sought refuge on the colony world of Henderson's Fall, as if by doing so he might distance himself from the pain of the tragedy.

And tonight he was returning to the source of that pain.

That evening I attended the party thrown by the president of Mali to welcome Nathaniel Maltravers to Sapphire Oasis. It was held in the president's own dome— he dabbled in photomontage—with a view across the desert to the telemass portal through which Maltravers was due to arrive at midnight. The dome was packed with eager guests: I recognised the two dozen or so serious artists who made up the nucleus of the Sapphire colony, faces familiar from Earth to the furthest settled world. Also present were the flamboyant Hoppers, attendant sycophants, and sombre-suited officials from the countries of Northern Africa and Europe.

I drank by myself beside the alcohol dispenser and thought about returning to my own dome. There was an atmosphere of excitement and expectation about the gathering that smacked of voyeurism. I was on my fourth drink when I admitted that the only reason *I* was here was to see for myself how the passage of years had treated Maltravers, and perhaps learn the real reason for his return.

At twelve we spilled out onto the balcony and marvelled at the exhibition of interstellar *son et lumiére* enacted to the south.

Until its activation, the portal was nothing more than an illuminated hexagonal frame through which could be seen a continuation of the starlit African sky. Within minutes all that had changed. The frame flickered, as if affected by a power drain; then a thunderous report rolled across the desert, and the scene through the portal was transformed. The guests gasped and applauded as an alien landscape appeared: a busy spaceport, distant blue mountains, and binary suns in a pink sky. As we watched, a bull-nosed bigship eased its way through the interface and entered the atmosphere of Earth. The ship came to rest on the apron of the spaceport at the foot of the portal.

We returned inside. As the flier carrying Maltravers raced across the desert towards the oasis, the conversation in the dome had about it a charged expectancy. I kept to myself by the dispenser; around me, guests quipped, exchanged stories, and looked frequently to the gates in anticipation of Maltravers's arrival.

I was thinking about my experience with the crystal that morning when a sudden hush fell upon the company. I stared through the diaphanous, curvilinear wall of the room as the flier banked over the colony and settled beside the lake.

Two figures climbed out, were met by the president and his entourage, and disappeared into the scimitar shaft that supported our dome. The conversation started up again, self-consciously, all eyes on the entrance across the room. The door opened and applause rippled through the gathering.

I can recall very little about Nathaniel Maltravers as he made his entry—I was too intent on watching the person who entered with him. While the guests flocked to congratulate Maltravers on his return, I had eyes only for his daughter.

Corrinda Maltravers surprised me on two counts. The first was that I had never thought of her as a young woman. If I thought of her at all, it was as a babe-in-arms, a cypher in the tragedy, untouched by the passage of time. The second was that she was as beautiful as her mother.

Maltravers moved from one group of guests to the next, and his daughter followed in his wake. This was the first time she had returned to Earth since the tragedy, and she appeared shy and bewildered at the reception. She was small, slim, wore a black tube dress that left her shoulders bare, hugged her hips, and finished just above the knees. I caught only a glimpse of her large green eyes and isosceles face—so painfully like her mother's—before she disappeared into an admiring throng of guests. I wondered how long it would be before she found herself waking up beside the next self-professed Picasso.

My reverie was interrupted by the arrival at my side of Maltravers and the president of Mali. They sipped their drinks and the president regaled Maltravers with a short history of his great country.

Nathaniel Maltravers was in his middle-fifties, tall and silver-haired, with the well-groomed, distinguished appearance of someone who has foregone the life of an artist for that of a sybarite. I could not reconcile the man beside me with the artist who had suffered the anguish of his wife's death and communicated it so harrowingly.

Then I noticed the distant, blitzed look in his grey eyes. I recalled the report that, during his self-imposed exile on Henderson's Fall, Maltravers had taken the easy way out. Before the possession of mem-erase became an offence, he had duly self-administered the process of wiping from his memory the entirety of his stay at Sapphire Oasis. His only knowledge of the tragic event was what he read in factual accounts, stripped of all emotion and pain.

Now he glanced my way, his eyes measuring me for size in the places he thought important. His gaze was less lecherous than professional, as if he were seriously considering me as a prospective model.

"Aren't you Eva Hovana?" he asked. "The creator of the *Persephone* crystal?"

I admitted that I was; it was an early piece and not one of my best.

"If I may say so"—he smiled—"I have always found your work rather derivative."

I was quick with the riposte, and immediately regretted it. "At least I don't get other people to do my work for me, however derivative it might be."

Stung, he moved off instantly. "As I mentioned earlier," he said to the president of Mali, "my next piece will be influenced by my obsession with symmetry."

The president hurried him across the room. "Ah... meet my friends from the Council of Europe..."

I escaped onto the balcony.

I gazed out over the body of water, glittering in the moonlight, and wondered what was keeping me at Sapphire Oasis. After all, I had experienced the crystal I had come to see.

I was contemplating a trip to Europe when I sensed someone beside me. I felt a hand on my arm, and turned.

Corrinda Maltravers stood before me, even shorter than she had seemed in the room, almost childlike. She had quickly withdrawn her hand when I started, and now regarded me uncertainly.

"I'm *so* sorry. My father. He..." She gestured.

I smiled. With her shock of sun-bleached hair, her green eyes, she was so much like the picture of her mother I had kept at my bedside during my uncertain youth.

She smiled in return, relieved at my acceptance. "My father *hates* women and artists. It's bad luck if you happen to be both." She had the habit of emphasising certain words as her mother had done.

I shrugged. "I can live with the hatred of men," I told her, and cursed myself for being so obvious.

She regarded me shyly. There was a diffident look in her eyes that could *not* be what I believed it to be. "I think your best work is the *Goddess of Lesbos*," she whispered.

My stomach fluttered. "You do?"

There were a thousand questions I wanted to ask her, about herself, about her mother, but I was frightened of being seen to be too forward, too eager.

Maltravers called her name and Corrinda almost winced.

"I *must* go. I'll see you again?" She smiled shyly. "I really meant what I said about your work."

She slipped through the sliding door with a small wave and disappeared into the crowd.

I decided to remain at Sapphire Oasis for a while.

Over the next few days, I saw Corrinda on a number of occasions. She was always with her father, and although she did not leave him to join me, she gave the distinct impression of *wanting* to do so. Or was I kidding myself? I was pushing forty and desperate, still searching for that which most people have either found at my age, or have given up hope of ever finding. Besides, I had to admit that it wasn't Corrinda I was attracted to; rather, I was obsessed with Cassandra Quebec and the tragedy of her death.

However much I tried, I could not bring myself to start work. I had brought with me several small crystals in various stages of completion, with the notion of dabbling with them should no new project inspire me. Not only did nothing come to mind, but I found it impossible to complete the crystals already begun. My thoughts were too occupied with Maltravers, his daughter, and the death of Cassandra Quebec. I was afraid of corrupting the unfinished work with my turbulent and unresolved emotions, and reluctant to begin a fresh crystal, perhaps on the subject of Quebec, for fear of being unoriginal. It had all been done before, and how might I bring some new and stimulating insight to the drama?

I spent more and more time beside the sparkling oasis, sipping long drinks and wondering whether my assumption the other night as to Corrinda's preferences had been nothing more than a drunken fantasy. Certainly, she did not join me as I sat in full view with my drink. But then, I told myself, perhaps this was because her father was in attendance so much of the time.

Maltravers spent a few hours each morning in his studio. Around noon he would emerge, showered and suited, and hold court in the bar. He had found himself lionised by the clique of Hoppers, and had proved himself a competitive drinker and an able raconteur. From my lounger by the water, I took the opportunity to watch him as he drank and illustrated his spiel with expansive gestures. I recalled the way he'd eyed my body at our first meeting, and during the course of the next few days I realised that he was likewise sizing up the women in his crowd.

He soon found what he was looking for. Within a week of his arrival he was escorting a willowy Nigerian Princess, a laser-sculptress with a penchant for scarlet gowns that emphasized the absolute ebony of her flesh. They spent the mornings in his studio, afternoons in the bar and the evenings partying at various other oases scattered about the desert. I heard one rumour that they were creating a crystal together, another that they were producing a sculpture.

As much as I disliked seeing a beautiful and talented artist used by him, it did have the advantage of keeping Maltravers occupied and out of the way. I lived in hope that Corrinda might take the opportunity to seek my company.

Then one evening as I watched the sun set and the moon rise, and was contemplating whether to go to the bar for another drink or to return to my dome, a shadow fell across my outstretched legs.

Corrinda smiled uncertainly. "Miss Hovana?"

"Eva, please. Won't you sit down?"

She perched herself on the edge of the chair across the table and gave a shy smile in lieu of words. She wore a spacer's silversuit, chopped at shoulders and thighs. I could not help but notice, on the tanned flesh of her limbs, white scars like tribal striations.

In mutual nervousness we both began speaking at once. We stopped, and I said, "Please, you first."

She shrugged, reddened. She seemed younger than when we first met. "I just . . . I wanted to *apologise* for not meeting you sooner. I was working."

I reached across the table and took her hand. "Working?"

She reacted to my touch with characteristic nervousness. "Didn't I tell you that I'm an artist?" she whispered.

"An artist?" I was surprised and delighted.

"Shhh! Not so *loud*—if it ever got back to my father. As I said before, he *hates* women and artists. What do you think it's like being his daughter?"

I made a small sound of commiseration.

She looked up from our hands. "That's what I wanted to see you about—my work. I've just finished a piece. I was wondering, *would* you like to see it?" She watched me with eyes so soft it seemed they could be bruised by rejection.

I said that I'd like nothing more, and she jumped up and led me around the curve of the oasis, talking earnestly in relief at my acquiescence. She took me through the lounge of her father's hanging dome and into her bedroom.

44

"I must keep it in here," she explained, hardly able to meet my gaze, "so that Father doesn't find out. There's no telling what he'd do."

She stood beside an angular object covered by a silken sheet, and unveiled it so shyly that she might have been uncovering her own nakedness. "What do you think? *Honestly?*"

I approached it slowly, aware of some choking emotion in my throat. It was a sculpture in some kind of glowing, off-world wood; perhaps half life-sized, it was of a naked woman seated on the ground, hugging her shins.

Corrinda was watching me. "It's you," she said in a small voice.

I touched the wood, caressed it. I wanted to cry, and yet did not want Corrinda to see me doing so—which was ridiculous. I wanted to cry because Corrinda had produced in the carved representation of myself all my loneliness, all my desire to want someone who wanted me.

The invitation was obvious, but I was too scared to trust her. She was so young, I told myself, while another voice asked what did age matter beside the fact of her compassion.

I bit my lip in a bid to stop the tears, turned to her. "And your father would put an end to this?"

"He's ruled by his hatred. Success makes him jealous."

"You should leave him!"

"He wanted me with him when he returned. He said that by returning here he could come to terms with what happened—then I *will* leave."

"You must hate him," I said.

Corrinda looked away.

In the silence that followed, I heard a sound from beyond the open door: the leathery creak and swoop of wings. I recognised the shape that flapped across the lounge and alighted on the back of the foamform.

I screamed.

Corrinda took my arm. "It's okay, Eva. It's not the same one, and anyway it's quite tame."

"But even so!"

"I know. It's sick. But, you see, my father is quite insane."

She reached out and pushed the door shut. "We'll be alone for the rest of the night," she said.

For the next week, at every available opportunity, Corrinda would leave her father's dome and visit me, and we would make love on my bed beneath the arching dome. I blessed each minute that Maltravers spent in the company of the Nigerian, creating his work of art.

The day before the twentieth anniversary of her mother's death, Corrinda sat cross-legged beside me on the bed. I stared at her naked body, her torso a sun-browned canvas on which a pattern of pale striations had been inscribed. Some incisions were more recent than others, and the tracery of mutilation was too symmetrical to be the result of an accident. I wondered what had driven her to this masochism that almost masqueraded as art.

She traced a scar on her thigh, and said, "Do you love me, Eva?"

I made some tired remark to the effect that we hardly knew each other, and that when she was my age she would come to doubt if anything such as love existed.

"I'm sorry. That's cynical. I like you a lot, Corrinda. Perhaps in time."

For so long I had hero-worshipped Cassandra Quebec that, having her daughter, I could not be sure if the girl I wanted to love was no more than an illusion of my fantasies, a substitution for the love that was impossible.

"I love you," she whispered.

I kissed her projecting knee. I wanted to tell her that she longed for a mother, and as I was both the right age and an artist . . . I glanced across the room at the statue, now installed in my bedroom, and convinced myself that even this was her subconscious grieving for her mother's absence, with myself as the transferred subject.

Ours was a union born of tragedy, and I kept asking myself how such a union might succeed.

I said, "Tomorrow we could visit the Museum of Modern Art. We could experience your parents' crystal."

Corrinda regarded me with a shocked expression. "My father would never allow it!"

"Why are you so imprisoned by your father's wishes?" I asked harshly.

Corrinda just shrugged, ignored the question. "I've read about the crystal, Eva. I *want* to experience it, to understand what my father went through. Then I might come to understand what makes him like he is. I might even be able to sympathise with him, instead of hating him."

"Then come with me tomorrow."

She shook her head. "He wouldn't like it."

In the silence that followed I realised that it was because of her father that Corrinda was so pathetically shy, her experience so circumscribed.

46

She changed the subject. She leaned over me and stared into my eyes. She could see, in my distant, shattered pupils, the tell-tale sign of addiction.

"You've used mem-erase!" she declared.

I told her that I had used it often in my twenties.

She shrugged. "But why? What did you need to erase?"

"Oh. I suspect periods of unhappiness, old lovers. Of course, I can't remember."

"But didn't you know it was dangerous?"

I shrugged. "Not at the time," I told her. Mem-erase was withdrawn from sale only when it was discovered that memories could never be truly erased. They were just blanked from the conscious, pushed into the subconscious, and could resurface at any time as trauma, psychosis.

"Have you ever thought of *replaying* those memories, reliving those affairs?" she asked. "Do you still have the pins?"

"I still have them. But no, I haven't thought of accessing them. I always thought that if they were sufficiently terrible for me to erase in the first place, then perhaps I shouldn't relive the experiences. Then again, perhaps I was mistaken. How can I claim to be an artist if I can't face my past and make something of it?"

Corrinda smiled timidly. "Would you erase *me* from your memory?" she asked.

I pulled her to me. "Of course not," I said, and I wondered how many times I had made that promise in the past.

I touched the scars that covered her body. "You still haven't told me, Corrinda."

"Please, Eva," she said, and would say no more.

That evening, as the sun sank beyond the dunes of the Sahara and a cool night breeze tempered the heat of the day, the entire colony turned out to witness the ceremonial unveiling of Maltravers's latest work of art. There was a full moon shining, and above our heads the bulb of his studio hung like a replica of the ivory satellite. There was no sign of the great work, and I was not alone in wondering just what form it might take. Corrinda had chosen not to join me; she said that she *absolutely hated* her father's latest production, but had refused to tell me why.

There was a patter of applause as Maltravers appeared on the balcony, resplendent in white suit and cravat, and gave a short speech. His latest creation, he claimed, represented living evidence of his contention that all art attempted to attain the symmetry of nature. I found the monologue vain and pretentious, but I had to admit that it did have the desired effect of creating a considerable air of anticipation.

He came to the end of his speech and gave a slight bow, the minimal courtesy suggesting a certain contempt for his audience. His Nigerian lover joined him on the balcony. She wore a vermilion gown, fastened at the throat and gathered at the crotch to form a pair of voluminous pantaloons.

Maltravers kissed her hand and, as we gazed up in expectation, he stepped behind the woman and unfastened the choker at her neck. The gown whispered down the curves of her body to reveal her terrible nakedness.

She struck a demure, Junoesque pose and the crowd gasped.

Her flesh had been sliced and flensed, the incisions opened, pulled back and pinned to reveal the inner organs in their precise, geometrical arrangement; the kidneys were displayed in positional harmony, the lungs likewise. The muscle of her abdomen had been turned back to create an elliptical orifice, through which could be seen the opalescent coils of her intestines. Her arms and legs too had undergone the depredations of Maltravers's scalpel: the ebony skin was scored and folded in a baroque series of curlicues and scrolls, repeating the motif of red on black.

But Maltravers's ultimate abomination—or masterstroke, depending on one's point of view—was the woman's heart. It perched between the orchids of her segmented breasts and throbbed like some grotesque alien polyp.

I recalled the scars on Corrinda's body and almost retched.

Maltravers stepped forward and took the woman's hand. She twirled. "My Symmetrical Goddess," he announced.

The stunned silence extended itself for several seconds, and then a Hopper whooped and clapped, and immediately the acclamation was taken up by the rest of the crowd. Maltravers and his model disappeared into the dome. Minutes later they strode out across the lawn, and there was a mad scramble to be the first to congratulate the pair.

I took refuge on the patio outside the bar and anaesthetized myself with alcohol. I alone seemed to understand that Maltravers's macabre violation of the woman's body had its source not so much in his desire to create new and outrageous art, but in some deep-seated psychological need known only to himself.

It was not long before my thoughts returned to Corrinda. I recalled her scarred body—her diffidence, which amounted almost to shame, at my insensitive questioning—and her refusal to attend the exhibition. I pushed myself unsteadily to my feet. I wanted suddenly to find her, to comfort her as best I could.

A party was raging in Maltravers's dome. The guests filled the various levels with a buzz of conversation, debate as to the man's genius and the occasional burst of laughter. I pushed through the groups of drinkers and searched for Corrinda, my desire to be with her increasing with every passing minute. I felt a surge of panic take hold of me, as if fearing that Corrinda, provoked by the extent of her father's latest perversion, might take it into her head to do something stupid. I wondered how much she hated Maltravers.

I found myself on a small, railed gallery overlooking a sunken bunker of loungers, which in turn overlooked the darkened desert. The mutilated Nigerian stood on a coffee table in the hub of the bunker, striking a series of extravagant poses. Light flashed off her exposed internal organs. "He took my heart," she was saying drunkenly to a posse of admirers, "and did with it that which no man has ever done."

I was overcome with revulsion and hurried around the circular gallery. The only place I had not yet looked for Corrinda was in her bedroom. I was about to make my way there when, across the lounge, I saw a door swing open and Maltravers stagger from his studio. His sudden appearance silenced the gathered drinkers; he became the focus of attention as, in evident distress, he pushed his way through the crowd. He paused at the rail, breathing heavily, saw his model and hurried down the steps into the bunker. He grabbed the woman by the arm, dragged her from the pedestal, and pushed her across to the outer membrane of the dome. The circle of admirers hastily evacuated the bunker; already, a crowd had gathered along the gallery rail opposite me. I stood directly above Maltravers and the woman, and I alone overheard what followed.

"Where is it?" Maltravers sounded all the more menacing for the low pitch of his question. He still gripped the woman's patterned arm, and she grimaced at the pressure and raised a hand, palm outwards, as if to protect herself from a blow.

"I have no idea what you're talking about!"

I noticed that, for all the violent intimacy of the assault, Maltravers could not bring himself to regard the woman. Her organs were highlighted, the line of liver and kidney duplicating the overhead fluorescents—but Maltravers stared past her at the desert outside, as if ashamed of his creation.

"You were the only person in the studio when I opened the locker." He was shaking with rage. "Where is it?"

Pinned inelegantly to the wall of the dome, the woman nevertheless affected disdain. "Where is *what*, exactly?"

Then he brought himself to regard her. He hissed something too low for me to hear, and the woman looked shocked. I could guess, from my knowledge of his past, from his haunted eyes, the reason for his secrecy.

I pushed myself from the rail and hurried through the dome to Corrinda's room. I opened the door without knocking and slipped quickly inside.

She was curled on her bed in the foetal position.

I paused by the door. "Your father still uses..." I began.

She looked up and stared at me through her tears. "After every session with the Nigerian and me," she whispered. "He didn't want to remember how much he enjoyed cutting us up."

I could barely make out her words. She seemed traumatised, present only in body. Her eyes stared through me.

Then I saw the mem-erase crown beside her on the bed.

"Corrinda."

"I had to!" she said. "I had to know what it was that made him do these things. I knew he was ill, but I didn't know *why*." She struggled into a sitting position, picked up the crown and held it out to me. "So I took this, found the relevant pin and accessed his past."

I accepted the crown. The silver head of the pin showed at the port. I looked at her.

"I replayed his memory of the death of my mother." She began to cry. "Take it! Access it for yourself!"

From another part of the dome I heard Maltravers calling his daughter. Corrinda looked up at me and smiled a terrible smile. I quickly kissed her and hurried from the room, at once eager to learn the reason for Corrinda's horror and yet dreading what I might find.

I left the dome as dawn touched the desert sky. The party was breaking up, the revellers leaving and making their way around the curve of the oasis.

In my own dome I poured myself a stiff drink, and then another. I sat down, picked up the mem-erase crown, and rechecked the setting. I placed the crown on my head, connected the probes and pushed the slide to activate the programme.

Instantly, I was inside his head. I saw what Maltravers had seen that day twenty years ago, experienced everything he'd heard and said. But his thoughts, as they were not my own, remained in the background, blurred and indistinct, full of nebulous anger.

He was in the studio, facing his wife—oh, so much like Corrinda!—across a floor littered with slabs of crystal, frames and crystal-cutters. The pterosaur, hunched and menacing, regarded him down the length of its scythe-like bill.

Cassandra stood in shirtsleeves next to her fused crystal, sunlight falling on her golden hair. "I don't understand your objection," she was saying. "The crystal will show my *love* for you. I want you to collaborate—"

"I want no part of it. It's your crystal, not mine."

"But you're part of me. How can the crystal be anything other than *both* of us?" She stared at him. "Are you frightened? Is that it, Nathaniel? You don't want the world to see you as you really are."

Maltravers turned at a sound from the door, and the nanny hurried away to tend the crying baby before he could find the words to censure her.

He slammed the door and turned to his wife.

"How can you talk of our love like that, after what you've been doing?"

Cassandra stared at him, stricken. "What do you mean?" It was barely a whisper.

Maltravers tried to laugh, but the sound he made was desperate. "How did you think you could keep it from me?"

She was staring at him, shaking her head.

"How long has it been going on? Before we came here?"

Cassandra was silent for a second, then said, "Two days—no more. I met her here. But she means nothing to me."

(Paralysed, on the edge of consciousness, I screamed.)

"Then why have an affair with her?" Maltravers cried. "It isn't even as if she's a good artist. Christ, the woman's third rate. She isn't even as good as me!"

(I wanted to hit the release stud, retreat into the safety of ignorance; but some other part of me, fascinated and appalled by this vision of the past, would not allow me so easy an exit.)

"Oh, Eva's much better than you, Nathaniel. That's what attracted me—her talent. But, please believe me—I don't love her. It was only a physical thing, an infatuation."

Maltravers's anger welled; I could feel it massing in my head like a thundercloud.

"Then if you think she's so good, why don't you stay with her?"

The pterosaur hopped from foot to foot in agitation. At any second, I thought, it would swoop across the room and tear Quebec to shreds.

"Because I love you!" Cassandra yelled through her tears.

"I don't want your love!" he cried. "I want your respect for the artist I am."

She broke; the walls of her reserve crumbled and she was no longer able to lie. She bent almost double and screamed at him.

"But, Nathaniel—*you are no artist!*"

His anger exploded, rocking me.

I knew, then, what was about to happen, and I suddenly understood the reason for Corrinda's terrible smile.

The pterosaur remained on its perch.

Maltravers rushed at his wife.

He lifted a crystal-cutter and in a blind rage attacked, slashed at her again and again as she stood before him and offered no resistance.

(I tried to shut out the vision as Cassandra Quebec was transformed before my eyes into a lacerated carcass, but the image played on in my head.)

Then Maltravers ceased his attack and Cassandra slipped to the floor, and realising what he'd done he fell to his knees, and his remorse swamped me. He saw the crystal, and something—perhaps some insane idea that this was the only way to immortalise his wife *and* her talent—moved him to lift her and lay her to rest on the slab of crystal. She died and gave her dying to the world, and Maltravers was overcome with a weight of guilt and regret that I was slowly coming to realise was my burden also.

I hit the release, tore the crown from my head, and sat staring through the dome, weeping at the new order of reality revealed to me.

Then I realised what day it was—the twentieth anniversary of Cassandra Quebec's passing—and something, some vague and disturbing premonition, reminded me of Nathaniel Maltravers's obsession with the symmetry of art. I could see, across the oasis in the artist's studio, the evil flapping form of the pterosaur. I pulled myself upright and staggered from the lounge.

I crossed the lawn in a daze of disbelief. I seemed to take an age to reach his studio, very aware of the terrible fact that my affair with Cassandra Quebec had brought tragedy upon two generations.

Just as I, denied the emotion of grief by my use of mem-erase all those years ago, had been brought here by my subconscious for motives of its own—to empathise with Quebec's death on its anniversary, to fall in love again with her through the medium of her daughter?—Maltravers too had been delivered here by his subconscious for its own sinister reasons.

I came to the scimitar support of Maltravers's dome and, sobbing with desperation, hauled open the door. I ran inside and up the escalator, numbed by the knowledge of what I might find.

I was crossing the lounge when I heard Corrinda's scream from the direction of the studio, and my relief that she was still alive was tempered by the knowledge that soon, if her father had his way, she would not be. I heard his curse, and the din of things being overturned from within the room. I reached the communicating door and tried to yank it open—but it was locked. Corrinda yelled my name, pleading with me to hurry, and I called out that I was coming. Through the frosted glass I could make out two indistinct figures circling each other with extreme wariness, and above them the pterosaur in flight.

I scanned the lounge for something with which to smash the door when I heard another cry: Maltravers, this time—though whether in victory or defeat I could not tell. Then silence. I hefted a carved statue, pitched it through the glass and stepped in after it.

The scene that greeted my eyes was a grotesque tableau, the aftermath of tragic events played out to their conclusion. Maltravers lay on his back on a slab of crystal, his throat slit and his torso, from gullet to abdomen, opened to his spine. Beside him, Corrinda braced herself against the faceted crystal, as if in exhaustion or in silent prayer.

Still gripping the crystal-cutter, she stared at me with eyes burning like emeralds.

"He attacked me," she whispered. "He had it all planned, the crystal set up."

Only then did I notice the rip in her one-piece and the bloody gash across her stomach. She stared at the cutter as if seeing it for the first time, then dropped it and reached out to me. "Eva."

"After all I've done?" I said.

"I *need* you!"

As I took her in my arms, the pterosaur swooped through the air, alighted on Maltravers's corpse and began picking at the bloody remains.

Corrinda looked at me and, together, we reached out to the crystal and experienced Maltravers's death. We shared his initial shock at the realisation of his end, and then his profound relief that his jealousy and guilt were drawing to a close. We experienced his macabre satisfaction in the symmetry—not quite that which he had planned, but symmetry nevertheless—that the crystal would come to represent.

Then, in a subtle underlay of emotion, I became aware of Corrinda's contribution to the crystal. I felt her joy that at last she was free, and her delight in the irony of creating a work of art at her father's expense.

I came to Sapphire Oasis in search of experience, or so I thought at the time.

HUNTING THE SLARQUE

In the mid-nineties I began a series of stories set on the exotic world of Tartarus, whose sun was due to go nova. The stories were about the people fleeing the imminent catastrophe, those who chose to remain, and the few hardy fools who, for reasons of their own, were returning to the doomed planet. Over the years I wrote eight long stories with this venue and they were collected in the fix-up novel The Fall of Tartarus *in 2005. "Hunting the Slarque" is about a man forced, by forces out of his control, to return to the planet of his death. It won the British Science Fiction Award for the best short story in 2000.*

HUNTING THE SLARQUE

HUNTER OPENED HIS EYES AND DIMLY REGISTERED A CRYSTAL DOME ABOVE him. Beyond, a thousand rainbows arched through the sky like the architraves of a cathedral ceiling. Below the rainbows, as if supporting them, mile high trees rose, dwellings of various design lodged within their branches. Large insects, on closer inspection he recognised them as *Vespula Vulgaris Denebian*, shuttled back and forth between the trees. He guessed he was on Deneb XV, The World of a Million Wonders.

He was on Million? He was *alive*? It was a miracle. Or was this a dream? Was he dying? Was this some cruel jest played by his embattled consciousness as he slipped into oblivion? Would this vision soon cease, to be replaced by total nothingness? The concept frightened him, even though he told himself that he had nothing to fear: dead, he would not have the awareness with which to apprehend the terrible fact of his extinction.

Now, however, he had. He tried to scream.

He could not open his mouth. Nor for that matter could he move any other part of his body. Come to that, he could feel nothing. He tried to move his head, shift his gaze. He remained staring through the dome at the rainbow sky.

Following his pang of mental turmoil, he seemed to sense his surroundings with increased clarity. The prismatic parabolas overhead struck him like visual blows, and for the first time he made out sound: the strummed music of troubadours, the cool chuckle of a waterfall, and muted chatter, as contented crowds promenaded far below.

Such fidelity could not be the product of a dwindling consciousness, surely? But the alternative, that he was indeed alive, was almost as hard to believe.

How could anyone have survived an attack of such ferocity?

In his mind's eye, dimly, like a half-remembered image from a dream, he recalled the attack: claws and teeth and stingers. He had experienced pain both physical—he had been torn savagely limb from limb—and mental, as he had known he was going to die.

And beyond that instant of mental terror?

Where had the attack taken place? How long ago? Had he been alone, or...?

He wanted more than anything to call her name, less to verify the fact of his own existence than to seek assurance of her safety.

"*Sam!*" But the sound would not form.

He felt his grasp on reality slacken. The colours faded, the sounds ebbed. He fell away, slipped—not into oblivion, as he had feared, but into an ocean of unconsciousness inhabited by the great dim shapes of half-remembered visions, like basking cetaceans. Hunter dreamed.

At length he felt himself resurface. The rainbows again, the stringed music and babble of water. He still could not shift his vision, not that this overly troubled him. He was more occupied by trying to shuffle into some semblance of order the images revealed in his dream.

He had been on Tartarus Major, he recalled, that great, ancient, smouldering world sentenced to death by the mutinous primary which for millennia had granted the planet its very life. He had been commissioned to catalogue and holopix Tartarean fauna, much of which had never been registered by the Galactic Zoological Centre, Paris, Earth—in the hope that some of the unique examples of the planet's wildlife might be saved from extinction, removed off-world, before the supernova blew.

He had been with Sam, his wife, his life and joy—Sam, carrying his child. He recalled her warning scream, and he had turned, too late to lift his laser. A charging nightmare: teeth and claws, and pain. Oh, the pain!

And, above everything, Sam's screams.

And his fear, as he died, for Sam's safety.

Now he wanted to weep, but he had not the physical wherewithal to do so; he felt as if his soul were crying for what might have become of Sam.

Unconsciousness claimed him, mercifully.

When next he awoke, what seemed like aeons later, the trapezoid lozenges of sky between the crosshatched rainbows were cerise with sunset, and marked with early stars. The achingly beautiful notes of a musical instrument, perhaps a clariphone, floated up from the thoroughfares below.

He tried to shift his gaze, move his head, but it was impossible. He had absolutely no sensation in any part of his body.

A cold dread surged through his mind like liquid nitrogen.

He had no body—that was the answer. He was but a brain, a pair of eyes. Only that much of him had survived the attack. He was the guinea pig of some diabolical experiment, his eyes fixed forever on the heavens, the stars he would never again visit.

Hunter. He was Hunter. For as long as he recalled, he had gone by that simple appellation. He had roved the stars, hunting down the more bizarre examples of galactic fauna, amassing a vast holo-library, as well as extensive case-notes, that were regarded as invaluable by the legion of zoologists and biologists from Earth to Zigma-Zeta. He was a scholar, an intrepid adventurer *non pareil*. He had often gone where lesser men feared to go, like Tartarus. He wondered how his death had been taken by the galaxy at large, how his friends had mourned, jealous colleagues smiled that at last his need to prove himself had instead proved to be his undoing.

Tartarus, a double danger: to go among beasts unknown, on a world in imminent danger of stellar annihilation. He should have swallowed his pride and left well alone. Instead, he had dragged Sam along with him.

He recalled, with a keening melancholy deep within him like a dying scream, that Sam had tried to talk him out of the trip. He recalled his stubbornness. "I can't be seen to back out now, Samantha."

He recalled her insistence that, if he did make the journey, then she would accompany him. He recalled his smug, self-righteous satisfaction at her decision.

As unconsciousness took him once again, he was aware of a stabbing pain within his heart.

Someone was watching him, peering down at where he was imprisoned. He had no idea how long he had been staring up at the lattice of rainbows, mulling over his memories and regrets, before he noticed the blue, piercing eyes, the ugly bald head at the periphery of his vision.

The man obligingly centred himself in Hunter's line of sight.

He stared at his tormentor, tried to order his outrage. He boiled with anger. *Do you know who I am?* he wanted to ask the man. *I am Hunter, famed and feted the galaxy over! How dare you do this to me!*

Hands braced on knees, the man looked down on him. Something about his foppish appearance sent a shiver of revulsion through Hunter. His captor wore the white cavalier boots of a nobleman, ballooning pantaloons, and a sleeveless overcoat of some snow-white fur. His face was thin, bloodless, almost as pale as his vestments.

He reminded Hunter of an albino wasp: the concave chest, the slim waist, the soft abdomen swelling obscenely beneath it.

Without taking his gaze off Hunter, the man addressed whispered words to someone out of sight. Hunter made out a muttered reply. The man nodded.

"My name is Alvarez," he said. "Do not be alarmed. You are in no danger. We are looking after you."

Oddly, far from reassuring him, the words put an end to the notion that he might still be dreaming, and convinced him of the reality of the situation.

He tried to speak but could not.

Alvarez was addressing his companion again, who had moved into Hunter's view: a fat man garbed in robes of gold and crimson.

Alvarez disappeared, then returned with a rectangular, opaqued screen on castors. He positioned it before Hunter, so that it eclipsed his view of the sky. Hunter judged, from the position of the screen and his captors, that he was lying on the floor, Alvarez and the fat man standing on a platform above him.

He stared at the screen as Alvarez flicked a switch on its side.

A work of art? A macabre hologram that might have had some significance to the jaded citizens of The World of a Million Wonders, who had seen *everything* before?

The 'gram showed the figure of a man, suspended—but the figure of a man as Hunter had never before witnessed. It was as if the unfortunate subject of the artwork had been flayed alive, skinned to reveal purple and puce slabs of muscle shot through with filaments of tendons, veins and arteries—like some medical student's computer graphic which built up, layer on layer, from skeleton to fully fleshed human being.

At first, Hunter thought that the figure was a mere representation, a static hologram—then he saw a movement behind the figure, a bubble rising through the fluid in which it was suspended. And, then, he made out the slight ticking pulse at its throat.

He could not comprehend why they were showing him this monster.

Alvarez leaned forward. "You have no reason to worry," he said. "You are progressing well, Mr Hunter, considering the condition you were in when you arrived."

Realisation crashed through Hunter. He stared again at the reflection of himself, at the monstrosity he had become.

Alvarez opaqued the screen, wheeled it away. He returned and leaned forward. "We are delighted with your progress, Mr Hunter." He nodded to his fat companion. "Dr Fischer."

The doctor touched some control in his hand, and Hunter slipped into blessed oblivion.

When he came to his senses it took him some minutes before he realised that his circumstances were radically altered. The view through the dome was substantially the same—rainbows, towering trees—but shifted slightly, moved a few degrees to the right.

He watched a vast, majestic star-galleon edge slowly past the dome, its dozen angled, multi-coloured sails bellying in the breeze. He monitored its royal progress through the evening sky until it was lost to sight—and then he realised that he had, in order to track its passage, moved his head.

For the first time he became aware of his immediate surroundings.

He was in a small, comfortable room formed from a slice of the dome: two walls hung with tapestries, the third the outer wall of diamond facets.

With trepidation, he raised his head and peered down the length of his body. He was naked, but not as naked as he had been on the last occasion he had seen himself. This time he was covered with skin—tanned, healthy-looking skin stretched over well-developed muscles. He remembered the attack in the southern jungle of Tartarus, relived the terrible awareness of being riven limb from limb.

And now he was whole again.

He was in a rejuvenation pod, its canoe-shaped length supporting a web of finely woven fibres which cradled him with the lightest of touches. It was as if he were floating on air. Leads and electrodes covered him, snaking over the side of the pod and disappearing into monitors beneath.

He tried to sit up, but it was all he could do to raise an arm. The slightest exertion filled him with exhaustion. But what did he expect, having newly risen from the dead?

He experienced then a strange ambivalence of emotion. Of course he was grateful to be alive—the fear of oblivion he had experienced upon first awakening was still fresh enough in his memory to fill him with an odd, retrospective dread, and a profound gratitude for his new lease of life. But something, some nagging insistence at the back of his mind, hectored him with the improbability of his being resurrected.

Very well—he was famous, was respected in his field, but even he had to admit that his death would have been no great loss to the galaxy at large. So why had Alvarez, or the people for whom Alvarez worked, seen fit to outlay millions to bring him back to life? For certain, Sam could not have raised the funds to finance the procedure, even if she had realised their joint assets. He was rich, but not *that* rich. Why, the very sailship journey from the rim world of Tartarus to the Core planet of Million would have bankrupted him.

He was alive, but *why* he was alive worried him.

He felt himself drifting as a sedative sluiced through his system.

Hunter opened his eyes.

He was in a room much larger than the first, a full quadrant of the dome this time. He was no longer attached to the rejuvenation pod, but lying in a bed. Apart from a slight ache in his chest, a tightness, he felt well. Tentatively, he sat up, swung his legs from the bed. He wore a short white gown like a kimono. He examined his legs, his arms. They seemed to be as he remembered them, but curiously younger, without the marks of age, the discolourations and small scars he'd picked up during a lifetime of tracking fauna through every imaginable landscape. He filled his chest with a deep breath, exhaled. He felt good.

He stood and crossed to the wall of the dome, climbed the three steps and paused on the raised gallery. A magnificent star-galleon sailed by outside, so close that Hunter could make out figures on the deck, a curious assortment of humans and aliens. A few stopped work to look at him. One young girl even waved. Hunter raised his arm in salute and watched the ship sail away, conscious of the gesture, the blood pumping through his veins. In that instant, he was suddenly aware of the possibilities, of the wondrous gift of life renewed.

"Mr Hunter," the voice called from behind him. "I'm so pleased to see you up and about."

Alvarez stood on the threshold, smiling across the room at him. He seemed smaller than before, somehow reduced. Within the swaddles of his fine clothing— rich gold robes, frilled shirts—he was even more insect-like than Hunter recalled.

"I have so many questions, I don't really know where to begin," Hunter said.

Alvarez waved, the cuff of his gown hanging a good half-metre from his stick-like wrist. "All in good time, my dear Mr Hunter. Perhaps you would care for a drink?" He moved to a table beneath the curve of the dome, its surface marked with a press-select panel of beverages.

"A fruit juice."

"I'll join you," Alvarez said, and seconds later passed Hunter a tall glass of yellow liquid.

His thoughts returned to the jungle of Tartarus. "My wife?"

Alvarez was quick to reassure him. "Samantha is fit and well. No need to worry yourself on that score."

"I'd like to see her."

"That is being arranged. Within the next three or four days, you should be re-united."

Hunter nodded, reluctant to show Alvarez his relief or gratitude. His wife was well, he was blessed with a new body, renewed life. So why did he experience a pang of apprehension like a shadow cast across his soul?

"Mr Hunter," Alvarez asked, "what are your last recollections before awakening here?"

Hunter looked from Alvarez to the tall trees receding into the distance. "Tartarus," he said. "The jungle."

"Can you recall the actual attack?"

"I remember, but vaguely. I can't recall what led up to it, just the attack itself. It's as if it happened years ago."

Alvarez was staring at him. "It did, Mr Hunter. Three years ago, to be precise."

Again, Hunter did not allow his reaction to show: shock, this time. Three years! But Sam had been carrying their child, his daughter. He had missed her birth, the first years of her life.

"You owe your survival to your wife," Alvarez continued. "She fired flares to frighten the beast that killed you, then gathered your remains." He made an expression of distaste. "There was not much left. Your head, torso. She stored them in the freeze unit at your camp, then returned through the jungle to Apollinaire, and from there to the port at Baudelaire, where she arranged passage off-planet."

Hunter closed his eyes. He imagined Sam's terror, her despair, her frantic hope. It should have been enough to drive her mad.

Alvarez went on, "She applied for aid to a number of resurrection foundations. My company examined you. They reported your case to me. I decided to sanction your rebirth."

Hunter was shaking his head. "But how did Sam raise the fare to Million?" he asked. "And the cost of the resurrection itself? There's just no way . . . " What, he wondered, had she done to finance his recovery?

"She had to arrange a loan to get the both of you here. She arrived virtually penniless."

"Then how . . . ?"

Alvarez raised a hand. There was something about the man that Hunter did not like: his swift, imperious gestures, his thin face which combined aspects of asceticism and superiority. In an age when everyone enjoyed the means to ensure perfect health, Alvarez's affectation of ill health was macabre.

"Your situation interested me, Mr Hunter. I knew of you. I followed your work, admired your success. I cannot claim to be a naturalist in the same league as yourself, but I dabble. I run many novel enterprises on Million. My very favourite, indeed the most popular and lucrative, is my Xeno-biological Exhibit Centre, here in the capital. It attracts millions of visitors every year from all across the galaxy. Perhaps you have heard of it, Mr Hunter?"

Hunter shook his head, minimally. "I have no interest in, nor sympathy with, zoos, Mr Alvarez."

"Such an out-dated, crude description, I do think. My Exhibit Centre is quite unlike the menageries of old. The centre furnishes species from around the galaxy with a realistic simulacra of their native habitats, often extending for kilometres. Where the species exhibited are endangered on their own worlds, we have instituted successful breeding programmes. In more than one instance I have saved species from certain extinction." He paused, staring at Hunter. "I have a large staff of experts in every field of xeno-biology," he went on, "though usually I hire operators from the planet in question to capture and transport the animals I require to update my exhibits. I would like you to—"

Hunter laid his drink aside, untouched. "I am a cameraman, Mr Alvarez. I hunt animals in order to film them. I have no expertise in capturing animals."

"What I need is someone skilled in the *tracking* of a certain animal. My team will perform the actual physical capture. On the planet in question, there are no resident experts, and as you are already *au fait* with the terrain."

Hunter interrupted. "Where?" he asked.

"Where else?" Alvarez smiled. "Tartarus, of course."

It took some seconds for his words to sink in. Hunter stared across the room at the dandified zookeeper. "Tartarus?" He almost laughed. "Madness. Three years ago, the scientists were forecasting the explosion of the supernova in two to three years at the latest."

Alvarez responded evenly. "The scientists have revised their estimates. They now think the planet is safe for another year."

Hunter sat down on the steps that curved around the room. He shook his head, looked up. "I'm sorry, Mr Alvarez. Tartarus holds too many bad memories for me. And anyway, it would be insane to go there with the supernova so imminent."

"I think you fail to understand the situation in which you find yourself, Mr

Hunter. You and your wife are in debt to me to the tune of some five million credits. You are now, legally, in my employ—"

"I didn't ask to be resurrected. I signed nothing!"

Alvarez smiled. "Your wife signed all the relevant forms. She wanted you resurrected. She agreed to work for me."

Hunter experienced a strange plummeting sensation deep within him. He whispered, "Where is she?"

"Six months ago, when it was obvious that your resurrection would be successful, she left for Tartarus to do some fieldwork, investigations and preliminary tracking."

Hunter closed his eyes. Alvarez had him.

He thought of his child. Surely Sam would not take an infant to Tartarus. "Who's looking after our child while Sam is on Tartarus?" he asked.

Alvarez shook his head apologetically. "I never actually met your wife. Our negotiations were conducted via intermediaries. I know nothing of her personal arrangements."

Hunter contemplated the view, the tall trees marching away into a slight mist, the canopy of rainbows and the star-galleons. It was against everything that Hunter believed in to hunt and trap an animal for captivity. How many lucrative commissions had he turned down in the past?

But there was one obvious difference in this case. If the animal that Alvarez wanted capturing was not tracked and taken from Tartarus, then it faced annihilation come the supernova.

And there was the added incentive that soon he would be reunited with Sam.

"I seem to have little choice but to agree to your demands."

Alvarez smiled thinly. "Excellent. I knew you would see sense, eventually. We need a man of your calibre in order to track the creature I require as the prize of my collection."

"Which is?" Hunter asked.

Alvarez paused for a second, as if for dramatic emphasis. "The Slarque," he said.

Hunter mouthed the word to himself in disbelief. Millennia ago, long before humankind colonised Tartarus, a sentient alien race known as the Slarque were preeminent on the planet. They built cities on every continent, sailed ships across the oceans, and reached a stage of civilisation comparable to that of humanity in the sixteenth century. Then, over the period of a few hundred years, they became extinct—or so some theorists posited. Others, a crank minority, held that the Slarque still existed in some devolved form, sequestered in the mountainous jungle terrain of the southern continent. There had been reports of sightings, dubious eyewitness accounts of brief meetings with the fearsome, bipedal creatures, but no actual concrete evidence.

"Mr Hunter," Alvarez was saying, "do you have any idea what kind of creature was responsible for your death?"

Hunter gestured. "Of course not. It happened so fast. I didn't have a chance—" He stopped.

Alvarez crossed the room to a wall-screen. He inserted a small disc, adjusted dials. He turned to Hunter. "Your wife was filming at the time of your death. This is what she caught."

The screen flared. Hunter took half a dozen paces forward, then stopped, as if transfixed by what he saw. The picture sent memories, emotions, flooding through his mind. He stared at the jungle scene. He could almost smell the stringent, putrescent reek peculiar to Tartarus, the stench of vegetable matter rotting in the vastly increased heat of the southern climes. He heard the cries and screams of a hundred uncatalogued birds and beasts. He experienced again the mixture of anxiety and exhilaration at being in the unexplored jungle of a planet which at any moment might be ripped apart by its exploding sun.

"Watch closely, Mr Hunter," Alvarez warned.

He saw himself, a small figure in the background, centre-screen. This was an establishing shot, which Sam would edit into the documentary she always made about their field trips.

It was over in five seconds.

One instant he was gesturing at the blood-red sky through a rent in the jungle canopy—and the next something emerged through the undergrowth behind him, leapt upon his back and began tearing him apart.

Hunter peered at the grainy film, trying to make out his assailant. The attack was taking place in the undergrowth, largely obscured from the camera. All he could see was the rearing, curving tail of the animal—for all the world like that of a scorpion—flailing and thrashing and coming down again and again on the body of its victim.

The film finished there, as Sam fired flares to scare away the animal. The screen blanked.

"We have reason to believe," Alvarez said, "that this creature was the female of the last surviving pair of Slarque on Tartarus—"

"Ridiculous!" Hunter cried.

"They are devolved," Alvarez went on, "and living like wild animals." He paused. "Do you see what an opportunity this is, Mr Hunter? If we can capture, and save from certain extinction, the very last pair of an alien race?"

Hunter gestured, aware that his hand was trembling. "This is hardly proof of its existence," he objected.

"The stinger corresponds to anatomical remains which are known to be of the Slarque. Which other species on Tartarus has such a distinctive feature?" Alvarez paused. "Also, your wife has been working hard on Tartarus. She has come up with some very interesting information."

From a pocket in his robe, he pulled out what Hunter recognised as an earphone. "A couple of months ago she dispatched this report of her progress. I'll leave it with you." He placed it on the tabletop beside the bed. "We embark for Tartarus in a little under three days, Mr Hunter. For now, farewell."

When Alvarez had left the room, Hunter quickly crossed to the bed and took up the phone. His hand trembled at the thought of listening to his wife's voice. He inserted the phone in his right ear and activated it.

Tears came to his eyes. Her words brought back a slew of poignant memories. He saw her before him, her calm oval face, dark hair drawn back, green eyes staring into space as she spoke into the recorder.

Hunter lay on the bed and closed his eyes.

Apollinaire Town. Mary's day, 33rd St Jerome's month, 1720—Tartarean calendar. By Galactic Standard it's . . . I don't know. I know I've been here for months, but it seems like years. Sometimes I find it hard to believe that anything exists beyond this damned planet. The sun dominates everything. During the day it fills the sky, bloated and festering. Even at night the sky is crimson with its light. It's strange to think that everything around me, the everyday reality of Tartarus I take for granted, will be incinerated in less than a year. This fact overwhelms life here, affecting everyone. There's a strange air of apathy and lassitude about the place, as people go about their business, marking time before the wholesale evacuation begins. The crime rate has increased; violence is commonplace. Bizarre cults have sprung up—and I mean even weirder than the Church of the Ultimate Sacrifice.

Alvarez, I want you to pass this recording on to Hunter when he's fit and well. I know you want a progress report, and you'll get one. But I want to talk to my husband, if you don't mind.

I'm staying at the Halbeck House hotel, Hunter, in the double room overlooking the canal. I'm dictating this on the balcony where we did the editing for the last film. I'm watching the sun set as I speak. It's unpleasantly hot, but at least there's a slight breeze starting up. In the trees beside the canal, a flock of nightgulls are gathering. You'll be able to hear their songs a little later, when night falls. A troupe of Lefevre's mandrills is watching me from the far balcony rail. I know you never liked the creatures, Hunter—but I find something inexpressibly melancholy in their eyes. Do you think they know their time is almost up?

(Oh, by the way, the hotel still serves the most superb lemon beer in Apollinaire. Mmmm.)

Okay, Alvarez, I know—you want to hear how I'm progressing.

Three days ago I got back from a month-long trip into the interior. I'd been getting nowhere in either Apollinaire or Baudelaire. The leads I wanted to follow up all ran out, people were reluctant to talk. A couple of people I wanted to interview—the freelance filmmaker who recorded *something* ten years ago, and the prospector who claimed he'd seen a Slarque. Well, the filmmaker left Tartarus a couple of years back, and the prospector is dead. I tried to make an appointment with the director of the Natural History Museum, but he was away and wasn't due back for a week. I left a message for him, then decided to take a trek into the interior.

Hunter, the ornithopter service no longer runs from Apollinaire. Gabriella's sold up and left the planet, and the new owner has re-sited the operation in Baudelaire. It's understandable, of course. These days there are few naturalists, geologists, or prospectors interested in the southern interior. The only visitors to the area are the members of one of the crackpot cults I mentioned, the so-called *Slarqists*, who come here on their way to the alien temples down the coast. I don't know what they do there. There are rumours that they make sacrifices to the all-powerful God of the Slarque. Don't ask me what kind of sacrifices.

Anyway, with no ornithopters flying, I hired a tracked bison and two armed guards and set off inland.

It took four days to reach the site of our first camp, Hunter—the rock pool beneath the waterfall, remember? From there it was another two days to the foot of the plateau, to the place where you . . . where the attack happened. It was just how I remembered it, the opening in the smaller *salse* trees, the taller, surrounding trees providing a high-level canopy that blotted out the sun. I left the guards in the bison and just stood on the edge of the clearing and relived the horror of what happened three years ago.

I can hear you asking why did I go back there, why did I torture myself? Well, if you recall, I'd set up a few remote cameras to record some of the more timorous examples of the area's wildlife while we went trekking. After the attack... I'd left the cameras and equipment in my haste to get to Baudelaire. It struck me that perhaps if the Slarque—if Slarque they were—had returned, then they might be captured on film.

That night in the clearing I viewed all the considerable footage. Plenty of shots of nocturnal fauna and grazing quadrupeds, but no Slarque.

The following day, I took forensic samples from the area where the attack happened—broken undergrowth, disturbed soil, etc., for Alvarez's people to examine when they get here. Then I set up more cameras, this time fixed to relay images back to my base in Apollinaire.

I decided to make a few exploratory forays into the surrounding jungle. We had food and water for a couple of weeks, and as the guards were being paid by the hour they had no reason to complain. Every other day we made circular treks into the jungle, finishing back at the campsite in the evening. I reckon we covered a good two hundred square kilometres like this. I filmed constantly, took dung samples, samples of hair and bone. Needless to say, I didn't come across the Slarque.

Just short of a month after leaving Apollinaire, we made the journey back. I felt depressed. I'd achieved nothing, not even laid the terror of that terrible day. It's strange, but I returned to Tartarus on this mission for Alvarez with extreme reluctance—if not for the fact that I was working for him to cover the cost of your treatment, I would have been happy to leave Tartarus well alone and let the Slarque fry when the sun blew. That was then. Now, and even after just a few days on the planet, I wanted to know what had killed you, if it were a Slarque. I wanted to find out more about this strange, devolved race.

I left the interior having found out nothing, and that hurt.

When I got back to Halbeck House, there was a message for me from the director of the Natural History Museum at Apollinaire. He'd seen and enjoyed a couple of our films and agreed to meet me.

Monsieur Dernier was in his early eighties, so learned and dignified I felt like a kid in his company. I told him about the attack, that I was eager to trace the animal responsible. It happened that he'd heard about the incident on the newscasts, and he was happy to help me. Now that it came to it, I was reluctant to broach the subject of the Slarque, in case Dernier thought me a complete crank, one of the many crazy cultists abroad in Apollinaire. I edged around the issue for a time, mentioned at last that some people, on viewing the film, had commented on how the beast did bear a certain superficial resemblance to fossil remains of the Slarque. Of course, I hastened to add, I didn't believe this myself.

He gave me a strange look, told me that he himself subscribed to the belief, unpopular though it was, that devolved descendants of the Slarque still inhabited the interior of the southern continent.

He'd paused there, then asked me if I'd ever heard of Rogers and Codey? I admitted that I hadn't.

Dernier told me that they had been starship pilots back in the eighties. Their shuttle had suffered engine failure and come down in the central mountains, crash-landed in a remote snowbound valley, and never been discovered. They were given up for dead—until a year later when Rogers staggered into Apollinaire, half-delirious and severely frostbitten. The only survivor of the crash, he'd crossed a high mountain pass and half the continent—it made big news even on Earth, thirty years ago. When he was sufficiently recovered to leave hospital, Rogers had sought out M. Dernier, as he'd heard that Dernier was an advocate of the extant Slarque theory.

Lt Rogers claimed to have had contact with the Slarque in their interior mountain fastness.

Rogers had repeated, over and over, that he had seen the Slarque, and that the meeting had been terrible—and he would say no more. Rogers had needed to confess, Dernier felt, but, when he came to do so, the burden of his experience had been too harrowing to relive.

I asked Dernier if he believed Rogers's story.

He told me that he did. Rogers hadn't sought to publicise his claim, to gain from it. He had no reason to lie about meeting the creatures. Whatever had happened in the interior had clearly left the lieutenant in a weakened mental state.

I asked him if he knew what had become of Lt Rogers, if he was still on Tartarus.

"Thirty years ago," Dernier said, "Lt Rogers converted, became a novice in the Church of the Ultimate Sacrifice. If he's survived this long in that bloody organisation, then he'll still be on Tartarus. You might try the monastery at Barabas, along the coast."

So yesterday I took the barge on the inland waterway, then a pony and trap up to the cliff-top Monastery of St Cyprian of Carthage.

I was met inside the ornate main gate by a blind monk. He listened to my explanations in silence. I said that I wished to talk a certain Anthony Rogers, formerly Lt Rogers of the Tartarean Space Fleet. The monk told me that Father Rogers would be pleased to see me. He was taking his last visitors this week. Three days ago he had undergone extensive penitent surgery, preparatory to total withdrawal.

The monk led me through ancient cloisters. I was more than a little apprehensive. I'd seen devotees of the Ultimate Sacrifice only at a distance before. You know how squeamish I am, Hunter.

The monk left me in a beautiful high garden overlooking the ocean. I sat on a wooden bench and stared out across the waters. The sky was white hot, the sun huge above the horizon as it made its long fall towards evening.

The monk returned, pushing a *bundle* in a crude wooden wheelchair. Its occupant, without arms or legs, jogged from side to side as he was trundled down the incline, prevented from falling forwards by a leather strap buckled around his midriff.

The monk positioned the carriage before me and murmured that he'd leave us to talk.

I... even now I find it difficult to express what I thought, or rather *felt*, on meeting Father Rogers in the monastery garden. His physical degradation, the voluntary amputation of his limbs, gave him the unthreatening and pathetic appearance of a swaddled infant, so perhaps the reason I felt threatened was that I could not bring myself to intellectually understand the degree of his commitment in undergoing such mutilation.

Also what troubled me was that I could still see, in his crew cut, his deep tan and keen blue eyes, the astronaut that he had once been.

We exchanged guarded pleasantries for a time, he suspicious of my motives, myself unsure how to begin to broach the subject of his purported meeting with the aliens.

I recorded our conversation. I've edited it into this report. I've cut the section where Fr Rogers rambled—he's in his nineties now and he seemed much of the time to be elsewhere. For long periods he'd stop talking altogether, stare into the distance, as if reliving the ordeal he'd survived in the mountains. In the following account I've included a few of my own comments and explanations.

I began by telling him that, almost three years ago, I lost my husband in what I suspect was a Slarque attack.

Fr Rogers: Slarque? Did you say Slarque?

Sam: I wasn't one hundred per cent sure. I might be mistaken. I've been trying to find someone with first-hand experience of...

Fr Rogers: The Slarque... Lord Jesus Christ have mercy on their wayward souls. It's such a long time ago, such a long time. I sometimes wonder... No, I know it happened. It can't have been a dream, a nightmare. It *happened*. It's the reason I'm here. If not for what happened out there in the mountains, I might never have seen the light.

Sam: What happened, Father?

Fr Rogers: Mmmm? What happened? What *happened*? You wouldn't believe me if I told you. You'd be like all the others, disbelievers all.

Sam: I have seen a Slarque, too.

Fr Rogers: So you say, so you say... I haven't told anyone for a long time. Became tired of being disbelieved, you see. They thought I'd gone mad. But I didn't tell anyone what really happened. I didn't want the authorities to go and find Codey, arrest him.

Sam: Codey, your co-pilot? But I thought he died in the crash-landing?

Fr Rogers: That's what I told everyone. Easier that way. He wanted people to think he hadn't survived, the sinner.

Sam: Father, can you tell me what happened?

Fr Rogers: It's... how long ago? Thirty years? More? There's little chance Codey will still be alive. Oh, he had supplies aplenty, but up here... up here he was sick and getting worse. He made me promise that I'd keep quiet about what he did, and until now I have. But what harm can it do now, with Codey surely long dead?

(He stopped here and stared off into the distance and the gothic monastery rearing against the twilight sky. Tears appeared in his eyes. I felt sorry for him. Part of me regretted what I was putting him through, but I was intrigued by the little he'd told me so far. I *had* to find out what he'd experienced, all those years ago.)

Sam: Father?

Fr Rogers: Eh? Oh, the crash-landing. We came down too soon. Don't ask me why. I can't remember. Miracle we survived. We found ourselves in a high valley in the central mountains, shut in by snow-covered peaks all around. We were a small ship, a shuttle. The radio was wrecked and we had no other means of communicating with the outside world. We didn't reckon the Fleet would waste much time trying to find us. We had supplies enough for years, and the part of the ship not completely stove in we used as living quarters. I made a few expeditions into the surrounding hills, trying to find a way out, a navigable pass that'd get us to the sea level jungle below the central range... But the going was too tough, the snow impassable.

It was on one of these abortive expeditions that I saw the first Slarque. I was coming back to the ship, wading through a waist-high snowdrift, frozen to the bone and sick with the thought that I'd never get away from this frozen hell.

The Slarque was on a spur of rock overlooking the valley. It was on all fours, though later I saw them standing upright. It was watching me. It was a long way off, and in silhouette, so I couldn't really make out much detail. I recognised the arched tail, though, whipping back and forth behind its back.

So when I returned to the ship I told Codey what I'd seen. He just stared at me for a long time—and I assumed he thought I'd gone mad. But then he began nodding, and he said, "I know. They've been communicating with me for the past three days." Then it was *my* turn to think *he'd* flipped.

(His gaze slipped out of focus again. He no longer saw the monastery. He was back in the mountain valley.)

Fr Rogers: Codey was strangely calm, like a man blessed with a vision. I asked him what he meant by "communicating." Looking straight through me, he just pointed to his head. "They put thoughts into here—not words, but thoughts: emotions, facts..."

I said, "Codey, you've finally gone, man. Don't give me any of that shit!" But Codey just went on staring through me like I wasn't there, and he began talking, telling me about the Slarque, and there was so much of it, so many details Codey just couldn't have known or made up, that by the end of it all I was scared, real scared, not wanting to believe a word of it, but at the same time finding myself half-believing...

Codey said that there were just two Slarque left. They were old, a couple of hundred years old. They'd lived near the coast in their early years, but with the arrival of humans on the southern continent, and the melting of the ice as the sun warmed, they'd retreated further south, into the snowfields of the central mountains. Codey told me that the Slarque had dwindled because a certain species of animal, on which they were dependent, had become extinct long ago. Codey said that the female Slarque was bearing a litter of young, that she was due to birth soon... He told me many other things that night, as the snow fell and the wind howled outside, but either I've forgotten what else he said, or I never heard it at the time through fear... I went straight out into that gale and rigged up an electric fence around the ship, and I didn't stop work until I was sure it'd keep out the most fearsome predator.

The next day or two, I kept out of Codey's way, as if he was contaminated. I ate in my own cabin, tried not to dwell on what he'd told me.

One night he came to my cabin, knocked on the door. He just stood there, staring at me. "They want one of us," he told me. As soon as he spoke, it was as if this was what I'd feared all along. I had no doubt who "they" were. I think I went berserk then. I attacked Codey, beat him back out of my cabin. I was frightened. Oh, Christ was I frightened.

In the morning he came to me again, strangely subdued, remote. He said he wanted to show me something in the hold. I was wary, expecting a trick. I armed myself and followed him down the corridor of the broken-backed ship and into the hold. He crossed to a suspension unit, opened the lid, and said, "Look."

So I looked. We were carrying a prisoner, a criminal suspended for the trip between Tartarus and Earth, where he was due to go on trial for the assassination of a Tartarean government official. I hadn't known what we were carrying. I hadn't bothered to check the manifest before take-off. But Codey had.

He said, "He'd only be executed on Earth."

"No," I said.

Codey stared at me. "It's either him or you, Rogers." He had his laser out and aimed at my head. I lifted my own pistol, saw that the charge was empty. Codey just smiled.

I said, "But...but when they've done with him—how long will he keep them satisfied? How long before they want one of us?"

Codey shook his head. "Not for a long while, believe me."

I ranted and raved at him, cried and swore, but the terrible inevitability of his logic wore me down. It was either the prisoner or me. So I helped him drag the suspension unit from the ship, through the snow to the far end of the valley, where we left it with the lid open for the Slarque. I...I have never forgiven myself to this day. I wish now that I'd had the strength to sacrifice myself.

(He broke down then, bowed his head and wept. I soothed him as best I could, murmured platitudes, my hand on the stump of his shoulder.)

Fr Rogers: That night I watched two shadowy ghosts appear at the end of the valley, haul the prisoner from the unit and drag him off through the snow. At first light next morning I kitted up, took my share of provisions and told Codey I was going to find a way out, that I'd rather die trying than remain here with him. I reckoned that with the Slarque busy with the prisoner, I had a slim chance of getting away from the valley. After that...who could tell?

Codey didn't say a word. I tried to persuade him to come with me, but he kept shaking his head and saying that I didn't understand, that they needed him. So I left him and trekked north, fearful of the aliens, the snow, the cold. All I recall is getting clear of the valley and the Slarque, and the tremendous feeling of relief when I did. I don't remember much else. The terror of what I was leaving was worse than the thought of dying alone in the mountains. They tell me it's one and a half-thousand kilometres from the central range to the coast. I don't know. I just walked and kept on walking.

(He was silent for a long, long time after that. At last he spoke, almost to himself.)

Fr Rogers: Poor Codey. Poor, poor Codey...

Sam: And...then you joined the Church?

Fr Rogers: Almost as soon as I got back. It seemed the only thing to do. I had to make amends, to thank God for my survival and at the same time to make reparations for the fact that I did survive.

We sat for a time in silence, Father Rogers contemplating the past while I considered the future. I knew what I was going to do. I unfolded the map of the southern continent I had brought with me and spread it across the arms of the invalid carriage. I asked him where the ship had come down. He stared at the map for a long time, frowning, and finally quoted an approximate grid reference coordinate. I marked the valley with a cross.

I sat and talked with Father Rogers for a while, and then left him sitting in the garden overlooking the sea, and made my way back to Apollinaire.

That was yesterday. Today I've been preparing for the expedition. Unfortunately I've found no one willing to act as my bodyguard this time—because of the duration of the planned trip and the sun's instability. I set off tomorrow in a tracked bison, with plenty of food, water and weapons. I've calculated that it'll take me a couple of months to cover the one and a half-thousand kays to the valley where the ship crash-landed. Fortunately, with the rise of the global temperature, the snow on the high ground of the central mountains has melted, so that leg of the journey should be relatively easy. With luck, the sun will hold steady for a while yet, though it does seem to be getting hotter every day. The latest forecast I've heard is that we're safe for another six to nine months.

I don't know what I'll find when I get to the valley. Certainly not Codey. As Father Rogers said, after thirty years he should be long dead. Maybe I'll hit lucky and find the Slarque? I'll leave transmitter beacons along my route, so you can follow me when you get here, whenever that might be.

Okay, Alvarez, that's about it. If you don't mind, I'd like the next bit to remain private, between Hunter and me, okay?

Hunter, the thought that sooner or later we'll be together again has kept me going. Don't worry about me, I have everything under control. Arabella is with me; I'm taking her into the interior tomorrow. And before you protest—don't! She's perfectly safe. I can't wait until we're reunited, Hunter, until we can watch our daughter grow, share her discoveries...I love you. Take care.

—.—

Hunter sat on the balcony of Halbeck House, where weeks before Sam had made the recording. He'd tried contacting her by radio upon his arrival, but the activity of the solar flares made such communication impossible.

He sipped an iced lemon beer and stared out across what had once been a pretty provincial town. Now the increased temperature of the past few months had taken its toll. The trees lining the canal were scorched and dying, and the water in the canal itself had evaporated, leaving a bed of evil-smelling mud. Even the three-storey timber buildings of the town seemed weary, dried out and warped by the incessant heat. Although the sun had set one hour ago, pulling in its wake a gaudy, pyrotechnical display of flaring lights above the crowded rooftops, the twilight song of the nightgulls was not to be heard. Nor was there any sign of Lefevre's mandrills, usually to be seen swinging crazily across the town's rooftops. An eerie silence hung in the air, a funereal calm presaging the planet's inevitable demise.

Hunter, Alvarez and his entourage had arrived on Tartarus by the very last scheduled sailship; they would entrust their departure to one of the illegal pirate lines still ferrying adventurers, thrill-seekers, or just plain fools, to and from the planet.

They had arrived in Apollinaire that morning, to find the town deserted but for a handful of citizens determined to leave their flight to the very last weeks.

Three days ago the sun had sent out a searing pulse of flame, a great flaring tongue, as if in derision of the citizens who remained. The people of Baudelaire and Apollinaire had panicked. There had been riots, much looting and burning, and another great exodus off-world. The regular shipping lines had been inundated by frantic souls desperate to flee, and the surplus had been taken by the opportunistic pirate ships that had just happened to be orbiting like flies around a corpse.

Technically, Halbeck House was no longer open for business, but its proprietor had greeted Hunter like a long-lost brother and insisted that he, Alvarez and the rest of the team make themselves at home. Then he had taken the last boat to Baudelaire, leaving a supply of iced beer and a table set for the evening meal.

Hunter drank his beer and considered Father Rogers's story, which he had listened to again and again on the voyage to Tartarus. Although the old astronaut's words had about them a kind of insane veracity which suggested he believed his own story, even if no one else did, it was stretching the limits of credulity to believe

76

that not only did a last pair of Slarque still exist in the central mountains, but that they had been in mental contact with Codey. And the beast that had attacked and killed Hunter? Sam's footage of the incident was not conclusive proof that the Slarque existed, despite Alvarez's assumptions otherwise.

The more he thought about it, the more he came to the conclusion that the trip into the interior would prove fruitless. He looked forward to the time when he would be reunited with Sam, and meet his daughter Arabella for the very first time.

He had expected Sam to leave a message for him at the hotel, maybe even a pix of Arabella. But nothing had awaited him, and when he asked the proprietor about his daughter, the man had looked puzzled. "But your wife had no little girl with her, Monsieur Hunter."

Dinner that evening was taken on the patio beside the empty canal. The meal was a subdued affair, stifled by the oppressing humidity and the collective realisation of the enormity of the imminent mission. Hunter ate sparingly and said little, speaking only to answer questions concerning the planet's natural history. The chest pains which had bothered him on Million had increased in severity over the past few days; that afternoon he had taken to his bed, wracked with what he thought was a heart attack. Now he felt the familiar tightness in his chest. He was reassured that Dr Fischer was on hand.

The rest of their party, other than himself, Alvarez and the doctor, consisted of a team of four drivers-cum-guards, men from Million in the employ of the Alvarez Foundation. They tended to keep to themselves, indeed were congregated at the far end of the table now, leaving the others to talk together.

Alvarez was saying, "I made a trip out to the St Cyprian Monastery this afternoon, to see if I could get anything more from Rogers."

Hunter looked up from his plate of cold meat and salad. "And?" He winced as a stabbing pain lanced through his lungs.

The entrepreneur was leaning back in his chair, turning a glass of wine in his fingers. He was dressed in a lightweight white suit of extravagantly flamboyant design. "I found Rogers, and a number of the other monks."

Dr Fischer asked, "Did you learn anything more?"

Alvarez shook his head. "A couple of the monks were dead. Rogers was still alive, but only just. They were strapped to great wooden stakes on the cliff-top greensward, naked, reduced to torsos. Many had had their eyes and facial features removed. They were chanting. I must admit that in a perverse kind of way, there was something almost beautiful in the tableau."

"As an atheist," Hunter said, "I could not look upon such depredation with sufficient objectivity to appreciate any beauty. As far as I'm concerned, their cult is a sick tragedy."

"They could be helped," Dr Fischer said tentatively.

Hunter grunted a laugh. "I somehow doubt that your ministrations would meet with their approval."

The three men drank on in silence. At length, talk turned to the expedition.

Alvarez indicated the huge tracked bison he had transported from Million. The vehicle sat in the drive beside the hotel, loaded with provisions—food, water, weapons and, Hunter noticed, a collapsible cage lashed to the side.

"All is ready," Alvarez said. "We set off at dawn. Your wife's radio beacons are transmitting, and all we have to do is follow their course through the jungle. Our progress should be considerably quicker than hers. We'll be following the route she has carved through the jungle, and as we have four drivers working in shifts we'll be able to journey throughout the night. I estimate that, if all goes well, we should arrive at the valley of the crash-landing within two weeks. Then you take over, Mr Hunter, and with luck on our side we should bring about the salvation of the Slarque."

Hunter restrained himself from commenting. The pain in his chest was mounting. He told himself that he should not worry. Dr Fischer had brought him back to life once; he could no doubt do so again, should it be necessary. But something instinctive deep within him brought Hunter out in hot and cold sweats of fear.

Alvarez leaned forward. "Hunter? Are you—?"

Hunter clasped his chest. Pain filled his lungs, constricting his breathing. Dr Fischer, with surprising agility for a man his size, rounded the table and bent over him. He slipped an injector from a wallet and sank it into Hunter's neck. The cool spread of the drug through his chest brought instant relief. He regained his breath little by little as the pain ebbed.

Dr Fischer said, "You've undergone a rapid resurrection programme, Mr Hunter. Some minor problems are to be expected. At the first sign of the slightest pain, please consult me." The doctor exchanged a quick glance with Alvarez, who nodded.

Hunter excused himself and retired to his room.

He lay on his bed for a long time, unable to sleep. The night sky flared with bright pulses of orange and magenta light, sending shadows flagging across the walls of the room. He thought of Sam, and the daughter he had yet to meet, somewhere out there in the interior. He cursed the day he had first heard of Tartarus Major, regretted the three years it had robbed from his life. He slept fitfully, troubled by dreams in which Sam was running from the teeth and claws of the creature that had killed him.

He was awoken at dawn, after what seemed like the briefest of sleeps, by the ugly klaxon of the tracked bison. The vehicle was equipped to sleep eight, in small compartments little wider than the individual bunks they contained. It was invitation enough for Hunter. He spent the first six hours of the journey catching up on the sleep he'd lost during the night. He was eventually awoken by the bucketing yaw of the bison as it made the transition from the relatively smooth surface of a road to rough terrain.

He washed the sweat from his face in the basin above his bunk, then staggered through the sliding door. A narrow corridor ran the length of the vehicle to the control cabin where a driver wrestled with the wheel, accompanied by a navigator. A ladder led up to a hatch in the roof. He climbed into the fierce, actinic sunlight and a blowtorch breeze. Alvarez and Fischer were seated on a bench, swaying with the motion of the truck.

Hunter exchanged brief greetings and settled to quietly watching the passing landscape. They had moved from the cultivated littoral to an indeterminate area of characterless scrubland, and were fast approaching the jungle-covered foothills that folded away, ever hazier, to a point in the distance where the crags of the central mountains seemed to float above a sea of cloud.

They were following a route through the scrub which he and Sam had pioneered years ago in their own bison. The landmarks, such as they were—towering insects' nests, and stunted, sun-warped trees—brought back memories that should have cheered him but which served only to remind him of Sam's absence.

As the huge sun surged overhead and the heat became furnace-like, Alvarez and Dr Fischer erected a heat-reflective awning. The three men sat in silence and drank iced beers.

They left the scrubland in their wake and accelerated into the jungle, barrelling down the narrow defile torn through the dense undergrowth by Sam's vehicle before them. It was minimally cooler in the shade of the jungle, but the absence of even a hot wind to stir the air only increased the humidity.

Around sunset they broke out the pre-packaged trays of food and bulbs of wine, and ate to the serenade of calls and cries from the surrounding jungle. Hunter recognised many of them, matching physical descriptions to the dozens of songs that shrilled through the twilight. When he tired of this he said goodnight to Alvarez and the doctor and turned in. He lay awake for a long time until exhaustion, and the motion of the truck, sent him to sleep.

This routine set the pattern for the rest of the journey. Hunter would wake late, join Alvarez and the doctor for a few beers, eat as the sun set, then retire and lie with his chaotic thoughts and fears until sleep pounced, unannounced. His chest pains continued, but, as Dr Fischer ordered, he reported them early, received the quelling injection and suffered no more.

To counter boredom, he pointed out various examples of Tartarean wildlife to his fellow travellers, giving accounts of the habits and peculiarities of the unique birds and beasts. Even this pastime, though, reminded him of Sam's absence: she would have told him to stop being so damned sententious.

Seven days out from Apollinaire, they came to the clearing where Hunter had lost his life. Alvarez called a halt for a couple of hours, as they'd made good time so far. The driver slewed the bison to a sudden stop. The comparative silence of the clearing, after the incessant noise of the engine, was like a balm.

Hunter jumped down and walked away from Alvarez and the others, wanting to be alone with his thoughts. The encampment was as Sam had left it on the day of the attack: the dome-tent located centrally, the battery of cameras set up peripherally to record the teeming wildlife. His heart pounding, Hunter crossed to where he judged the attack had taken place. There was nothing to distinguish the area; the disturbed earth had scabbed over with moss and plants, and the broken undergrowth in the margin of the jungle had regrown. He looked down the length of his new body, apprehending the miracle of his renewed existence. Overcome by an awareness of the danger, he hurried back to the truck.

Sam had been this way—the tracks of her bison had patterned the floor of the clearing—but if she had left any recorded message there was no sign, only the ubiquitous radio transmitter which she had dropped at intervals of a hundred kilometres along her route.

They ate their evening meal in the clearing, a novelty after having to contend with the constant bucking motion of the truck at mealtimes. No sooner had the sun set, flooding the jungle with an eerie crimson night light, than they were aboard the bison again and surging through the jungle into territory new to Hunter.

Over the next six days, the tracked bison climbed through the increasingly dense jungle, traversing steep inclines that would have defeated a lesser vehicle. They halted once more, two days short of their destination, at a natural pass in the mountainside which had been blocked, obviously since Sam's passage, by a small rock fall.

While Alvarez's men cleared the obstruction, Hunter walked back along the track and stared out over the continent they had crossed. They were at a high elevation now, and the jungle falling away, the distant flat scrubland and cultivated seaboard margin, was set out below him like a planetary surveyor's scale model. Over the sea, the red giant sphere of the dying sun was like a baleful eye, watching him, daring their mission to succeed before the inevitable explosion.

Alvarez called to Hunter, and they boarded the truck on the last leg of the journey.

The night before they reached the valley where the starship had crash-landed, Hunter dreamed of Sam. The nightmare was vague and surreal, lacking events and incidents but overburdened with mood. He experienced the weight of some inexpressible depression, saw again and again the distant image of Sam, calling for him.

He awoke suddenly, alerted by something. He lay on his back, blinking up at the ceiling. Then he realised what was wrong. The truck was no longer in motion; the engine was quiet. He splashed his face with cold water and pulled on his coverall. He left his cabin and climbed down into the burning sunlight, his mood affected by some residual depression from the nightmare. He joined the others gathered around the nose of the bison and stared without a word into the valley spread out below.

In Father Rogers's story, the valley had been snow filled, inhospitable, but over the intervening years the snow had melted, evaporated by the increased temperature, and plant life in abundance had returned to this high region. A carpet of grass covered the valley floor, dotted with a colourful display of wild flowers.

Hunter was suddenly aware of his heartbeat as he made out the broken-backed shape of a starship, its nose buried in a semi-circular mound it had ploughed all those years ago, grassed over now like some ancient earthwork. Little of the original paintwork was observable through the cocoon of grass and creepers that had captured the ship since the thaw.

Then he made out, in the short meadow grass of the valley, the tracks of Sam's vehicle leading to the ship. Of her bison there was no sign. He set off at a walk, then began running towards the stranded ship.

He paused before the ramp that led up to the entrance, then cautiously climbed inside. Creepers and moss had penetrated a good way into the main corridor. He called his wife's name, his voice echoing in the silence. The ship seemed deserted. He returned outside, into the dazzling sunlight, and made a complete circuit of the ship. Sam's truck wasn't there—but he did see, leading away from the ship to a distant, higher valley, the parallel imprint of vehicle tracks in the grass.

Beside the ramp was a radio beacon. Tied to the end of its aerial was Sam's red-and-white polka-dotted bandanna. Hunter untied it and discovered an earphone.

Up the valley, the others were approaching in the bison. Before they reached him, Hunter sat on the ramp, activated the phone and held it to his ear.

The sound of Sam's voice filled him with joy at first, then a swift, stabbing sadness that he had only her voice.

Somewhere in the interior... Luke's day, 26th, St Bede's month, 1720, Tartarean Calendar.

I've decided to keep a regular record of my journey, more for something to do before I sleep each night than anything else.

I set off from Apollinaire eight days ago and made good time, driving for ten, twelve hours a day. I preferred the days, even though the driving was difficult—the nights seemed to go on forever. It didn't occur to me until I stopped on that first evening that I'd never camped alone in the interior before, and it was a long time before I got to sleep. The following nights were a bit better, as I got used to being alone. On the morning of the fourth day I was awoken by a great flare from the sun. I nearly panicked. I thought this was it, the supernova. Then I recalled all the other times it'd done that, when you were with me, Hunter. It wasn't the end, then—but perhaps it was some kind of warning. Nothing much else to report at the moment. Long, hot days. Difficult driving. I stopped yesterday at the clearing where... *it* happened. It brings back terrible memories. I'm missing you. I can't wait till you're with me again. Arabella is well.

The interior. Mary's day, 34th, St Bede's month.

I've spent the last few days trying to find the best route through the damned foothills. The map's useless. I've tried three different routes and I've had to turn back each time, wasting hours. Now I think I've found the best way through.

The Central Mountains. Mathew's day, 6th, St Botolph's month.

Well, I'm in the mountains now. The going is slow. What with a map that's no damned good at all, and the terrain clogged with new jungle since the thaw, I'm making precious little progress. Sometimes just ten kays a day. I haven't had a proper wash for ages, but I'm eating and sleeping well. I'm okay.

—.—

82

Central Mountains. John's day, 13th, St Botolph's month.

Another frustrating week. I suppose it's a miracle that I've been able to get this far, but the bison's a remarkable vehicle. It just keeps on going. I reckon I'm three weeks from Codey's Valley, as I've started to think of it. At this rate you won't be far behind me. I've decided to leave the recording on one of the radio beacons somewhere, so you'll know in advance that I'm okay. So is Arabella.

Central Mountains. Mark's day, 22nd, St Botolph's month.

I've been making good progress, putting in sometimes fourteen hours at the wheel. I've had some good luck. Found navigable passes first time. I should make Codey's Valley in a week, if all goes well.

Central Mountains. Mary's day, 27th, St Botolph's month.

I'm just two or three days from Codey's Valley, and whatever I'll find there. I must admit, I haven't really thought about what might be awaiting me. I've had too much to concentrate on just getting *here*, never mind worrying about the future. It'll probably just be a big anti-climax. I'll wait for you there, at the ship.

It's dark outside. I'm beneath a great overhanging shelf of rock that's blocking out the night sky's light. I can't hear or see a single thing out there. I might be the only living soul for kilometres. I just want all this to be over. I want to get away from this damned planet. Promise me we'll go on a long, relaxing holiday when all this is over, Hunter, okay?

Codey's Valley. I don't know what date, St Cyprian's month.

A lot has happened over the past couple of weeks. I hardly know where to begin. I've spent maybe ten, eleven days in a rejuvenation pod—but I'm not really sure how long. It seems like ages. I'm okay, but still a bit woozy...I'm getting ahead of myself. I'll go back a bit—to the 28th, I think, when it happened.

I was a day away from the valley, according to the map. I was feeling elated that I was nearly there, but at the same time...I don't know, I was apprehensive. I could think of nothing else but the Slarque, what they'd done to you. What they might do to me if they chose to...Anyway, perhaps I wasn't concentrating for thinking about this. I was driving up a ravine, crossing the steep slope. I'd had little trouble with the bison until then, so I think what happened was my fault. I lost control. You know how you feel in that terrible split-second when you realise something life threatening is about to happen . . . Well, the truck rolled and I couldn't do a thing about it. I was knocked unconscious.

I don't know how long I was out, maybe a day or two. The pain brought me around a few times, then put me under again, it was that bad. I thought I'd cracked my skull, and there was something wrong with my pelvis. I couldn't move. The bison was on its side, with all the loose contents of the cab piled up around me. When I tried to move . . . the pain! Then wonderful oblivion.

When I came to my senses, the truck was no longer on its side. It was upright again—and I wasn't where I'd been, in the cab. I was stretched out in the corridor, something soft cradling my head.

Then the truck started up and roared off up the side of the ravine, the motion racking me with pain. I was delirious. I didn't know what the hell was happening. I cried out for the truck to stop, but I couldn't make myself heard over the noise of the engine.

When I regained consciousness, night was falling. I'd been out for hours. The truck was moving, but along a flat surface that didn't cause me pain. I tried to look down the length of my body, into the cab, and as I did so the driver turned in his seat and peered down at me.

I knew it was Codey.

Spacers never lose that look. He was short and thickset, crop-headed. I reckoned he was about seventy, and while his body looked younger, that of someone half his age, his face was old and lined, as if he'd lived through a hundred years of hardship.

I passed out again. When I came to, I thought I'd dreamed of Codey. The truck had stopped, its engine ticking in the silence. Then the side door opened and Codey, wearing old Fleet regulation silvers, climbed up and knelt beside me. He held an injector.

He told me not to worry, that he was going to take me to the ship, where he had a rejuvenation pod. He told me that my pelvis was broken and that a few days in the pod would fix it. He placed the cold nozzle to my upper arm and plunged.

I felt nothing as he lifted me and carried me from the bison, across to the ship. He eased me down long corridors, into a chamber I recognised as an astrodome— the glass all covered and cloaked with creepers—and lay me in the pod. As I slipped into sleep, he stared down at me. He looked worried and unsure.

Yesterday, I awoke feeling . . . *rejuvenated.* Codey assisted me from the pod and led me to a small room containing a bunk, told me to make myself at home. The first thing I did was to hurry out to the truck and root around among its tumbled contents until I found the container, then carried it back to my new quarters. Codey watched me closely, asked me what it was. I didn't tell him.

I remembered what Fr Rogers had said about him, that he thought Codey had flipped. And that was *then*. For the past thirty years he'd lived up here, *alone*. When I looked into his face I saw the consequence of that ordeal in his eyes.

Codey's Valley. Mark's day, 16th, St Cyprian's month.

Early this morning I left my cabin, went out to the truck, and armed myself. If the story Father Rogers had told me in the monastery garden was true, about Codey and the Slarque...

I remained outside the ship, trying to admire the beauty of the valley.

Later, Codey came out carrying a tray of preheated food. He offered it to me and said that he'd grown the vegetables in his own garden. I sat on the ramp and ate, Codey watching me. He seemed nervous, avoided eye contact. He'd not known human company in thirty years.

We'd hardly spoken until that point. Codey hadn't seemed curious about me or why I was here, and I hadn't worked out the best way to go about verifying Father Rogers's story.

I said that Rogers had told me about the crash-landing.

I recorded the following dialogue:

Codey: Rogers? He survived? He made it to Apollinaire?

Sam: He made it. He's still there.

Codey: I didn't give him a chance of surviving...They monitored him as far as the next valley down, then lost him.

Sam: *They?*

Codey: The Slarque, who else? Didn't Rogers tell you they were in contact with me?

Sam: Yes—yes, he did. I didn't know whether to believe him. Are you still in contact?

Codey: *They're* in contact with me...You don't believe me, girl?

Sam: I...I don't know.

Codey: How the hell you think I found you, ten klicks down the next valley? They read your presence.

Sam: They can read my mind?

Codey: Well, let's just say that they're sympathetic to your thoughts, shall we?

Sam: Then they know why I'm here?

Codey: Of course.

Sam: So... If they're in contact with you, you'll know why I'm here...

(Codey got up suddenly and strode off, as if I'd angered him. He stood with his back to me, his head in his hands. I thought he was sobbing. When he turned around, he was grinning... insanely.)

Codey: They told me. They told me why you're here... Listen, they don't want your help. They don't want to be saved. They have no wish to leave Tartarus. They belong here. This is their home. They believe that only if they die with their planet will their souls be saved.

Sam: But... but we can offer them a habitat identical to Tartarus, practically unbounded freedom.

Codey: Their religious beliefs would not allow them to leave. It'd be an act of disgrace in the eyes of their forefathers if they fled the planet now.

Sam: They... they have a religion? But I thought they were animals...

Codey: They might have devolved, but they're still intelligent. Their kind have worshipped the supernova for generations. They await the day of glory with hope.

Sam: And you?

Codey: I belong here, too. I couldn't live among humans again. I belong with the Slarque.

Sam: Why? Why do they tolerate *you*? One... one of them killed my husband.

Codey: I performed a service for them, thirty years ago, the first of two such. In return they keep me company... in my head... and sometimes bring me food.

Sam: Thirty years ago? You gave them the prisoner?

Codey: They commanded me to do it! If I'd refused... Don't you see, they would have taken me or Rogers. I had no choice, don't you understand?

Sam: My God. Three years ago... my husband? Did you...?

Codey: I... I was monitoring your broadcasts, the footage you beamed to Apollinaire. You were out of range of the Slarque up here, and they were desperate. I had to do it, don't you see? If not... they would have taken me.

Sam: But why? Why? If they bring you food, then why did they want...?

Codey broke down then. He fled sobbing up the ramp and into the ship. I didn't know whether to go after him, comfort him, and try to learn the truth. In the event I remained where I was, too emotionally drained to make a move.

It's evening now. I've locked myself in my cabin. I don't trust Codey, and I don't trust the Slarque. I'm armed and ready, but I don't know if I can keep awake all night.

Oh, my God. Oh, Jesus. I don't believe it. I can't...

He must have over-rode the locking system, got in during the night as I slept. But how did he know?

The Slarque, of course. If they read my mind, knew my secret...

I didn't tell you, Hunter. I wanted it to be a surprise.

I wanted you to be there when Arabella was growing up. I wanted you to see her develop from birth, to share with you her infancy, her growth, to cherish her with you.

Two and a half years ago, Hunter, I gave birth to our daughter. Immediately I had her suspended. For the past two years I've carried her everywhere I've been, in a suspension container. When we were reunited, we would cease the suspension, watch our daughter grow.

Last night, Codey stole Arabella. Took the suspension container. I'm so sorry, Hunter. I'm so...

I've got to think straight. Codey took his crawler and headed up the valley to the next one. I can see the tracks in the grass.

I'm going to follow him in my truck. I'm going to get our daughter back.

I'll leave this recording here, for when you come. Forgive me, Hunter... Please, forgive me.

He sat on the ramp of the starship with his head in his hands, the sound of his pulse surging in his ears as Alvarez passed Sam's recording to Dr Fischer. Hunter was aware of a mounting pain in his chest. He found himself on the verge of hysterical laughter at the irony of crossing the galaxy to meet his daughter, only to have her snatched from his grasp at the very last minute.

He looked up at Alvarez. "But why? What can they want with her?"

Alvarez avoided his gaze. "I wish I knew—"

"We've got to go after them!"

Alvarez turned and addressed his men. Hunter watched, removed from the reality of the scene before him, as Alvarez's minions armed themselves with lasers and stun rifles and boarded the truck.

He rode on the roof with Alvarez and Dr Fischer. As they raced up the incline of the valley, towards the v-shaped cutting perhaps a kilometre ahead, he scanned the rocky horizon for any sign of the vehicles belonging to Sam or Codey.

Sam's words rang in his ears, the consequences of what she'd told him filling him with dread. For whatever reasons, Codey had supplied the Slarque with humans on two other occasions. Sam had failed to see that she had been led into a trap, with Arabella as the bait.

They passed from the lower valley, accelerated into one almost identical, but smaller and enclosed by steep battlements of jagged rock.

There, located in the centre of the greensward, stood Codey's crawler and Sam's truck.

They motored cautiously towards the immobile vehicles.

Twenty metres away, Hunter could wait no longer. He leapt from the truck and set off at a sprint, Alvarez calling after him to stop. The pain in his chest chose that second to bite, winding him.

Codey's crawler was empty. He ran from the vehicle and hauled himself aboard Sam's truck. It, too, was empty.

Alvarez's men had caught up with him. One took his upper arm in a strong yet gentle grip, led him back to Alvarez who was standing on the greensward, peering up at the surrounding peaks.

Two of his men had erected the collapsible cage, then joined the others at strategic positions around the valley. They knelt behind the cover of rocks, stun rifles ready.

An amplified voice rang through the air. "Hunter!"

"Codey . . ." Alvarez said.

"Step forward, Hunter. Show yourself." The command echoed around the valley, but seemed to issue from high in the peaks straight ahead.

Hunter walked forward ten paces, paused and called through cupped hands, "What do you want, Codey? Where's Sam and my daughter?"

"The Slarque want you, Hunter," Codey's voice boomed. "They want what is theirs."

Hunter turned to Alvarez, as if for explanation. "What does he mean, 'What is theirs'?"

Alvarez licked his lips and said, "Believe me, it was the only foolproof way we had of luring the Slarque."

Hunter shook his head. "*What* was?"

"To use you," Alvarez said.

"Use me?" Hunter was aware of the heat of the sun, ringing blows down on his head. "I don't understand," he said. "Use me?"

Dr Fischer made an impatient gesture. "For God's sake, tell him!"

Alvarez stared at Hunter. "Three years ago," he said, "when the Slarque attacked and killed you, it laid the embryos of its young within your remains, as has been their way since time immemorial. The animals they used began to die out millennia ago; hence the fall of the Slarque. It so happened that humans are also a suitable... repository. Of course, when Sam rescued your remains and had them suspended, the embryos too were frozen. We discovered them when we examined your remains on Million."

Hunter was shaking his head. "You used me."

"It was part of the deal, Hunter. For your resurrection, you would lead us to the Slarque."

"But if you wanted the Slarque, you had them! Why didn't you raise the embryos for your exhibition?"

"The young would not survive more than a few months. We examined the embryos and found they'd been weakened by inbreeding, by cumulative genetic defects. I suspect that the brood incubated in the body of the prisoner thirty years ago did not survive. We need the only existing pair of adult Slarque. Then we can modify their genes, so that they might breed true, again."

Something moved within Hunter's chest. He winced.

Dr Fischer stepped forward. "A painkiller."

Hunter was unable to move, horrified at what Alvarez had told him but at the same time needing the analgesic to quell the slicing pain. Fischer plunged the injector into his neck and he gasped with relief.

Codey's voice rang out again. "Step forward, Hunter! Approach the south end of the valley. A simple trade: for the Slarque young, your wife and daughter."

Hunter stepped forward, began walking.

Behind him, Alvarez said, "Stop right there, Hunter. Let the Slarque come to you... Remember our deal?"

Hunter hesitated, caught between obeying the one man capable of granting him life, and the demands of the Slarque who held his wife and daughter.

The pain in his chest was almost unbearable, as if his innards were being lacerated by swift slashes of a razor blade. My God, if this was the pain with the sedative...

He cried out, staggered forward.

"Hunter!" Alvarez called.

He turned. He saw Alvarez raise the laser to his shoulder, take aim. He dived as Alvarez fired, the cobalt bolt lancing past him with a scream of ionised air.

He looked up the valley, detecting movement. Two figures emerged from behind a jagged rock. They were at once grotesquely alien and oddly humanoid: scaled, silver creatures with great hooked, Scorpion tails. What invested them with humanity, Hunter thought, was their simple desire to rescue their young. And even as he realised this, he was overcome by the terror of their initial attack, three years ago.

Behind him, he heard Alvarez give the order to his men. He turned in time to see them raise their stun guns and take aim at the Slarque.

A quick volley of laser fire issued from a single point in the rocks high above. The first vector hit Alvarez, reducing him to a charred corpse. The succeeding blasts accounted for the others, picking them off one by one.

Only Dr Fischer remained, hands in the air, terrified.

Hunter hauled himself to his feet and cried Sam's name, trying to ignore the pain in his chest.

The Slarque approached him. As they advanced, Hunter tried to tell himself that he should not feel fear: their interest in him was entirely understandable.

"Sam!" he cried again.

In his last few seconds of consciousness, Hunter saw his wife run from the cover of the rocks and dash past the Slarque. He was suddenly struck by the improbable juxtaposition of ugliness and extreme beauty. Behind her, he saw a thin, bedraggled human figure—the madman Codey. He wondered if Codey's action in killing Alvarez meant that he, Hunter, would die without hope of resurrection on this infernal planet.

He keeled over before Sam reached him, and then she was cradling him, repeating his name. He lay in her arms, stared up at her face eclipsing the swollen sun.

He felt the lifeforms within him begin to struggle—a sharp, painful tugging as they writhed from his chest and through his entrails, the tissue of his stomach an easier exit than that of his ribcage.

"Sam," he said weakly. "Arabella...?"

Sam smiled with reassurance through her tears. Behind her, Hunter saw the monstrous heads of the Slarque as they waited. He tried to raise his face to Sam's, but he was losing consciousness, fading fast. He was aware of a sudden loosening of his stomach muscles as the alien litter fought to be free.

The he cried out, and died for the second time.

——.——

Aboard the *Angel of Mercy*, orbiting Tartarus Major, 1st, May, 23210—Galactic Reckoning.

I need to make this last entry, to round things off, to talk.

With Dr Fischer I collected the remains—the bodies of Alvarez and his men—and your body, Hunter. Fischer claims he'll be able to resurrect Alvarez and the other men lasered by Codey, but he didn't sound so sure. Personally, I hope he fails with Alvarez, after what he put you through. The man doesn't deserve to live.

I've negotiated a price for our story with NewsCorp—they've promised enough to pay for your resurrection. It'll be another three years before you're alive again. It's a long time to wait, and I'll miss you, but I guess I shouldn't complain. Of course, I'll keep Arabella suspended. I look forward to the day when together we can watch her grow.

The final exodus has begun. Through the viewscreen of my cabin I can see Tartarus and the giant sphere of the sun, looming over it. Against the sun, a hundred dark specks rise like ashes—the ships that carry the citizens to safety. There's something sad and ugly about the scene, but at the same time there's something achingly beautiful about it, also.

By the time we're together again, Hunter, Tartarus will be no more. But the exploding star will be in the heavens still, marking the place in space where the Slarque and poor Codey, and the other lost souls who wished for whatever reasons to stay on Tartarus, perished in the apocalypse.

I can't erase from my mind the thought of the Slarque, those sad, desperate creatures who wanted only the right to die with their young in the supernova, and who, thanks to Codey and you, will now be able to do so.

DARK CALVARY

"Dark Calvary", though chronologically the very last story in the Fall of Tartarus *sequence, was one of the first written. (And it was hell to get right—I think I rewrote the tale a dozen times before I was satisfied.) It's a trifle bleaker than my usual stories, and pretty well sums up what I think of religion. The image of the Abbot is like something from a nightmare, and I'd like to go back some day and write more about the holy fool. The story was first published in* SF Age, *edited by Scott Edelman.*

DARK CALVARY

He BURIED FRANCESCA IN THE RICH JUNGLE SOIL OF TARTARUS MAJOR while the sky pulsed with the photon haemorrhage of the supernova and the Abbot of the Church of the Ultimate Sacrifice knelt and chanted prayer.

And he thought that was the end of the affair.

Hans Cramer met Francesca when she was eighteen, two decades his junior but wise beyond her years, and already a second-class helio-meteorologist aboard one of the Fleet's finest nova observation vessels. Cramer was employed as an itinerant lecturer, teaching philosophy and theology to the reluctant crews of the various ships of the Zakinthos Line. His posting to the observation sailship *Dawn Light* was just another move, but one that changed his life.

Francesca was a regular at his rambling lectures in the vast auditorium of the city-sized sailship. She was distinguished by her striking Venezuelan face and jet-black mass of hair—an affectation in space, where so many crew members went partly shorn or bald. What attracted him initially was not so much her physical aspect as her youth, and that she attended every one of his lectures. She was that rarity among spacers: a student who wanted to learn. After years of having his talks received with boredom, or at best polite apathy, Cramer found her attentiveness exhilarating. It was natural that he should single her out for special tuition. He gave her one-to-one lessons, and she responded. He prided himself on the fact that she excelled herself, absorbed everything he had to offer, and was still hungry for more.

Inevitably, perhaps, they transcended the teacher-pupil relationship and became lovers. It was a gradual process, but one which culminated in an event that informed them both that their feelings for each other were reciprocated. They had been discussing the physics of spatial dimensions congruent to singularities, and the conversation continued well beyond the time Cramer usually allotted for her tuition. The talk turned general, and then personal. There was a period of silence, and Cramer looked into the depths of her Indian eyes—and he was suddenly aware of his desire, affection, and overwhelming need to be responsible for Francesca.

For the next year Cramer lectured aboard the *Dawn Light* as it sailed from star to unstable star, and their love deepened into a thorough understanding of one another. She told Cramer that which she had never told anyone before: how, at the age of ten, she had lost her father. He had been a scientist, working on the planet of a sun due to go nova, when the sun blew before its time and killed him and his scientific team . . . This, Cramer thought, helped to explain the choice of her profession.

Cramer became for Francesca a combination of lover-teacher-protector, as well as a friend and confidant . . . And for him Francesca was the first person in his life to remind him that he was not, contrary to nearly forty years of assumptions otherwise, the fulcrum of the universe. Her naivety, her vitality and honesty, her willingness to learn, her trust in others—he was in awe of all these things. Sometimes he wanted to protect her from herself when others might take advantage, but at the same time he learned from her that openness and trust can bring its own rewards: contact with one's fellows, even friendships, which for long enough he had shunned. Her youth and enthusiasm were a foil to Cramer's age and cynicism, and though at times he found it exhausting, more often than not he was swept along heedless by the tide of her passion.

Francesca had her dark side, though.

Six months after they became lovers, she slipped into a sullen, uncommunicative depression. Often he found her in tears, his entreaties ignored. He assumed that the chemical magic that had attracted her to him had soured, that their time together had run its course.

Then, one rest period, Cramer found her in a personal nacelle which obtruded through the skin of the ship and afforded a magnificent view of the blazing variable below. Francesca had sought privacy in which to brood. He lowered himself in beside her and waited.

After a period of silence, she asked in a whisper, "What do you believe, Hans?"

Cramer had never spoken to her about his beliefs, or lack of—perhaps fearing that his apathy might frighten her away. "I was once a nihilist," he said, "but now I believe in nothing."

She slapped his face. "Be serious!"

He was being serious. "Nothing," he said.

She was silent, a small frown of puzzlement denting her forehead. At last she murmured, "I need belief. I need to believe in something...something *more* than all this." She made a spread-fingered gesture to indicate everything, all existence. "Life is so meaningless, if this is all there is to it—*life*. There must be something more!"

He stroked a strand of hair from her Indian eyes.

She looked at him. "Don't you fear death? Don't you wake up panicking in the early hours, thinking, 'One day I'll be dead for all eternity'?"

He could not help but smile. "At one time I did," he said. "But no more." He told her that it was as if his subconscious had become inured to the fact of his mortality, was no longer daunted by the inevitability of his death.

Francesca was crying. "I hate being alive," she sobbed, "if all it will end in is death."

Cramer held her, soothed her with comforting noises, secretly relieved that he knew the reason for her depression. He told himself that it was nothing more than a stage through which everyone must pass—but, perhaps, he should have seen in her terror the seeds of a consuming obsession.

Six months later Cramer was posted to another ship—there was nothing he could do to avoid the transfer—and he saw Francesca only once every three months or so, when their dirtside leaves coincided. He had feared that the separation might have worked to dampen Francesca's ardour, but the reverse was true. Their hurried, stolen weeks together were the happiest times of their lives.

And then, three years after their first meeting, Francesca was promoted, transferred to a ship bound for the Rim, to study the effects of an imminent supernova on the world of Tartarus Major.

Cramer was on Earth, on long-service leave from the Fleet and teaching part-time at the University of Rio. Francesca was due back in a week, when her boat would dock at the Santiago shipyards for refurbishment. Cramer had a trekking holiday planned in the Andes, followed by a fortnight in Acapulco, before they said goodbye again and her ship whisked her off to some far, unstable star.

He could recall precisely where he was, what he was doing—even trivial things like what he was wearing at the time, and what mood he was in—when he heard about the crash-landing: in a café on the Rio seafront, drinking coffee and reading *El Globe*, wearing the kaftan Francesca had brought back from the Emirate colony of Al Haq, and feeling contentment at the thought of her imminent return. The wall-screen was relaying news to the café's oblivious, chattering clientele. He took notice only when it was announced that a Fleet observation vessel had crash-landed on the Rim world of Tartarus Major. "*The Pride of Valencia* was mapping Tartarus for stress patterns and went down two days ago," said the reporter. "Casualty figures are not yet known. Other news..."

His soul released its pent up breath; relief flooded him. For perhaps five seconds Cramer existed in a glorious state of reprieve, because he knew—didn't he?—that Francesca was aboard the observation vessel *Dawn Light?* Then, crashing through his consciousness like a great wave, came the awareness that she had left the *Dawn Light* months ago, had been promoted to the *Pride of Valencia.*

Cramer returned to his apartment, shock lending him a strange sense of calm in which he felt removed from the reality of his surroundings. He contacted the Fleet headquarters in Geneva, but was told that no details of the incident would be forthcoming until accident investigators had reported from Tartarus Major. Unable to bear the wait, the feeling of redundancy, he knew that the only course of action was to make his way independently to Tartarus. He booked passage on a sailship leaving Earth the following day, and spent the duration of the voyage under blissful sedation.

He had no idea what to expect on landing, but it was not the decrepit, medieval city of Baudelaire. It seemed to him that he had stepped back in time. Not only was the architecture and atmosphere of the place archaic, but the bureaucracy and services were likewise mired in the past. The prevailing ethos of the government departments he petitioned seemed to be that the loss of any sailship— and minor officials seemed unsure as to whether a sailship *had* been lost on Tartarus Major—was not the responsibility of their department, and Cramer was advised to see so-and-so at such-and-such a bureau. Added to which confusion, the entire population of the planet seemed to be packed into the capital city, eager to catch a ship off-planet before the supernova blew. Eventually, and with scant regard for his feelings, he was advised to check at the city morgue. Beside himself, he battled through the bustling streets until he came upon the relevant building. The chambers and corridors of the morgue were packed with the stiffened, shrouded figures of the dead. Here, tearful and in obvious distress, he had his first stroke of luck. He happened upon a harassed Fleet official, checking charred remains against the crew list of the *Pride of Valencia.*

Cramer explained his predicament, and the official took sympathy and went through the names of the dead for that of Francesca.

She was not, apparently, in the morgue. All the bodies had been recovered from the site of the crash. According to the official, Cramer was in luck: he was advised to try the infirmary, where the twelve surviving crewmembers were receiving treatment.

Given hope, he was filled with fear now at the thought of Francesca's having survived—or rather he feared the state in which she might have survived. Would he find Francesca reduced to a brain-dead wreck, a hopelessly injured cripple? He considered only the worst-case scenario as he made his way to the infirmary. He explained his situation to a doctor who escorted him to the ward where the survivors lay. As the medic checked the records, Cramer strode down the line of beds—not rejuvenation pods, in this backward hole, but beds!—fearful lest he should come upon Francesca, yet petrified that he should not.

She was not on the ward.

The doctor joined Cramer; the medic had located the crew list of the *Pride of Valencia,* and a memo. There was one name outstanding, accounted for neither in the morgue nor in the hospital: Francesca Maria Rodriguez.

Cramer was in turmoil. "Then where the hell is she?"

The doctor placed a soothing hand on his shoulder. "Apparently two of the injured were found in the jungle by an order of monks who took them in and treated their wounds. One male crewmember died. The other, Rodriguez, is still undergoing treatment."

"Is she badly injured?"

"I'm sorry. I have no records..." He paused. "You might try the Church of the Ultimate Sacrifice, just along the street. They should be able to help you."

Cramer thanked him and, filled with a mixture of despair and hope that left him mentally exhausted, he almost ran from the infirmary. He found the church without difficulty: in a street of mean timber buildings, it was the only stone-built edifice, a towering cathedral along classical lines.

He hurried inside. A cowled figure riding an invalid carriage barred his way. Desperately Cramer explained himself. The disabled cleric told him to wait, and propelled his carriage up the aisle. While he was gone, Cramer gazed about the sumptuous interior. He noticed the strange, scorpion-like statue above the altar, flanked by a human figure bound to a cross—its arms and legs removed so that it resembled the remains of some ancient statue. He could not help but wonder what perverted cult he had stumbled upon.

The monk returned and gestured that Cramer should follow him. He led the way to a small study behind the altar. "The Abbot," he murmured as Cramer passed inside.

Behind a large desk was an imposing figure garbed in a black habit, his face concealed by a deep cowl.

Nervously, Cramer sat down. Prompted by the Abbot's silence, he babbled his story.

Halfway through, he paused and peered into the shadow of the Abbot's hood. The holy man seemed to have his eyes closed. Cramer noticed two dried, discoloured orbs tied to his right wrist, but failed to make the connection.

He continued with what the doctor had told him about Francesca. When he had finished, the Abbot remained silent for some time. He placed his fingertips together in a miniature facsimile of the spire that surmounted the cathedral. He seemed to be contemplating.

He said at last, his voice a rasp, "Are you a believer, Mr Cramer?"

"In your religion?" Cramer shifted uncomfortably.

"In any."

"I . . . I have my own beliefs."

"That sounds to me like another way of admitting you're an atheist."

"Does it matter?" he asked. He contained his anger. The Abbot was, after all, his only link with Francesca.

The holy man seemed to take an age before he next spoke. "I can help you, Mr Cramer. Francesca is in the jungle."

"How badly . . . ?" he began, the words catching in his throat.

"Do not worry yourself unduly. She will live."

Cramer sat back in his seat, relief washing over him. He imagined Francesca recuperating in some remote jungle hospital.

"But how badly injured . . . ?" he began.

The Abbot said, "I am afraid I do not have that information."

"When can I see her?"

"Tomorrow I return to the jungle to resume my pilgrimage. If you wish, you may accompany me."

Cramer thanked him, relieved that at last his search was almost over.

"I leave at first light," said the Abbot. "You will meet me here." And he gestured—parting his spired hands—to indicate that the audience was over.

That night Cramer found expensive lodging in a crowded boarding house. In the morning the sun rose huge and brooding over the parched city, though the sky had been lit all night long with the primary's technicolour fulminations. He had slept badly, apprehensive as to the state in which he might find Francesca. At dawn he returned to the cathedral and met the Abbot, and they hurried through narrow alleyways to a jetty and a barge painted in the sable and scarlet colours of the Church.

The crew of two natives cast off the moorings and the barge slipped sideways into mid-stream before the engines caught. Cramer sat on the foredeck, in the shade of a canvas awning, and shared a thick red wine with the Abbot. The holy man threw back his cowl, and Cramer could not help but stare. The Abbot's ears and nose had been removed, leaving only dark holes and scabrous scar tissue. His eyelids, stitched shut over hollowed sockets, were curiously flattened, like miniature drumheads. He kept his eyeballs, dried and shrunken, on a thong of optic nerves around his wrist.

The barge proceeded upriver, against a tide of smaller craft streaming in the opposite direction. The Abbot cocked his head towards their puttering engines. "Some believed the things which were spoken," he quoted, "and some did not. Once, sir, all Tartarus believed. Now the faith is defended by a devout minority."

Cramer murmured something non-committal in reply. He was not interested in the Abbot's belief system and its macabre extremes. For fifteen years he had taught students the rudiments of the various major faiths. Now religion, every religion, sickened him. In his opinion, superstitious belief systems were just one more political tool that man used to subjugate, terrorise, and enslave his fellow man.

He sat and drank and watched the passing landscape. At one point they idled by an ancient temple complex. Many of the buildings were in ruins; others, miraculously, considering their age, stood tall and proud. Towers and minarets of some effulgent stone like rose-coloured marble, they were sufficiently alien in design to inspire wonder. As the barge sailed slowly by, Cramer made out six statues—tall, scorpion-like insects, their tails hooked as if in readiness.

He finished his wine, excused himself, and retreated to his cabin. He drew the shutters against the light and, despite the heat, enjoyed the sleep he had been denied the night before.

He awoke hours later, much refreshed, hardly able to believe after the trials of the past two days that Francesca would soon be in his arms. He climbed to the deck. The sun was directly overhead—he must have slept for five or six hours. The barge was pulling into a jetty. A tumbledown collection of timber buildings lined the riverbank. The Abbot appeared at Cramer's side. "Chardon's Landing," he said. "From here we walk. It is thirty kilometres to the plateau."

With scarcely a delay they set off into the jungle, Cramer marvelling at the blind man's sure tread as he navigated his way through the jungle. At first the trek was not arduous. The way had been cleared, and they followed a well-defined path through the undergrowth. Only later, as they put twenty kilometres behind them, and the path began to climb, did Cramer begin to feel the strain. They slowed, and halted often to swallow water from leather canteens.

They continued through the long, sultry hours of afternoon; at last, when Cramer thought he could continue no more, they came to a clearing. Before them, the plateau fell away in a sheer drop, affording an open panorama of treetops stretching all the way to the northern horizon beneath a violent, actinic sky.

Only then did Cramer notice the tent, to one side of the clearing.

He turned to the Abbot. "Where are we?"

The holy man gestured. "Francesca's tent," was his only reply.

"But this can't be the mission..." Cramer began.

He heard a sound from across the clearing, and turned quickly. He stared in disbelief as Francesca drew aside the tent flap and stepped out. His heart began a laboured pounding. She stood, tiny and trim in her radiation silvers. He searched her for any sign of injury—but she seemed whole and perfect, as he had dreamed of her all along. She stared at him, appearing uncertain at his presence. A smile came hesitantly to her lips.

He crossed the clearing and hugged her to his chest.

She pulled away, shaking her head. "I meant to contact you. It's just..." Cramer had expected tears; instead, she was almost matter-of-fact.

"Francesca... What's happening? The Abbot—" He nodded towards the holy man, who was busying himself with a second tent across the clearing. "He said that you were injured, in hospital—"

She looked pained. "Come. We have a lot to talk about." She took his hand and drew him into the tent.

They sat facing each other. He scanned her for injuries, but saw no bandages, compresses, or scabs of synthetic flesh.

She read his gaze, and smiled. "Cuts and bruises, nothing serious."

Cramer felt a constriction in his throat. "You were lucky."

She lowered her head, looked at him through her lashes. "You don't know how lucky," she murmured.

A silence developed, and he wished at that moment that silence was all that separated them; but they seemed divided by more than just the inability to meaningfully communicate.

Then he saw the book beside her inflatable pillow. Embossed in scarlet upon its black cover was the symbol of a scorpion beside a dismembered human figure.

"Francesca..." he pleaded. "What's happening?"

She did not meet his gaze. "What do you mean?"

He indicated the holy book.

It was some time before she could bring herself to respond. At last she looked up, her eyes wide, staring, as if still in shock from the trauma of the crash-landing.

"After the accident," she began, "I regained consciousness. I lay in the wreckage, surrounded by the others . . . my friends and colleagues. They were dead." She paused, gathered herself. "I couldn't move. I saw a figure, the Abbot, and then other robed monks, moving among the crew, giving blessings, first aid where they could. Eventually the Abbot found me. They loaded me onto a stretcher, knocked me out. The next thing I remember, I was in the mission hospital at Chardon's Landing,"

"And the Abbot did all this without eyes?"

"He was sighted then," Francesca said. "Only later did he return to Baudelaire to petition for *penance physicale.*" She paused, continued, "Before that, while I recuperated, he told me about his faith, his quest."

Cramer echoed that last word, sickened by something in her tone.

"The Abbot is searching for the lost temple of the Slarque," Francesca went on, "the race which lived on Tartarus before humankind. This temple is of special significance to his religion."

Something turned in his stomach. He gestured towards the book. "Do you believe *that?*" he said.

She stared at him with her green and vital eyes. "I'm intrigued by the extinct aliens," she replied. "I was always interested in xeno-archaeology. I want to help the Abbot find the temple."

He felt betrayed. "You act as his eyes?"

She nodded, then reached out and took his hand. "I love you, Hans. I always have and always will. This . . . this is something I must experience. Please, don't obstruct me."

The Abbot called that a meal was prepared.

The sun was dipping below the horizon, presaging the nightly show of tattered flames and flares like shredded banners. They sat in the shade of the jungle— Cramer was relieved when Francesca chose to sit next to him—and ate from a platter of meat, cheese and bread. He recalled her words, her avowal of love, but they did nothing to banish his jealousy.

The Abbot poured wine and spoke of his religion, his belief that only through physical mortification would his God be appeased and the sun cease its swelling. Cramer listened with mounting incredulity. From time to time he glanced at

Francesca. The girl he knew of old would have piped up with some pithy remark along the lines that the holy man's fellow believers had been sawing bits off themselves for centuries, and still the sun was unstable. But she said nothing. She seemed hypnotised by the Abbot's words.

Cramer was drunk with the wine, or he would have held his tongue. "A lot your mortification has achieved so far," he slurred, indicating the burning heavens.

"Once we locate the temple of the Slarque," said the Abbot, "our efforts will be rewarded. Be glad and rejoice, for the Lord will do great things." According to his holy book, he said, strange feats and miracles were to be expected in the alien ruins—but by this time Cramer had heard enough, and concentrated on his drinking.

He shared Francesca's tent that night. He sat cross-legged, a bottle of wine half-full in his lap. Francesca lay on her back, staring up at the sloping fabric.

He processed his thoughts and carefully ordered his words. "How . . . how can you be sure that you'll find the temple before the sun—?"

"The Abbot and his minions have searched most of the jungle. There is only this sector to go. We *will* find the shrine."

"You sound in little doubt."

She turned her head and stared at him. "I am in no doubt," she said.

He determined, then, that he would not let her go. He would restrain her somehow, drag her back to Baudelaire and then to Earth.

"When do you set out on this . . . this *expedition*?" he asked.

"Tomorrow, maybe the day after." There was defiance in her tone.

"Then you'll return?" He could not bring himself to say, *"to me?"* Instead he said, "You'll re-join the Fleet?"

She glanced at him, seemed to be searching for the words with which to explain herself. "Hans . . . I joined the Fleet believing that through science we might do something to stabilise these novae. Over the years, I've come to realise that nothing can be done." She frowned. "I can't go back, re-join the Fleet." She hesitated, seemed to want to go on, but instead just shook her head in frustration.

She turned her back on him and slept.

Her words echoing in his head, Cramer drank himself unconscious.

He was awoken by a sound, perhaps hours later. He oriented himself and reached out for Francesca, but she was gone. He gathered his wits, peered from the tent. Across the clearing he made out Francesca's short figure next to the tall form of the Abbot. They were shouldering their packs, their movements careful so as not to wake him. Cramer felt the smouldering pain of betrayal in his gut. From his pack he drew his laser and slipped from the tent. As he moved around the clearing, keeping to the shadows, he was formulating a plan. He would stun both Francesca and the Abbot, then flee with her back to the port and take the first ship home. The girl was not in her right mind, could not be held responsible for her actions.

Francesca saw him coming. She stared at him, wide-eyed.

Dry of throat, Cramer said, "You were leaving me!"

"Do not try to stop us," the Abbot warned.

Francesca cried, "I must go! If you love me, if you trust me, then you'll let me go."

"What have you done to her?" he yelled at the Abbot.

"You cannot stop us," the holy fool said. "The way of the pious will not be impeded by those of scant faith!"

Cramer raised his laser, clicked off the safety catch.

Francesca was shaking her head. "No..."

His vision swam. A combination of the heat, the drink, the emotional consequences of what was happening conspired to addle his wits.

Francesca made to turn and go.

He reached out, caught her arm. The sudden feel of her, the hot flesh above her elbow, reminded Cramer of what he was losing. He pulled her to him. "Francesca..."

Her eyes communicated an anger close to hatred. She struggled. She was small, but the determination with which she fought was testament to her desire to be free. He was incensed. He roared like a maniac and dragged her across the clearing towards the tent. She screamed and broke free.

Then Cramer raised his laser and fired, hitting her in the chest and knocking her off her feet, the large-eyed expression of disbelief at what he'd done still on her face as she hit the ground.

The Abbot was feeling for her pulse. He stared blindly in Cramer's direction. "You've killed her! My God, you've killed her!"

"No..." Cramer collapsed and held the loose bundle of Francesca in his arms. There was no movement, no heartbeat. Her head lolled. He cried into her hair that he had not meant to...

The Abbot fell to his knees and chanted a doleful prayer. Cramer wanted to hate him then, revile the holy man for infecting Francesca with his insane belief, but in his grief and guilt he could only weep and beg forgiveness.

At the Abbot's suggestion, Cramer buried Francesca in the rank jungle soil, while the night sky pulsed and flared with all the colours of Hell.

When it was done, and they stood above the fresh mound of earth, Cramer asked, "And you?"

"I will continue on my quest."

"Without eyes?"

"We walk by faith, not by sight," the Abbot said. "If God wishes me to find the shrine, that is his will."

Cramer remained kneeling by the grave for hours, not quite sane. As the sun rose he set off on the long trek south, the Abbot's dolorous chant following him into the jungle. He caught one of the many ferries bound for Baudelaire, and the following day bought passage aboard a slowboat to Earth.

He lost himself in Venezuela's vast interior, relived his time with Francesca, wallowed in grief and guilt and cursed himself for her death.

Four months later he was sitting on the porch of his jungle retreat, the abandoned timber villa of some long-dead oil prospector, when he had a visitor. It was not yet noon and already his senses were numbed by alcohol. The encroaching jungle, the variation of greens and the odd splash of colour from bird or flower, reminded him of Tartarus—though the sky, what little of it could be seen through the tree-tops, was innocent of the baleful eye of the supernova.

The rattle of loose boards sounded through the humid air.

He sat up, fearful of trouble. He checked the pistol beneath the cushion at his side.

The walkway rose from the river in an erratic series of zigzags, and only when the caller negotiated the final turn could Cramer make him out. With his long sable habit and peaked hood, he looked the very image of Death itself.

The boards were loose and treacherous. The Abbot had to tread with care, but not once did he reach for the side rails—and only when he arrived at the verandah did Cramer realise why. The Abbot had had his arms removed since their last encounter.

To each his own mortification, Cramer thought. He hoisted his bottle in greeting.

"What the hell brings you here?" he asked. "You've finally abandoned your damn-fool quest?"

The holy man lowered himself to the deck and sat cross-legged before Cramer, a feat of some achievement considering the absence of arms. He tipped his head back, and his cowl slipped from his bald pate to reveal his face ravaged by the depredations of his piety.

Cramer noted that his dried eyeballs were now fastened about his left ankle, bolas-like.

"In two days I return to Tartarus," the Abbot said in his high, rasping voice. His stitched-shut eye-sockets faced Cramer's approximate direction. "My quest is almost over."

Cramer raised his drink. "You don't know how pleased I am," he sneered. "But I thought no one knew the whereabouts of your precious shrine?"

"Once, that was true," the Abbot said, unperturbed by Cramer's rancour. "Explorers claimed they'd stumbled upon the alien temple, and then just as conveniently stumbled away again, unable to recall its precise location. But then two weeks ago a miracle occurred."

Cramer took a long pull from the bottle and offered his guest a shot. The Abbot refused.

"There is a pouch on a cord around my waist," he said. "Take it. Retrieve the items within."

Cramer made out the small leather pouch, its neck puckered by a drawstring. He could not reach the Abbot from his seat. He was forced to kneel, coming into contact with the holy man's peculiar body odour—part the putrid stench of septic flesh, part the chemical reek of the analgesics that seeped from his every pore.

Cramer opened the pouch and reached inside.

Three spherical objects met his fingertips, and he knew immediately what they were. One by one he withdrew the image apples. He did not immediately look into their depths. It was as if some precognition granted him the knowledge of what he was about to see. Only after long seconds did he raise the first apple to his eyes.

He gave an involuntary sob.

Image apples were not a fruit at all, but the exudations of an amber-like substance, clear as dew, from tropical palms native to Tartarus. Through a bizarre and unique process, the apples imprinted within themselves, at a certain stage in their growth, the image of their surroundings.

Bracing himself, Cramer looked into the first apple again, then the second and the third. Each crystal-clear orb contained a perfect representation of Francesca as she strode through the jungle where the apples had grown.

The first apple had captured her full-length, a short, slim, childlike figure striding out, arms swinging, all radiation silvers and massed midnight hair. In the second apple she was closer; just her head and shoulders showed. Cramer stared at her elfin face, her high cheekbones, her jade green eyes. Then the third apple: she was striding away from the tree, only her narrow back and fall of hair visible. Tears coursed down his cheeks.

He held the apples in cupped hands and shook his head. He was hardly able to find the words to thank the Abbot. Just the other day he had been bewailing the fact that he had only half a dozen pix of Francesca. That the holy man had come all the way to Earth to give him these . . .

"Thank you. I don't know what to say."

Then Cramer stopped. Perhaps the whisky had clouded his senses. He stared at the Abbot.

"How did you find these?" he asked.

"When you left," said the Abbot. "I continued north. At the time, if you recall, I was following directions given to me by a boatman on the river St Augustine. They proved fallacious, as ever, and rather than continue further north and risk losing my way, I retraced my steps, returned to the plateau where we had camped." He was silent for a time. Cramer was back on Tartarus Major, pained by memories of what had happened upon the plateau.

"When I reached the clearing, it occurred to me to pray for Francesca. I fell to my knees and felt for the totem I had planted to mark her resting place, only to find that it was not there. Moreover, I discovered that the piled earth of the grave had been disturbed, that the grave was indeed empty."

Cramer tried to cry out, but no sound came.

"In consternation I stumbled back to my tent. She was waiting for me."

"No!"

"Yes. Francesca. She spoke to me. 'Abbot, do not fear. Something wondrous has occurred.'"

Cramer was shaking his head. "No, she was dead. Dead. I buried her with my own hands."

"Francesca lives," the Abbot insisted. "She told me that she knew the whereabouts of the holy temple. She would show me, if I did as she bid."

"Which was?"

He smiled, and the approximation of such a cheerful expression upon a face so devastated was ghastly to behold. "She wanted me to come to Earth and fetch you back to Tartarus. She gave me the image apples as proof."

Cramer could only shake his head like something clockwork. "I don't . . . I don't believe it."

"Look upon the images," he ordered.

Cramer held the baubles high. "But surely these are images of Francesca *before* I arrived on Tartarus, *before* her death?"

"Look closely, man! See, she carries your laser, the one you left in your flight from the clearing."

He stared again, disbelieving. He had overlooked it in the apples before, so slight a sidearm it was. But sure enough—strapped to Francesca's thigh was the silver length of his personal pulse laser.

"She wants you," the Abbot said in a whisper.

Cramer wept and raged. He hurled his empty whisky bottle through the air and into the jungle, which accepted it with hardly a pause in the cacophonous medley of insects, toads, and birds.

"But the sun might blow at any time," he cried.

"Some experts say a month or two." The Abbot paused. "But vain and rapacious men still pilot illegal boats to Tartarus, to raid the treasures that remain. I leave the day after tomorrow. You will accompany me, I take it?"

Sobbing, unable to control himself, racked with guilt and a fear he had no hope of understanding, Cramer said that he would indeed accompany the Abbot. How could he refuse?

And so Cramer returned to Tartarus Major, cursing the twisted machinations of fate. Four months ago he had set out on his first voyage to the planet, in a bid to find a Francesca he feared was surely dead—and, now, he left with the Abbot aboard a ramshackle sailship to be reunited with a Francesca he knew for sure to be dead, but somehow miraculously *risen*...

He chose to spend the voyage under sedation.

The first he knew of the landing was when the Abbot coaxed him awake with his croaking, cracking voice. Cramer emerged reluctantly from his slumber, recalling vague, nightmare visions of Francesca's death, only to be confronted by another nightmare vision: the Abbot's mutilated visage, staring down at him.

"To your feet. Tartarus awaits."

He gathered his scant belongings—six flasks of whisky, the image apples—and stumbled from the ship.

As he emerged into the terrible daylight, the assault of Tartarus upon his every sense seemed to sober him. He stared about like a man awakening from a dream, taking in the stench and the panorama of ancient wooden buildings around the port, their façades and steep, tiled roofs seeming warped by the intense heat.

Theirs was the only ship in sight, its silver superstructure an arrogant splash of colour against a sun-bleached dun and ochre city. A searing wind soughed across the port, blowing hot grit into Cramer's face. He gazed at the magnesium-bright sun that filled half the sky. The very atmosphere of the planet seemed to be on fire. The air was heavy with the reek of brimstone, and his every breath was a labour.

The captain of the ship stood beneath the nose cone. "We set sail for Earth in two days," he said. "If you want passage back, be here at dawn. We'll not be waiting."

Cramer calculated how long it might take to reach the jungle plateau, and return—certainly longer than any two days. He trusted there would be other pirate boats to take him back to civilisation.

Already the Abbot was hurrying across the port, his armless gait made fastidious with concentration. His dried eyeballs scuffed around his ankles as he went, striking random patterns in the dust. Cramer shouldered his bag and followed.

Unerringly, the holy man led the way down narrow alleys between the tall timber buildings of the city's ancient quarter. Just four months ago these by-ways had been thronged with citizens streaming to the port, eager to flee the impending catastrophe. Now they were deserted. The only sound was that of their footsteps, and the dry rasp of the Abbot's eyeballs on the cobbles. Between the overreaching eaves, the sky dazzled like superheated platinum. All was still, lifeless.

They descended to the banks of the St Augustine, its broad green girth flowing slowly between the rotten lumber of dilapidated wharves and jetties. The river, usually choked with trading vessels from all along the coast, was empty now of boats—though rotting, bloated corpses, of men and animals, drifted on the sluggish tide.

An urchin fell into step beside the Abbot and tugged at his robes. They came to a boathouse, and the Abbot shouldered open the door and stepped carefully aboard a long-boat. Cramer climbed in after him and seated himself on cushions beneath the black and scarlet awning. The Abbot sat forward, at the very prow of the launch, while the boy busied himself with the engine. It spluttered into life, a blasphemy upon the former silence, and the boat surged from the open-ended boathouse and headed upriver, into the interior.

Cramer pulled a flask of whisky from his bag and chugged down three mouthfuls, the quantity he judged would keep him half-sedated until the serious drinking began at sunset. The Abbot had thought to provision the launch with a container of food: biltong, rounds of ripe cheese, cobs of black bread and yellow, wizened fruit like pears. A goblet suggested that they should take from the river for their refreshment: Cramer decided to stick to his whisky. He ate his fill, lay back and closed his eyes as the boat puttered upstream. He must have dozed; when he next opened his eyes he saw that they had left the city far behind. Flat fields spread out to either side; tall crops, perhaps green once, were scorched now the colour of straw beneath the merciless midday sun.

He thought of Francesca, considered the possibility of her resurrection, and somehow withheld his tears. To busy himself, to take his mind off what might lie ahead, he dipped the goblet into the brackish river and carried it to where the Abbot was seated cross-legged at the prow like some proud, macabre figurehead.

He raised the brimming goblet to the holy man's lips. Graciously, the Abbot inclined his head and drank thirstily. When the cup was dry, he murmured his thanks.

Cramer remained seated beside him. Already he was soaked with sweat and uncomfortable, and he wore the lightest of jungle wear. The Abbot was surely marinating within the thick hessian of his habit.

Cramer nodded to where his sleeves were tucked inside their shoulder holes. "Yet more penance since we last met," he observed, his tone sarcastic.

He wondered when the Abbot would have his tongue cut out, his legs amputated, his testicles removed—if they had not been removed already.

"After finding Francesca," the Abbot said, "I made my way back to Baudelaire. I informed the Church Council of the miracle in the jungle, and petitioned them for permission to undergo further *penance physicale*. The following day the Surgeon Master removed my arms."

Cramer let the silence stretch. He felt dizzy with the heat. The glare of the sun seemed to drive needles into his eyes.

"And Francesca?" Cramer whispered.

The Abbot turned his cowl to Cramer, suggesting inquiry.

Cramer cleared his throat. "Why does she want me with her?"

"She did not say." The Abbot paused. "Perhaps she loves you, still."

"But what exactly did she tell you?"

"She said that I was to bring you back to Tartarus. In return, she would guide me to the temple."

Cramer shook his head. "How does she know its whereabouts? Months ago, like you, she had no idea."

"She was bequeathed its location in her sleep."

He cried aloud. "In her sleep? *Sleep?* She was dead. I buried her myself," he cried. "How can she possibly be alive?"

111

The Abbot would say no more, no matter how much Cramer pleaded. He lowered his head, and his lips moved in soothing prayer.

Cramer took sanctuary beneath the awning. He sucked down half a flask of whisky as night failed, as ever, to fall. The bloated sun dipped below the flat horizon, but such was the power of its radiation that the night sky was transformed into a flickering canopy of indigo, scarlet and argent streamers. The light show illuminated the entirety of the eastern sky, and against it the Abbot was a stark and frightening silhouette.

Cramer drank himself to sleep.

He was awoken by a crack of thunder such as he had never heard before. He shot upright, convinced that the sun had blown and that Tartarus had split asunder. Sheet lightning ignited the river and the surrounding flatlands in blinding silver explosions, a cooling breeze blew, and a warm rain lashed the boat. He slept.

It was dawn when he next awoke. The sun was a massive, rising semicircle on the horizon, throwing harsh white light across the land. They were approaching a dense tangle of vegetation with leaves as broad as spinnakers, waxy and wilting in the heat. The river narrowed, became a chocolate-coloured canal between the overgrown banks. When the sun was hidden partially by the treetops, they were spared its direct heat, yet the humidity increased so that every laboured inhalation was more a draught of fluid than a drawn breath.

Cramer breakfasted on stale bread and putrescent cheese, thirst driving him to forego his earlier circumspection as to the potability of the water, and draw a goblet from the river. He gave the Abbot a mouthful of the rank liquid and fed him bread and biltong so that the holy fool might not starve.

They proceeded on a winding course along the river, ever farther into the dense and otherwise impenetrable jungle.

Hours later they came to Chardon's Landing. Cramer made the launch fast to the jetty and assisted the Abbot ashore. They paused briefly to take a meal, and then began the arduous slog to the plateau where Cramer had buried Francesca.

The air was heavy, the light aqueous, filled with the muffled, distant calls of doomed animals and birds. The trek to the plateau was tougher than he recalled from his first time this way. After months of drunkenness Cramer was in far from peak condition, and without his arms the Abbot often stumbled.

As the hours passed and they slogged through the cloying, hostile heat, Cramer considered what the holy man had said about Francesca's resurrection. Clearly, he had not killed her in the clearing all those months ago, but merely stunned her—and she had discovered the whereabouts of the temple from the survey photographs made by the *Pride of Valencia*... Then again, there was always the possibility that the Abbot was lying, that Francesca had not risen at all, that he had lured Cramer here for his own sinister purposes. And the image apples, which seemed to show Francesca in possession of the laser which had killed her? Might she not have been carrying a laser similar to his own after the crash-landing, but before his arrival?

They came at last to the clearing. The two tents were as he recalled them, situated thirty metres apart. Francesca's grave, in the jungle, was out of sight.

Cramer hurried across to Francesca's tent and pulled back the flap. She was not inside. He checked the second tent, also empty, and then walked towards the edge of the escarpment. He looked out across the spread of the jungle far below, gathering his thoughts.

He knew that he would find Francesca's grave untouched.

"If you claim she is risen," he called to the Abbot, "then where is she?"

"If you do not believe me," the Abbot said, "then look upon the grave."

Cramer hesitated. He did not know what he feared most, that he should find the grave empty... or the soil still piled above Francesca's cold remains.

He crossed the clearing to the margin of jungle where he had excavated her resting place. The Abbot's cowl turned, following his progress like some gothic tracking device. Cramer reached out and drew aside a spray of ferns. The light fell from behind him, illuminating a raw furrow of earth. He gave a pained cry. The mound he had so carefully constructed was scattered, and only a shallow depression remained where he had laid out her body.

He stumbled back into the clearing.

"Well?" the Abbot inquired.

Before Cramer could grasp him, beat from him the truth, he saw something spread in the centre of the clearing. It was a detailed map of the area, based on aerial photographs, opened out and held flat by four stones.

The Abbot sensed something. "What is wrong?"

Cramer crossed the clearing and knelt before the map. Marked in red was the campsite, and from it a dotted trail leading down the precipitous fall of the escarpment. It wound through the jungle below, to a point Cramer judged to be ten kilometres distant. This area was marked with a circle, and beside it the words, 'The Slarque Temple,' in Francesca's meticulous, childish print.

"My God," Cramer whispered to himself.

"What is it!"

Cramer told the Abbot, and the holy man raised his ravaged face to the heavens. "Thanks be!" he cried. "The Age of Miracles is forever here!"

Cramer snatched up the map, folded it to a manageable size, and strode to the edge of the escarpment. He turned to the Abbot. "Are you up to another hard slog?"

"God gives strength to the pilgrim," the holy man almost shouted. "Lead the way, Mr Cramer!"

For the next two hours they made their slow way down the incline. So steep was the drop in places that the Abbot was unable to negotiate the descent through the undergrowth, and Cramer was forced to carry him on his back.

He murmured holy mantras into Cramer's ear.

He found it impossible to assess his emotions at that time, still less his thoughts— perhaps disbelief, maybe even fear of the unknown. He entertained the vague hope that Francesca, having completed her quest and found the temple, might return with him to Earth.

They came to the foot of the incline and pressed ahead through dense vegetation. From time to time they came across what Cramer hoped was the track through the undergrowth that Francesca might have made, only to lose it again just as quickly. Their progress was slow, with frequent halts so that Cramer could consult the map and the position of the bloated sun. He wondered if it was a psychosomatic reaction to the events of the past few hours, or a meteorological change, that made the air almost impossible to breathe. It seemed sulphurous, infused with the miasma of Hell itself. Certainly, the Abbot was taking laboured breaths through his ruined nose-holes.

At last they emerged from the jungle and found themselves on the edge of a second great escarpment, where the land stepped down to yet another sweep of sultry jungle. Cramer studied the map. According to Francesca, the temple was situated somewhere along this ledge. They turned right and pushed through fragrant leaves and hanging fronds. Cramer could see nothing that might resemble an alien construction.

Then, amid a tangle of undergrowth ten metres ahead, he made out a regular, right-angled shape he knew was not the work of nature. It was small, perhaps four metres high and two wide, a rectangular block of masonry overgrown with creepers. He detected signs that someone had passed this way, and recently: the undergrowth leading to the stone block was broken, trampled down.

"What is it?" the Abbot whispered.

Cramer described what he could see.

"The shrine," the holy man said. "It has to be ... "

They approached the Slarque temple. Cramer was overcome with a strange disappointment that it should turn out to be so small, so insignificant. Then, as they passed into its shadow, he realised that this was but a tiny part of a much greater subterranean complex. He peered, and saw a series of steps disappearing into the gloom. Tendrils, like trip-wires, had been broken on the upper steps: someone had passed this way, and recently.

Cramer took the Abbot's shoulder and assisted him down the steps. Just as he began to fear that their way would be in complete darkness, he made out a glimmer of light below. The steps came to an end. A corridor ran off to the right, along the face of the escarpment. Let into the stone of the cliff-face itself, at regular intervals, were tall apertures like windows. Great shafts of sunlight poured in and illuminated the way.

He walked the Abbot along the wide corridor, its ceiling carved with a bas-relief fresco of cavorting animals. In the lichen carpet that had spread across the floor over the millennia, he made out more than one set of footprints: the lichen was scuffed and darkened, as if with the passage of many individuals.

At last, after perhaps a kilometre, they approached the tall, arched entrance of a vast chamber. At first he thought it a trick of his ears, or the play of the warm wind within the chamber, but as they drew near he heard the dolorous monotone of a sustained religious chant. The sound, in precincts so ancient, sent a shiver down his spine.

They paused on the threshold. From a wide opening at the cliff-face end of the chamber, evening sunlight slanted in, its brightness blinding. When his eyes adapted Cramer saw, through a haze of tumbling dust motes, row upon row of grey-robed, kneeling figures, cowled heads bowed, chanting. The chamber was the size of a cathedral and the congregation filled the long stone pews on either side of a central aisle. The heat and the noise combined to make Cramer dizzy.

He felt a hand grip his elbow, and thought at first that it was the Abbot. He turned—a monk stood to his left, holding his upper arm; the Abbot was on Cramer's right, his broken face suffused with devotional rapture.

He felt pressure on his elbow. Like an automaton, he stepped into the chamber. The monk escorted Cramer up the aisle. The continuous chanting, now that they were amidst it, was deafening. The front of the chamber was lost in shadow. He could just make out the hazy outline of a scorpion-analogue statue, and beside it the representation of a torso upon a cross.

Halfway down the aisle, they paused.

The monk's grip tightened on his arm. The Abbot whispered to Cramer. His expression was beatific, his tone rapturous. "In the year of the supernova it is written that the Ultimate Sacrifice will rise from the dead, and so be marked out to appease the sun. Too, it is written that the sacrifice will be accompanied by a non-believer, and also by the Abbot of the true Church."

Cramer could hardly comprehend his words.

The monk pushed him forward. The chanting soared.

He stared. What he had assumed to be the statue of a body on a cross was not a statue at all. His mind refused to accept the image that his vision was relaying. He almost passed out. The monk held him upright.

Francesca hung before him, lashed to the vertical timber of the cross, the ultimate sacrifice in what must have been the most God-forsaken Calvary ever devised by man. Her head was raised at a proud angle, the expression on her full lips that of a grateful martyr. Her eyelids were closed, flattened like the Abbot's, and stitched shut in a semicircle beneath each eye. The threads obtruded from her perfect skin, thick and clotted like obscene, cartoon lashes.

Her evicted eyes, as green as Cramer remembered them, were looped about her neck.

Her arms and legs had been removed, amputated at shoulder and hip; silver discs capped the stumps. They had even excised her small, high breasts, leaving perfect white, sickle-shaped scars across her olive skin.

Cramer murmured his beloved's name.

She moved her head, and that tiny gesture, lending animation to something that by all rights should have been spared life, twisted a blade of anguish deep into his heart.

"Hans!" she said, her voice sweet and pure. "Hans, I told you that I loved you, would love you for ever." She smiled, a smile of such beauty amid such devastation. "What greater love could I show you than to allow you to share in the salvation of the world? Through our sacrifice, Hans, we will be granted eternal life."

He wanted, then, to scream at her—to ask how she could allow herself to believe in such perversion? But the time for such questioning was long gone.

And, besides, he knew . . . She had always sought something more than mere existence, and here, at last, she had found it.

"Hans," she whispered now. "Hans, please tell me that you understand. Please hold me."

Cramer stepped forward.

He felt the dart slam into the meat of his lower back. The plainsong crescendoed, becoming something sublime and at the same time terrible, and he pitched forward and slipped into oblivion.

He surfaced slowly through an ocean of analgesics and sedatives. He found himself in darkness, something wet tied around his neck. With realisation came pain, and he cried aloud. They laid him out again and put him under, and though he wanted to rage and scream at the injustice, the futility of what they were doing to him, all he could manage was a feeble moan of protest.

He came to his senses to find himself tied upright—to a cross?—four points of numbness where his arms and legs had been. Beside him he could hear the Abbot, moaning in masochistic ecstasy. He considered what a gruesome trinity they must present upon the altar.

"Francesca," he whispered. "Oh, Francesca, the pain..."

"The pain, Hans," she replied, "the pain is part of the sacrifice."

He laughed, and then wept, and then fell silent.

Francesca continued, her voice a whisper. She lovingly detailed what further sacrifices they would be called upon to make. Next, she said, would come the expert excision of their genitalia; after that they would be skinned alive. And then the Master Surgeon would remove their internal organs one by one: kidneys, liver, lungs, and finally their hearts, while all the time they were conscious of what was taking place, the better to appreciate their sacrifice.

"Hans," she whispered. "Can you feel it? Can you? The wonder, the rapture, the joy?"

He could feel nothing but pain, and lapsed into unconsciousness. He awoke from time to time, unable to tell how long he'd spent in blessed oblivion, or what further surgical mutilations they had carried out upon his body.

What followed was a nightmare without respite. During the day, when the heat was at its most intense, they were lifted from the altar and set side by side in the opening of the cliff-face, while the congregation chanted their medieval, monotone chant in hope of miracles. The pain was constant, at its worst in the heat of the day, dulling to a tolerable agony during the night.

Towards the end, Cramer dreamed of rescue: he hallucinated the arrival of a pirate ship come to set them free. Then he came to his senses and realised that for him there would be no release, no return to physical well-being. He was a prisoner of Tartarus, a jail more secure than any of ancient myth.

On the very last day they were carried outside and positioned before the scalding glare of the sun. Cramer sensed heightened activity among the monks, hurried movement and hushed conversation suggesting panic and disbelief. He felt the heat of the sun searing his flesh, and laughed aloud at the knowledge of his victory.

Francesca maintained her faith until the very end. In mounting fear she intoned: "And it is written that the Ultimate Sacrifice *shall* rise from the dead, and *will* guide the faithful to the lost temple of the Slarque, and through the sacrifice of the holy trinity the sun *will* cease its swelling..."

Cramer was torn between exacting revenge upon the person responsible for his torture and keeping the one he loved in ignorance. A part of him wanted to impose upon Francesca his rationalisation of what had happened, explain that there had been no miracles at all.

He said nothing. If he were to make her comprehend the tragedy and evil of their predicament, the insane fanaticism of the accursed Church, he would only inflict upon her a greater torture than that she had suffered already.

The end came within the hour, and swiftly. He felt his flesh shrivel in the intense heat, and was aware of Francesca and the Abbot to his left and right. Francesca was murmuring a constant prayer, and the Abbot from time to time laughed in manic ecstasy.

All around them sounded the monks' frantic chanting, the entreaties of the faithful to their oblivious God.

In rapture, Cramer heard the detonation of multiple thunder, and the roar of the approaching firestorm as the sun exploded and unleashed its terrible freight of radiation.

He turned his head. "Abbot!" he called out with his very last breath. "So much for your superstition! You bastards didn't get my heart!"

The holy man could only laugh. "For our sacrifice," he began, "we will be granted life ever—"

Cramer should have known that the righteous would forever have the last word.

"Hans!" He heard the small voice to his left. She was crying, now. "Hans, please say you love me..."

But before he could speak, before he could accede to Francesca's final wish, the blastfront reached the surface of Tartarus Major with a scream like that of a million souls denied, and Cramer gave thanks that his suffering was at a blessed end.

STEPS ALONG THE WAY

I have no idea where the idea for this short story came from, but I recall that I had the idea one morning and wrote the tale that afternoon. It was quite unlike anything I'd written until that point, and I've written nothing similar since. I don't write many post-human tales (and to be honest they're not my favourite sub-genre of SF), but this story couldn't have been done in any other way. It first appeared in Peter Crowther's Moonshots *anthology, and the American editor Gardner Dozois bought it twice for different anthologies.*

STEPS ALONG THE WAY

O N THE EVE OF MY FIVE HUNDREDTH REBIRTHDAY, AS I STROLLED THE
gardens of my manse, a messenger appeared and informed me that I had a
visitor.

"Severnius wishes to consult you on a matter of urgency," said the ball of light.
"Shall I make an appointment?"

"Severnius? How long has it been? No—I'll see him now."

The light disappeared.

It was the end of a long autumn afternoon, and a low sun filled the garden with
a rich and hazy light. I had been contemplating my immediate future, quite how I
should approach the next century. I am a man methodical and naturally circum-
spect: not for me the grand announcements of intent detailing how I might spend
my *next* five hundred years. I prefer to plan ahead one hundred years at a time,
ever hopeful of the possibility of change, within myself and without. For the past
week I had considered many avenues of enquiry and pursuit; but none had
appealed. I had awoken early that morning, struck with an idea like a revelation:
Quietus.

I composed myself on a marble bench beneath an arbour entwined with fragrant
roses. The swollen sun sank amid bright tangerine strata, and on the other side of
the sky the moon rose, full yet insubstantial, above the manse.

Severnius stepped from the converter and crossed the glade. He always wore
his primary somaform when we met, as a gesture of respect: that of a wise man of
yore, with flowing silver-grey hair and beard. He was a Fellow some two thousand
years old, garbed in the magenta robes of the Academy.

We embraced in silence, a short communion in which I reacquainted myself
with his humanity.

"Fifty years?" I asked.

He smiled. "More like eighty," he said, and then gave the customary greeting of these times: "To your knowledge."

"Your knowledge," I responded.

We sat and I gestured, and wine and glasses appeared upon the bench between us.

"Let me see, the last time we met you were still researching the Consensus of Rao."

"I concluded that it was an unworkable proposition, superseded by the latest theories." I smiled. "But worth the investigation."

Severnius sipped his wine. "And now?"

"I wound down my investigations ten years ago, and since then I've been exploring the Out-there. Seeking the new..."

He smiled, something almost condescending in his expression. He was my patron and teacher; he was disdainful of the concept of the new.

"Where are you now?" he asked. "What have you found?"

"Much as ever, permutations of what has been and what is known." I closed my eyes, and made contact. "I^2 is on Pharia, in the Nilakantha Stardrift, taking in the ways of the natives there; I^3 is climbing Selerious Mons on Titan, and I^4 is in love with a quasi-human on a nameless moon half a galaxy away."

"It appears that you are... waiting?" he said. "Biding your time with meaningless pursuits. Considering your options for the next century."

I hesitated. It occurred to me then how propitious was his arrival. I would never have gone ahead with Quietus without consulting him.

"A thought came to me this morning, Severnius. Five hundred years is a long time. With your tutelage and my enquiries, I have learned much, dare I say everything? I was contemplating a period of Quietus."

He considered my words. "A possibility," he agreed. "Might I enquire as to the duration?"

"It really only occurred to me at dawn. I don't know—perhaps a thousand years."

"I once enjoyed Quietus for five hundred," said Severnius. "I was reinvigorated upon awakening—the thrill of change, the knowledge of all the learning to be caught up with."

"Precisely my thoughts."

"There is an alternative, of course."

I stared at him. "There is?"

He hesitated, marshalling his words. "My Fellows at the Academy last week

Enstated and Enabled an Early," he said. "The process, though wholly successful physiologically, was far from psychologically fulfilled. We had to wipe his memories of the initial awakening and instruction. We are ready to try again."

I stared at him. The Enstating and Enabling of an Early was a rare occurrence indeed. I said as much.

"You," Severnius said, "were the last."

Even though I had been considered a success, my rehabilitation had required his prolonged patronage. I thought through what he had told me so far, the "urgency" of his presence here.

He was smiling. "I have been watching your progress closely these past eighty years," he said. "I submitted your name to the Academy. We agreed that you should be made a Fellow, subject to the successful completion of a certain test."

"And that is?" I asked, aware of my heartbeat. All thought of Quietus fled at the prospect of becoming a Fellow.

"The patronage and stewardship of the Early we Enstated and Enabled last week," Severnius said.

It was a while before I could bring myself to reply. It was a great honour to be considered by the Academy, but at the same time I fully understood the difficulties of patronage. "You said that the subject was psychologically damaged."

Severnius gestured. "You studied advanced psycho-healing in your second century. We have confidence in your abilities."

"It will be a considerable undertaking. A hundred years, more?"

"When we Enstated and Enabled you, I was your steward for almost fifty years. We think that perhaps a hundred years might suffice in this case."

"*Perhaps*," I said, "before I make a decision I might meet the subject?"

"By all means," Severnius said.

And while he gave me the details of the Early, his history, I closed my eyes and made contact. I recalled I^2 from his studies on Pharia, I^3 from Titan, and I^4 from his affair with the alien.

I^2, I^3, and I^4 followed each other from the converter and stepped across the glade, calling greetings to Severnius. They appeared as younger, carefree versions of myself, before age and wisdom had cured me of vanity. I stood and reached out, and we merged.

Their thoughts, their respective experiences on Pharia, Titan and the nameless moon, became mine—and while they had revelled in their experiences, to me they were the antics of children, and I learned nothing new. I resolved to edit the memories when an opportune moment arose.

Severnius, with the etiquette of the time, had averted his gaze during the process of merging. Now he looked up and smiled. "You are ready?"

I stood. We crossed to the converter, and then, before stepping upon the plate, both paused to look up at our destination.

The moon, riding higher now, and more substantial against the darker sky, gazed down on us with a face altered little since time immemorial. The fact of its immutability, in an age replete with the boundless possibilities of change, filled me with awe.

We converted.

The Halls of the Fellowship of the Academy occupied the Sea of Tranquillity, an agglomeration of domes scintillating in the sunlight against the absolute black of the lunar night.

We stepped from the converter and crossed the regolith towards the Academy. Severnius led me into the cool, hushed shade of the domes and through the hallowed halls. He explained that if I agreed to steward the Early, then the ceremony of acceptance to the Fellowship would follow immediately. I glanced at him. He clearly assumed that I would accept without question.

The idea of ministering to the psychological well-being of an Early, for an indefinite duration, filled me with apprehension.

We came to the interior dome. The sight of the subject within the silver hemisphere, trapped like some insect for inspection, brought forth in me a rush of memories and emotions. Five hundred years ago I too had awoken to find myself within a similar dome. Five hundred years ago, I presume, I had looked just as frightened and bewildered as this Early.

A gathering of Fellows—academics, scientists, philosophers—stood in a semicircle around the dome, watching with interest and occasionally addressing comments to their colleagues. Upon the arrival of Severnius and myself, they made discreet gestures of acknowledgement and departed, some vanishing through their own converters, others choosing to walk.

I approached the skin of the dome and stared.

The Early was seated upon the edge of a low foamform, his elbows lodged upon his knees, his head in his hands. From time to time he looked up and stared about him, his clasped hands a knotted symbol of the fear in his eyes.

I felt an immediate empathy, a kinship.

Severnius had told me that he had died at the age of eighty-two, but they had restored him to a soma-type approximately half that age. His physique was lean and well muscled, but his most striking attribute was his eyes, piercingly blue and intelligent.

I glanced at Severnius, who nodded. I walked around the dome, so that I would be facing the Early when I entered, and stepped through the skin of the hemisphere. Even then, my sudden arrival startled him. He looked up, his hands gripping his knees, and the fear in his eyes intensified.

He spoke, but in an accented English so primitive that it was some seconds before I could understand his words.

"Who the hell are you?" he said. "What's happening to me?"

I held up a reassuring hand and emitted pheromones to calm his nerves. In his own tongue I said, "Please, do not be afraid. I am a friend."

Despite the pheromones and my reassurances, he was still nervous. He stood quickly and stared at me. "What the hell's going on here?"

His agitation brought back memories. I recalled my own awakening, my first meeting with Severnius. He had seemed a hostile figure, then. Humankind had changed over the course of thirty thousand years, become taller and more considerate in the expenditure of motion. He had appeared to me like some impossibly calm, otherworldly creature.

As I must have appeared to this Early.

"Please," I said, "sit down."

He did so, and I sat beside him, a hand on his arm. The touch eased him slightly.

"I'd like to know what's happening," he said, fixing me with his intense, sapphire stare. "I know this sounds crazy, but the last I remember . . . I'd been ill for a while, and then the hospitalisation . . ."

He shook his head, tears appearing in his eyes as he gazed at his hands—the hands of a man half the age of the person he had been. I reached out and touched his arm, calming him.

"And then I woke up here, in this body. Hell, you don't know what it's like, to inhabit the body of an old man, and then to wake up suddenly . . . suddenly young again."

I smiled. I said nothing, but I could well recall the feeling, the wonder, the disbelief; the doubt and then the joy of apprehending the reality of renewal.

He looked up at me, quickly, something very much like terror in his eyes. "I'm alive, aren't I? This isn't some dream?"

"I assure you that what you are experiencing is no dream."

"So this is . . . Afterlife?"

"You could say that," I ventured. "Certainly, for you, this is an afterlife." I emitted pheromones strong enough to forestall his disbelief.

He merely shook his head. "Where am I?" he asked in little more than a whisper.

"The time is more than thirty thousand years after the century of your birth."

"Thirty thousand years?" He enunciated each word separately, slowly.

"To you it might seem like a miracle beyond comprehension," I said, "but the very fact that you are here implies that the science of this age can accomplish what in your time would be considered magic. Imagine the reaction of a stone age man, say, to the wonders of twentieth century space flight."

He looked at me. "So... to you I'm nothing more than a primitive—"

"Not at all," I said. "We deem you capable of understanding the concepts behind our world, though it might take a little time." This was a lie—there were many things that would be beyond his grasp for many years, even decades.

Severnius had told me that the subject had evinced signs of mental distress upon learning the disparity between his ability to understand and the facts as they were presented. I would have to be very careful with this subject—if, that was, I accepted the Fellowship.

"So," he said, staring at me. "Answer my question. How did you bring me here?"

"Very well..." I proceeded to explain, in terms he might understand, the scientific miracle of Enstating and Enabling. It was a ludicrously simplistic description of a complex process, of course, but it would suffice.

His eyes bored into me. His left cheek had developed a quick, nervous tic. "I don't believe it..."

I touched his arm, the contact calming him. "Please... why would I lie?"

"But how could you possibly recover my memories, my feelings?"

"Think of your childhood," I said, "your earliest memories. Think of your greatest joy, your greatest fear. Tell me, have we succeeded?"

His expression was anguished. "Christ," he whispered. "I can remember every-thing... *everything*. My childhood, college." He shook his head in slow amazement. "But... but my understanding of the way the universe works... It tells me this can't be happening."

I laughed. "Come! You are a man of science, a rationalist. Things change: what was once taken as written in stone is overturned; theory gives way to established fact, which in turn evolves yet more fundamental theory, which is then verified... and so proceeds the advance of scientific enlightenment."

"I understand what you're saying," he said. "It's just that I'm finding it hard to believe."

"In time," I said, "you will come to accept the seeming miracles of this age."

Without warning he stood and strode towards the concave skin of the dome. He stared at his reflection, and then turned to face me.

"In time, you say? Just how long have I got?" He lifted his hand and stared at it. "Am I some laboratory animal you'll get rid of once your experiment's through?" He stopped and considered something. "If you built this body, then you must be able to keep it indefinitely . . ."

He stopped again, this time at something in my expression.

"You are immortal," I said.

I could see that he was shaken. The tight skin of his face coloured as he tried to come to terms with my casual pronouncement of his status.

"Thirty thousand years in the future," he whispered to himself, "the world is inhabited by immortals."

"The galaxy," I corrected him. "Humankind has spread throughout the stars, inhabiting those planets amenable to life, adapting others, sharing worlds with intelligent beings."

Tears welled in his eyes. He fought not to let them spill, typical masculine product of the twentieth century that he was.

"If you did this for me," he said, "then it's within your capability to bring back to life the people I loved, my wife and family—"

"And where would we stop?" I asked. "Would we Enstate and Enable the loved ones of everyone we brought forward?" I smiled. "Where would it end? Soon, everyone who had ever lived would live again."

He failed to see the humour of my words. "You don't know how cruel that is," he said.

"I understand how cruel it seems," I said. "But it is the cruelty of necessity." I paused. I judged that the time was right to share my secret. "You see, I too was once like you, plucked from my death bed, brought forward to this strange and wondrous age, fearful and little comprehending the miracles around me. I stand before you as testament to the fact that you will survive this ordeal, and come to understand."

He stared at me, suspicious. At last he said, "But why? Why you and me?"

"They, the people of this age, considered us men of importance in our time— men whose contribution to history were steps along the way to the position or pre-eminence that humankind now occupies. Ours is not to wonder, but to accept."

"So that's all I am—a curiosity? A specimen in some damned museum?"

"Not at all! They will be curious, of course; they'll want to hear all about your time... But you are free to learn, to explore, to do with your limitless future what you will—with the guidance and stewardship of a patron, as I too was once guided."

The Early walked around the periphery of the dome. He completed a circuit, then halted and stared at me. "Explore," he said at last, tasting the word. "You said explore? I want to explore the worlds beyond Earth! No—not only the worlds beyond Earth, the worlds beyond the worlds you've already explored. I want to break new ground, discover new worlds..." He stopped and looked at me. "I take it that you haven't charted all the universe?"

I hesitated. "There are places still beyond the explored expanses of space," I said.

"Then I want to go there!"

I smiled, taken by his naïve enthusiasm. "There will be time enough for exploration," I said. "First, you must be copied, so that you can send your other selves out to explore the unexplored. There are dangers—"

He was staring at me in disbelief, but his disbelief was not for what I thought. "Dangers?" he scoffed. "What's the merit of exploration if there's no risk?"

I opened my mouth, but this time I had no answer. Something of his primitivism, his heedless, reckless thirst for life which discounted peril and hardship, reminded me of the person I had once been, an age ago.

I considered the next one hundred years, and beyond. I had reached that time of my life when all experience seemed jejune; I had come to the point, after all, where I had even considered Quietus.

To go beyond the uncharted, to endanger oneself in the quest for knowledge, to think the unthinkable...

It was ridiculous—but why, then, did the notion bring tears to my eyes?

I hurried across the dome and took his arm. "Come," I said, leading him towards the skin of the hemisphere.

"Where?" he began.

But we were already outside the dome, and then through the skin of another, and walking across the silver-grey regolith of the lunar surface.

He stopped and gazed about him in wonder. "Christ," he whispered. "Oh, Christ, I never thought..."

"Over here," I said, leading him.

We crossed the plain towards the display, unchanged in thirty thousand years. He stared at the lunar module, stark beneath the unremitting light of the sun. We stood on the platform encircling the display and stared down at the footprints the first astronauts had laid upon the surface of another world.

He looked at me, his expression beatific. "I often dreamed," he said, "but I never thought I'd ever return."

I smiled. I shared the emotions he experienced, then. I knew how much it meant to return. I recalled the time, not long after my rebirth in this miraculous age, when I had made the pilgrimage to Earth and looked again upon the cell where over thirty thousand years ago I, Galileo Galilei, had been imprisoned for my beliefs.

Haltingly, I told Armstrong who I was. We stared up into the dark sky, past the Earth and the brilliant sun, to the wonders awaiting us in the uncharted universe beyond.

We embraced for a long minute, and then turned and retraced our steps across the surface of the moon towards the domes of the Academy, where Severnius would be awaiting my decision.

The Miracle of Kallithéa

I wrote the first draft of "The Miracle of Kallithéa" in December '96, then sent it out to Keith Brooke and Stephen Baxter for their criticism. With their comments to hand, I set about the final draft, completing it to my satisfaction sometime around the middle of '97. It was accepted by Paul Fraser and published in his magazine Spectrum SF 3, *August 2000.*

It is, like much of my work, about the effects of technological innovation on human beings, rather than about the innovation itself. In Charles Sinclair I found a flawed character whose past was weighted with guilt, and whose future was without hope, until . . .

THE MIRACLE AT KALLITHÉA

THE SEARING HEAT AND THE RASP OF CICADAS BROUGHT SINCLAIR TO semi-consciousness. He was lying on the camp bed in his studio, still wearing his shorts and paint-streaked shirt. The stench of ouzo rose from the pillow. He sat up and stared through the window at the olive groves and the distant sea. Christ, but there was nothing like a Greek summer to make him feel better, physically if not mentally. And the ouzo helped. He'd tried Metaxa over the years, and then raki, but the punishing hangovers rather than the warnings of the island's only doctor, "Three years, Mr Edward, if you continue to drink this poison," had warned him off. He'd taken to ouzo. "Very good, Mr Edward," the doctor had said, pointing to the platoon of empty bottles on the packed-earth floor. "Maybe five years, now."

The idea of drinking himself to death appealed to Sinclair: there was something suitably cowardly in the slow suicide of alcohol poisoning. Also, the after-effects of ouzo were enjoyable. Now he felt neither hung over nor nauseous—just wonderfully lightheaded, and woozy, detached from the reality of his stone-built studio and the start of another day.

He left the building and crossed the clearing to the well, drawing a plastic bucket of cold water. He tipped it over his head, massaging sensation back into his alcohol-benumbed features. He used the front of his shirt to dry his face, then noticed that his big, awkward hands were smeared with streaks of oil paint: Naples yellow, rose madder, burnt sienna—flesh-tones. Had he been painting yesterday, for the first time in months?

He returned to the studio. All the canvases he'd completed during the past eight years, perhaps a hundred, were stacked facing the walls: he had no desire to look upon these works. He had sold none of them, not because there was no demand—parasitical dealers were clamouring to offer him outrageous sums—but because he had no desire to unleash upon the world visual representations of what he was feeling.

For the past year he had painted nothing at all.

He crossed the studio, pulled the cover from the easel, and stared at the work revealed.

It was vile! A self-portrait, done with all his accustomed skill, and honest, but because of that very honesty impossible for him to contemplate. His face was a livid series of mottled pink slabs, his eyes buried and guilty, his mouth twisted with the knowing leer of self-hatred.

With shaking fingers he filled the wood-stove with off-cuts of frame and twists of lighted newspaper. He ripped the canvas from its working frame and rolled it, buckling it in anger, and forced it into the greedy belly of the stove. The canvas detonated in an explosion of blue and orange flame.

He stood back, breathing deeply with accomplishment. Soon the odour of canvas, oils and primer filled the studio, the perfume heady and intoxicating, at once beautiful and terrible.

He heard the sound of the car engine with disbelief, and hurried into the clearing. A silver Mercedes braked on the cart track between the olive trees.

The driver climbed out. "Ah... Monsieur Edward Sinclair?"

"What do you want?" The question was more aggressive than he'd intended. He saw that the stranger was carrying two thick books.

"I came merely to introduce myself," the man said, his swift glance taking in Sinclair's unkempt state. There was something defensive about his explanation, as if he detected the hostility in Sinclair's manner, or had heard about his legendary reclusiveness.

He was perhaps fifty, but dressed much younger: brand-name white sneakers, Calvin Klein pre-faded jeans, a white silk Versace shirt. His hair was as silver as the coachwork of his automobile, and his face tanned.

Sinclair felt suddenly tired, hardly up to the mental effort of telling the man that he should go. "I'm sorry," he said, "I'm rather busy." And he cursed himself for sounding so apologetic. Damn it, the bastard's invading my space and time—I'm entitled to tell him to piss off.

"Deauchamps. Pierre Deauchamps." He held up one of the books, and Sinclair mentally winced to see that it was his unauthorised biography. "I've been reading about your life and work. I find it fascinating."

Sinclair interrupted. "Do you know how he got that? Have you any idea?"

"Excuse me?"

"Mitchell, the hack who wrote that?" He pointed to the book that Deauchamps was still holding. "Do you know how he duped me into confiding in him? He pretended to be Cartwright. Set up a studio across the valley, went out sketching when he knew I left my studio. Contrived a chance meeting. Told me he was Justin Cartwright, the abstract expressionist. Fooled me completely. I hadn't seen a photograph of Cartwright in years. He knew what he was talking about, too. Stayed on the island three months, came over practically every bloody night—with booze, of course. The bastard milked me dry. I talked, told him things..." Sinclair stopped, pained at the memory of the deception, his confessions.

"I thought the book an incredible insight..."

"Did you? Well, he got it wrong. He listened to me and formed his own impressions, made ridiculous interpretations. The whole thing's a mess of guesswork and supposition."

"I'm sorry. Of course, I respect your word. Nevertheless"—and here Deauchamps held up the second book, the Thames and Hudson *Complete Works of Edward Charles Sinclair*—"I am a student of your work."

Sinclair rubbed his eyes wearily. "Just what do you want, Mr Deauchamps?"

The Frenchman shrugged. "I would like to talk to you, Monsieur Sinclair," he explained. "You see, five years ago I lost my daughter, Sabine."

They sat outside the studio on folding chairs, sipping ouzo as the afternoon progressed. For perhaps two hours they talked of nothing else but Sinclair's paintings. Deauchamps had an exhaustive knowledge of his work—more, a deeply felt understanding of what Sinclair had been trying to achieve. Only rarely, Sinclair told himself, do we come upon people with whom we immediately connect, people whose views and outlooks uncannily mirror our own. Pierre Deauchamps, Sinclair felt, was one of these people.

Nevertheless, some residual cynicism in Sinclair, a suspicion fed by years of disappointment in friends and loved ones, urged caution.

He refilled the Frenchman's glass. On contact with the water, the ouzo turned opaque.

A silence came between the men, but there was nothing awkward or embarrassing about the sudden absence of dialogue. At last, as if he had been considering the move for some time, Deauchamps took a calfskin wallet from the breast pocket of his shirt. He opened it and removed, tweezered between index and fore-finger, a small colour snapshot. He passed it to Sinclair.

"Sabine," he said.

Sinclair felt his heart lurch. A part of him wanted to tell Deauchamps that he would rather not look at the photograph, did not want to experience the pain. Then he was looking down at the pretty, blonde little girl, perhaps five or six years old. She was staring into the camera, her eyes squinting against the sun, and Sinclair felt his throat constrict and tears burn his eyes. He passed the snapshot back, unable to bring himself to speak.

"That's the last picture I took of her," Deauchamps said, "on holiday in Monaco. Six months later I noticed she appeared listless. She developed bruising. We, my wife and I, we took her to a doctor, who recommended a specialist. An oncologist. My daughter was diagnosed with leukaemia a few days later. I thought... you know, in these modern times... I'd heard of so many cases of the disease being cured. But Sabine had a particularly rare form, which was incurable. Can you imagine that, Monsieur Sinclair?"

Sinclair shook his head.

"We never gave up hope," Deauchamps went on. "In retrospect, with knowledge of what transpired, you wonder how you coped—but at the time you are sustained by hope. She died a few days before her sixth birthday."

Sinclair hoped that his mute inability to express sympathy might be construed by the Frenchman as genuine commiseration. He wanted to respond, to repay Deauchamps' openness with an account of his own loss, but something prevented him. He told himself that he did not know the man well enough to open up just yet, but if he were honest with himself he knew that he would never be able to express the pain of his own bereavement, never do justice with mere words to the incommunicable tragedy of loss and its consequences.

He feared that Deauchamps, in the aftermath of his own confession, might ask him about what had happened eight years ago. But he thought not; Deauchamps was too intelligent and sensitive to demand such a crass reciprocation. In any case, their meeting was brought to a close when Deauchamps' mobile phone bleeped in counterpoint to the hum of the cicadas. He slipped the miniature device from the pocket of his jeans—its compact size surprising Sinclair, reminding him how long he had sequestered himself from the world—and spoke in rapid French.

Deauchamps stood and apologised for imposing himself on Sinclair. "I wonder, if it is okay with you... perhaps we might talk again?"

And to his surprise Sinclair found himself agreeing, suggesting the following day. "But perhaps a little later," he added. "Say, the early evening? I usually work during the day." And hating himself for the lie, he watched the Mercedes back out of the clearing and disappear down the cart track.

They had been talking for almost five hours. The sun was setting over the olive groves. As the sky darkened to an indigo twilight, Sinclair sat with his thoughts and drank himself to sleep.

He woke late the following morning. He sat on the step of his studio and chewed on stale bread and wizened olives, washed down with cold well water. As he gradually came to his senses he went over his meeting with Deauchamps. He recalled the photograph of Deauchamps' dead daughter, and he realised, with a sudden pang of panic, that the image of the little girl had eclipsed his eight-year-old memory of another child.

He found himself filling a plastic bottle with water. He left the studio and walked up the hillside through the olive groves towards the whitewashed church, the building icing-sugar white and miniaturised by distance like some improbable cake decoration. On the way he picked a single wild flower—he had no idea of its name, but the delicate blue of its petals reminded him of a child's trusting eyes.

He had not visited Rachel's grave for many years. His memories were painful enough, without subjecting himself to the torture of a pilgrimage to the meaningless reliquary of her bones. He had no belief in a god of any kind, and he had not wanted her funeral to be conducted in the church, much less for her to be buried. He had desired the clean finality of cremation, but Sophia, his estranged wife falling back on religion in her distress, had demanded a church service and burial. Sinclair had been unable to bring himself to disagree.

He kept no photographs of Rachel in his studio: he had bundled them together eight years ago and lodged them in a deposit box in the island's only bank. His memory would suffice, he'd told himself, more than adequately—and had done so until this morning. Now he thought of his daughter and saw instead only the smiling face of Sabine Deauchamps.

He came to the sprawling graveyard and walked among the headstones. He was disoriented by the rows of additional graves—Rachel's had marked the furthest extent of the churchyard on his last visit—and it was some minutes before he located her small white headstone.

He approached it with something like trepidation, as if fearing what he might find. He sat before the headstone on the plot of parched grass and reached out to touch the cool marble. Another of his wife's demands had been that the headstone should bear Rachel's photograph, in the Greek tradition. She came from Paris every year to renew the sun-bleached snapshot, briefly visiting Sinclair to torture him with her silent accusation, her bitterness.

He removed the pane of glass from the frame and slipped the photograph out. It was faded, its bright primary colours washed to a wan pastel. Rachel stared up at him, her long blonde hair framing a knowing gaze, her wide mouth serious.

Along with her image came a sudden painful surge of recollected incidents and events. She moved in his memory, and spoke to him, and he was overcome with a wave of renewed emotion: his love for this innocent child, his fear for her, his desire for her to have everything it was in his power to provide.

The pain of grief filled his chest like an exploding coronary. He wanted to scream in rage at the unfairness of the world, but instead he just hung his head and wept.

Eight years ago, following the separation from his wife, Rachel had spent the summer with Sinclair on the island. The holiday was drawing to a close, and she was due to return to her mother in Athens, when they set off to the beach for the very last time.

While Sinclair painted, Rachel explored the rock pools of the foreshore. He had watched her for a while, delighting in her bubbling excitement as she jumped from one pool of captured seawater to the next, shrieking at her discoveries.

Then he lost himself in his painting; time passed, but Sinclair was oblivious. At midday he surfaced, released from his concentration on the canvas by the need for food. He packed away his paints and shouted for his daughter. They would dine at the nearby taverna as they did two or three times every week, Sinclair enjoying an Amstel lager while Rachel told him of her finds.

There was no reply from Rachel. He strolled towards the rocky outcrop where he had last seen her. He called again, not unduly worried. She was an inquisitive and adventurous child: she had often gone off like this, to turn up hours later musing abstractedly at some discovered shell or starfish. She could come to no harm on an island where everyone knew everyone else. Occasionally she had disappeared from his studio, to be returned in due course by a smiling islander.

This time she would never return.

He found her body facedown in a deep rock pool, something almost beautiful in the grace with which she floated, arms and legs outstretched, staring down with open eyes at the wonder of the underwater world.

She had fallen and cracked her head on a rock and slipped into the water and drowned, while he had been lost in contemplation of the sea and the limitless sky.

Even now, as he recalled the details of the discovery, the stark visual fact of her end, he was unable to recall his precise feelings or thoughts at the time. He had staggered from the rocks with his daughter in his arms, laid her on the sand and attempted to resuscitate her. He was joined by a small crowd of locals who relieved him one by one, battling to breath life into the tiny body while he looked on in disbelief.

When no hope remained he took her in his arms and walked from the beach. She was lighter than he recalled, as if the departure of life had robbed her body of a certain weight. Her thin, tanned arms and legs hung lazily, their swinging movement investing her with a cruel semblance of life. The expression on her face was serene.

Word of the tragedy had reached the village. As Sinclair walked up the main street to his studio, locals came from their houses, crossed themselves and murmured prayers.

He recalled little of the following few days; the summoning of his wife, the details of the funeral, the burial itself. He wondered how he had survived that period, the grief and the guilt. Over and over he said to himself, *If only . . . if only they had not gone to the beach that day, if only he had kept watch on her, if only she had not slipped and fallen . . .*

He did not paint for over a year. He was consumed with emotions he had no desire to commit to canvas. He drank, and numbed with alcohol in time began to paint again, bleak visions of hopelessness, which he did not show to anyone or try to sell.

It had seemed to him that everything in his life, his studio, the island, was a painful reminder of Rachel's non-existence. He had contemplated leaving the island, abandoning the place from which the physical fact of his daughter had been removed—but it came to him that this would be a betrayal of her memory, a cowardly running away from her essence which, he told himself, still dwelt in the hills and the olive groves and the beach.

In his imagination, as the years passed by, Rachel existed as a child of eight, a girl of ten, then a teenager—now she would be fifteen, and on the verge of womanhood. She was a phantom child who haunted his waking dreams with the beauty of the person she would never become.

Sinclair told himself that he rarely ventured out because he had no desire to be recognised. But the truth was far more painful. How often had he found himself, on his infrequent visits to the town, staring in grief-stricken amazement at some golden-haired Nordic girl-child? On more than one occasion he had had to stop himself from following a lanky, tanned teenager, suddenly convinced by some mannerism or glance that she was the daughter he had lost. The world out there seemed populated by versions of Rachel as she might have been, and the realisation was intolerable.

He replaced the photograph behind the square of glass and stood. Resolving not to return to the grave for a long, long time, he slowly made his way down the hill and through the olive groves to his studio.

Pierre Deauchamps returned at sunset that evening, bearing a bottle of ouzo. They sat in the cooling breeze and talked, drinking slowly as the twilight deepened. Deauchamps did not mention his daughter, and for this Sinclair was grateful; he would have been unable to respond with the story of his own loss. He felt that he did not possess the vocabulary with which to articulate the essence of what had happened. He had never been that good with words, which perhaps was why he had become a painter. He seemed to have a talent for the communication of emotions, feelings and ideas through the abstraction of pattern and colour—or, rather, had *had* a talent. He no longer thought of himself as a man with a talent for anything much but self-pity.

During the following week Deauchamps dropped by two or three times. The course of each evening would be much the same. He would question Sinclair as to his ideas on a certain school of artists, and if Sinclair had any ideas at all he would share them. More often than not, he would admit that apathy had won out and he had no ideas or opinions on the school of so-and-so. Then Deauchamps would begin, "Well, I have a theory..." And Sinclair would sit back, amused and often interested, as his guest talked knowledgeably long into the night.

A week after their first meeting a lull in the conversation seemed to suggest that they had exhausted the history of art, at least for the time being. Deauchamps looked across at Sinclair, as if wondering whether to broach a subject with him. At last he said, "You have been very hospitable, Edward."

"You do supply a superior brand of ouzo."

"I was thinking, perhaps you would care to come up to the station one evening this week?"

"The station?" Sinclair said. He realised, then, that Deauchamps had never mentioned what he was doing on the island.

"I am the Director of the Trans-Omega Research Station," Deauchamps said. "It's situated a kilometre up the hill. You must have seen it."

Sinclair shook his head. "I rarely venture out these days, Pierre. What do you do up there?"

"What do you know about quantum physics?"

"Good God! Nothing. Absolutely nothing at all."

"Then I'll explain," Deauchamps said, "on Saturday night, if that's convenient with you?"

"Fine—but what day is it today?"

Deauchamps smiled. "Today is Thursday. I'll pick you up around sunset. My colleagues usually leave at six. We'll have the place to ourselves."

Sinclair nodded. "I'll look forward to that," he said, not sure if he was telling the truth.

It was the first time he had been in an automobile for more than a decade, and he found the short ride to the Research Station a suitably novel experience. He was impressed by the sprung comfort of the seat, the silence of the vehicle as it swept effortlessly around the broad curves of the road. Deauchamps steered with one hand on the wheel, keeping up a stream of small talk until they reached the gates of the station. Beyond the diamond-mesh fencing, the building was an ugly, single-level concrete block, its flat roof sprouting a forest of rusted iron staves in typical Greek fashion, rods with which to found the second storey should one be required.

A uniformed security guard opened the gates without a second glance at Sinclair. The Mercedes crunched across the gravel and around the building.

Deauchamps unlocked a pair of polished double doors and gestured Sinclair in before him. The foyer was sumptuous: thick red carpeting, pine panelling, a vast reception desk, and on the wall behind it the Trans-Omega logo: the Greek letter omega, shot through with an arrow.

Deauchamps crossed to a door beyond the desk, unlocked it and indicated that Sinclair should follow. Then they were in the main body of the building, a long chamber which was revealed in successive, flickering stages as the Frenchman switched on the fluorescent strip-lighting.

Sinclair stared at the banks of computer terminals which lined the two long walls, each console attended by an empty swivel seat. The floor of the chamber was tiled with black and white squares, like an elongated chessboard. At the far end, opposite the entrance, was a plinth bearing an oval golden frame perhaps three metres high. In the frame a light glowed with a bright opaline intensity. Before the oval was a shorter array of terminals, and four black leather seats conspicuously vacant.

Deauchamps walked towards the oval frame, his footsteps ringing. Sinclair followed. It had been a long time since he had entered a building so thoroughly contemporary, and he felt obscurely uncomfortable with the chamber's modern, minimalist aesthetics.

Standing before the console, Deauchamps tapped a keyboard, glancing up at the frame from time to time. The opalescent light strobed. Sinclair gazed about him, at the banked computers lining the long walls, then back to the oval frame.

"What the hell is this place?" he asked.

Deauchamps left the console and stood before the frame. He lodged a foot on the first step of the plinth, staring up. "Watch," he said.

The opal glow flickered, went out. At first Sinclair saw only an ellipse of darkness. Then his eyesight adjusted and he made out trees and lights beyond. The frame was a window through the wall, he saw, overlooking the hillside and the island.

He glanced at Deauchamps, seeking an explanation, but the Director was intent on the night-time scene.

Sinclair returned his attention to the frame, and only then did he notice something amiss. If the view through the wall were to correspond with what might be seen from this position, then where was the diamond-mesh fence, the gate and the sentry post? For that matter, what had happened to the gravel floor of the compound? In the wash of light that spilled through the ellipse, he saw only tufts of grass and the occasional olive tree.

Deauchamps returned to the console and tapped at the keyboard again. The frame began to move rotate, turning edge on, and then stopped. The men moved around the frame so that they were looking through the aperture—which now, Sinclair saw, was showing a view *up* the hillside.

He took half a dozen cautious steps towards the plinth, staring.

Through the golden ellipse he saw a building, a villa, perhaps ten metres beyond the oval.

He turned to Deauchamps. "I don't understand... What the hell is this?"

He was sure that there was no villa situated ten metres up the hillside.

Someone appeared at the villa's window, looking out at the lighted verandah.

In the brief second that the man was visible, Sinclair noticed something eerily familiar about him, about his outline, his forward-leaning stance.

"Pierre?"

"The other day I asked you what you knew about quantum physics," the Director said. "I thought you might have read about the latest research projects backed by the European Union."

"I haven't read a paper in years," Sinclair said. "What research?"

"My investigations began a decade ago when I was leading a team on the European particle accelerator," Deauchamps said. "We noticed ... let's say, *anomalies* ... in the behaviour of certain subatomic particles. We devoted much study to nonlinearity in quantum wave functions ... " Deauchamps went on, and Sinclair understood not one word of the explanation.

Through the window of the villa, he saw people moving.

"Put simply, Edward, we were certain that we had evidence for the existence of parallel realms ... "

"What?" The phrase meant nothing to Sinclair. *"Parallel realms?"*

"Five years ago I gained funding from the Union to set up my own research unit in the south of France, before relocating here. We made our first breakthrough last year, and established visual contact with the realm we call Kallithéa Two."

Through the frame, Sinclair saw a bright light flicker above the long table on the verandah of the villa. As he watched, Deauchamps' words slowly percolating through his consciousness, someone stepped through the fly-screen door of the building, carrying a salad bowl. The man set the bowl in the centre of the table, and in the illumination from the overhead light ...

Sinclair stared, shocked.

The figure on the verandah was himself.

His knees felt week. Deauchamps had a swivel chair ready. Sinclair sat down, watching the figure—watching the other Sinclair—enter the house and return with place mats and cutlery. It was a Sinclair slightly weightier than himself, and prosperous looking. He wore a pair of gold-framed glasses that he, in this world, had never bothered to buy. This version of himself, he saw, was smiling.

"Jesus Christ, Pierre. What the hell's going on?"

"Imagine a million worlds, Edward, a billion, an infinite series of worlds like this one, but each one slightly different to the next—some differing only in details as minor as the arrangement of photons, others so different that we would have difficulty in recognising them. Worlds where humans did not evolve as the dominant life-form, where life was destroyed by the impact of a comet millennia

143

ago—an infinite number of worlds and *possibilities*. The reality you see through there is very close to our own, varying in minor details only. So far we have been able to achieve contact with just Kallithéa Two, but we know that there are many, many more worlds out there."

Sinclair shook his head. "I don't believe it."

Deauchamps smiled. "I know how you feel. Imagine my reaction when my theories were proved correct. Even now I sometimes find it hard to believe. I wake up thinking that it's all been a dream."

Sinclair's heart commenced a slow and laboured thudding as he stared through the frame. The other Sinclair stepped out onto the verandah, paused to talk to someone inside the villa.

"Why?" Sinclair said. "Why are you showing me this?"

Deauchamps smiled to himself and said, "Why do you think, Edward?"

Sinclair could only stare. His mouth went dry and his stomach turned sickeningly. The other Sinclair seated himself at the table. It was, he saw, set for two.

Then the screen door swung open. A figure stepped onto the verandah.

Crying out, Sinclair stood and stared as the second figure moved around the table and sat down.

"In this world," Deauchamps was saying, "your daughter did not drown at the age of seven. Rachel is fifteen now, and lives with you on the island."

Sinclair stared at his daughter and tears rolled down his cheeks.

She was the phantom who had haunted his dreams for so long, the teenager he had extrapolated from the seven-year-old Rachel who had left him so cruelly eight years ago. She sat cross-legged on a dining chair, elbows on the table, fork dangling over her plate. Her gestures and mannerisms were a sophisticated extension of those of the little girl she had been. She moved her hands when she spoke, gestured with her fork to emphasise a point. In her face Sinclair recognised his Rachel, the same small nose and wide, humorous mouth. Her hair was long and fair and two strands, on either side of her high cheekbones, were braided with a rosary of coloured beads.

Sinclair stared at the other Sinclair as "he" looked across the table at Rachel, listening to what she had to say and occasionally sipping a glass of red wine. His other self looked... Sinclair tried to find the right word—not so much bored but complacent, as if this meal was just one of many, as if the company of his daughter was to be taken for granted. Which, of course, for this Sinclair it was.

He wanted to yell at his alter ego that what he had was precious, that he should not let familiarity devalue the miracle of his daughter's presence. As he stared at the other Sinclair he saw a plump, self-satisfied man, someone who had never suffered what he had suffered, and he felt a sudden stab of envy at the other's good fortune.

He turned his attention to Rachel, drank in her every movement and mannerism. She was telling her father a long, complicated tale, from time to time forking pasta, but eating little.

Sinclair half-turned to Deauchamps, reluctant to take his gaze from Rachel. "Can we get closer? Is it possible to move the frame a little?"

The Director bent over the console. The image in the golden frame containing the portrait of Rachel, more amazing than any work of art, expanded. Sinclair approached the frame. It was as if he was at the table with them, as if he had only to reach out to touch Rachel's slim, tanned arm.

"Is it possible to hear what they're saying?" he asked. "Can sound transmit through the frame?"

"We *can* achieve sonic transference," Deauchamps told him. "But the power drain is tremendous. Perhaps, briefly, some other time."

"I can come here again?" Sinclair sounded awe-struck, even to his own ears.

Deauchamps smiled. "Perhaps once a week. I wouldn't want my colleagues to know what we are doing—this is supposed to be a top-secret project."

Rachel was pouring more wine, laughing at something the other Sinclair had said. She twisted around in her seat, her knees tucked up before her chest, and stared from the verandah. She appeared to be looking directly at Sinclair.

"Can they . . . ? I mean, they can't see us, can they?"

"That is not possible, Edward. The interface is one-way only. We can see them, but they are oblivious to our presence."

Sinclair nodded, formulating his next question. At last he said, "I don't suppose it would be possible to . . . to enter that world? Step through . . . ?"

"Impossible, Edward. There can be no possible transfer of mass between the realms."

Through the frame, the other Sinclair reached across the table and covered Rachel's hand with his, and Sinclair could only imagine the pleasure of the contact.

He sat and watched the meal progress like a critic at some private viewing. He considered the fact of what was before him, its implications. He thought about the chance, the stroke of luck, that in the other world had allowed Rachel to live past the age of seven.

It came to him that this was not the only change on the other world. He gestured at the interface. "In that world what happened to the Research Station? Where is it—or doesn't it exist there?"

"It exists, Edward—back in France. In that world, we never made the move from Montpellier to here. You see, I wasn't driven to move to Kallithéa."

Sinclair glanced at the Director. "Driven?"

"Edward, in that world your daughter did not die when she was seven. That was why I did not petition for the move to Greece."

"I'm not sure that I understand..." Sinclair began.

"It is all linked, Edward. Three years ago I read Mitchell's biography. I read his account of Rachel's accident, of how it affected you. I knew what you had suffered—I had gone through similar torment with Sabine, after all.

"An idea occurred to me. I brought a smaller, prototype version of the interface to the island and tested it at various sites. At last I discovered 'you' here, and Rachel. I returned to France, suggested the move to Greece on grounds of security, and last year we relocated. In the other world Rachel did not die, so I did not read of your bereavement, and therefore was not moved to transfer the station here."

Sinclair looked from the Frenchman to the vision of Rachel, dribbling red wine down her chin and laughing in tipsy delight.

He said at last, gesturing to the frame, "But... but why me, Pierre? I mean, what about...?" He stopped himself.

Deauchamps was smiling to himself. "What about Sabine? Don't you think I investigated the possibility?" He shook his head. "In that world, too, Sabine succumbed to leukaemia."

"Christ... I'm sorry. I'm so sorry." He stared at Rachel through the golden frame. "I don't know how to thank you, Pierre."

The Frenchman smiled. "Watching you tonight has been thanks enough."

In the other world, Sinclair and Rachel were clearing the table. He watched his daughter move from the verandah and into the villa.

"I think the show is over for tonight," Deauchamps said. "Perhaps Tuesday evening, if you are free?"

That night, back at the studio, Sinclair could not sleep. He sat beneath the stars, opened a bottle of ouzo and took the occasional sip. He did not want to get raging drunk tonight, did not want to wake in the morning and wonder if the events of the evening had been nothing but a dream. He considered the fact of the parallel worlds, thought of all the many Rachels existing out there... and laughed aloud in amazement.

———.———

He could think of nothing but the time he would next set eyes on his daughter. Tuesday seemed a long while coming. The days dragged. He found that he did not need alcohol to ease him into unconsciousness. Sleep came easily, and his dreams were no longer filled with the terror of his loss. Now he saw Rachel smiling, laughing, talking to him across a laden table.

Tuesday came and seemed to last forever, the hours until sunset drawn out through the merciless heat of the afternoon. Sunset came and went without the arrival of the Director. Towards eight, just as Sinclair was beginning to worry, the silver Mercedes appeared through the trees.

"I'm sorry for the delay," Deauchamps called through the open window. "I had trouble getting rid of a technician. Hop in."

Deauchamps backed from the olive grove and accelerated up the road. "Is Rachel...?" Sinclair began.

The Director smiled. "You're in for a treat. There's some kind of party. A celebration. Earlier Rachel gave 'you' a present."

"Good God..." He laughed at how out of touch he was. "What month is it, Pierre?"

"June—June the twenty-fourth." Deauchamps smiled. "Your birthday, Edward."

Sinclair shook his head. "Fifty-five today, damn it. I never realised."

Deauchamps smiled across at him as they drove through the gates of the station. "In that case I think we should celebrate," he said. "How about if we try for sound tonight?"

He led the way inside and across the deserted chamber to the ellipse of the interface. Sinclair imagined the view into the other world: soon he would be looking up the length of the garden, towards the single-storey villa.

While the Director worked at the console, Sinclair pulled up a chair and seated himself before the strobing white light.

The interface flickered, and the pearly glow was replaced by an *al fresco* party scene. Hurricane lamps on poles illuminated men and women on the lawn, dancing to silent bouzouki music. The table had been moved from the verandah to the lawn and piled with food. Those guests not dancing stood about in groups of two or three, drinking and chatting.

Sinclair stood up and moved to the frame. He looked for Rachel, but could not find her. Instead he recognised faces from the past, people he had not seen, in this world, for many years. There was Helmut Ganz, his agent, a rotund German in his fifties who seemed not to have aged a day since they had last met five years ago. He was chatting to Hirst, the installation artist Sinclair had known briefly during his London days. He recognised acquaintances he hadn't bothered to contact over the years—the sophisticated *habitués* of the European art scene, fellow artists, critics, the occasional actor.

"Prepare yourself for sound, Edward," Deauchamps called. "Coming through now!"

Then the chamber was filled with the high, fast music of multiple bouzoukis, the crowd's chatter and laughter. The dancers turned like the multi-coloured tesserae in a kaleidoscope, and at last Sinclair caught sight of Rachel, an angel in a long white cheesecloth dress with a black velvet choker at her neck.

She was hanging onto her father's arm, staring up at him with adoration in her eyes, while he smiled around at the assembled guests. Sinclair had difficulty in considering that he and the plump, well-groomed figure of the other Sinclair were essentially one and the same. Their life experiences had diverged eight years ago, the other Sinclair continuing with his successful, self-satisfied existence, while he . . . He stopped himself from following that line of thought. He should not let his jealousy of his other self get the better of him. Christ, until eight years ago he had been that man, just as smug and complacent and thankless of his good fortune, his talent and his love for his daughter.

"Speech!" the guests were calling. "Come on, man, say something!"

The band stopped playing and the dancers gathered round.

Sinclair raised a hand. "Very well! If you insist!" He removed his glasses and polished them with a cloth, smiling to himself. "First of all," he went on, "this party was a damned surprise, and you know, Rachel, how I hate surprises! There I was, down in the studio, working away . . . thinking that everyone had forgotten that it was my birthday . . . "

A chorus of "ohs" and "poor man"; an enterprising violinist set up a doleful lament.

Sinclair laughed. "And I come home to this! Arranged brilliantly and unexpect-edly by Rachel. I have my hands full keeping her on the straight and narrow, but she's not that bad a girl, really."

He held up his hands. "One more thing, while you're all here. After a lot of thought, Rachel and I have decided that, fantastic though life on Kallithéa is, we're ready for a change. So in two weeks we're moving to London. And, yes, we'll be throwing a party to celebrate!" He reached out and hugged Rachel to him, and finished, "Thank you all so much for coming. I'll talk to you all later. Now enjoy the party!"

Polite applause; murmurs of appreciation and laughter.

Sinclair turned to Deauchamps, the consequence of his alter ego's words just dawning on him. "Two weeks," he said. "In two weeks they'll be gone, Pierre."

Deauchamps avoided his gaze. "I will arrange things so that you can come up here more often until then, okay?"

Shell-shocked, Sinclair said, "Yes. Yes, I'd appreciate that."

Later that night, when Deauchamps had dropped him off, Sinclair sat outside his studio and drank. He had become practised at the game of self-pity over the years, and the aptitude came in useful now. *Two weeks,* he thought, over and over.

He contrasted the hand fate had dealt him, compared with the straight flush his other self—the smug bastard Sinclair in the other world—had found himself holding.

Then he rallied, told himself not to be so bloody pitiful. Christ, he knew now that out there somewhere Rachel had not died, was alive and vital, and loving life. He should be thankful for that, instead of selfishly wishing that he could continue to watch her, possessively, through the interface.

But, he told himself, love *was* selfish. It was natural to bewail the ill fortune that was taking Rachel from him. He could not hold her in his arms, or talk to her—and now his only form of contact would soon be denied.

He smiled through his tears. He had two weeks, he thought. Another few visits to the station to look upon his daughter. He must make the most of these visits, do his best to cherish the memory of her beauty.

Because after that he would be without her for a very long time.

Sinclair did not see Deauchamps for another week. The following Tuesday, Sinclair sat and watched the stars appear in the sky above the clearing. He began drinking shortly after eight, taking his ouzo neat and feeling its anaesthetic balm numb the pain of his disappointment.

The following day he maintained the hope that Deauchamps would turn up that night, full of apologies and excuses. When evening came with still no sign of the Director, Sinclair felt betrayed. Hell, every passing day brought closer the time of Rachel's departure... Why hasn't he contacted me, offered a word of explanation?

On Thursday evening the Director again failed to appear, and Sinclair began to fear the worst. Perhaps his illicit visits to the station had been discovered; perhaps

Deauchamps had been reprimanded, or worse, by the people who financed the project.

Perhaps he would never again set eyes on Rachel in the other world...

At sunset the following evening he could stand the suspense of ignorance no more. He would wash, change, walk up to the station and demand to see the Director. He drew a bucket of water from the well and carried it inside. He was splashing his face when he heard the grumble of a car engine. He moved to the door as Deauchamps' Mercedes halted and the Director climbed out, and Sinclair experienced a surge of joy and self-censure that he'd ever doubted his friend.

"I'll be with you in a minute, Pierre!" he called. "Sit down."

Instead, the Director paced, moving back and forth restlessly. He paused at the far end of the clearing, staring off into the trees.

Sinclair stepped from the studio, something in Deauchamps' manner filling him with an awful premonition. "Pierre...?"

Deauchamps turned, walked towards him.

"What is it?" Sinclair said.

"Something's happened," Deauchamps said.

"They've already left the island?" Sinclair began.

"No. No, nothing like that." The Director indicated the chairs and they sat down. He ran a hand through his silver hair. "I don't know where to begin..."

"Pierre?" Sinclair laughed, uneasy.

"Something has happened in the other world, Edward. Last week, the day after the party. That's why I haven't been round since. I've been trying to work out... I'm sorry, I should at least have called by."

"For Christ's sake, Pierre! What are you on about?" Sinclair felt a knot of fear in his belly.

"Listen, the other you—the Sinclair in the other world—he went out in his dinghy the day after the party. From what we've been able to piece together, a storm blew up. The dinghy capsized. It was found washed up a day later on the rocks off the eastern cape."

"What happened to him?"

Deauchamps was shaking his head. "His body hasn't been found. You know what the waters of the strait are like. If it hasn't been found in a week, the chances are it never will be. The currents would have carried it out into the Med."

"Christ...Oh, God, poor Rachel..." Oddly, he could not bring himself to mourn the loss of his other self.

"They've given up hope of his survival. They held a service on the island this morning. There was a gathering at the villa afterwards. Rachel was distraught, of course. She worshipped you."

Sinclair almost pointed out that it was the other Sinclair that Rachel had worshipped, but stopped himself.

He wanted to go to the station, but the desire was dampened by the thought of seeing Rachel in distress.

"Ever since the accident," Deauchamps went on, "or rather since they've given up hope of finding Sinclair, I've been considering the possibilities..."

Sinclair looked up. "What do you mean?"

Deauchamps held his gaze for what seemed like ages.

"The other week," he said, "when I told you that it was impossible to transfer mass from this world to the other..."

"Oh, sweet Jesus Christ," Sinclair whispered to himself.

"It isn't true," Deauchamps said. "I didn't want to put the idea into your head that you could go through and join your daughter, what with the other Sinclair there."

"I don't believe it."

"We can effect the transfer. I can open the interface for five, six seconds—long enough for you to step through."

Sinclair stood and paced to the far end of the clearing, shaking with shock. He turned and faced Deauchamps. "What about... I mean, what if the other Sinclair's body is found? What then?"

"I know. What do you think I've been worrying about for the past few days?" Deauchamps shook his head. "But it has been almost a week, Edward. The body would be unrecognisable by now. I know, I know—dental records might identify him, but they aren't always a hundred per cent accurate. And anyway—you'd be there. Who'd doubt the fact that you were who you said you were? It'd be one hell of a mystery, but—and this is what I've been considering—don't you want to be reunited with Rachel?"

The question required no reply. Sinclair shook his head in disbelief. "When?" he said at last. "When can I go?"

"Tonight. Now. Some friends stayed with Rachel at the villa for a few nights, but they left today. She insisted she'd be okay. If you go through now you won't be seen."

"But what about... about here? I'll suddenly disappear..."

Deauchamps looked at him. "Edward, you're a recluse. Who'd notice that you were no longer around? And then, when your absence was discovered..." He shrugged. "Perhaps it would be assumed that your grief, eventually got the better of you."

Briefly Sinclair considered his few friends in London who would be stricken by his disappearance . . .

Deauchamps moved towards his car. He stopped and asked, "What are you waiting for?"

Sinclair was looking at the studio, and around the clearing. He felt a strange sense of misplaced nostalgia for the place where he'd spent the last few years of his life—and then he told himself not to be so stupid. The studio, the clearing, existed where he was going. He was leaving nothing behind, absolutely nothing. Except, he told himself, so many years of bad, self-pitiful art, and tragic memories.

He joined Deauchamps and they drove through the olive groves to the station.

The Director unlocked the double doors and ushered Sinclair inside. They passed into the chamber, the opalescent oval at the far end strobing a bright, white light. Sinclair hurried towards it, halted before the plinth as Deauchamps worked at the console. The light was replaced by darkness. Sinclair made out the night-time garden, the villa against stars. All was still, silent.

"I'll open the 'face," Deauchamps said. "When I give the signal, step through."

Sinclair turned to the Director. "I don't know how to thank you."

"I don't want your thanks—but I would like your help."

"Anything."

"I need information about the other world, a record of the differences, local and world-wide, cultural and political. For the next few weeks I'll open the 'face, with sound, every evening at seven, by the cypress tree at the end of the garden. Don't worry if you can't make it, but I'd appreciate the occasional report. And of course I want to know how you and Rachel . . . "

Sinclair smiled. "I'll do that."

He turned to face the other world. He was about to make the most momentous journey of his life, and it felt odd to be doing so without baggage. He smiled and told himself that, where he was going, he would have everything he might ever need.

The image of the garden seemed to flicker. "Now!" Deauchamps called. "Step through now, Edward. *Bon voyage!*"

He embraced Deaucahmps, then stepped onto the plinth and hesitated. The Director urged him on. "Go, Edward. Quickly!"

Sinclair stepped forward, his heart pounding. As he crossed the threshold of the interface he felt a wave of heat pass through his body, and then he was on the other side, standing in the darkened garden of the other world. He turned and looked back. A faint opalescent glow hung in the air, marking the location of the door into his old world. Then the glow vanished and Sinclair felt inexplicably alone.

Except, of course, that now he was far from alone.

He moved towards the villa, a dark, low-lying shape against the stars. Then he stopped, staring, a strange emotion of longing and joy swelling in his chest.

A dark shape sat the top step of the verandah. Rachel was hugging her legs to her chest, leaning against the supporting post and crying quietly to herself. If he had been a sculptor, he would have been unable to carve a figure more expressive of bereavement and heart-rending grief.

He opened his mouth to call her name, but no sound came.

He tried again.

The figure started suddenly, sat up.

"Rachel . . . " Sinclair called.

She jumped to her feet, cried out, and fumbled for the light switch on the post. The fluorescent flickered on, bathing Rachel in its radiance, the harsh light freezing on her face a look of absolute amazement and rapture.

He held out his arms, and in that instant he was taken back eight years: he was walking through the town from the beach, and in his arms he carried the body of his dead daughter, and he had never been subject to an emotion that intense, until now.

Rachel screamed and sprinted towards him and launched herself into his arms, and the impact almost knocked him to the ground. He crushed her to him, flesh to flesh, tears to tears. "Dad, Dad . . . " She said this over and over, like a mantra, as if the repetition could magically ensure that he had truly returned from the dead, was not some fantasy of her grief-stricken mind.

He held her in his arms, smelled her girlness, the odour of her young body. He felt as though his heart was about to burst.

He carried her into the villa. He found the lounge and sat on a sofa in the darkness and pressed Rachel to him, lightheaded with joy and disbelief.

She tried to speak, but all that came out was a series of hiccoughing sobs, fragments of sentences. He shushed her like the child she was, stroked her hair and told her that it was all right, that they were together again, and that was all that mattered. Then the words caught in his throat, and he knew he could not go on without breaking down. He just sat and held her to him, overwhelmed by the miracle of her physicality.

"I . . . " she began. "I thought you were dead . . . after so long. We all—all thought you were dead. I'd given up hope!"

"Don't cry. I'm back. I'm safe. We're together now."

"Oh, the past week . . . it's been so terrible! I hardly believe . . . I didn't sleep at all, couldn't sleep. All I could think of was that I'd never see you again."

He manufactured a series of events to account for his absence. He told her that he'd overturned in a swell in the straits, then managed to swim ashore on a remote part of the island. He'd lain unconscious and delirious for days, before making his slow way back way to the villa.

"I've just thought!" she half-laughed. "I need to tell everyone! Tell them you're alive! And a doctor—you need to see a doctor!"

"Rachel, Rachel. Later, okay? There's plenty of time. And I'm fine. Just tired, that's all. For now all I want is to be with you."

"You don't know what it was like," she whispered, "to think for so long that you were dead . . . and then to get you back."

He slept, his daughter in his arms, and when he awoke the sun was slanting in through the window. He blinked himself awake and stared around the strange room. He looked down at Rachel, still sleeping, and could hardly bring himself to believe his good fortune.

Her face was pale and drawn, bruise-coloured semicircles beneath her eyes. He touched her cheek, traced the line of her chin with his big, clumsy fingers. He whispered her name, saw in the face of this young woman the dead girl he had carried through the village all those years ago.

He eased himself from her embrace and stood up. The phone rang—no doubt someone checking on Rachel—but he ignored it, and his daughter, exhausted, slept on through its persistent summons.

Today he would have to endure the solicitude of friends and strangers, a medical check up, the attention of well-wishers and no doubt, in time, the pursuit of the press.

And after that, when the incident blew over . . . then he would spend time in getting to know the girl who was Rachel.

He moved to the kitchen overlooking the verandah and the garden. From the refrigerator he took out a carton of orange juice and drank. He stood by the window and stared out. He wondered if the interface was open today, if Deauchamps and his men were watching...

His reverie was interrupted by something he noticed out there, across the straits. On one of the rocky, uninhabited islets in the channel...He peered, squinting. He saw the lazy drift of smoke slanting from the islet, but told himself that it could not be, that it was some shepherd or tourist. But even as he tried to rationalise the sight of the smoke, he knew that no shepherds worked on the isle, and certainly no tourists visited the barren, inhospitable rock.

He wondered why he was so convinced that he knew the origin of the smoke signal. Even now, even after the miracle that had occurred last night, he could not really bring himself to believe his luck. Even now he thought that something could go wrong to spoil the future.

He hurried into the lounge. Rachel was still asleep, breathing deeply. He told himself that he was being paranoid, that he should ignore the smoke—but what, he asked himself, if it *was* the original Sinclair? What if he had managed to survive? What if he returned to the villa? What would become of him, the interloper, then?

He dashed from the room, from the villa, almost ran down the track to the coast. As he reached the town he slowed for the sake of propriety. It was mid-afternoon and the seafront was crowded with strolling tourists. He hurried along the harbour wall—hoping he would go unnoticed by acquaintances in this world—towards a line of rowing boats tethered to the wall.

Sinclair climbed down a sundried ladder, unshipped the oars and began to row away from the harbour.

He had underestimated the effort required to pull a boat through the open sea, and the exercise soon exhausted him. The sea fought his every heave on the oars, and the heat of the sun was punishing. The isle approached by degrees, the fateful pall of smoke billowing from a crevice of rock close to the coastline.

He headed towards a narrow curve of beach, the last ten metres seeming to take an eternity, before the keel of the boat scraped the shelving sand. He climbed out, shaking as much from exhaustion as from fear at what he might find, and hauled the boat up the beach beyond the reach of the waves.

He set off towards the outcropping, the deep sand slowing his progress. The smoke fanned along the beach, choking him. He came to the rock, scrambled over, and at last stood and stared down into the angled crevice.

He realised, then, that somewhere along the way he had picked up a heavy, sea-tumbled rock. As he made out the face of the injured man through the flagging smoke, he wondered if this was what he had intended all along—to come here and kill the other Sinclair, so that he might have his daughter to himself? It would be so easy... For so many years he had hated himself, and now, as he stared down at Sinclair, semiconscious beneath him, he was gripped with the overwhelming desire to smash the familiar face to pulp—and he realised, at that instant, that it was not only the desire to remain in this world that made him want to kill the other Sinclair, but rather the desire to punish himself. It was as if all the years of self-hatred and guilt were culminating in this single event...

He dropped the stone and jumped down into the crevice. He kicked aside the fire of driftwood and sea-wrack, ignited with the lens of the other Sinclair's spectacles, and knelt beside the man. His alter ego looked pale and feeble, hardly aware that he was being rescued, let alone who his saviour was. He pulled the other Sinclair to his feet, half-carried him along the beach to the waiting boat, and eased him over the side. Then he pushed off through the waves, hauled himself aboard, unshipped the oars and began the journey back.

He headed not for the populous harbour but towards the stretch of deserted coastline beneath the olive groves. As he rowed he checked on the condition of the other Sinclair. The man was dazed, whether from his ordeal or from being rescued by a doppelgänger, Sinclair could not tell. He passed in and out of consciousness, from time to time muttering to himself.

The strip of beach backed by olive groves came into sight, and after five minutes of laboured hauling on the oars he brought the boat to shore. He half-lifted, half-dragged his other self from the boat and staggered with him to the cover of the trees. Once within their cool, protective shade he began to feel a measure of relief. Sinclair hung onto him and groaned, now and again protesting at the enforced walk.

They came to a fork in the path: to the right lay his studio; to the left the path continued towards the villa. Sinclair half-carried his other self on the last leg of the journey. Within minutes the stone-built studio came into sight, identical to the one he had left in his own world. He crossed the clearing and kicked open the door.

He assisted Sinclair over to an old chesterfield and laid him down. He turned to leave, to return to the villa, but he found himself wanting to confront Sinclair, in some way communicate to the other man the fact of his good fortune.

"What...?" the other Sinclair whispered. He gestured feebly, unable even to lift his head from the cushions.

Sinclair found a cup and fetched water from the well. He sat beside Sinclair, lifted his head and tipped the water to his lips. Sinclair drank thirstily. He lay back and stared up at Sinclair, mystification in his eyes.

"Listen to me," Sinclair said. "You don't know how lucky you are. Rachel... your daughter, she loves you. More than anything else you possess in this world, the greatest thing is the love of your daughter." He paused, shaking his head. "Don't take her for granted, do you understand? Even your art is worth nothing, *nothing*, beside what you have in Rachel. I've saved your life, Sinclair, so that you can show Rachel how much she means to you."

The other Sinclair stared up at him. Something almost like fear, or awe, showed in the man's eyes.

"Who..." he managed at last, "who the hell are you?"

Sinclair shook his head. "Call me your conscience," he said.

He stood and moved from the door, the other man's eyes following him all the way, and then hurried out and up the path towards the villa.

He crossed the garden and stepped onto the verandah, wanting more than anything to look upon Rachel again, to talk to her. As he passed through the kitchen he glanced at the wall clock: it was almost seven. With luck, Deauchamps would soon be opening the interface so that he might make his report. He had only minutes to be with Rachel.

She was no longer sleeping on the couch, but seated beside the far window in her dressing gown. She leaped up when she saw him and ran across the room. "So there you are!" she laughed. "I thought I'd lost you again."

He smiled. "I needed time to think," he said, holding her, "to realise how fortunate I am."

She reached up to kiss his cheek, and Sinclair wanted to somehow communicate to her the extent of his pain.

"I'm going for a quick shower, Dad, okay?"

"Rachel!" he called, halting her.

He reached out and held her. She pressed against him, and he felt a painful ache within his chest. "It's... it's so good to be back," he said.

She smiled at him, a smile he would never forget, and then hurried from the room. Sinclair watched her go, imprinting on his memory the sight of her slim form, her dancing hair.

He found a pen and a scrap of paper, wrote that he was down in the studio, and left it on the coffee table.

He hurried from the lounge. It was one minute past seven. He crossed the garden to the designated cypress and paused before its gnarled trunk.

"Deauchamps!" he called in an urgent whisper. He gathered his thoughts. "I've got to come back, Pierre. The other Sinclair is alive in this world. He survived the accident. You've got to open the interface and let me back."

He stopped there, unsure whether to repeat himself. He wondered how long it might take the Director to effect the opening. Minutes passed . . . What if Deauchamps had not opened the interface today? Then he would have to hide himself, come back tomorrow and hopefully avoid being seen by Rachel and the other Sinclair.

Five minutes elapsed and he repeated his message, desperately this time. He imagined Rachel finishing her shower, finding him here like this and demanding to know what he was doing. He was beginning to give up hope when something happened.

A faint white glow emanated from the tree trunk, and formed itself into a perfect ellipse.

He turned back one last time, as if hoping to catch a final glimpse of Rachel, but the villa was silent in the twilight and there was no sign of his daughter.

Sinclair stepped through the interface and into the Research Station.

The following evening Deauchamps visited Sinclair and invited him up to the station. Sinclair told him that he would rather not see his daughter tonight, or any other night. He had his memories, and he said that he would find Rachel's proximity, so real and alive but so unattainable, impossible to bear.

The Director nodded his understanding. "Rachel went down and found the other Sinclair in the studio," he said. "She helped him back to the villa and they talked. Sinclair could not recall anything of the day before, his return to the villa and his reunion with Rachel. He told her that he'd hallucinated, or dreamed, that someone had helped him from the island, rowed him ashore . . . but he could recall nothing else."

"And Rachel? She doesn't suspect anything?"

"She has her father back, and that is all she cares about." Deauchamps was watching him. "And you, Edward? How are you?"

He smiled. "I think I'm very much better," he said.

A few days later Sinclair began a new painting, the piece that would mark his return to full-time production. He carried his easel and canvas into the clearing and began tentatively—apprehensive, as always at this stage, that his talent would prove unequal to his intent.

He had a title for the piece. He would call it *The Miracle at Kallithéa*.

As he painted, a simple garden scene full of life and colour, the figure of a young girl began to take shape. She appeared from nowhere like a phantom, but a phantom that no longer haunted his waking dreams. She came to life, dominated the piece, and filled Sinclair with feelings of longing and loss—and at the same time, as he became increasingly confident that he had created something meaningful and of worth, also with a certain sense of guilt assuaged.

As he painted, a second figure materialised unbidden beside the girl, a mysterious presence which at first he thought might unbalance the symmetry of the work. Later it came to him that he need not have worried. The composition was perfect.

The second figure in the painting was himself.

THE CHILDREN OF WINTER

In the introduction to his fine story collection, Songs of Stars and Shadows, *George R. R. Martin called himself an "unabashed romantic," rather than an "incurable romantic," as romanticism is a literary-philosophic tradition, not a disease. I identify with that whole-heartedly. I love stories set on colony worlds, love writing about aliens, and have a soft spot for love stories. All three come together in "The Children of Winter", which was first published in* Interzone 163, *and won the BSFA best short story award in 2002.*

The Children of Winter

IN MY EIGHTEENTH TERM, WHICH WAS ALSO THE LAST TERM OF WINTER, I fell in love with a Blue, lost my youth, and learned the truth—and to learn the truth, after so long living in ignorance, can be a terrible revelation.

The three of us were inseparable, then. After lessons we skated the ice canals of Ak-helion beneath the sable skies of winter. At night we'd huddle around the brazier of an itinerant food-vendor, chewing on roasted tubers. The square was a scintillating sheet of ice, framed on three sides by the ugly stone buildings of the city; the fourth side looked down into the mountain valley, or would do so when the sun arrived to light the view.

We were swaddled in protective clothing like lagged boilers, so that it was an effort to bend our arms to eat the tubers. Nani giggled as she tried to nibble the long, steaming root. Oh, she was so beautiful, her every gesture a delight. She was, also, inaccessible: we had been friends for most of our lives, but she was in love with Kellor, and how could I begrudge my best friend the love of the girl I also secretly cherished?

The vendor closed his brazier, picked up its reins and dragged it away on its skates to another venue, leaving behind a puddle of slush that froze over within seconds.

Kellor whooped with the delight of being young and skated away on one leg, showing off to Nani. I looked around the square, at the dark buildings that merged with the night, and then I saw it. Between the Governor's manse and the library building, a tiny bright pinprick in the dark sky, the Star.

"Kellor!" I cried. "Nani! Come here!"

They skated to my side, each catching a shoulder to halt themselves, and almost dragged me to the ground.

THE DISCIPLES OF APOLLO

"What is it, Jen?" Nani panted.

"Look," I said, "the Star..."

We stared, our breaths clouding the air before us.

Nani whispered something to herself. Kellor said, "To the city wall!"

We set off pell-mell. We careered down ice canals and alleys, taking corners at speed with little thought for other skaters. The city wall was a long dam-like structure built across the valley, where often after lessons we met to stare in wonder at the fiery magnificence of the galactic spiral as it flung its starry arms high overhead.

Today it was as if our Star had detached itself from the shoal and was drifting towards us—but that was just my poetic imagination.

When we were nine terms old, Kellor, a practical-minded scientist even then, had explained to me the physics of our celestial situation.

He had taken me to the square and skated in an oval around the brazier of a food vendor, tilting his blades to score a long ellipse in the ice. Then he returned and took my arm, dragging me with him.

"I thought you were going to show me—" I began.

He laughed in indulgent reprimand and explained. "We—us two—are our planet, Fortune," he said. "That"—pointing to the distant brazier—"is the Star. We move around it in an oval orbit. Now we are far away, so far away that we cannot feel the heat of the Star. But, as we approach—see, the coals grow brighter. We move closer and feel the heat, and as we pass by the heat is intense, but only briefly. The period of our summer lasts for just four terms—any longer and Fortune would burn to a cinder. And then we begin the long, slow arc into winter again, the Star diminishing behind us as we move away. The winter lasts for eighteen terms, the cold and ice descends, the Star virtually disappears—until, in time, we swing back towards the Star for another short and fiery summer. Now do you understand, you dreamer?"

I was dumbstruck with the wonder of it. "But," I began, coming to understand something for the very first time, "that is why they call us the Children of Winter. We were born with the coming of winter, and will be initiated when winter ends!"

Kellor, even at nine, managed an adult's patronising smile. "When we are eighteen terms old," he said grandly, "the ice will melt and our initiation will coincide with the emergence of the starship."

Now we were eighteen, that magical age, and it seemed to me that life had never been so rich and full of promise.

Our initiation was just one week away.

We screamed down a steep conduit that in spring would drain the melt-water from the city and into the valley, but which now was a near vertical channel of breakneck ice. The conduit levelled out and we raced onto the span of the wall. To our right was the lambent arch of the galaxy; straight ahead, low in the night sky, the lone light of the setting Star.

We huddled in a niche in the wall, out of the rapier-keen wind from the north. Nani stared down the valley, her big eyes highlighting the glow of the galactic aura, and I felt my heart leap with love. She shook her head with finality. "I can't see the starship," she reported.

"The sun's not bright enough, yet," Kellor said. "It sheds little light. And anyway, the ship's a mile or more away, and hidden in a ravine. Only when the ice melts..."

I felt my heart hammer with another emotion. How fortunate we were! We were the Children of Winter, and our initiation ceremony would take place with the emergence of the starship—actually *within* the hallowed vault of the ship itself. Other citizens, those born either side of winter, would not share our luck: either their eighteenth term would come about when the starship was still entombed in layers of ice, or when the molten heat of high summer made a pilgrimage to the ship impossible.

I felt Nani's mittened hand grip mine. "Jen," she whispered. "Recite your poem."

Kellor snorted. He had little time for my sentimental verse.

I cleared my throat and stared at the distant light of the Star. "We are winter's children," I began. "Conceived with summer's last breath. Born to the first steel-hard frosts of winter. Our characters, our very souls, forged in sunless hardship and sleeting snows. To learn the truth when summer unveils the ship..."

"The truth," Kellor laughed. "Mark my word, it'll be nothing but political mumbo-jumbo. Our elders exhorting us to high morals and good citizenship."

"I don't think so," I said. "I've watched those who've been initiated in the past. They seem..." I shook my head. "I don't know, somehow *changed*. As if life seems different in light of what they've learned."

Kellor was derisory. "You'd think that this so-called truth would leak out, no? That some initiate wouldn't be able to contain themselves, that they'd tell us what they've learned."

"Perhaps the truth is so...so shattering that they cannot bring themselves to talk—" I began.

A sound from along the wall halted our speculation. We froze, listening. From afar came the muffled chug of a steam engine. "Blues!" Kellor cried in delight.

We peered from the niche. Sure enough, below us on the road that ran parallel with the city wall, a great steam-wagon made its lumbering way. Its spiked wheels bit into the ice, clawing it forward, and two figures could be seen riding high in the uncovered cab.

The Blues were native to Fortune and it seemed to me that, by their aloof manners and insistence that they keep contact with us to a minimum, they resented our arrival here millennia ago. Even their erect postures spoke of some genetic disdain. But perhaps what I found most daunting about these creatures, similar to us though they were, was their pale blue skins and their ability to go without winter clothing. It was as if their acceptance of the cold mocked my dependency—I was winter-born, after all—on thick breeches, a quilted overcoat, hat and gloves.

"Let's attack them!" Kellor cried, and so saying scraped up a snowball from the ground and lobbed it at the passing wagon. Nani followed suit, but I held back.

The Blues lived in the high mountains, far to the north of Ak-helion. They came in their steam-wagons from time to time, trading pots and utensils for the harl-meat and the other foodstuffs we produced. A few Blues lived in the city, liaising between their kind and our traders. Whenever I saw one I was struck dumb by their otherness, their silence and grace, their strange ethereal beauty. I could never bring myself to despise these people, as we were taught to do. Still less could I bring myself to pelt them with snowballs.

They passed beneath us, dignified in their dismissal of the missiles falling around them. As I watched, the passenger turned its head and stared up at us. She was a female of fragile beauty, her face as pale blue and translucent as the egg of a snowbird. It seemed that for a second our gazes met, and I willed into my expression an apology for the behaviour of my compatriots.

When the steam-wagon had departed, we raced the length of the city wall, whooping with the fact of our being eighteen and free, and soon to be initiated.

For an hour we huddled in the lee of the wall and chattered about the initiation, and then Kellor looked up at the rearing galactic arm. From the mass of stars displayed he declared it late and time for bed.

He departed with Nani, but I guessed from their manner—the almost coy propinquity of the intimate—that they would not be sleeping alone tonight.

—.—

I set off home. I skated slowly along the city wall and climbed the ice-bound stone steps to the city proper. I crossed the square where we had eaten tubers. It was late; even the food-vendors had doused their braziers and retired. Only the harl, the shaggy quadrupeds that drew passenger-sleds during the day, occupied the shadows, emitting steam and contented snores.

I was skating down the broad boulevard towards the street on which I lived, in a big government house with my mother and father, when I heard the noise.

At first I thought it was a harl in distress. I slid to a halt and listened. The sound came again, a thin, high sobbing. I moved towards its source, peering into the stone channel which flanked the road. At the foot of a steep flight of stairs to a tall townhouse, I made out a figure lying in the shadows. Impeded by my skates, I climbed down.

"It's okay," I said. "I'll get help."

I stopped, then, for the face of a Blue was staring up at me. I stood and backed off.

It reached out a hand. "Please. I fell and hurt my ankle." The voice was soft, a mere breath, and feminine. "If you could assist me inside." And she gestured to the door at the top of the steps.

My first impulse was to run; my second, to my credit, was to aid the Blue as she requested. I removed my skates, then knelt and lifted her to her good foot; I put an arm around her and assisted her slowly up the steps. She leaned against me, and I was astonished at how light and insubstantial she was. At the top of the steps she pushed open the door and pointed down the corridor to another.

With my help she moved around her apartment turning on yellow, glowing lamps. The room, revealed, was much like any other: perhaps I had expected something as alien as the Blue herself. Oils of winter landscapes adorned the walls, sculptures of winter-stark trees stood on shelves and tables. I had, in my ignorance, never credited the aliens with an appreciation of the arts.

She sat on a chair beside a glowing lamp and inspected her ankle. For the first time I became aware of what she was wearing: a thin red dress and a black, hooded cape. She was probing her ankle with delicate fingers, and wincing.

I knelt and took her foot in my hand. "I don't think it's broken," I said. "Perhaps it's just badly twisted. Ah... maybe a bandage?" I looked up, and was shocked to behold the regard of her great black eyes.

"It *is* you," she said. "I thought so."

"Excuse me?"

"Earlier, upon the city wall. Two children cast balls of ice at our wagon. You were with them, but did not join the attack."

167

"You were in the wagon," I said. I recalled the cool regard of the Blue passenger, and my shame at the antics of my friends.

"I ... I'm sorry. It was ... they didn't mean to hurt you. It was just a game."

She regarded me with a quizzical expression. For all our differences, our far-flung origins, we had much in common. She said, "But you refrained from joining in the attack. I thought your people deemed us beneath contempt. Certainly that is the impression I receive from those of you I work with from day to day."

"We aren't all like that. Some of us ... " I stopped myself, for fear of sounding sanctimonious.

"Do you know that many of your kind would have let me lie there all night," she said. "I am indeed fortunate that you were passing."

Her stare was making me uncomfortable. She smiled and told me that I would find a bandage in the kitchen. I stood and hurried into the adjacent room.

When I returned I saw that she had taken off her cloak. I could not help but notice the delicacy of her arms and legs, her high-cheekboned face framed in a long fall of jet-black hair.

Clumsily I wrapped the bandage around her swollen ankle.

"What is your name?" she asked.

"Jen," I whispered, not meeting her eyes.

"And how old are you, Jen?"

"Eighteen."

"But so am I!" she declared. "And my name is Ki."

"You're eighteen? But I thought ... " She seemed much older; something in her poise, her confidence, suggested the maturity of an adult.

"Among my people, at sixteen terms we are considered mature, and we can go about the business of the elders." Her large black eyes seemed to bore into me. "If you are eighteen terms," she said, "then very soon you will be initiated."

"In six days," I began.

Something in her regard made me uneasy. I stood suddenly. "I must go," I said. "It's late. Be careful with the ankle. Don't put any weight on it." I hurried to the door. "Goodbye."

A half-smile played on her lips as she watched me leave the room. I put on my skates and sped home, only then realising what had occurred. I had conversed with a Blue; I had broken the unspoken rule that contact between our races was forbidden, except in certain circumstances. I wondered what Kellor and Nani might have to say about my encounter, not that I intended to tell them.

My mother and father were still up when I returned, reading by lamplight in the front room. I slipped past the door and hurried up to bed. I was not close to them at the best of times, but something—was it shame?—stopped me from pausing to wish them goodnight.

That night I dreamed of Ki. It was a dream full of horror and . . . something else. I awoke in a sweat, an hour before I had to rise for college, and tried to recall the rapidly vanishing images of Ki, naked, in my arms.

The words "day" and "night," Kellor once explained to me, were derived from the time when Fortune experienced its brief, hot summer. The planet, he said, turned on its axis every twenty hours, so that for successive periods of ten hours every day during summer the sky above Ak-helion was light and then dark. During winter the sky was perpetually dark, but even so we still divided the day into periods of hours, and called one lot day and another night, for convenience. I had lived all my life in night-time darkness, and found it hard to imagine a daylight sky.

However, change was on the way. Now the Star was in the sky during the day, and at night it set. At college the following day, after my encounter with Ki, I sat at my desk and stared through the thick glass window at the small beacon of the Star, contemplating the forthcoming initiation and the changes that would follow.

In less than half a term the ice with which I was so familiar would be no more. It would melt and like drinking water run off down the mountain, leaving the rocks bare and inhospitable, and then the heat would start to rise. Soon it would be impossible to live out in the open, and we would retire, the entire population of the city, to a cool sanctuary excavated deep below the mountain long ago. Four or five terms later we would re-emerge to populate Ak-helion again. I wondered if I would adapt to life underground.

I sat with Kellor and Nani in the refectory at lunch. Soon the conversation came around to the subject of the starship.

"I've been thinking," Kellor said, smiling slyly at me, "why don't we leave the city and go to the ravine of the starship ourselves, sneak a quick look before the ceremony?"

The suggestion was as foolhardy as it was profane. Nani gasped at the very idea.

I laughed. "You're not serious, are you?"

"Aren't I? Why not?"

Nani said, "Because it isn't allowed!" She made a chopping gesture with her mittened hand. "It just *isn't* allowed!"

"If we were caught . . . " I began, heartened that Nani was on my side. I had never heard of anyone trying to view the starship before the ceremony. I looked at Kellor as if he were mad.

"We'll talk about it later, okay?" Kellor said. "Meet you on the square at eight."

That evening the housemaid served me dinner and I ate alone. My parents were important civil servants, and were attending a meeting at the government assembly buildings. Afterwards I left the house and skated towards the square. On the way I passed the tall building in which Ki had her apartment. On impulse, without analysing my motives, I bought some food—bread and harl cheese—from a nearby shop, returned, and climbed the steps.

Her door at the end of the corridor was ajar, spilling yellow light. I unfastened my skates and knocked tremulously. After a second or two I heard a faint, "It's open," and cautiously pushed my way inside.

She was seated upon a settee, her leg outstretched, foot resting on a cushioned stool. Her thin lips tightened into an indecipherable line at my appearance, her eyes widening.

I held up the bread and cheese. "I . . . I thought you might need something. I brought you these."

She smiled, and the sudden movement of her lips, conferring gratitude, filled me with relief.

"That is so kind of you. Please, put them here." She indicated the cushion beside her.

I could not take my eyes from that portion of her upper body not covered by her white dress, the delicate bone-work of sternum and clavicle.

It was cold in the room. I would have suffered without my thick coat. That she was happy in this environment brought home to me the fact of her alienness.

"I'm pleased that you came," she said. "I've been lonely here, with no one to talk to."

"Your people . . . ?"

She laid her head to one side and looked at me. "They do not like to come into the city. There is just one other liaison officer in Ak-helion, but as we work shifts I rarely see him."

"Why did you become a liaison officer?" I asked.

"Because I was curious. I wanted to know whether the stories my people told me about you were true. I wanted to see if you were really as hostile as they claimed."

I wondered if she were mocking me, this young girl who was my age, but much, much older. "And are we?"

"In general, yes," she said, and I blushed in shame. "I have experienced the most unwarranted acts of petty cruelty, bigotry and ignorance during my time in Ak-helion."

I shook my head.

"And then all my assumptions, my conclusions, are thrown into confusion by the random kindness of a total stranger."

I did not know what to say, and so said nothing.

"I am curious," she said. "I want to know why—why are you not like the others? Why did you help me?"

I shook my head, and then blurted words I regretted at once. "Because I think you're beautiful," I said.

Oh, you fool, you young, besotted, inexperienced fool! I cringe when I think about the boy I was, the pain and confusion that filled me then.

But I was honest, I'll grant my young self that. I said what I felt, and to my vast relief the Blue girl did not laugh at me.

She smiled.

She must have been aware of my naivety and pain: she was experienced beyond her age. "That is one of the nicest things anyone has ever said to me, Jen. Thank you."

We talked. It seemed that a tension had been removed from our encounter, and we conversed as friends. She told me of her people, her life in the city far to the north. They were, it seemed, an advanced race—but quite how advanced she refrained from telling me. I tried to question her about the technology of her city, but with a wave of her fingers and a smile she changed the subject.

She was, like me, an only child; and also like me she had experienced no love from or for her parents. She had excelled at school and developed an interest in the people who shared her planet; she had studied hard and applied to become a liaison officer, was taken on, trained, and despatched to the city of Ak-helion.

I told her about myself, my parents and friends, my schoolwork and passion for poetry; this last was a painful admission to make—many people might have laughed at my romanticism—but Ki smiled softly and expressed a love of poetry and music, too. I think it was then that I fell in love with her.

An hour passed, then two. It was almost eight. I remembered that I had agreed to meet Kellor and Nani in the square.

I told Ki that I had enjoyed talking to her, but that I had to go.

"Do you? Do you really? Can't you stay?" She reached out, laid a soft blue hand on mine. To my astonishment I found the touch of her fingers warm, not frost-cold as I had expected.

Her hand moved to my cheek, and drew my head as if by magic towards hers, and her kiss was the consummation of all my dreams.

She stood awkwardly and whispered something. I assisted her to the adjacent room, where she undressed me until I stood, naked and shivering like some sacrificial beast. Then she slipped from her simple dress and, amazingly naked, eased me onto the bed and warmed me with her love.

I was surprised, as I grappled inexpertly with the Blue girl, that this should seem so natural. I was fearful at first, afraid of her alienness and difference—but Ki gave me pleasure I had never imagined, and I could not conceive how sex, even with my own kind, could be any better.

Later, I reached out to the bedside table and examined the glowing ball that illuminated the room. It was unlike anything I had every seen, and remarkable, but not half as remarkable as the experience bequeathed me by the alien girl who slept quietly at my side.

I replaced the lambent sphere, dressed without waking her, and slipped from the apartment. I made my slow way home through the darkness, filled with a confusion of emotions: love and shame, joy and fear, elation at what I had shared with Ki, and uncertainty as to the future.

I awoke early the following morning and, unable to sleep or face breakfast, left home and skated down the deserted ice canals. The thought of going to lessons never entered my head; last night had been special to me, had been a turning point, and I needed time in which to digest what had happened. I was drawn to Ki's apartment, even reached the corner of the boulevard, but stopped myself from going any closer. I wanted to reacquaint myself with the pleasures of her body, but at the same time I did not want to throw myself at her. Yet, I told myself, if she felt for me what I felt for her, then surely she would be pleased to see me... I was a young boy in love for the first time, and confused. I was by turns elated at the thought of what we had found in each other, and then fearful of how our relationship might be viewed by my elders and so-called betters.

I explored the city three times over until exhausted, and then found a covered tea cabin and sat with off-duty ice trimmers and harl jockeys as they huddled over steaming pots of spiced milk and traded ribald jokes and jibes. I watched the Star rise high into the sky, surely a little larger than it had been yesterday, and considered the future.

It was a measure of my youthful naivety that, after just one brief liaison with Ki, I considered myself in love and fearful for that love. Soon the ice would melt, daylight would come to Fortune, and the citizens of Ak-helion would migrate below ground. As for the Blues, they would leave their city and trek even further north, to the pole of the planet where they would wait out the fierce heat in the relative cool of their summer city. Next winter they would return, and Ki with them. But the thought of waiting four or five terms! I would have left college by then, and entered a profession. I would be an adult, and my parents would be looking to arrange a marriage with a suitable girl. And would Ki even remember me? I laugh to think, now, of the yearning and heartache I suffered that day, with first love still fresh in my heart.

At eight I made my way to the square.

The galactic arms were fiery and spectacular that night. Crowds thronged the ice, staring up at the umber and magenta whorls. Food vendors and spiced-milk sellers were doing a brisk trade. I found Kellor and Nani.

"Why didn't you meet us last night?" Kellor asked. "And where have you been today?"

Nani was smiling with a warm soft glow that suggested contentment after intimacy.

"I was sick," I lied. "Must've eaten a bad tuber."

I was torn with the desire to tell them about the night I had spent with Ki, and yet chary of their ridicule. I knew they would be wrong to condemn me; what Ki and I shared was just as precious as anything between Kellor and Nani, but of course they would be unable to see that.

"We've decided to go," Kellor said proudly, as if announcing their betrothal.

I was confused, lost as I was in my own thoughts. "Go where?" I asked, and instantly recalled Kellor's boast of the day before.

He was nodding at my sudden expression of disbelief. "We made up our minds and we're going for it."

I looked to Nani, who yesterday had been as horrified as I.

Kellor had evidently talked her round. She shrugged. "Why not, Jen? If we're careful... Just think of it, to see the starship before anyone else!"

"But you won't," I pointed out, disappointed at her capitulation. "What about all the Church Elders preparing the ceremony, and the guards? They'll have seen it before you."

"You know what we mean," Kellor said. "We'll see it before anyone else of our age. We'll be the first."

"And if you're caught, what then? Anything might happen. You might be expelled from college, even jailed."

"We won't be caught," Kellor assured me. "We're young and fit. We can out-skate any feeble Elder."

"But you don't even know the way," I said.

"The High Elders make their way to the ravine every day," Kellor said. "We'll simply follow their tracks through the ice and snow."

"You're fools," I said. "I'll tell you now, you'll regret it."

"So you're not coming with us?" This was Nani, taunting me.

I merely shook my head and turned away.

"We leave from the square at eight tomorrow evening, if you change your mind and want to join us," Kellor said. "See you later." He took Nani's hand and tugged her off, weaving through the crowd towards her parents' place.

I skated around the square for a while, wondering who was the more foolish— Kellor and Nani for wanting to satisfy their curiosity ahead of time, or myself for loving a Blue? Perhaps my disdain for their venture was merely envy of their daring, as opposed to the cowardly doubt I felt at my own transgression.

The thought of Ki drove me from the square. I skated at speed across the city, turned down the wide boulevard and slid to a halt outside her building. Ensuring that there was no one about, I removed my skates and carefully climbed the stairs. I pushed through the outer door and knocked on the door of her apartment.

My heart leaped at the sound of her voice. "Who is it?"

"Me. Jen."

"Jen!" It was a cry. "Well, come in. Don't just stand there!" And no sooner had I pushed open the door and stepped over the threshold than she limped, wincing, into my arms.

"But where did you disappear to this morning?" she asked, all concern. "And why didn't you come earlier?"

I laughed in relief at her welcome. "I had to go home," I began. "My parents..."

"I missed you, Jen," she said. "I thought you were never coming back."

I carried her into the bedroom and lay with her on the bed. We held each other and talked of our respective pasts. I found myself telling her of incidents I thought I had forgotten, found that I had the ability to imbue stories with humour and excitement that had the Blue girl laughing in delight.

174

In the early hours I climbed from bed, and the movement woke Ki. I kissed her. "I must go. If my parents found out..."

"Tonight," she whispered. "Come back tonight, Jen. Please."

I promised, left her and made my way home. I slipped into the house and up to my room without disturbing the mundane sleep of my mother and father. It gave me strength and confidence to know that, for the first time in my life, I was acting without their knowledge or consent.

The following day at college I sat through lessons in a daze, waiting only for the end of the day so that I could visit Ki. Kellor and Nani were unusually quiet, and it was a while before I recalled what they had planned for tonight.

"You're fools if you go through with it," I whispered at lunch in the vast refectory hall. "Look, in four days it's the initiation ceremony anyway. Why not just wait?"

But they didn't even grace my concern with replies, just smiled to themselves and resumed their meal.

At five, rather than leave with them as I usually did, I strapped on my skates and sped away from the college, along the ice canals towards Ki's boulevard. I made sure no one saw me and slipped into the building.

She was waiting for me. I hugged her as if I had been away for terms.

Her delighted laugh was the trill of a snowbird.

We made love in her bed and then lay beneath the sheets, holding each other close; animal passion spent, I lazed in the glow of intimacy with the only person I had ever loved or wholly trusted.

Ki leaned on one elbow, a sheen of sweat coating her face and breasts. She pulled back the blankets to let the air of the room cool her nakedness, while I shivered.

"Tell me about your initiation, Jen," she said.

I laughed. "That would be like telling you about... I don't know... the Star," I said. "How can I tell you about something that I've never experienced?"

She pulled a pretty face. "But you *must* know what happens at the ceremony. Surely your Elders have said something?"

"All I know is that on initiation day a hundred of us, maybe more, will be taken to the ravine of the starship." My voice had become hushed, as if with awe.

"The starship," she said. I would recall, only later, the shadow that passed across her features then.

I nodded. "We enter the ship and the High Elder of the Church of Fortune addresses us. What he says, I don't know. But it's said that he vouchsafes us the Truth."

Ki looked at me, dubious. "The Truth? Just like that? Why is it that you've never heard the Truth before now?" A smile played on her lips.

"I don't know." I shrugged. "Initiates are sworn to secrecy."

"Jen," she said, staring at me seriously with her great black eyes, "will you tell me the Truth when you know it?"

I kissed her high forehead. "Yes, Ki," I said.

"Promise?"

"Of course I promise." I looked about the room, at the glow-spheres that not only afforded light but also heat. The bedroom was always warmer than the other room, though still cool to my sensibilities.

I picked up a glow-sphere from the bedside table. "I've told you what I know about the initiation. Now you tell me about these. I've never seen anything like them, Ki."

She took the ball from me and held it on her open palm; her staring eyes reflected the object. "Aren't they beautiful? But I'm no scientist, Jen. I don't know how they work."

"But you make them—the Blues, I mean?"

"Of course." She laughed. "Who else?" She frowned at me. "We aren't the savages you take us for, Jen. Who do you think sold you the invention of steam?"

I shrugged. I had always assumed that it was we who had invented steam power.

"We are a technological race, with many inventions you would never dream of," Ki said. "In time we will give you the secret of the glow-spheres, among other things."

She saw my gaze straying to the window, and the rise of the galaxy betraying the lateness of the hour. She laid a hand on my chest, pressing me to the bed. "Don't go, Jen. Stay a little longer, please."

What did it matter if I arrived home now or in three hours, just so long as my parents never discovered my absence? Ki's pleading was impossible to resist. I pulled the sheets over us, creating a scented darkness, and we made love again.

Later I considered the ceremony of the initiation, the approach of the Star, and all that this would entail.

"Ki," I said. I could hardly bring myself to broach the subject. "When the ice melts..."

She stilled my lips with a fingertip. "Shhh. Don't even think about it."

"I can think of nothing else! I don't want to lose you."

"Nor do I want to lose you."

"Then stay, come with us beneath the mountain..." But even as I spoke I realised the absurdity of my words.

She smiled sadly. "You know I couldn't do that. Your people..." She paused. "In five terms I will be back, Jen. I'll come for you."

"But five terms? I'll go mad just waiting!"

"And so will I, but then we'll have each other to ease our madness."

Later I dressed and tore myself away from Ki, and skated along the deserted ice canals of Ak-helion in a dismal frame of mind. A torch burned outside my parents' house, and I wondered if my father or mother intended an early start. I crept into the hall with especial care.

They were waiting for me. They emerged from the front room as I crossed the hall, and stared at me.

"Jen," my father said, something uncompromising in his tone. I feared they had found out about my relationship with Ki.

"Where have you been?"

"I..." I realised I was stammering. My knees felt weak. My father seemed like a stranger to me at the best of times: now he appeared as a condemning judge. "I've been with friends."

"Who?" he asked, sharply. "Kellor and Nani?"

Something, some inkling of what had happened, made me shake my head. "No. No, someone else—"

"Who?" he asked again, unrelenting.

I stared him in the eye. "A girl," I said. "I've been with a girl I met in a tea cabin."

My mother lowered her head and cried quietly. I burned with embarrassment at her knowing that I was no longer her innocent child.

"You're lying, Jen," my father said.

"I'm not. It's true... I'm sorry."

"You were with Kellor and Nina. Do not deny it!"

I repeated their names. "Why?" I managed at last. "What has happened?"

My father fixed me with a gaze colder than any northern wind. "Tonight Kellor and Nani were arrested by Church Elders close to the ravine of the starship. They are in serious trouble. If I find that you were with them..." His tone implied that if I were lying then he would flay me alive. "Go to your room."

I fled. I felt at first relief that my liaison with Ki had not been discovered, and then shame at that relief, and only then solicitude for my friends.

177

The following morning at breakfast my father did not mention the likely fate of Kellor and Nani, and I could not bring myself to ask; nor did he question me about my affair, for which I was relieved. I suspected that he would try to find out who I was seeing by other means, and I determined to ensure I was never followed to Ki's apartment.

Before I left the table, my father informed me that until my initiation I must be home by seven. I agreed with good grace, secretly mourning the hours I would lose with Ki.

At college that day all talk was about the fate of Kellor and Nani, who were notable by their absence. Classmates took great delight in imagining their punishment, from lengthy incarceration to ten strokes of the lash. I absented myself from all such speculation, sickened. I wondered if, had I not been involved with Ki, I might have weakened and joined my friends on their abortive pilgrimage.

After lessons I made my way to Kellor's house, but the windows were darkened and my summons went unanswered. I skated to Nani's apartment and knocked in desperation, but her parents too ignored my summons.

Then I crossed the city to Ki's boulevard, making various detours, and waited on the corner until there was not a soul in sight. I stayed with her until just before seven, and returned to share the evening meal with my parents like a dutiful son.

For the next three days, before the ceremony at the starship, I visited Ki immediately after lessons, my few hours with her at these times all the more precious for being stolen and curtailed. Of Nani and Kellor there was no word.

At college, on the day before the ceremony, an atmosphere of anticipation and excitement filled the cloisters and classrooms. The continued absence of Kellor and Nani dampened my sense of expectation, and at lunchtime in the refectory my worst fears were confirmed.

A small boy, whose father was a High Elder in the Church of Fortune, approached my table, "Are you Jen, a friend of Kellor and Nani?"

"What of it?"

"Their case is being heard today," he said with inflated self-importance. "If found guilty, their initiation will be set back six terms."

Six terms! I stared at him in shock, unable to reply. The rest of the day passed in a blur, and at five I fled across the city to Ki.

Another shock awaited me at her apartment. I knocked on the door and entered. She called to me from the bedroom. I looked about the outer room, sure that something had changed. It was some seconds before I noticed that various items, tree-sculptures and paintings, were missing.

When I stepped into the bedroom I saw that she was packing. She stood gingerly on her damaged ankle, placing wrapped objects in crates.

"Ki . . . ?"

She limped across the room and took me in her arms. "Jen . . . Oh, Jen. We've been recalled. The liaison officers. The time has come for the migration north. I leave Ak-helion in two days."

"Two days?" I repeated like an idiot, disbelieving. I shook my head. "In two days you'll be gone?"

The concept was too terrible to imagine.

She stared into my eyes, brushing hair from my forehead. "We have two days," she whispered. "I'll make them special, Jen, so that you'll remember me until I return."

I broke down and wept, then, like the young boy I was. She held me in her arms and tried to console me, with the care and concern of the woman she was.

I stayed with her throughout the night, regardless of my father's curfew. Damn him, I thought. I would not let him deny me precious hours with the girl I loved, no matter what the consequences. At dawn, as the Star rose in the dark sky, I made my way home and defiantly joined my parents at breakfast. That morning, the day of the ceremony, we ate in strained silence and they elected not to reprimand me for ignoring the curfew.

It seemed that the entire population of Ak-helion had gathered on the city wall to wish us on our way. Escorted by the Elders of the Church, we set off in a torch-lit procession along the downward path chiselled through the ice. The cheers of the crowd ringing in my ears, I looked around at the bright, expectant faces for any sign of Kellor and Nani, but saw neither.

We left the city behind us and entered territory new to me, vast sloping fields of snow, gullies sliced through slabs of ice washed orange in the torchlight. All around us were signs of the thaw: from overhangs and lips of ice, water poured in muscled, quicksilver torrents. We seemed to trek for miles through this eerie, flame-lit landscape, our thoughts on the forthcoming initiation. For all my sorrow at my friends' absence, I was more preoccupied with what might lie ahead.

Perhaps an hour later I made out, in the distance, the rosy glow of massed torches emanating from a hollow in the ground. We approached, and as we did so the robed Church Elders in our midst began a dolorous chant. My heart set up a laboured pounding.

We neared the lip of the ravine and stared down, and I saw first the sweeping flight of steps cut into the ice, and then the starship itself.

I had had no idea what to expect. The reproduction of pictures and icons representing the ship was prohibited by the Church, and from stray comments and hints dropped by adults I had in mind that the starship might resemble a tall stalagmite of ice, an edifice of silver metal reaching for the stars.

I stopped in my tracks and gazed in slack-jawed amazement. Silver it was indeed, and tall, but I would never have guessed how silver, or how tall. It coruscated like diamond and was fully five times as high as the highest building in Ak-helion. Set into its towering, triangular length were a hundred observation nacelles and viewports, alternating with vast numerals and decals excoriated by its journey through the gulf of space. Seeing the reality of the ship for the very first time, I was filled with heart-breaking pride at the achievements of my race, at the feat of survival represented by this rearing leviathan.

Gasps and cries of wonder broke out all around me as we naïve initiates stared, but no sooner had we feasted our eyes than the Church Elders hurried us down the ice steps. As we dropped into the ravine, so the starship seemed to gain height. Soon we had to crane our necks to make out the antennae bristling at its very pinnacle.

At the foot of the stairway, before the great arched entrance of the ship, we halted. There was a commotion among our group as initiates turned and stared. I felt elation swell within me at what I saw then. Climbing down the steps after us, escorted by two stern-faced Elders, were Kellor and Nani.

I made my way back through the throng and embraced my friends under the disapproving gazes of the Elders.

"What happened?" I gasped.

"We were reprimanded," Kellor said. "That's all—just reprimanded!" He and Nani seemed dazed at the fact of their reprieve, and shocked as we all were at the sight of the starship.

We were called to order by the Church High Elder, resplendent in his silver robes, and ushered into the hold of the ship.

There we stood like the worshippers we were, in this ultra-modern cathedral, while the High Elder climbed onto a podium before us and gave his speech.

I only heard fragments of what he said. It was much as Kellor had forecast: an exhortation to us, the new men and women of Ak-helion and the future of our race, to abide by established principles and prove ourselves worthy citizens.

I was disappointed that an experience of such grandeur should end like this.

"We of Ak-helion represent a proud and noble race, my friends. Through the void of space our kind came in search of new, habitable planets, came from a world more hospitable than ours, found Fortune, and settled. We overcame hardship, intemperate seasons and hostile climes, to survive, and not only survive, but flourish. And yet..." the words rang out above our heads, and he paused to stare at each one of us in turn, "and yet our ancestors had much to overcome, initially."

He paused again, and Nani found my hand and gripped. Involuntarily I reached out and clasped Kellor's hand. "This is it," I said. "The Truth."

"When our forbears made landfall in the starship," intoned the High Elder, "we were met with the opposition of not only the harsh seasons, the fire of summer and the ice of winter, but an even more uncompromising foe..."

He went on, and I heard his words, but so benumbed was my brain by the enormity of his address that I could take in barely half of what he said. "And before our ancestors could establish contact with the natives to assure them of our peaceful intentions, we were attacked. The natives were primitive by our standards, but they had the element of surprise, and vast forces, and we almost succumbed. We lost many a colonist during that first terrible week, many specialist and scientist who would have made our existence on Fortune that much less hazardous."

Nausea swelled in my belly, sickening me.

"That is why," he was saying, "our relations with the natives are limited and strictly controlled. How can we trust a race who once—millennia ago, granted—did its very best to annihilate our innocent ancestors?" The High Elder stared at us and asked, "How can we bring ourselves to trust the Blues?"

I felt dizzy. My pulse pounded in my ears. The High Elder spoke next of an oath of silence, and allegiance to the Church. One by one we moved to the front of the gathering, knelt and received his blessing, his hand upon our heads, and repeated the oath.

Then we found ourselves outside the ship, and filing away from the hallowed vessel, up the steps towards the city that was home, but which would never again be quite the same. I recall little of the return journey, save Kellor by my side, tears streaming down his face as he cursed the Blue-skinned barbarians of this planet. Those were his exact words, and I could tell from the reaction of the group that they shared his sentiments. Our initiation had achieved its aim: never again would we look upon a Blue in quite the same light.

Except... I loved Ki, and knew her for a caring, compassionate being.

There was a banquet thrown for the initiates at the college, to which families and friends were invited. I went through the motions of eating the lavish meal, listening to rousing speeches by government officials and Church Elders. It was as if we had been made one by the events of the initiation, as if we were unified against adversity and future hardship—except that I felt truly apart and isolated. I listened to Kellor and Nani chatter about the bravery of our intrepid ancestors, and could take no more. At the first opportunity I excused myself from the company of my parents and friends, ostensibly going outside for fresh air, and then made my escape. In the cloakroom, I found my skates and raced from the college building, across the city to Ki.

She was sitting alone, surrounded by packed crates and boxes, when I pushed into the room. She looked so forlorn, and I saw that she had been crying.

She stood and limped into my arms. "Jen," she said. "I have been thinking—considering our situation. Why don't you . . . " she paused, staring at me seriously, "why don't you come with me, to the city at the pole, and wait out summer there? It would be possible."

Something in my expression stopped her words. Go with her, I thought, go with her and live among the people who had once attacked my ancestors? How might I be received, a descendant of the invaders?

"Jen? Jen, what's wrong?"

I stared at her. Did she know? Was she aware of the events of the past that had so irrevocably divided our people?

"You don't know, do you?" I said. "They never told you."

She stared, wide-eyed. "Jen?"

I took a breath. "Today was the ceremony of initiation," I said. "Today I learned the Truth. I promised that I'd tell you . . . "

She raised a hand and touched my cheek. "Tell me what?" she asked in a small voice.

"Tell you what happened when we arrived on Fortune," I said, "what happened to our ancestors."

I recounted the events of the ceremony, what the High Elder told us about what had occurred all those terms ago. I was objective in my account of the initiation, showing her that, whatever might have happened in the past, I did not agree with the Church's chauvinistic reinforcement of enmity and xenophobia.

When I finished I looked into her eyes. "So how could I go with you, Ki—how would your people accept me?"

Her face slipped into an expression of infinite pity. She kissed my lips softly, then drew away and shook her head.

"Oh, Jen," she said. "Oh, my love, can't you see...?"

I stared at her, taken aback. "What?"

"Jen, please listen to me." She pushed me onto the settee and sat down by my side. "This might be hard for you to accept, Jen, but please believe me. I wouldn't lie to you—you know that. I love you, and I would not tell you one single untruth." She took my face between her palms and said, "Jen, please believe me when I say that you, your people, did not arrive on Fortune aboard the starship."

I stared at her, trying to make sense of her words.

It came to me, then, with sudden insight.

Why had I been so blind? The glow-spheres, Ki's talk of superior technology... It was not we who had travelled through space aboard the ship, but the Blues.

Then I wondered if it might have been *we* who had attacked the space-faring Blues...

Later, to atone for our collective guilt and to maintain the status quo of life in Ak-helion, had the Church initiated the lie of the initiation ceremony?

"You..." I said. "You came here aboard the starship?"

She stared at me, as if pitying my ignorance.

"Jen," she said, sadly. "Jen, both our races are native to this planet. We *both* evolved here."

I shook my head, confused. "But the ship," I cried. "It's out there. I saw it. If we didn't come in the ship, then who did?" I stopped.

"Who else?" she asked. "A third race, who call themselves Humans. It was they who came to Fortune aboard the starship."

My mind was reeling. "Humans?" I whispered. "But... but I always thought that we, that my people..."

She was shaking her head.

"How do you know this?" I asked in a feeble whisper. "Why didn't you tell me before?"

"Because my people are sworn to secrecy—we cannot tell you the truth of the past for fear of rekindling old enmities. Before the arrival of the starship, you people of the south were at war with us. You were a terrible warrior race..." She paused, then went on, "Then the Humans arrived. Their ship was malfunctioning and they had to make a forced landing—they would never have chosen to settle on Fortune if not for the failure of their ship's guidance systems. And then, Jen, your people attacked. You killed many of the Humans. Only six survived. We rescued them, took them to the sanctuary of our city in the north. How do you think we gained the knowledge to develop the technology we now possess? It was the Humans, Jen, who gave us that knowledge."

I sat in silence for a long time. At last I said, "But how can you be sure, Ki? How can you *know* for certain? I mean, it's all so confusing, it all happened so long ago—how can anyone be sure?"

She was watching me with compassion. "Because, in our northern city, two Humans still live with us."

"No!" I exclaimed. "That isn't possible! The starship landed *millennia* ago. How could they have survived?"

She took my hand. "Jen, they live much longer than we do. They live for thousands of terms. They live with us now, as free citizens, in the north." She paused, squeezing my hand. "Jen, listen to me—you cannot stay here in this city of lies and repression. A steam-wagon leaves in three hours. Come with me and learn the truth, Jen. Come with me to the north and meet the Humans for yourself."

I left Ki then, telling her that I needed time in which to think. I skated to the city wall and stared into the dark sky, at the Star growing in luminosity hour by hour. I considered the initiation ceremony, and the terrible lie I had learned there.

I thought of the summer that was coming to Fortune, the claustrophobic interment beneath the mountain that my people would be forced to undergo to escape the merciless heat of the sun. I thought of Kellor and Nani, good people diminished by conditioned ignorance.

As the Star set slowly in the east, I left the city wall and made my way to where the steam-wagon was waiting in the boulevard.

Ki was standing beside its huge front wheel, her back to me, staring nervously along the boulevard.

"Ki," I said.

She turned with speed and fear, and stared at me. I saw that she had been crying. She opened her mouth to speak, but words would not come.

At last she managed, "Jen? Have you . . . ? Will you come with me?"

Until I heard those words, the desperation in her voice, I had been undecided. Or perhaps a part of me had known what I might do all along, but had been too fearful to acknowledge the fact.

To live so long in ignorance, and then to learn the truth, can be a terrible revelation.

Slowly, without a word, I reached out and took her hand.

Then we boarded the steam-wagon and began the long journey north to the polar city of the Blues.

THE KÉTHANI INHERITANCE

In the mid-nineties I had the idea for a story about a race of aliens
who came to Earth and conferred upon humankind the gift of
immortality. When individuals died, the Kéthani would take the dead
to their homeplanet and bring them back to life. The subjects would
then be immortal, and given the choice of either returning to Earth
and their lives there, or acting as ambassadors to the Kéthani amongst
the stars. I soon realised that the idea was too big to limit to one story,
and over the course of the next ten years wrote a series about the
effect of immortality on the people of Earth: quiet, character-based
tales in which the aliens never made a physical appearance. The fix-
up novel, Kéthani, was published in 2008.

"The Kéthani Inheritance" is about a lonely man, his past blighted
by his relationship with his father, and how his life changed thanks to
the aliens and a good woman. It first appeared in Spectrum SF 7, in
2001.

THE KÉTHANI INHERITANCE

THAT WINTER, TWO EVENTS OCCURRED WHICH CHANGED MY LIFE. MY father died and, for the first time in thirty years, I fell in love. I suppose the irony is that, but for my father's illness, I would never have met Elisabeth Carstairs.

He was sitting in the lounge of the Sunny View nursing home that afternoon, chocked upright in his wheelchair with the aid of cushions, drooling and staring at me with blank eyes. The room reeked of vomit with an astringent overlay of bleach.

"Who're you, then?"

I sighed. I was accustomed to the mind-numbing, repetitive charade. "Ben," I said. "Benjamin. Your son."

Sometimes it worked, and I would see the dull light of recognition in his rheumy eyes. Today, however, he remained blank.

"Who're you, then? What do you want?"

"I'm Ben, your son. I've come to visit you."

I looked around the morning room, at the other patients—or "guests" as the nurses called them; they all gazed into space, seeing not the future, but the past.

"Who're you, then?"

Where was the strong man I had hated for so long? Such was his decrepitude that I could not bring myself to hate him any longer; I only wished that he would die. I had wished him dead so many times in the past, and now it came to me that he was having his revenge: he was protracting his life purely to spite me.

In Holland, I thought, where a euthanasia law had been passed years ago, the old bastard would be long dead.

I stood and moved to the window. The late afternoon view was far from sunny. Snow covered the hills to the far horizon, above which the sky was mauve with the promise of evening.

I was overcome with a sudden, soul-destroying depression.

"What's this?" my father said.

I focussed on his apparition reflected in the plate-glass window. His thin hand had strayed to his implant.

"What's this, then?"

I returned to him and sat down. I would go through this one more time—for perhaps the hundredth time in a year—and then say goodbye and leave.

His frail fingers tapped the implant at his temple, creating a hollow timpani.

"It's your implant," I said.

"What's it doing there?"

It sat beneath the papery skin of his temple, raised and rectangular, the approximate size of a matchbox.

"The medics put it there. Most people have them now. When you die, it will bring you back to life."

His eyes stared at me, then through me, uncomprehendingly.

I stood. "I'm going now. I'll pop in next week." It would be more like next month, but, in his shattered mind, all days were one now.

As I strode quickly from the room I heard him say, "Who're you, then?"

An infant-faced Filipino nurse beamed at me as I passed reception. "Would you like a cup of tea, Mr Knightly?"

I usually refused, wanting only to be out of the place, but that day something made me accept the offer.

Serendipity. Had I left Sunny View then, I might never have met Elisabeth. The thought often fills me with panic.

"Coffee, if that's okay? I'll be in here." I indicated a room designated as the library, though stocked only with Mills & Boon paperbacks, *Reader's Digest* magazines, and large-print Western novels.

I scanned the chipboard bookcases for a real book, then gave up. I sat down in a big, comfortable armchair and stared out at the snow. The coffee arrived. The nurse intuited that I wished to be left alone.

I drank the coffee and gazed at my reflection in the glass: I felt like a patient, or rather a "guest".

I think I was weeping when I heard, "It is depressing, isn't it?"

The voice shocked me. She was standing behind my chair, gripping a steaming mug and smiling.

I dashed away a tear, overcome with irritation at the interruption.

She sat down in the chair next to mine. I guessed she was about my age—around thirty—though I learned later that she was thirty-five. She was broad and short with dark hair bobbed, like brackets, around a pleasant, homely face.

"I know what it's like. My mother's a guest here. She's senile." She had a direct way of speaking that I found refreshing.

"My father has Alzheimer's," I said. "He's been in here for the past year."

She rolled her eyes. "God! The repetition! I sometimes just want to strangle her. I suppose I shouldn't be saying that, should I? The thing is, we were so close. I love her dearly."

I found myself saying, "In time, when she dies, her memory will—" I stopped, alarmed by something in her expression.

It was as if I had slapped her.

Her smile persisted, but it was a brave one now in the face of adversity. She shook her head. "She isn't implanted. She refused."

"Is she religious?"

"No," she said, "just stubborn. And fearful. She doesn't trust the Kéthani."

"I'm sorry."

She shook her head, as if to dismiss the matter. "I'm Elisabeth, by the way. Elisabeth Carstairs."

She reached out a hand, and, a little surprised at the forthright gesture, I took it. I never even thought to tell her my own name.

She kept hold of my hand, turning it over like an expert palm-reader. Only later did I come to realise that she was as lonely as I was: the difference being, of course, that Elisabeth had hope, something I had given up long ago.

"Don't tell me," she said, examining my weather-raw fingers. "You're a farmer, right?"

I smiled. "Wrong. I build and repair dry-stone walls."

She laughed. "Well, I was almost there, wasn't I? You do work outdoors, with your hands."

"What do you do?" I would never have asked normally, but something in her manner put me at ease. She did not threaten.

"I teach, for my sins. The comprehensive over at Bradley."

"Then you must know Jeff Morrow. He's a friend."

"You know Jeff? What a small world."

"We meet in the Fleece every Tuesday." I shrugged. "Creatures of habit."

She glanced at her watch and pulled a face. "I really should be getting off. It's been nice talking..." She paused, looking quizzical.

I was slow on the uptake, then realised. "Ben," I said. "Ben Knightly. Look, I'm driving into the village. I can give you a lift if you..."

She jangled car keys. "Thanks, anyway."

I stood to leave, nodding awkwardly, and for the first time she could see the left-hand side of my face.

She stared, something stricken in her eyes, at where my implant should have been.

I hurried from the nursing home and into the raw winter wind, climbed into my battered ten-year-old Sherpa van, and drove away at speed.

The following evening, just as I was about to set off to the Fleece, the phone rang. I almost ignored it, but it might have been a prospective customer and I was going through a lean spell.

"Hello, Ben? Elisabeth here, Elisabeth Carstairs. We met yesterday."

"Oh...Of course, yes." My heart was thudding, my mouth dry: the usual reactions of an inexperienced teenager to being phoned by a girl.

"The thing is, I have a wall that needs fixing. A couple of cows barged through it the other day. I don't suppose...?"

"Always looking for work," I said, experiencing a curious mixture of relief and disappointment. "I could come round tomorrow, or whenever's convenient."

"Sometime tomorrow afternoon?" She gave me her address.

"I'll be there between two and three," I said, thanked her and rang off.

That night, in the snug of the Fleece, I was on my third pint of Timothy Taylor's Landlord before I broached the subject of Elisabeth Carstairs.

The conversation was desultory. We'd been meeting in the same pub, sitting at the same table beside the log fire, and drinking the same beer for almost five years now. As might be expected the talk had grown somewhat predictable.

Jeff Morrow was forty-five, a quiet, thoughtful man who shared my interest in football and books. He'd come to the village just over five years ago, and once, after a few too many pints, had told me the reason he'd fled his last school. He'd had an affair with an eighteen-year-old pupil, which had ended in tragedy. She had not been implanted—he never said why not—and had taken her life for reasons that he had also never divulged.

He carried a photograph of her in his wallet: a slim, beautiful French girl called Claudine. Five years before that, and a year before the Kéthani came, his wife had died in a car accident.

An accretion of sadness showed in his eyes.

He had never once commented on the fact that I was not implanted, and I respected him for this.

The third member of our party was Richard Lincoln, the local ferryman. I'd always viewed people in his profession in the same light as undertakers, which in a way is what they were. He was a big, silver-haired man in his early sixties. His wife had died six years ago, and was now somewhere out-there, an ambassador of the Kéthani.

I suppose we gravitated towards each other because we were all single at the time, liked a regular pint, and enjoyed the company of quiet people to whom silences were natural.

"I met a woman called Elisabeth Carstairs yesterday," I said. "She teaches at your school, Jeff."

"Ah, Liz. Lovely woman. Good teacher. The kids love her. One of those naturals."

That might have been the end of that conversation, but I went on. "Is she married?"

He looked up. "Liz? God, no."

Richard traced the outline of his implant with an absent forefinger. "Why 'God, no,' Jeff? She isn't . . . ?"

"No, nothing like that." He shrugged, uncomfortable. Jeff is a tactful man. He said to me, "She's been looking after her mother for the past fifteen years. As long as I've known her, she's never had a boyfriend."

Richard winked at me. "You're in there, Ben."

I swore at him. Jeff said, "Where did you meet?"

I told him, and conversation moved on to the health of my father—on his third stroke, demented, but still hanging on—and then by some process of convoluted logic to Leeds United's prospects this Saturday.

Another thing I liked about Jeff and Richard was that they never made digs about the fact that I'd never had a girlfriend since they'd known me—since my early twenties, if the truth be known.

I'd long ago reconciled myself to a life mending dry-stone walls, reading the classics, and sharing numerous pints with the likes of Morrow and Lincoln.

And I'd never told anyone that I blamed my father: some wounds are too repulsive to reveal.

It was midnight by the time I made my way up the hill and across the moors to the cottage. I recall stopping once to gaze at the Onward Station, towering beside the reservoir a mile away. It coruscated in the light of the full moon like a stalagmite of ice.

As I stared, a beam of energy, blindingly white, arced through the night sky towards the orbiting Kéthani starship, and the sight, I must admit, frightened me.

"I tried repairing it myself," Elisabeth said, "but as you can see I went a bit wrong."

"It's like a jigsaw puzzle," I said. "It's just a matter of finding the right piece and fitting it in."

It was one of those rare, brilliantly sunny November days. There was no wind, and the snow reflected the sunlight with a twenty-four carat dazzle.

I dropped the last stone into place, rocked it home, and then stood back and admired the repair.

"Thirty minutes," Elisabeth said. "You make it look so easy."

I smiled. "Matter of fact, I built this wall originally, twelve years ago."

"You've been in the business that long?"

We chatted. Elisabeth wore snow boots and a padded parka with a fur-lined hood that made her look like an Eskimo. She stamped her feet. "Look, it's bitter out here. Would you like a coffee?"

"Love one."

Her house was a converted barn on the edge of the moor, on the opposite side of the village to my father's cottage. Inside it was luxurious: deep pile carpets, a lot of low beams and brass. The spacious kitchen was heated by an Aga.

I stood on the doormat, conscious of my boots.

"Just wipe them and come on in," she said, laughing. "I'm not house-proud, unlike my mother."

I sat at the kitchen table and glanced through the door to a room full of books. I pointed. "Like reading?"

"I love books," she said, handing me a big mug of real coffee. "I teach English, and the miracle is that it hasn't put me off reading. You?" She leaned against the Aga, holding her cup in both hands.

We talked about books for a while, and I think she was surprised at my knowledge.

Once I saw her glance at my left temple, where the implant should have been. I felt that she wanted to comment, to question me, but couldn't find a polite way of going about it.

The more I looked at her, and the more we talked, the more I realised that I found her attractive. She was short, and a little overweight, and her hair was greying prematurely, but her smile filled me with joy.

Romantic and inexperienced as I was, I extrapolated fantasies from this meeting, mapped out the future.

"How often do you visit your mother?" I asked, to fill a conversational lull.

"Four times a week. Monday, Wednesday, Friday and Sunday."

I hesitated. "How long has she been ill?"

She blew. "Oh . . . when has she ever been well! She had her first stroke around fifteen years ago, not long after we moved here. I've been working part-time and looking after her ever since. She's averaged about . . . oh, a stroke every three years since. The doctors say it's a miracle she's still with us."

She hesitated, then said, "Then the Kéthani came, and offered us the implants and I thought all my prayers had been answered."

I avoided her eyes.

Elisabeth stared into her cup. "She was a very intelligent woman, a member of the old Labour Party before the Blair sell-out. She knew her mind. She wanted nothing to do with afterlife, as she called it."

"She was suspicious of the Kéthani?"

"A little, I suppose. Weren't we all, in the beginning? But it was more than that. I think she foresaw humanity becoming complacent, apathetic with this life when the stars beckoned."

"Some people would say she was right."

A silence developed. She stared at me. "Is that the reason you . . . ?"

There were as many reasons for not having the implant, I was sure, as there were individuals who had decided to go without. Religious, philosophical, moral . . . I gave Elisabeth a version of the truth.

Not looking her in the eye, but staring into my empty cup, I said, "I decided not to have the implant, at first, because I was suspicious. I thought I'd wait, see how it went with everyone who did have it. A year passed, two . . . And it really was as the Kéthani said. We had nothing to fear." I looked up quickly to see how she was taking it.

She was squinting at me. "So, why didn't you . . . ?"

"By that time," I said, "I'd come to realise something. Living on the edge of death, staring it in the face, made life all the more worth living. I'd be alone, on some outlying farm somewhere, and I'd be at one with the elements . . . and, I don't know, I came to appreciate being alive."

Bullshit, I thought. It was the line I'd used many a time in the past, and though it contained an element of truth, it was not the real reason.

Elisabeth was intelligent; I think she saw through my words, realised that I was hiding something, and I must admit that I felt guilty about lying to her.

I thanked her for the coffee and made to leave.

"How much for the work?" she said, gesturing through the window at the repaired wall.

I hesitated. I almost asked her if she would like to go for a meal, but stopped myself just in time. I told myself that it would seem crass, as if she had to accept the invitation in payment. In fact, the coward in me shied away from escalating the terms of our relationship.

"Call it fifty," I said.

She gave me a fifty-euro note and I hurried from the house, part of me feeling that I had escaped, while another part was cursing my fear and inadequacy.

I found myself, after that, visiting my father on Monday, Wednesday, Friday, and Sunday. Sunny View seemed a suitably neutral venue in which to meet and talk to Elisabeth Carstairs.

I even found myself looking forward to the visits.

About two weeks after I repaired her wall, I was sitting in the lounge with my father. It was four o'clock and we were alone. Around four-thirty Elisabeth would emerge from her mother's room and we would have coffee in the library.

I was especially nervous today because I'd decided to ask her if she would like to come for a meal the following day, a Thursday. I'd heard about a good Indonesian place in Harrogate.

I'd come to realise that I liked Elisabeth Carstairs for who she was, her essential character, rather than for what she might represent: a woman willing to show me friendship, affection, and maybe even more.

We had a lot in common, shared a love of books, films, and even a similar sense of humour. Moreover, I saw in Elisabeth a fundamental human decency, perhaps borne out of hardship, that I detected in few other people.

"Who're you, then?"

"Ben," I said absently, my thoughts miles away.

He regarded me for about a minute, then said, "You always were bloody useless!"

I stared at him. He had moments of lucidity: for a second, he was back to his old self, but his comment failed to hurt. I'd heard it often before, when the sentiment had been backed by an ability to be brutal.

"Dry-stone walls!" he spat.

"Is that any worse than being a bus driver?" I said.

"Useless young..." he began, and dribbled off.

I leaned forward. "Why don't you go to hell!" I said, and hurried from the room, shaking.

I sat in the library, staring out at the snow and shaking. I wondered if, when my father was resurrected and returned, he would have any memory of the insult.

"Hello, Ben. Nice to see you."

She was wearing her chunky primrose parka and, beneath it, a jet-black cashmere jumper. She looked lovely.

"You don't look too good," she said, sitting down and sipping her coffee.

I shrugged. "I'm fine."

"Some days he's worse than others, right? Don't tell me. Mum's having one of her bad days today."

More than anything I wanted to tell her that I cared nothing for my father, but resisted the urge for fear of appearing cruel.

We chatted about the books we were reading at the moment; she had loaned me Chesterton's *Tales of the Long Bow*, and I enthused about his prose.

Later, my coffee drunk, I twisted the cup awkwardly and avoided her eyes. "Elisabeth, I was wondering... There's a nice Indonesian restaurant in Harrogate. At least, I've heard it's good. I was wondering—"

She came to my rescue. "I'd love to go," she said, smiling at me. "Name a day."

"How about tomorrow? And I'll pay."

"Well, I'll get the next one, then. How's that sound? And I'll drive, if you like."

"Deal," I said, grinning like an idiot.

I was working on a high sheepfold all the following day, and I was in good spirits. I couldn't stop thinking about Elisabeth, elation mixed equally with trepidation. From time to time I'd stop work for a coffee from my thermos, sit on the wall I was building and stare down at the vast, cold expanse of the reservoir, and the Onward Station beside it.

Ferrymen came and went, delivering the dead. I saw Richard Lincoln's Range Rover pull up and watched as he unloaded a coffin and trolleyed it across the car park and into the station.

At five I made my way home, showered and changed and waited nervously for Elisabeth to pick me up.

The meal was a success. In fact, contrary to my fears, the entire night was wonderful. From the time she picked me up, we began talking and never stopped.

The restaurant was quiet, the service excellent and the food even better. We ate and chattered, and it seemed to me that I had known this friendly, fascinating woman all my life.

I could not see in Elisabeth the lonely, loveless woman that Jeff had described; she seemed comfortable and at ease. I feared I would appear gauche and naïve to her, but she gave no indication of thinking so. Perhaps the fact was that we complemented each other: two lonely people who had, by some arbitrary accident, overcome the odds and discovered each other.

We drove back through a fierce snowstorm and stopped outside her converted barn. She turned to me in the darkness. "You'll come in for a coffee, Ben?"

I nodded, my mouth dry. "Love to," I said.

We sat on the sofa and drank coffee and talked, and the free and easy atmosphere carried over from the restaurant. It was one o'clock by the time I looked into my empty mug and said, "Well, it's getting on. I'd better be..."

She reached out and touched my hand with her fingers. "Ben, stay the night, please."

"Well... If it's okay with you."

"Christ," she said, "what do you think?" And, before I knew it, she was in my arms.

I had often wondered what the first time would be like, tried to envisage the embarrassment of trying to do something that I had never done before. The simple fact was that, when we undressed each other beside the bed, and came together, flesh to soft, warm flesh, it seemed entirely natural, and accomplished with mutual trust and affection—and I realised that I'd never really had anything to fear, after all.

I was awoken in the night by a bright flash of light. I rolled over and held Elisabeth to me, cupped her bottom in my pelvis and slipped a hand across her belly.

The window overlooked the valley, the reservoir and the station.

High-energy pulse beams lanced into the stratosphere.

"You 'wake?" she murmured.

"Mmm," I said.

"Isn't it beautiful?" she whispered. Shafts of dazzling white light bisected the sable sky, but more beautiful to me was holding a warm, naked woman in my arms.

"Mmm," I said.

"I always keep the curtains open," she whispered. "I like to watch the lights when I can't sleep. They fill me with hope."

I watched the lights with her. Hard to conceive that every beam of energy contained the newly dead of Earth.

"Elisabeth," I said.

"Hmm?"

"Have you read much about the Kéthani?"

She turned to face me, her breasts against my chest. She stroked my face and lightly kissed my lips. "Just about everything there is to read."

"Something I don't understand," I said. "Millions of humans die, and are taken away and resurrected. Then they have a choice. They can either come back and resume their lives on Earth, or they can do the bidding of the Kéthani, and go among the stars, as explorers, ambassadors."

"Or they can come to Earth, live a while, and then leave for the stars."

"That, too," I said.

The Kéthani discovered billions of stars in thousands of galaxies. They found millions of habitable, and inhabited, planets, and they need minions to go abroad and explore, contact, report on these worlds. There were not enough Kéthani to do this, so they employed humankind, and as payment they brought us back to life.

"And we trust them?" I said.

"We do now. At first, millions of us didn't. Then the reports started to come back from those who had died, been resurrected, and gone among the stars. And the stories they told, the accounts of a wondrous and teeming universe . . ."

"I've seen the documentaries. But . . ."

"What?"

"What about all those humans who are . . ." I tried to think of a diplomatic phrase, "let's say, unsuited even for life on Earth. I mean, thugs and murderers, dictators, psychopaths."

My father . . .

"Hard to imagine Pol Pot acting as an ambassador for an enlightened alien race," I said.

She stroked my hair. "They're changed in the resurrection process, Ben. They come back . . . *different*. Altered. Still themselves, but with compassion, humanity." She laughed, suddenly.

"What?" I asked.

"The irony of it," she said. "That it takes an alien race to invest some people with humanity!"

She reached down and took me in her fingers, and guided me into her. We made love, again, bathed in the blinding light of the dead as they ascended to heaven.

THE DISCIPLES OF APOLLO

———.———

Our parents died the following week, within days of each other.

On the Monday afternoon I was working on the third wall of the sheepfold when my mobile rang. "Hello, Ben Knightly here," I called above the biting wind.

"Mr Knightly? This is Maria, from Sunny View. Your father was taken into Bradley General at noon today. The doctor I spoke to thinks that it might only be a matter of hours."

I nodded, momentarily at a loss for words.

"Mr Knightly?"

"Thanks. Thank you. I'll be there as soon..." I drifted off.

"Very well, Mr Knightly. I'm so sorry."

I thanked her again and cut the connection.

I continued the section of wall I was working on, placing the stones with slow deliberation, one by one, ensuring a solid finish.

I had anticipated this day for months: it would mark the start of a temporary freedom, an immediate release from the routine of visiting the nursing home. For six months I would be free of the thought of my father on Earth, demanding my attention.

It was perhaps two hours after receiving the call that I drove into the car park at Bradley General and made my way along what seemed like miles of corridors to the acute coronary ward. My father had suffered a massive heart attack. He was unconscious when I arrived, never came round, and died an hour later.

The sudden lack of a regular bleep on his cardiogram brought me from my reverie: I was staring through the window at the snow-covered fields, thinking that a few walls out there could do with attention.

Then the bleep changed to a continuous note, and I looked at my father. He appeared as he had before death: grey, open-mouthed, and utterly lifeless.

A ferryman came for him, asked me if I would be attending the farewell ceremony—I declined—and took him away in a box they called a container, not a coffin. I signed all the necessary papers, and then made my way to Elisabeth's house.

That night, after making love, we lay in bed and watched the first energy beam leave the Onward Station at ten o'clock.

"You're quiet," she said.

I hesitated. "My father died today," I told her.

She fumbled for the light, then turned and stared at me. "Why on earth didn't you say something earlier?"

I reached out for her and pulled her to me. "I didn't think it mattered," I said.

She stroked my hair. I had never told her of my relationship with my father, always managed to steer the subject away from our acrimony.

She kissed my forehead. "He'll be back in six months," she soothed. "Renewed, younger, full of life."

How could I tell her that that was what I feared most?

The following Thursday I finished work at five and drove to Elisabeth's. The day after my father died, she had asked me to move in with her. I felt that our relationship had graduated to another level; I often had to pause and reminded myself how fortunate I was.

We settled into a routine of domestic contentment. We took turns at cooking each other meals more daring and spectacular than any we would have prepared for ourselves alone.

I was expecting, that night, to be assailed by the aroma of cooking meat when I entered the kitchen, but instead detected only the cloying fragrance of air freshener. The light was off.

Then I made out Elisabeth. She was sitting on the floor by the far wall, the receiver of the phone cradled redundantly in her lap.

I saw her look up when I came in, and I reached instinctively for the light.

Her face, revealed, was a tear-stained mask of anguish.

My stomach flipped, for I knew immediately.

"Oh, Ben," she said, reaching for me. "That was the nursing home. Mum died an hour ago."

I was across the room and kneeling and hugging her to me, and for the first time I experienced another person's heartfelt grief.

The funeral was a quiet affair at the village church—the first one there, the vicar told me, for years. A reporter from a national newspaper was snooping, wanting Elisabeth's story. I told him where to go in no uncertain terms. There was less I could do to deter the interest of a camera crew from the BBC, who kept their distance but whose very presence was a reminder, if any were required, of the tragedy of Mary Carstairs's death.

Every day we walked up to the overgrown churchyard, and Elisabeth left flowers at the grave. If anything, my love for her increased over the next few weeks; I had

201

never before felt needed, and to have someone rely on me, and tell me so, made me realise in return how much I needed Elisabeth.

One evening I was cooking on the Aga when she came up behind me very quietly, slipped her arms around my body and laid her head between my shoulder blades. "God, Ben. I would have gone mad without you. You're the best thing that's ever happened to me."

I turned and held her. "Love you," I whispered.

She joined us on Tuesday nights, and it was as if her presence injected a well-needed dose of life into the proceedings. The conversation became more varied, and others joined our table. We made friends with another ferryman, Dan Chester, who lived in the old coach house a few doors down from the Fleece, and with Khalid Azzam, an implant surgeon over at Bradley General, and his wife Zara.

Four months after my father's death, Richard Lincoln came into the Fleece one Tuesday night and handed me a package. "Special delivery from the Onward Station," he said.

I turned the silver envelope over. It was small and square, the size of the DVD I knew it would contain. My name and address were printed on both sides, below the double star logo of the Kéthani.

"A message from your father, Ben," Richard said.

I could not bring myself to enjoy the rest of the evening: the package was burning a hole in my pocket.

When we returned home, Elisabeth said, "Well?"

I laughed, wrestling her towards the bedroom. "Well, what?"

"Aren't you going to play it?"

"Don't think I'll bother."

She stared at me. "Aren't you curious?"

"Not particularly."

"Well, if you aren't, I am. Come on, we'll play it on the TV in the bedroom."

I lay in bed, staring out at the rearing obelisk of the station, while she inserted the DVD into the player. Then, with Elisabeth in my arms, I turned and stared at the screen.

My father had decided against a visual recording: only his broad, bluff Yorkshire voice came through, while the screen remained blank. I was relieved that I would be spared the sight of his new, rejuvenated image.

"Ben, Reg here. I'm well. We still haven't seen the Kéthani—can you believe that? I thought I'd catch a glimpse of them at least." He paused. The fact that his voice issued from a star three hundred light years distant struck me as faintly ridiculous. "I'm in a group with about a dozen other resurrectees, all from different countries. We're learning a lot." He paused. "I still haven't decided what I'm doing yet, when I get back. Well, that's about it for now." His murmured farewell was followed by a profound silence.

And that was it, as casual as a postcard from Blackpool; except, I told myself, there was something almost human in his tone, an absence of hostility that I had not heard in years.

But that did nothing to help lessen my dread of the bastard's return.

Whenever Elisabeth broached the topic of implants, however tenuously, I managed to change the subject. In retrospect, I was ashamed at how my reluctance to undergo the implantation process affected her; at the time, selfishly, I could apprehend only my own frail emotions.

More than once, late at night, when we had made love, she would whisper that she loved me more than anything in the world, and that she did not want to lose me.

A week before my father was due to return, she could no longer keep her fears to herself.

She was sitting at the kitchen table when I returned from work. She indicated the letter I'd received that morning from the Onward Station. My father was returning in seven days; he had asked to meet me at a reception room in the station.

It was the meeting I had dreaded for so long.

She was quiet over dinner, and finally I said, "Elisabeth, what is it?" I imagined that the news of my father's return had reminded her again of her mother's irrevocable demise.

She was silent for a while.

"Please don't avoid the issue this time," she said at last. "Don't change the subject or walk away." Her hand was shaking as she pushed away her plate.

"What is it?" I asked, stupidly.

She looked up, pinned me with her gaze.

"I can't stand the thought of losing you, Ben." It was almost a whisper.

"Don't worry, you won't. I have no intention of leaving you."

"Don't be so crass!" she said, and her words hurt. "You know what I mean." She shook her head, fighting back the tears. "Sometimes I experience a kind of panic. I'm on my own, driving to school or whatever, and I imagine you've been in some accident... and you can't begin to understand how that makes me feel. I don't want to lose you."

"Elisabeth..."

She hit the table with the ham of her right hand. "What if you're in a car crash, or drop dead of a heart attack? What then? You'll be dead, Ben! Dead forever. There'll be no bringing you back." She was crying now. "And I'll be without you *forever.*"

"What are the chances of that?" I began.

"Don't be so bloody rational!" she cried. "Don't you see? If you were implanted, then I wouldn't worry. I could love you without the constant, terrible fear of losing you." She paused, and then went on, "And this thing about not being implanted making you appreciate being alive all the more." She shook her head. "I don't believe it for a minute. You're hiding something. You fear the Kéthani or something."

"It's not that."

"Ben, listen to me." Her tone was imploring. "When you're implanted, it invests you with a wonderful feeling of... of liberation. Of freedom. You really do appreciate being alive all the more. We've been afraid of death for so long, and then the Kéthani came along and gave us the greatest gift, and you spurn it."

We sat in silence for what seemed an age, Elisabeth staring at me, while I stared at the tabletop.

She could have said, then, "If you love me, Ben, you'll have the implant," and I wouldn't have blamed her. But she wasn't the type of person who used the tactics of blackmail to achieve her desires.

At last I said, "My father made my life a misery, Elisabeth. My mother died when I was ten, and from then on he dominated me. He'd hit me occasionally, but far worse was the psychological torture. You have no idea what it's like to be totally dominated, to have your every move watched, your every word criticised, whatever you do put down and made worthless." I stopped. The silence stretched. I was aware of a pain in my chest, a hollowness. "I've never been able to work out why he was like that. All I know is that, until eighteen months ago, I lived in fear of him."

I stopped again, staring at my big, clumsy hands on the tabletop. "His criticism, his snide comments, his lack of love... they made me feel worthless and inadequate. I hated being alive. I'd often fantasise about killing myself, but the only thing that stopped me was the thought that my father would gain some sick satisfaction from my death." I looked up, tears in my eyes. "He turned me into a lonely, socially inept wreck. I found it hard to make friends, and the thought of talking to women..."

She reached out, gently, and touched my hand.

I shook my head. "Ten years ago he had his first stroke, and I had to look after him. The bastard had me just where he wanted me, and he made my life even worse. I dreamed of the day he'd die, freeing me.

"And then the Kéthani came, with their damned gift, and he was implanted, and the thought of him living forever..." I took a long, deep breath. "I wasn't implanted, Elisabeth, because I wanted to die. As simple as that. I hated being alive, and I was too weak and inadequate to leave and start a life of my own."

"But now?" she asked, squeezing my fingers.

"But now," I said, "he's coming back next week."

We went to bed, and held each other in silence as the white light streaked into the air above the Onward Station.

At last Elisabeth whispered, "Don't be afraid any longer, Ben. You have me, now."

I left the van in the car park and approached the station. I had never seen it at such close quarters before, and I had to crane my neck in order to view its sparkling summit, a thousand metres overhead.

I felt as cold as the surrounding landscape, my heart frozen. I wanted to get the meeting over as soon as possible, find out what he intended to do.

I passed the letter to a blue-uniformed woman at a reception desk, and another woman led me down a long white corridor. A cold, sourceless light pervaded the place, chilling me even further.

With the fixed smile of an airhostess, the woman ushered me into a small white room, furnished with two sofas, and told me that my father would be along in five minutes.

I sat down. Then I stood up and paced the room.

I almost panicked, recalling the sound of his voice, his silent, condemnatory expression.

A door at the far side of the room slid open and a figure in a sky blue overall walked through.

All I could do was stand and stare.

It was a version of my father I recalled from my teenage years. He looked about forty, no longer grey and bent, but upright, with a full head of dark hair.

For so long, in my mind's eye, I had retained an image of my father in his sixties, and had vented my hatred on that persona. Now he was the man who had blighted my early years, and I was the young boy again, abject and fearful.

He stepped forward, and I managed to stand my ground, though inside I was cowering.

He held out a hand. "Ben," he said.

And the sound of his voice was enough. I had a sudden memory, a vivid flash of an incident from my youth not long after my mother's death: he had discovered me in my bedroom, crying over the faded photograph of her I kept beside my bed. He had stared at me in bitter silence for what seemed like an age, and then, with his big, clumsy hands, he had unbuckled his belt and pulled it from his waist. His first, back-handed blow had laid me out across the bed, and then he had set about me with the belt, laying into me with blows that burned red-hot in time to his words, "You're a man, now, Ben, and men do not cry!"

His beatings had become regular after that; he would find the slightest excuse in my behaviour to use his belt. Later it occurred to me that my beatings were a catharsis that allowed him to vent his perverted grief.

But now, when he stepped forward and held out his hand, I could take no more. I had intended to confront my father, ask him what he intended, and perhaps even tell him that I did not want him to return. Instead, I fled.

I pushed my way from the room and ran down the corridor. I was no longer a man, but the boy who had escaped the house and sprinted onto the moors all those years ago.

I left the Onward Station and stopped in my tracks, as if frozen by the ice-cold night.

I heard a voice behind me. "Ben..." The bastard had followed me.

Without looking round, I hurried over to the van. I fumbled with the keys, my desire to find out his intentions forgotten in the craven need to get away.

"Ben, we need to talk."

Summoning my courage, I turned and stared at him. In the half-light of the stars, he seemed less threatening.

"What do you want?"

"We need to talk, about the future."

"The future?" I said. "Wasn't the past bad enough? If you think you can come back, start again where you left off, spoil the life I've made since you died..." I was amazed that I had managed to say it. I was shaking with rage and fear.

"Ben," my father said. "My own father was no angel... but that's no excuse."

"What do you want?" I cried.

He stared at me, his dark eyes penetrating. "What do *you* want, Ben? I have a place aboard a starship heading for Lyra, if I wish to take it. I'll be back in ten years. Or I can stay here. What do you want me to do?"

He left the question hanging, and the silence stretched. I stared at him as the cold night invaded my bones. The choice was mine; he was giving me—for the first time in my life, so far as he was concerned—a say in my destiny. It was so unlike my father that I wondered, briefly, if in fact the Kéthani *had* managed to instil in him some small measure of humanity.

"Go," I found myself saying at last, "and in ten years, when you return, maybe then . . ."

He stared at me for what seemed like an age, but I would not look away, and finally he said, "Very well, Ben. I'll do that. I'll go, and in ten years . . ."

He looked up, at the stars, and then lowered his eyes to me for the last time. "Goodbye, Ben."

He held out his hand, and after a moment's hesitation I took it.

Then he turned and walked back into the station, and as I watched him go I felt an incredible weight lift from my shoulders, a burden that had punished me for years.

I looked up into the night sky, and found myself crying.

At last I opened the door of the van, climbed inside, and sat for a long time, considering the future.

Much later I looked at my watch and saw that it was seven o'clock. I started the engine, drove slowly over the moors to Bradley, and did what I had to do there.

It was ten o'clock by the time I arrived at the Fleece.

I had phoned Elisabeth and told her to meet me there, saying that I had a surprise for her. I'd also phoned Jeff Morrow, Richard Lincoln, and Dan Chester, to join in the celebration. They stood at the bar, smiling to themselves.

Elisabeth entered the lounge, and my heart leapt.

She hurried over and sat down opposite me, looking concerned and saying, "How did it go with . . . ?"

I reached across the table and took her hand. "I love you," I said.

She stared at me, tears silvering her eyes. Her lips said my name, but silently.

Then she moved her hand from mine, reached up and, with gentle fingers, traced the outline of the implant at my temple.

ULLA, ULLA

H. G. Wells's The War of the Worlds *and* The Time Machine *were among the first science fiction novels I ever read, and they made a big impression on me. I recall the depiction of a ruined London in the former work and the wonder of the description of the desolate beach and the swollen sun in the latter. The sound of the Martian's dying call, "Ulla, ulla, ulla, ulla." fills me with a strange frisson to this day. In the following tale I enjoyed juxtaposing the old with the new, as I've done in a few other stories. It first appeared in Mike Ashley's* The Mammoth Book of Science Fiction, *2002.*

ULLA, ULLA

AFTER THE DEBRIEFING, WHICH LASTED THREE DAYS, ENRIGHT LEFT THE Kennedy Space Center and headed for home.

He drove south to the Keys in his '08 Chevrolet convertible, taking his time now that he was alone for the first time in three years. For that long he had been cooped up in the *Fortitude* on its voyage to Mars and back. Even on the surface of the planet, beneath the immensity of the pink sky, he'd never felt truly alone. Always there were the voices of McCarthy, Jeffries, and Spirek on his com, and the prospect of the cramped living quarters on his return to the lander.

Ten miles south of Kennedy, on the coast road, he pulled into a parking lot overlooking the sea, climbed out and stared into the evening sky.

There was Mars, riding high.

He considered the mission, but he had no original take on what they had discovered beneath the surface of the red planet. He was as baffled as everyone else. One thing he knew for certain, though: everything was different now. At some point, inevitably, the news would break, and things would change forever.

He had been allowed a couple of hours with Delia after quarantine, before being whisked off to the intensive debriefing. He had not been cleared to discuss their findings with her, the one person in his life with whom he had shared everything. She had sensed something, though, detected in his manner that all was not right. She had been at mission control when the first broadcast came through from Mars, but Director Roberts had cut the transmission before anything major had leaked.

He shivered. The wind was turning cold.

He climbed back into his Chevrolet, reversed from the lot, and drove home.

—·—

He left the car in the drive and walked around the house.

The child's swing, in situ when they had bought the place four years ago, had still not been removed. Delia had promised him that she would see to it while he was away.

She was sitting in the lighted conservatory, reading. She looked up as he pushed through the door, but made no move to rise and greet him.

"You weren't due back until tomorrow," she said, making it sound like an accusation.

"Let us off a day early. Thought I'd surprise you." He was aware of the distance between them, after so long apart.

Over dinner, they chatted. Small talk, the inconsequential tone of which indicated that they both knew they were avoiding deeper issues. She was back teaching, three days a week at the local elementary school. Ted, her nephew, had been accepted at Florida State.

He wanted to tell her. He wanted to tell her everything that had happened on Mars. He had always shared everything with her in the past. So why not now?

Mission confidentiality? The papers he had signed seven years back on being accepted by NASA?

Or was it because what they had discovered might have been some kind of collective hallucination? And Delia might think that he was losing it, if he came out and told her?

A combination of all the above, he realised.

That night they made love, hesitantly, and later lay in a parallelogram of moonlight that cut across the bed.

"What happened, Ed?" she asked.

"Mmm?" He tried to feign semi-wakefulness.

"We were there, in mission control. You were out with Spirek. Something happened. There was a loud ... I don't know, it sounded like a landslide. You said, 'Oh my God ...'. Roberts cut the link and ushered us out. It was an hour before they got back to us. An hour. Can you imagine that? I was worried sick."

He reached out and stroked away her tears.

"Roberts gave us some story about subsidence," she said. "Then I heard you again, reassuring us that everything was okay."

They had staged that, concocted a few lines between them, directed by Roberts, to reassure their families back home.

He shrugged. "That's it. That's what happened. I was caught in a landslide, lost my footing." Even to his own ears, he sounded unconvincing.

Delia went on, "And then three days ago, I could tell something wasn't right. And now... You're hiding something."

He let the silence stretch. "I'm hiding nothing. It's hard to readjust. Imagine being stuck in a tin can for three years with cretins like Jeffries and McCarthy."

"You're too sensitive, Ed. You're a geologist, not an astronaut. You should have stayed at the university."

He embraced her. "Shh," he said, and fell silent.

He dreamed that night. He was back on Mars. He could feel the regolith slide away beneath his boots. The sensation of inevitable descent and imminent impact turned his stomach as it had done all those months ago. He fell, tumbling, and landed in a sitting position. In the dream he opened his eyes—and awoke suddenly, the image of what he had seen down there imprinted on his waking consciousness.

He gasped aloud and reached out, grabbing the headboard. Then it came to him that he was no longer weightless, floating in his sleeping bag. He was on Earth. He was home. He reached out for Delia and held her.

In the morning, while Delia was at school, Enright took a walk. The open space, after so long cramped in the *Fortitude*, held an irresistible allure. He found himself on the golf course, strolling along the margin of the second fairway in the shade of maple trees.

He came to a bunker and stopped, staring at the clean, scooped perfection of the feature. He closed his eyes, and jumped. The sensation was pretty accurate. He had stepped out onto Mars again. He felt the granular regolith give beneath his boots.

When he opened his eyes, he saw a young girl, perhaps twelve years old and painfully pretty. She was standing on the lip of the bunker, staring down at him.

She was clutching a pen and a scrap of paper.

Beyond her, on the green, two men looked on.

"Mr Enright, sir?" the kid asked. "Can I have your autograph?"

He reached up, took the pen and paper, and scrawled his name.

The girl stared at the autograph, as if the addition of his signature upon the paper had invested it with magical properties. One of the watching men smiled and waved a hand.

Delia was still at school when he got back. The first thing he did on returning was to phone a scrap merchant to take away the swing in the back yard. Then he retired to his study and stared at the pile of unanswered correspondence on his desk, and the hundreds of emails on his PC.

He leafed through the mail.

One was from Joshua Connaught, in England. Enright had corresponded with the eccentric for a number of years before the mission. The man had said he was writing a book on the history of spaceflight, and wanted Enright's opinion on certain matters.

They had exchanged letters every couple of months—Connaught loathed email, he said—moving away from the original subject and discussing everything under the sun. Connaught had been married, once, and he too was childless.

Enright set the envelope aside, unopened.

He sat back in his armchair and closed his eyes.

He was back on Mars again, and falling . . .

It had been a perfect touchdown.

The first manned craft to land on another planet had done so at precisely 3:33 a.m., Houston time, September 2nd, 2025.

Enright recalled little of the actual landing, other than his fear. He had never been a good flyer—plane journeys had given him the shakes: he feared the take-off and landings, while the bit in between he could tolerate. The same was true of spaceflight. The take-off at Kennedy had been delayed by a day, and then put on hold for another five hours, and by the time the *Fortitude* did blast off from pad 39A, Enright had been reduced to a nervous wreck. Fortunately, his presence at this stage of the journey had been token. It was the others who did the work—just as when they came in to land, over eighteen months later, on the broad, rouge expanse of the Amazonis Planitia.

Enright recalled gripping the arms of his seat to halt the shakes that had taken him, and staring through the viewscreen at the rocky surface of Mars which was rushing up to meet them faster than seemed safe.

Jeffries had seen him and laughed, nudging McCarthy to take a look at his funk. Fortunately, the Air Force man had been otherwise occupied. Only Spirek sympathised with a smile; Enright received the impression that she too was not enjoying the descent.

The retros cut in, slamming the seat into Enright's back and knocking the wind from his lungs. The descent of the lander slowed appreciably. The boulder-strewn terrain seemed to be floating up to meet them, now.

Touchdown, when it came, was almost delicate.

McCarthy and Jeffries were NASA men through and through, veterans of a dozen space station missions and the famous return to the moon in '20. They were good astronauts, lousy travelling companions. They were careerists who were less interested in the pursuit of knowledge, of exploration for its own sake, than in the political end-results of what they were doing—both for themselves personally and for the country. Enright envisaged McCarthy running for president in the not too distant future, Jeffries ending up as some bigwig in the Pentagon.

They tended to look upon Enright, with his PhD in geology and a career at Miami University, as something of a makeweight on the trip.

Spirek. Enright could not quite make her out. Like the others, she was a career astronaut, but she had none of the brash bravado and right-wing rhetoric of her male counterparts. She had been a pilot in the Air Force, and was along as team medic and multi-disciplinary scientist: her brief, to assess the planet for possible future colonisation.

McCarthy was slated to step out first, followed by Enright. Fancy that, he'd thought on being informed at the briefing, Iowa farm-boy made good, only the second human being ever to set foot on Mars.

After the landing, Jeffries had made some quip about Enright still being shit-scared and not up to taking a stroll. He'd even made to suit up ahead of Enright.

"I'm fine," Enright said.

Spirek had backed him up. "Ed's A-OK for go, Jeffries. You don't want Roberts finding out you pulled a stunt, huh?"

Jeffries had muttered something under his breath. It had sounded like "Bitch," to Enright.

So he'd followed McCarthy out onto the sun-bright plain of the Amazonis Planitia, his pulse loud in his ears, his legs trembling as he climbed the ladder and stepped onto the surface of the alien world.

There was a lot to do for the two hours he was out of the lander, and he had only the occasional opportunity to consider the enormity of the situation.

He took rock samples, drilled through the regolith to the bedrock. He filmed what he was doing for the benefit of the geologists back at NASA who would take up the work when he returned.

He recalled straightening up on one occasion and staring, amazed, at the western horizon. He wondered how he had failed to notice it before. The mountain stood behind the lander, an immense pyramidal shape that rose abruptly from the surrounding volcanic plain to a height, he judged, of a kilometre. He had to tilt his head back to take in its summit.

Later, Spirek and Jeffries took their turn outside, while Enright began a preliminary analysis of the rock samples and McCarthy reported back to mission control.

Day one went like a dream, everything A-OK.

The following day, as the sun rose through the cerise sky, Enright and Spirek took the Mars-mobile out for its test drive. They ranged a kilometre from the lander, keeping it in sight at all times.

Spirek, at the wheel, halted the vehicle at one point and stared into the sky. She touched Enright's padded elbow, and he heard her voice in his earpiece. "Look, Ed." And she pointed.

He followed her finger, and saw a tiny, shimmering star high in the heavens.

"Earth," she whispered, and, despite himself, Enright felt a strange emotion constrict his throat at the sight of his homeplanet, so reduced.

But for Spirek's sighting of Earth at that moment, and her decision to halt, Enright might never have made the discovery that was to prove so fateful.

Spirek was about to start up, when he glanced to his left and saw the depression in the regolith, ten metres from the Mars-mobile.

"Hey! Stop, Sally!"

"What is it?"

He pointed. "Don't know. Looks like subsidence. I want to take a look."

Sal glanced at her chronometer. "You got ten minutes, okay?"

He climbed from the mobile and strode towards the rectangular impression in the red dust. He paused at its edge, knelt and ran his hand through the fine regolith. The first human being, he told himself, ever to do so here at this precise location . . .

He stood and took a step forward.

And the ground gave way beneath his feet, and he was falling. "Oh, my God!"

He landed in a sitting position in semidarkness, battered and dazed but uninjured. He checked his life-support apparatus. His suit was okay, his air supply functioning.

Only then did he look around him. He was in a vast chamber, a cavern that extended for as far as the eye could see.

As the dust settled, he made out the objects ranged along the length of the chamber.

"Oh, Christ," he cried. "Spirek . . . *Spirek*!"

He stood in the doorway of the conservatory and watched the workmen dismantle the swing and load it onto the back of the pickup.

He'd been home four days now, and he was falling back into the routine of things. Breakfast with Delia, then a round of golf, solo, on the mornings she worked.

They met for lunch in town, and then spent the afternoons at home, Delia in the garden, Enright reading magazines and answering emails.

He was due back at the university in a week, to begin work on the samples he'd brought back from Mars. He was not relishing the prospect, and not just because it would mean spending time away from Delia: the business of geology, and what might be learned from the study of the Martian rocks, palled beside what he'd discovered on the red planet.

Roberts had phoned him a couple of days ago. Already NASA was putting together plans for a follow-up mission. He recalled what McCarthy and Jeffries had said about their discovery, that it constituted a security risk. Enright had forced himself not to laugh out loud, at the time. And yet, amazingly, when he returned to Earth and heard the talk of the back-room boys up at Kennedy, that had been the tenor of their concern. Now Roberts confirmed it by telling him, off the record, that the government was bankrolling the next Mars mission. There would be a big military presence aboard. The disaster of bellicose US foreign policy repeating itself again, he thought: as if we hadn't learned from Iraq and Iran and Venezuela. He wondered if McCarthy and Jeffries were happy now.

The workmen finished loading the swing and drove off. Delia was kneeling in the border, weeding. He watched her for a while, then went into the house.

He fetched the papers from the sitting room where he'd discovered them yesterday, slipped under the cushion of the settee.

"Delia?"

She turned, smiling.

She saw the papers and her smile faltered. Her eyes became hard. "I was just looking them over. I wasn't thinking of . . ."

"We talked about this, Delia."

"What, five years ago, more? Things are different now. You're back at university. I can quit work. Ed," she said, something like a plea in her tone, "we'd be perfect. They're looking for people like us."

He sat down on the grass, laid the brochure down between himself and his wife. The wind caught the cover, riffled pages. He saw a gallery of beseeching faces staring out at him, soft focus shots designed to pluck at the heartstrings of childless couples like themselves.

He reached out and stopped the pages. He stared at the picture of a small blonde-haired girl. She reminded him of the kid who'd asked for his signature at the golf course the other day.

And, despite himself, he felt a longing somewhere deep within him like an ache.

"Why are you so against the idea, Ed?"

They had planned to start a family in the early years. Then Delia discovered that she was unable to bear children. He had grown used to the idea that their marriage would be childless, though it was harder for Delia to accept. Over the years he had devoted himself to his wife, and when five years ago she had first mentioned the possibility of adoption, he had told her he loved her so much that he would be unable to share that love with a child. He was bullshitting, of course. The fact was that he did not want Delia's love for him diluted by another.

And now? Now, he felt the occasional craving to lavish love and affection on a child, and he knew he would find it hard to explain his uneasiness to Delia.

Look at the world, he wanted to say to her. Look at the mess we've made of the place: it's one disaster after another, war after ecological foul-up after war . . . Was the world really any place in which to bring up a child? Even if they adopted, then how would he sleep at night knowing that the future would be hideously bleak for a child he loved?

He shook his head, wordlessly, then stood and returned to the house.

The following day Delia sought him out in his study. He'd retreated there shortly after breakfast, and for the past hour had been staring at his replica sixteenth-century globe of the world. He considered the crude, formless shapes that over the years had been redefined as countries and continents.

Terra incognita . . .

A sound interrupted his reverie. Delia paused by the door, one hand touching the jamb. She was carrying a newspaper.

She entered the room and sat down on the very edge of the armchair beside the bookcase. He managed a smile.

"You haven't been yourself since you got back."

"I'm sorry. It must be the strain. I'm tired."

She let the silence develop. "Did you know, there were stories at the time? The 'net was buzzing with rumours, speculation."

He smiled at that. "I should hope so. Humankind's first landing on Mars . . . "

"Besides that, Ed. When you fell, and the broadcast was suddenly cut."

"What were they saying? That we'd been captured by little green men?"

"Not in so many words. But they were speculating, said you might have stumbled across some sign of life up there." She stopped, then said, "Well?"

"Well, what?"

"What happened?"

He sighed. "So you'd rather believe some crazy press report—"

She stopped him by holding out the morning paper. The headline of the *Miami Tribune* ran: Life on Mars?

He took the paper and read the report.

Speculation was growing today surrounding man's first landing on the red planet. Leaks from NASA suggest that astronauts McCarthy, Jeffries, Enright, and Spirek discovered ancient ruins on their second exploratory tour of the red planet. Unconfirmed reports suggest that . . .

Enright stopped reading and passed the paper back to his wife.

"Unconfirmed reports, rumours. Typical press speculation."

"So nothing happened?"

"What do you want me to say? I fell down a hole, but I didn't find Wonderland down there."

Later, when she left without another word, he chastised himself for such a cheap parting shot.

He hadn't found Wonderland down there, but something far stranger instead.

So the leaks had begun. Maybe he should tell Delia, before she found out from the paper.

For the rest of the morning, he went through the letters that had accumulated during his absence. He replied to a few and discarded others. Just as he was about to break for lunch, he came upon the letter from Connaught in England, with its distinctive King's head stamp.

He wondered what strange theory his eccentric pen pal might have come up with this time.

He opened the letter and unfolded a single sheet of high-quality notepaper. Usually there were dozens of pages in his tiny, meticulous handwriting.

Enright read the letter, no more than three short paragraphs. Then he read it again, his mouth suddenly dry. He lay the sheet on his knee, and his hands were trembling.

Dear Ed, he read, *I have been following your exploits on the red planet with interest and concern. By now you will have returned, and I hope you will read this letter at the earliest opportunity. I was watching the broadcast from the Amazonis Planitia, which was suddenly terminated in strange circumstances . . . I wondered if humankind had at last found that life once existed on Mars. Ed, my friend, if you did indeed discover something beneath the sands of Mars, I think I can furnish an explanation.*

If you would care to visit me at the manor at the earliest opportunity, I have a rather interesting story to tell.

If you need further convincing that your trip might prove worthwhile, I can but write the words: Ulla, ulla . . .
Your very good friend,
Joshua Connaught

Enright read the letter perhaps a dozen times, before folding it away and staring at the far wall for long minutes.

If the original discovery had struck him as an irresolvable enigma, then this only compounded the sense of mystery.

He reached for the phone and made immediate plans to fly to England.

Over lunch, he told Delia that NASA had recalled him. He'd be up at the Space Center for just under a week.

"Is it about what happened on Mars?"

How much to tell her? "Delia, when I get back . . . I think I'll be able to tell you something, okay?"

She smiled and squeezed his hand.

And the words Connaught had scrawled at the end of his letter came back to him.

Ulla, ulla.

He had fetched up on his butt at the bottom of the landslide and stared about him in wonder. The dust had settled, and bright sunlight penetrated the chamber for the first time in who knew how long.

Through the dust and the glare he made out an array of towering shapes ranged along the walls of the chamber. He had fallen perhaps fifty feet, and the shapes— the machines—were almost that tall.

"Oh, Christ," he cried. "Spirek . . . *Spirek!*"

In his ear he heard, "You okay, Ed? You hear me? Are you okay?"

"Sal! You gotta see this."

"Ed, where are you?"

He looked up. Sal was a tiny, silver-suited figure bobbing about on the lip of the drop, trying to see him.

He waved. "Get yourself down here, Sal. You've gotta see this!"

In his headset he heard McCarthy shouting, "What's going on out there, Enright? Spirek?"

"You getting the pics, McCarthy?" Enright asked.

"Is your camera working? The picture went haywire when you fell."

He checked the camera. It had ceased filming at some point during his descent. He activated it again and swept the head-mounted lens around the chamber. He could see now that a section of the ceiling had sunk over the years, and the pressure of his weight upon it had brought the slab crashing down, and tons of sand with it.

McCarthy: "It's all hazy, Enright. Can't see much."

Enright stood, tested his limbs. He was fine. No breaks. He stepped forward, out of the direct sunlight, and stared at the ranked machinery that disappeared into the perspective.

"Hellfire in heaven!" Jeffries murmured.

Spirek was still peering down at him, unsure whether to negotiate the landslide.

"Ed, are you gonna tell me?"

He peered up at her. "Get yourself down here, Sal!"

She hesitated, then stepped forward and rode the sliding sand down to him like a kid on a dune.

She lost her footing and sprawled on her back. Enright helped her up. He was still holding her hand, staring past her faceplate to watch her expression, as she turned and looked down the length of the chamber.

She said nothing, but tears welled in her eyes.

Then, without a word, spontaneously, they embraced.

Hand in hand, like frightened kids, they walked down the chamber.

They approached the machinery, the *craft*, rather. There were dozens of them, each one tall and columnar and bulky. They were dark shapes, seemingly oiled, silent, and static, and yet every one upright and aimed, seemingly poised with intent.

Then they came to a smaller piece of machinery, perhaps half the height of the columns. Enright stopped, and stared.

He could not help himself: he began weeping.

"Ed?" Sal said, gripping his hand in sudden fear.

He indicated the looming, legged, vehicle.

She shook her head. "So what? I don't see...?"

In his headset, Enright heard McCarthy, "Hey, you two oughtta be heading back now. Sal, how much air you got there?"

Sal swore. "Dammit, Ed. We gotta be getting back."

He was staring up at the vehicle, mesmerised. "Ed!" Sal called again.

Reluctantly, Enright turned and followed Sal back up the landslide to the Marsmobile.

England, in contrast to sun-soaked Florida, was caught in the grip of its fiercest winter for years. From the window seat of the plane as it came in to land, Enright stared down at a landscape sealed in an otherworldly radiance of snow. This was the first time he had seen snow for almost twenty years, and he thought the effect cleansing: it gave mundane terrain a transformed appearance, bright and pristine: it looked like a land where miracles might easily occur.

He caught a Southern Line train from Heathrow to the village of Barton Humble in Dorset, and from there a taxi to Brimscombe Manor.

For the duration of the ten-mile drive, Enright stared out at a landscape every bit as alien and fascinating as the terrain of Mars. He seemed to be travelling deep into the heart of ancient countryside: everything about England, he noted, possessed a quality of age, of history and permanence, entirely lacking in the American environment to which he was accustomed. The lanes were deep and rutted, with high hedges, more suited to bullock-carts than automobiles. They passed an ancient forest of oak, the dark, winter-stark trees bearing ghostly doppelgängers of themselves in the burden of snow that limned every branch.

Brimscombe Manor, when it finally appeared, standing between the forest and a low rise of hills, was vast and sprawling, possessed of a tumbledown gentility that put Enright in mind of fading country houses in the quaint black and white British films he'd watched as a child.

The driver took one look at the foot-thick mantle of snow that covered the drive of the manor, and shook his head. "Okay if I drop you here?"

Enright paid him off with unfamiliar currency, retrieved his bag from the backseat, and stood staring at the imposing façade of the manor as the taxi drove away.

He felt suddenly alone in the alien environment. He knew the sensation well. The last time he had experienced this gut-wrenching sense of dislocation, he had been on Mars.

What the hell, he wondered, am I doing here? He had the sudden vision of himself, a US astronaut, standing forlornly in the depths of the English countryside on a freezing December afternoon, and smiled to himself.

"Ulla, ulla," he said, and his breath plumed in the icy air before him, the effect at once novel and disconcerting. "I'm going mad."

He set off through the snow. His boots compacted ice crystals in a series of tight, musical squeaks.

A light burned, orange and inviting, behind a mullioned window in the west wing of the manor. He climbed a sweep of steps and found the bell push.

The vast timber door swung open, and heat and light flooded out to greet him.

"Mr Enright, Ed, you can't imagine how delighted I am . . . "

Within seconds of setting eyes upon his long-term correspondent, Enright felt at ease. Connaught had the kind of open, amiable face that Enright associated with English character-actors of the old school: he guessed Connaught was in his early sixties, medium height, with a full head of grey hair, a wide smiling mouth, and blue eyes.

He wore tweeds, and a waistcoat with a fob watch on a silver chain.

"You must be exhausted after the journey. It's appalling out there." He escorted Enright across the great hallway. "Ten below all week. Record, so I'm told. Coldest cold snap for sixty years. You'll want a drink, and then dinner. I'll show you to your room. As soon as you've refreshed yourself, join me in the library."

He indicated a room to the right, through an open door. Enright glimpsed a roaring open fire and rank upon rank of books. "This is the library, and right next door is your room. I hope you don't mind sleeping on the ground floor. I live here alone now, and since Liz passed away I don't bother with the upstairs rooms. Cheaper, you see. Here we are."

He showed Enright into a room with a double bed and an *en suite* bathroom, then excused himself and left.

Enright sat on the bed, staring through the window at the snow-covered lawn and the drive. The only blemish in the snow was his footprints, which a fresh fall was already filling in.

He showered, changed, and ventured next door to the library.

Connaught stood beside a trolley of drinks. "Scotch? Brandy?"

He accepted a brandy and sat on a leather settee before the open fire. Connaught sat to the right of the fire in a big, high-backed armchair.

He surprised himself by falling into a polite exchange of small talk. His curiosity was such that all he wanted from Connaught was an explanation of the letter which he carried, folded, in his hip pocket.

Ulla, ulla . . .

He fitted sound bites and observations around Connaught's questions and comments.

"The flight was fine—a tailwind pushed us all the way, cutting an hour and a half off the expected time...

"England surprises me. Everything seems so old, and *small*...

"I'm impressed by the manor. We don't have anything quite like this back home."

And then they were discussing the history of manned space exploration. Connaught was extremely knowledgeable, indeed more so than Enright, in his grasp of the political cut and thrust of the space race.

An hour had elapsed in pleasant conversation, and still he had not broached the reason for his visit.

Connaught glanced at the carriage clock on the mantelshelf. "Eight already! Let's continue the conversation over dinner, shall we?"

He ushered Enright along the hall and into a comfortable lounge with a table, laid for two, in a recessed area by the window.

A steaming casserole dish, a bowl of vegetables, and a bottle of opened wine, stood on the table.

Connaught gestured to a seat. "I hire a woman from the village," he explained. "Heavenly cook. Comes in for a couple of hours a day and does for me."

They ate. Steak-and-kidney casserole, roast potatoes, carrots, and asparagus. They finished off the first bottle and started into a second.

The night progressed. Enright relaxed, drank more wine.

The amicable tenor of their correspondence was maintained, he was delighted to find, in their conversation. He contrasted the humane Connaught with the bullish egomaniac of McCarthy.

Ulla, ulla...

Suddenly, the conversation switched—and it was Connaught who instigated the change.

"Of course, I watched every second of the Mars coverage. I was glued to the TV. I hoped and prayed that your team might discover something there, though of course I was prepared for disappointment... I'll tell you something, Ed. I harboured the desire to be an astronaut myself, when I was young. Just a dream, of course. Never did anything about it. I fantasised about discovering new worlds, alien civilisations."

Enright smiled. "I never had that kind of ambition. I slipped into the space program almost by accident. They wanted a geologist on the mission, and I volunteered." He hesitated. "So when I stepped out onto Mars, of course the last thing on my mind was the discovery of an alien civilisation."

"I was watching the broadcast when you fell. The moment you said those words, I knew. Your tone of disbelieving wonder told me. I just knew you'd found something."

Connaught refilled the glasses. "What happened, Ed? Tell me in your own words how you came to ... "

So he recounted the landing, his first walk on the surface of Mars, and then his second. He worked up to his fall, and the discovery, like an expert storyteller. He found he was enjoying his role of raconteur ...

They arrived back at the lander, after the discovery, with just two minutes' air supply remaining.

McCarthy and Jeffries were standing in the living quarters when they cycled through the hatch and discarded their suits. They were white-faced and silent.

Enright looked around the group, shaking his head. Words, at this moment, seemed beyond him.

McCarthy said, "Mission control went ballistic. You should hear Roberts. Wait till this breaks!"

Sal Spirek slumped into a seat. "We're famous, gentlemen. I think that this just might be the most momentous occasion in the history of humankind, or am I exaggerating?"

They stared around at each other, trying to work out if she was indeed exaggerating.

Enright was shaking his head.

"What is it?" Sal asked.

He could not find the words to articulate what even he found hard to believe. "You don't understand," he began.

Sal said, "What's wrong?"

"Those things back there," Enright said, "the cylindrical rockets and three-legged machines." He stared around at their uncomprehending faces. "Have none of you ever read *The War of the Worlds*?"

Six hours later, with the go-ahead of Roberts at mission control, all four astronauts suited up and rode the Mars-mobile to the subterranean chamber.

As he negotiated the sloping drift of red sand, Enright half-expected to find the cavern empty, the cylinders and tripods revealed to be nothing other than a figment of his imagination.

He paused at the foot of the drift, Sal by his side, McCarthy and Jeffries bringing up the rear and gasping as they stared at the alien machinery diminishing in perspective.

He and Sal walked side by side down the length of the chamber, passing from bright sunlight into shadow. He switched on his shoulder-mounted flashlight and stared at the vast, cylindrical rockets arrayed along the chamber. They were mounted on a complex series of frames, and canted at an angle of a few degrees from the perpendicular.

They paused before a smaller machine, consisting of a cowled dome atop three long, multi-jointed legs.

McCarthy and Jeffries joined them.

"Fighting Machines," Enright said.

McCarthy looked at him. "Say again?"

"Wells called them Fighting Machines," he said. "In his book—"

He stopped then, as the implications of what he was saying slowly dawned on him.

He walked on, down the aisle between the examples of an alien culture's redundant hardware. The atmosphere within the chamber was that of a museum, or a mausoleum.

McCarthy was by his side. "You really expect us to believe . . . ?" he began.

Spirek said, "I've read *The War of the Worlds*, McCarthy. Christ, but Wells got it right. The cylinders, the Fighting Machines . . . "

"That's impossible!"

Enright said, "It's all here, McCarthy. Just as Wells described it."

McCarthy looked at him, his expression lost in the shadow behind his faceplate. "How do you explain it, Enright?"

He shrugged. "I don't. I can't. God knows."

"Here!" Spirek had moved off, and was kneeling beside something in the shadow of a tripod.

"The hardware wasn't all Wells got right." She gestured. "Look . . . "

Mummified in the airless vault for who knew how long, the Martian was much as the Victorian writer had described them in his novel of alien invasion, one hundred and twenty years before.

It was all head, with two vast, dull eyes the size of saucers, and a beak, with tentacles below that—tentacles that Wells had speculated the aliens had walked upon. It was, Enright thought, more hideous than anything he had ever seen before.

Enright walked on, and found more and more of the dead aliens scattered about the chamber.

Jeffries said, "I'll get all this back to Roberts. We need to work out strategy."

Enright looked at him. "Strategy?"

Jeffries gestured around him. "This is a security risk, Enright. I'm talking an AI security risk, here. How do we know these monsters aren't planning an invasion right now? Isn't that what the book was about?"

Enright and Spirek exchanged a glance.

"The Martians are dead, Jeffries," Spirek said. "Their planet was dying. They lived underground, but air and food was running out. They died out before they could get away."

"You don't know that, Sal," Jeffries said. "You're speculating."

Enright strode off. He needed isolation in which to consider his discovery.

He found other chambers through giant archways, and a series of ramps that gave access to even lower levels. He imagined an entire city down there, a vast underground civilisation, long dead.

Sal Spirek joined him. "How did Wells know?" she asked. "How could he possibly have known?"

Enright recalled the last time he had read the novel, in his teens. He had been haunted by the description of a ravaged, desolate London in the aftermath of the alien invasion. He recalled the cry of the Martians as they succumbed to a deadly Terran virus, the mournful lament that had echoed eerily across an otherwise deathly silent London. "Ulla, ulla, ulla, ulla..."

He had left Spirek and the others, wanting to be alone with his thoughts, and descended a ramp to another, deeper chamber. He came to a great door in the wall of the chamber, and through a wide triangular viewscreen or window had seen something which had sent his pulse racing. He turned and ran, clumsily, hardly able to believe what he had seen.

"Enright? You okay?" Jeffries was in the entrance of the chamber. "You seen something?"

Aware that he had to keep what he had seen to himself, he had said, "Nothing. Just more machinery and dead Martians..."

And he had followed Jeffries back up the ramp.

He told Connaught everything, barring his final discovery in the chamber.

"What was it like when I looked upon those ranked machines?" Enright shook his head. "I *felt* more than I *thought*, Joshua. I was overwhelmed with disbelief, and then elation, and then later, back at the ship, when I thought about it, a little fear. But at the time, when I first saw the machines ... it came as one hell of a shock when I realised why they were so familiar."

Connaught was nodding. "Wells," he said.

Enright let the silence stretch. "How did you know?" He leaned forward. "How did Wells know?"

Connaught stood. "How about a whiskey? I have some fine Irish here."

He moved across the room to a mahogany cabinet and poured two generous measures of Bushmills.

He returned to the table. Enright sipped his drink, feeling the mellow burn slide down his throat like hot velvet.

"My great-grandfather, James Connaught," he said, "inherited the manor from his father, who built the house in 1870 from profits made in the wine trade. James was a writer—unsuccessful and unpublished. He wrote what was known then as scientific romances. He self-published a couple of short books, to no great notice. To be honest, his imagination was his strong point—his literary ability was almost negligible. To cut a long story short, he was friendly with a young and aspiring writer at the time—this was the early 1890s. Chappie by the name of Wells. They spent many a weekend down here and swapped stories, ideas, plots, etc ... One story James told him was about the invasion of Earth by creatures from Mars. They came in vast cylinders, and stalked the earth aboard great marching war machines. Apparently, my great-grandfather had tried to write it up himself, but didn't get very far. Wells took the idea, and the rest is history. *The War of the Worlds*. A classic."

Connaught paused, staring into his glass.

Enright smiled, his mind full of H. G. Wells and James Connaught discussing story ideas in this very building, all those years ago.

"How," he asked at last, "how did your great-grandfather know about the Martians?"

He realised that he was drunk, his speech slurred. The sense of anticipation he felt swelling within him was almost unbearable.

"One night way back in 1880," Connaught said, "James was out walking the grounds. This was late, around midnight. He often took a turn around the garden at this time, looking for inspiration. Anyway, he saw something in the sky, something huge and fiery, coming in from the direction of the coast. It landed with a loud explosion in the spinney to the rear of the manor."

Enright leaned forward, reached for the whiskey bottle, and helped himself.

"James ran into the spinney," Connaught continued, "after the fallen object, and found there... He found a huge pit gouged into the ground, and in that pit a great cylindrical object, glowing red and steaming in the cold night."

Enright sat back in his chair and shook his head.

Joshua Connaught smiled. "You don't believe me?"

"No, it's just... I do believe you. It's just that it's so fantastic."

Connaught smiled. "I've heard it called threshold shift," he said. "Your consciousness of what is possible undergoes a shift, a moment of conceptual breakthrough, and nothing is ever the same again."

Enright laughed. "You can say that again."

Connaught went on, "My great-grandfather excavated the pit and built an enclosure around it, and it exists to this day. I've shown no one since Elizabeth."

Enright experienced a sudden dizziness. He made a feeble gesture.

Connaught smiled. "It's still there, Ed."

Enright shook his head. "*It?* You mean...?"

"The Martian cylinder, and other things."

Enright downed the last of his whiskey, felt it burning his throat.

Connaught stood. "Shall we go?"

Enright stood also, unsteadily. "Please, after you." Swaying, he followed Connaught from the room.

He expected to be taken outside, but instead Connaught led him through a narrow door and down a flight of even narrower steps. A succession of bare, low-watt bulbs illuminated a series of vaulted cellars, the first chambers stocked with wine, the later ones empty and musty.

They walked along a narrow red brick corridor.

"We're now passing from the manor and walking beneath the kitchen garden towards the spinney," Connaught reported over his shoulder.

Enright nodded, aware that he was sobering rapidly with the effects of the cold and the notion of what might imminently be revealed.

The corridor extended for five hundred yards, and terminated abruptly at a small wooden door.

Connaught drew a key from the pocket of his waistcoat and opened the door. He stood aside, gesturing for Enright to enter.

Cautiously, he stepped over the threshold.

He faced an abyss of darkness, until Connaught reached past him and threw a switch.

A dozen bare bulbs illuminated a vast rectangular redbrick room perhaps a hundred feet long. The walls were concave, bowed like the hull of a galleon. A series of rough wooden steps led down to the floor, again of red brick.

The cylinder lay in the centre of the room, a long, gunmetal grey column identical to those he had seen in the chamber on Mars. At the facing end of the cylinder was a circular opening. Beside the cylinder, laid out lengthways, was one of the Fighting Machines.

Enright climbed down the steps, aware that his mouth was hanging open. He walked around the cylinder, its dimensions dwarfing him and Connaught. He reached out and touched the icy cold surface of the cylinder, something he had been unable to do on Mars. He inspected the tripod, marvelling at the intricacy of the metalwork—crafted far away on Mars by a race other than human.

"According to the story," Connaught said, "that night James crouched on the edge of the pit and watched fearfully as the great threaded stopper slowly unscrewed and fell out. He waited, but hours elapsed and nothing emerged other than a strange, otherworldly cry, 'Ulla, ulla, ulla, ulla.' It was daybreak before he plucked up the courage to scramble down into the pit and approach the cylinder. There were three beings in the craft, he could see by the light of dawn, but they were dead. Fortunately, the spinney was on his land, and anyway the trees concealed the pit from view. Over the course of the following year, working alone, he built this construction around the craft, and then devoted the rest of his life to the study of its contents. He and his son, my grandfather, found the tripod inside the cylindrical ship, pulled it out piece by piece, and reconstructed it. They even attempted to preserve the dead aliens, but they rotted almost to nothing with the passage of years."

Enright looked up. "Almost nothing?"

Connaught walked over to a raised wooden platform. Upon this was a big desk, and piles of papers and manuals, illuminated by a reading lamp. He gestured to a bulbous preserving jar, floating in which was a grey-brown scrap of what looked like hide.

"This is all that remains of the first alien beings to arrive on planet Earth," Connaught said.

"Did James show Wells all this?" Enright asked.

Connaught shook his head. "It was a strict secret, at the time known only to James and his son. As I said, he gave Wells the idea as a fiction, but supplied him with detailed drawings of the cylinder and the other machinery, and even of the aliens themselves, and their death cry."

"And you've never shown anyone outside the family, until now?"

Connaught smiled. "By the time my father found out, the truth of what had happened was lost in time. My grandfather was old when he showed my father the cylinder—his memory was not what it was. My father took the story with a pinch of salt. He rationalised that James had manufactured the cylinder himself, and the tripod. My father sealed the chamber, and only showed it to me when I was down here exploring, and asked about the mysterious bricked-up door."

"And yet you believed James's story?" Enright said.

Connaught hesitated. "I was at Oxford in the seventies," he said, "studying ancient literature. Later I found myself working for the government, decrypting codes . . . When I inherited the manor, I inspected this chamber and everything it contained."

He moved to the desk and unlocked a drawer. From it he produced a thick, silver object that looked something like a book.

He laid it upon the desk and opened the cover. The pages were also silver, manufactured from some thin metallic material, and upon each leaf of the book Enright made out, in vertical columns, what might have been lines of script. But it was a script unlike any he had ever seen before.

"James discovered this in the cylinder. For years and years he worked at decoding the book from the stars, as he called it. He failed. When I came across it, I began where my great-grandfather had left off."

Enright stared at him. "And you succeeded?"

Connaught bent and unlocked another drawer. From this he lifted a more conventional manuscript, a ream of A4 paper in a clip folder.

"I succeeded," he said, "and last year finished translating the book. Much of it is an encyclopaedia of their world, a history of their race. Mars was dying, Ed. Millennia ago, the beings that had dwelled on the surface of the planet were forced to move underground, out of the inhospitable cold. Their numbers dwindled, until only tens of thousands survived. They realised that they had to leave their planet."

"And invade Earth," Enright finished.

But Connaught was smiling and shaking his head. "They were a peaceful people. Only in Wells's fiction were they belligerent."

He reached out and opened the cover of his translation. "Please," he said.

Enright stepped forward, his pulse pounding, and read the first paragraph.

We of the fourth planet of the solar system, the planet we call Vularia, come to the third planet on a mission of peace. Although our kind has known enmity, and fought debilitating wars, we have outgrown this stage of our evolution. We come with the hope that our two races might join as one and explore the universe together...

Enright stopped reading, aware of the constriction in his throat. He leafed through more than five hundred pages of closely printed text.

He thought of McCarthy, and Jeffries, and the military operation underway right at this minute.

"Over half a million words," Connaught said. "You can hardly begin to conceive what a treasure it is."

Enright turned and walked away from the desk. He stared at the cylinder, and the so-called Fighting Machine.

Behind him, Connaught was saying, "My great-grandfather guessed that they were dying before they arrived on Earth—that it was not an earthly virus that ended their existence, but one of their own. How wonderful it might have been, had they survived."

Enright smiled to himself.

He turned and looked at Connaught. "Why, Joshua? Why have you shown me all this? Your translation?"

"Why else? This has been a secret long enough. Now, my life's work is finished, the translation done—I would like to receive acknowledgement, in due course. I summoned you here so that you might take this copy of the translation back to America, to answer the mystery of what you discovered beneath the sands of Mars."

He gestured towards the door. "Come, it's cold in here. Shall we retire to the library for a nightcap?"

With one last glance at the Martian machines, he turned and followed Connaught from the chamber.

Later, before the open fire, Enright said, "They're sending a military mission to Mars, Joshua."

The old man smiled. "Forgive me if I say that that is typical of your government." He laughed. "A military mission to rout the ghosts of long-dead Martians!"

Enright looked up from his whiskey and stared at Connaught. "Joshua, there's something I haven't told you. Something I've told no one, yet." He paused and smiled to himself, then said, "I'm sickened by the thought of my government sending a hostile mission to Mars—"

"But, Ed, all they'll find is..."

The old man stopped, his words halted by something in Enright's expression.

"They'll find a race of Martians," he said. "The survivors. I saw them in one of the lower chambers. Dozens of them. I have no doubt that we would have rounded them up and imprisoned them, at best. Perhaps, if I take your document to the right people, the more farsighted among my countrymen might see sense..."

They raised their glasses in a toast to that.

On the flight back to America, Enright dreamed. He was in London, but a London laid waste by some apocalyptic war. He strode through the ruins, listening. He was not alone. Beside him was a child, a small girl, and when he looked upon her he was filled with a strange sense of hope for the future, a hope like elation. The girl slipped a hand in to his, and at that moment Enright heard it. Faint at first, and then stronger. It was the saddest, most haunting sound he had ever heard in his life.

"Ulla, ulla, ulla, ulla..."

Then he saw the Martian standing amid the ruins, and it came to him that its call was not one of desolation, after all.

He awoke with a start. The sensation of the small, warm hand in his was so real that he glanced at the seat beside him, but it was empty.

The plane was banking. They were coming in to land at Orlando.

Enright pulled his briefcase containing the Martian translation from beneath the seat and held it tight.

We of the fourth planet of the solar system, the planet we call Vularia, come to the third planet on a mission of peace...

He smiled to himself, closed his eyes, and thought of Delia, and home, and the future.

THURSDAY'S CHILD

Although not in any way religious myself, I'm interested in religion, the religious impulse, and what a belief in a higher power can drive people to do, for good and for bad. The following story, one of the Kéthani sequence, examines the polarised viewpoints of two people with very different opinions about the arrival of aliens from the stars and their gift of immortality to the human race.

THURSDAY'S CHILD

I CRESTED THE HILL, PULLED THE RANGE ROVER INTO THE SIDE OF THE lane and stared through the windscreen. There was something about the freezing February landscape, with the westering sun laying a gold leaf patina over the snow-covered farmland in the valley bottom, that struck me as even more beautiful than the same scene in summer.

I took a deep breath and worked to control my anger. It was always the same when I collected Lucy from Marianne. I had to stop somewhere and calm myself.

I was on call for the next hour, but calculated that the chances of being summoned during that time were slight. Marianne would object to my early arrival, but Lucy would be eager to get away. I told myself that I arrived early on these occasions so that I'd have an extra hour with my daughter, but I wondered if, subconsciously, I did it on purpose to spite Marianne.

I started the engine and cruised down the hill. Three minutes later I entered the village of Hockton and pulled up outside a row of cottages, each one quaintly bonneted with a thick mantle of snow.

A light glowed behind the mullioned window of Marianne's front room. Lucy would be watching a DVD of her latest favourite film.

I pressed the horn twice, my signal to Lucy that I was here, and climbed out.

Lucy had hauled the door open before I reached the gate, and only the fact that she was in her stockinged feet prevented her rushing out to meet me.

She was a beautiful skinny kid, six years old, with a pale elfin face and long black hair. My heart always kicked at the sight of her, after an absence of days.

She seemed a little subdued today: usually she would launch herself into my arms. I stepped inside and picked her up, her long legs around my waist, and kissed her nose, lips, neck in an exaggerated pantomime of affection which made her giggle.

"Love you," I said. "Bag packed?"

"Mmm."

"Where's your mum?"

"I think in the kitchen."

"Get your bag and put some shoes on. I'll just pop through and tell her I'm here."

She skipped into the front room and I moved towards the kitchen, a psycho-somatic pain starting in my gut.

Marianne was peeling carrots at the draining board, her back to me. "You're early again, Daniel," she said without turning. She knew I disliked the long form of my name.

I leaned against the jamb of the door. "I was in the area, working."

She turned quickly, knife in her hand, and stared at me. "You mean to say you have a body with you?"

She was a small, pretty woman, an adult version of Lucy. In the early days of our separation, alternating with the anger, I had experienced a soul-destroying sorrow that all the love I'd felt for this woman had turned to hate.

I should have seen what might have happened before we married, extrapolated from her beliefs—but at the time my love for her had allowed no doubt.

Lately she had taken to wearing a big wooden crucifix around her neck. Her left temple was not implanted and neither, thanks to her, was Lucy's.

"Not all my work involves collection," I said. "What time should I bring her back on Thursday?"

"I'm working till five." She turned and resumed her peeling.

I pushed myself away from the door and moved to the lounge. Lucy was sitting on the floor, forcing her feet into a pair of trainers. I picked up her bag and she ran into the kitchen for a goodbye kiss. Marianne, the bitch, didn't even come to the door to wave her off.

I led Lucy to the Range Rover and fastened her into the car-seat in the back. When I started collecting her, a year ago, she had said that she wanted to sit in the front, next to me. "But why can't I?" she had wailed.

How could I begin to explain my paranoia? "Because it's safer in case of accidents," I'd told her.

I set off along the road back to Oxenworth, ten miles away over the moors.

"Enjoying your holidays?" I asked.

"Bit boring."

I glanced at her in the rear-view mirror. "You okay?"

She hesitated. "Feeling a bit rough," she said, and to illustrate pantomimed a hacking cough into her right fist.

"Did Mum take you to the doctor's?"

I saw her nod.

"And?" I asked.

"He gave me some pills."

"Pills?" I said. "What did he say was wrong?"

She looked away, through the window. "I don't know."

"Do you have the pills with you?" Perhaps I'd be able to determine her ailment from the medication.

She shook her head. "Mummy said I didn't need them."

I decided to ring Marianne when we got back, find out what was going on. Or was this yet another manifestation of my paranoia?

We drove on in silence for a while. Cresting the snow-covered moorland, we passed the glittering obelisk of the Onward Station. It never failed to provoke a feeling of awe in me—and I saw the Station every working day. Quite apart what it represented, it was perhaps aesthetically the most beautiful object I had ever seen.

I wondered if it was the sight of it which prompted Lucy to say, "Daddy, the girls at school have been making fun of me."

I glanced at her in the rear-view mirror. "Why's that?"

"It's because I'm not implanted. They say I'll die."

I shook my head, wondering how to respond. "They're just being silly," I said.

"But if I have an accident..." she began.

"Don't worry," I said, marvelling at the fact that she was only six years old, and yet had worked out the consequences of not being implanted. "You won't have an accident."

Then she asked, "Why aren't I implanted?"

It was the first time she had ever mentioned the fact, and it was a while before I replied. "Because Mum doesn't want you to be," I said.

"But *why* doesn't she?"

"I think you'd better ask her that yourself," I said. I changed the subject. "How about a meal at the Fleece when we get back? Would you like that?"

"Mmm," she said, without her usual enthusiasm for the idea, and fell silent.

———.———

We were a couple of miles from home when my mobile rang. I cursed.

"Dan Chester here," I said, hoping the collection would be nearby.

"Dan." It was Masters, the Controller at the Station. "I've just had a call from someone over in Bradley. This is most irregular. They've reported a death."

I slowed down, the better to concentrate. "I don't understand. Was the subject implanted?"

"Apparently so—"

"Then why didn't it register with you?"

"Exactly what I was wondering. That's why I want you to investigate. I'm sending a team from the Station straight away, but I thought that as you're in the area..."

I sighed. "Okay. Where is it?"

Masters relayed the address.

"Right. I'll be in touch when I've found out what's going on." I cut the connection.

Bradley was only a mile or two out of my way. I could be there in ten minutes, sort out the problem in the same time, and be at the Fleece with a pint within the half-hour.

I glanced back at Lucy. She was asleep, her head nodding with the motion of the Rover.

The Grange, Bradley Lower Road, turned out to be a Georgian house tucked away in a dense copse a mile down a treacherous, rutted track. The Range Rover negotiated the potholes with ease, rocking back and forth like a fairground ride.

Only when the foursquare manse came into view, surrounded by denuded elm and sycamore, did I remember hearing that the Grange had been bought at a knockdown price a few years ago by some kind of New Age eco-community.

A great painted rainbow decorated the façade of the building, together with a collection of smiley faces, peace symbols and anarchist logos.

A motley group of men and women in their thirties had gathered on the steps of the front door, evidently awaiting my arrival. They wore dungarees and oversized cardigans and sweaters; many of them sported dreadlocks.

Lucy was still sleeping. I locked the Rover and hurried over to the waiting group, a briefcase containing release forms and death certificates tucked under my arm.

A stout woman with a positive comet's tail of blonde dreadlocks greeted me. I was pleased to see that she was implanted—as were, a brief glance told me, most of the other men and women standing behind her. Some radical groups I'd heard of were opposed to the intervention of the Kéthani, and openly hostile to their representatives.

"Dan Chester," I said. "I'm the ferryman from the Station."

"Dan, I'm Marsha," the woman said. "Welcome to New Haven. I'll show you to..."

The press parted, and Marsha escorted me across a garishly painted hallway and down a corridor.

Marsha was saying, "Sanjay was against the resurrection process, Dan. We were surprised when he decided to be implanted, a couple of weeks ago." She paused outside a door, pushed it open and stood back. I stepped over the threshold and stopped in my tracks.

Sanjay lay on a mattress in the corner of the room. He had opened the vein of his left arm all the way from the wrist to the crook of his elbow.

Blood had spurted up the far wall, across the window, and soaked into the mattress around the body.

"Billy found him about thirty minutes ago," Marsha was explaining. "We knew Sanjay was depressed, but we never thought..."

I took in the scene, and knew immediately that there was something not quite right about the corpse. By now the nanomechs released by his implant should have been effecting repairs on the wound. The body should have the relaxed appearance of someone asleep, not the stone-cold aspect of a corpse.

I glanced over my shoulder; Marsha and half a dozen others were watching him from the door. "If I could be left alone for a minute or two..." I said.

They retreated, closing the door behind them.

I pulled out my mobile and got through to Masters at the Station.

"Dan here," I said. "I'm with the subject. You're not going to believe this—he's implanted, but he's dead."

"That's impossible."

"Perhaps... I don't know. I've never heard of a malfunction before. But there's always a first time."

"No way," Masters said. "They can't go wrong."

"Well, it looks as though this one has." I paused. "What the hell should I do?"

"The team should be with you any minute. I've called the police. They'll take over once they arrive."

I cut the connection, moved to the window and stared out, touching my own implant. I avoided another glance at the corpse, but I knew I would see the man's agonised expression for a long time to come. He had been implanted, and had taken his own life, fully expecting to be resurrected to begin a new life among the stars.

Five minutes later I watched another Range Rover draw up beside mine, followed by a police car. Four Station officials, led by Richard Lincoln, hurried across the snow-covered drive and up the steps, two constables in their wake.

A minute later Richard appeared at the door, along with the officials and the police officers.

"What the hell's going on, Dan?" Richard said.

"I wish I knew." I indicated the corpse and went though my findings. The other officials recorded my statement and took video footage of the room.

Richard questioned Marsha and a few of the others, while the Station officials fetched a container and eased the body inside.

I followed Richard outside and climbed into the Rover. Lucy was still asleep.

Richard tramped through the snow and I wound down the window. "We'll take the body back to the Station," he said, "try to find out what happened with the implant."

I looked beyond him, to the posse of communees on the steps of the Grange, silent and watchful.

"Has anyone told them?"

Richard shook his head. "I'll come back and explain the situation when we've found out exactly what happened. See you later, Dan."

I fired the engine and headed up the track. The Fleece beckoned. I considered a rich pint of Taylor's Landlord and a hot meal, and tried to forget about what I'd seen back at the Grange.

The Fleece was one of those horse-brass and beams establishments that had resisted the tide of modernisation sweeping the country. Norman, the landlord, had the twin assets of a good publican: friendliness and the ability to keep a good pint. The food wasn't bad, either.

It was seven o'clock by the time we settled ourselves in the bar room, a little too early for the regular Tuesday night crowd. I ordered a pint of Landlord and steak and kidney pie with roast potatoes, and for Lucy a fresh orange juice and chicken nuggets with chips.

The food arrived. Lucy was far from her lively self tonight; she was tired and hardly talked, answered my questions with monosyllabic replies and pushed her food around the plate with a distinct lack of interest.

I put my arm around her shoulders and pulled her towards me. "Home and an early night for you, m'girl."

"Can I watch TV for a bit before I go to bed? *Please.*"

"Okay, seeing as there's no school in the morning."

I was about to suggest we leave when Khalid pushed through the door, a swirl of snow entering with him, and signalled across to me. He mimed downing a pint and pointed at my empty glass. I relented and gave him the thumbs-up.

No doubt Lucy would tell Marianne that I'd kept her at the pub way past her bedtime, and I wouldn't hear the last of it the next time I picked her up. Marianne thought alcohol the tipple of the devil, and all who drank it damned.

Khalid ferried two pints from the bar and sat down across the table from me.

"Hi, sleepyhead," he said to Lucy. Her eyelids were fighting a losing battle.

"Just the man," Khalid said to me. "I hoped you'd be here."

"It's Tuesday night," I said. "What's wrong?"

"The implanted suicide you investigated today . . . "

Khalid Azzam was a medic working at Bradley General, in charge of the Implant ward. I'd met him a couple of years ago when he moved to the village from Bradford. He and his wife Zara were regulars on Tuesday nights.

"Masters contacted you?" I asked.

"They brought the body in and I inspected the implant."

I voiced what I'd been dreading since discovering the dead man. "It mal-functioned, right?"

"Malfunctioned?" Khalid shook his head and accounted for the top two inches of his pint. He sighed with satisfaction. "I'd say that was well nigh impossible."

"So . . . ?"

"This is only the second case I've come across, but I've heard rumours that they're more widespread than we first believed."

He took another mouthful.

"What," I said, unable to stop myself smiling, "is more widespread?"

"This is between you and me, okay? Don't tell Masters I said anything. Your people at the Station have yet to come out with an official statement." He leaned forward, a little melodramatically—only Old Wilf was at the bar, and he was stone deaf. "Some cowboys have started pirating fake implants."

I lowered my pint and stared at him. "Why on earth . . . ?" I began.

"It was only a matter of time," Khalid said. "Think about it. There are thousands of people out there who refuse for whatever reasons to be implanted . . . " His eyes flickered, almost imperceptibly, towards Lucy. "They're . . . what? . . . one in a few hundred thousand? A minority, anyway. And like any minority, they occasionally suffer victimisation. Wouldn't it be easier, they reckon, if they could have something that looked like, but wasn't, an implant? They'd blend in, become one of the crowd. They would no longer stand out."

"It makes a kind of sense," I said. "And so some enterprising back-street surgeon has started offering the service?"

"Doesn't have to be a surgeon. Anyone with a little medical knowledge can perform the operation. A quick slit, insert something the same shape as an implant, and seal the wound with synthiflesh. Thirty minutes later you're back out on the street."

I thought through the implications. "But if these people don't inform friends, loved ones?"

He was nodding. "Exactly. Like today. Sanjay's friends thought he was implanted, and fully expected him to be resurrected."

"Christ," I said. "The whole thing's tragic."

"And there are thousands of people going around out there with these fake, useless implants. Masters said something about a law to make them illegal. He's talking to a few politicians tomorrow."

Lucy had stretched out on the seat next to me and was snoring away. Had she been awake and bored, guilt might have driven me homeward. As it was, I owed Khalid a pint, and at that very second Ben Knightly and Elisabeth Carstairs dashed in from the snowstorm that was evidently raging outside. I was off work for a couple of days, and I could treat myself to a lie-in in the morning.

I pointed to Khalid's empty glass. "Another?"

"You've twisted my arm."

I bought a second round. Ben and Elisabeth joined us and we stopped talking shop.

It was another hour, and two more pints, before conscience got the better of me. I refused all offers of more beer, eased the still sleeping Lucy into my arms, and carried her from the bar and along the street.

The cold had awoken her by the time I pushed through the front door. I carried her to her room, where she changed into her pyjamas. Five minutes later she was snuggling into my lap before the fire and we were watching a DVD of a French mime act, which apparently was the latest craze in kids' entertainment.

She was asleep ten minutes later, and I turned down the sound and switched over to a news programme. Half-awake myself, and cradling my daughter in my arms, I allowed a succession of images to wash over me and considered how lucky I was.

So I might have married the last religious zealot in North Yorkshire, but from that match made in Hell had issued Lucy Katia Chester. And to think that, back in my twenties, I'd vowed never to have children. I sometimes shudder to think of the joy I would have missed had I stuck to my bachelor principles.

A newscaster was reporting anti-Kéthani riots in Islamabad, but by then I was fading fast.

I took Lucy to Bolton Abbey the following day. I bundled her up in her chunky yellow parka, bobble hat and mittens against the biting cold, and we walked through the trees along the riverbank. Down below, the river was frozen for the first time in living memory, its usual quicksilver torrent paused in shattered slabs of grey and silver. Later we lobbed snowballs at each other among the stark ruins of the Abbey. It was quiet—no one else had dared to venture out, with the thermometer fifteen below zero—and to hear her laughter echoing in the stillness was a delight. I had quite forgotten to ring Marianne last night, to enquire about Lucy's illness, but she seemed fine today so I decided not to bother.

We had lunch in the Devonshire Arms across the road from the Abbey, and in the afternoon visited Marsworld, a couple of miles north of Skipton. We wandered around the replica rockets that had carried the scientific team to the red planet a couple of years ago, then visited mock-ups of the dozen domes where the explorers were living right at that moment. I had worried that Lucy might find it boring, but she turned out to be fascinated; she'd had lessons about the mission at school, and actually knew more about it than I did.

We drove home through the narrow lanes at four, with dusk rapidly falling. I proceeded with a caution I would not have shown had I been alone: I carried a precious cargo on the back seat... The only time I was truly content, and could rest easy, was when Lucy was with me. At other times, I envisaged, perhaps unfairly, the unthinking neglect with which Marianne might treat her.

"Do you know what would be nice, Daddy?" Lucy said now.

"What?" I asked, glancing at her in the rear-view.

"I would really like it if you and Mummy would live together again."

She had said this before, and always I had experienced a hopeless despair. I would have done anything to secure my daughter's happiness, but this was the one thing that I could not contemplate.

"Lucy, we can't do that. We have our separate lives now."

"Don't you love mummy any more?"

"Not in the same way that I once did," I said.

245

"But a little bit?" she went on.

"A little bit," I lied.

She was quiet for a time, and then said, "Why did you move away, Daddy? Was it because of me?"

I slowed down and looked at her in the mirror. "Of course not. What made you think—?"

"Mummy said that you stopped loving her because you couldn't agree about me," she said.

I gripped the wheel, anger welling. I might have hated the bitch, but I had kept that animosity to myself. Never once had I attempted to turn Lucy against her mother.

"That's not true, Lucy. We disagreed about a lot of things. What you've got to remember is that we both love you more than anything else, okay?"

We underestimate children's capacity for not being fobbed off with platitudes. Lucy said, "But the biggest thing you disagreed about was me, wasn't it? You wanted me to be implanted, and Mummy didn't."

I sighed. "That was one of the things."

"Mummy says that God doesn't want people to be implanted. If we're implanted, then we don't go to heaven. She says that the aliens are evil—she says that they're in the same football league as the Devil."

I smiled to myself. I just wanted to take Lucy in my arms and hug her to me. I concentrated on that, rather than on the anger I felt towards Marianne.

"That isn't true," I said. "God made everyone, even the Kéthani. If you're implanted, then you don't die. Eventually you can visit the stars, which I suppose is a kind of heaven."

She nodded, thinking about this. "But if I die, then I'll go to a different heaven?" she asked at last.

If you die without the implant, I thought, you will remain dead forever and ever, amen, and no Christian sky-god will effect your resurrection.

"That's what your mum thinks," I said.

She was relentless with her dogged six-year-old logic. "But what do *you* think, Daddy?"

"I think that in twelve years, when you're eighteen, you can make up your own mind. If you want, you can be implanted then." Twelve years, I thought: it seemed like an eternity.

"Hey," I said, "we're almost home. What do you want for dinner? Will you help me make it?"

"Spaghetti!" she cried, and for the rest of the journey lectured me on the proper way to make Bolognese sauce.

That evening, after we'd prepared spaghetti together and eaten it messily in front of the TV, Lucy slept next to me while I tried to concentrate on a documentary about ancient Egypt.

I could not erase memories of Marianne from my mind's eye.

I had met her ten years ago, when I was thirty. She was twenty-six, and I suspected that I was her very first boyfriend. At that time her Catholicism had intrigued me, her moral and ethical codes setting her apart in my mind from the hedonism I saw all around. The Kéthani had arrived the year before, and their gift of the implants had changed society forever: in the early days, many people adopted a devil-may-care attitude towards life—they were implanted, they could not die, so why not live for the day? Others opposed the changes.

I was implanted within a year of the Kéthani's arrival. I was not religious, and had always feared extinction: it had seemed natural to accept their gift of immortality, especially after the first returnees arrived back on Earth with the stories of their resurrection on the homeplanet of the Kéthani.

Not long after my implantation, I trained to become a ferryman—and but for this I might never have met Marianne. Her mother, an atheist and implanted, had died unexpectedly of a cerebral haemorrhage, and I had collected the body.

I had been immediately attracted to Marianne's physicality, and found her world view—during our many discussions in the weeks that followed our first date— intriguing, if absurd.

She thought the Kéthani evil, the implantation process an abomination in the eyes of the Lord, and looked forward to the day when she would die and join the virtuous in heaven.

She was appalled by my blithe acceptance of what I took to be our alien saviours.

We were married six months after our first meeting.

I was in love, whatever I thought that meant at the time. I loved her so much that I wanted to save her. It was only a matter of time, I thought, before she came to see that my acceptance of the Kéthani was sane and sensible.

She probably thought the reverse: given time, her arguments would bring about my religious salvation.

We had never spoken about what we might do if we had children. She was a successful accountant for a firm in Leeds, and told me that she did not want children. She fell pregnant despite our precautions, but I often wondered since whether she had intended conceiving a child, and whether she had consciously planned what followed.

During the course of her pregnancy, I refrained from raising the topic of implants, but a couple of days after Lucy was born I presented the implantation request form to Marianne for her signature.

She would not sign, and because both our signatures were required, Lucy could not undergo the simple operation to ensure her continual life.

We remained together for another year, and it was without doubt the worst year of my life. We argued—I accused my wife of terrible crimes in the name of her mythical god, while she called me an evil blasphemer. Our positions could not be reconciled. My love for Lucy grew in direct proportion to my hatred of Marianne. We separated at the end of the year, though Marianne, citing her religious principles, would not grant me a divorce. She gained custody of our child.

I saw Lucy for two or three days a week over the course of the next five years, and the love of my daughter sustained me, and at the same time drove me to the edge of sanity, plagued continually by fear and paranoia.

That night, in the early hours, Lucy crept into my bed and snuggled up against me, and I dozed, utterly content.

We slept in late the following morning, lunched at the Fleece, and then went for a long walk. At five we set off for Hockton, Lucy quiet in the back seat.

I led her from the Range Rover to the front door, where I knelt and stroked a tress of hair from her face. I kissed her. "See you next week, poppet. Love you."

She hugged me and, as always, I had to restrain myself from weeping.

She hurried into the house and I left without exchanging a word with Marianne.

I threw myself into my work for the next five days. We were busy; Richard Lincoln was away on holiday, and I took over his workload. I averaged half a dozen collections a day, ranging across the length and breadth of North Yorkshire.

Tuesday night arrived, and not a day too soon; I was due to pick up Lucy in the morning and keep her for the duration of my three-day break. I celebrated with a few pints among congenial company at the Fleece. The regulars were present: Khalid and Zara, Ben and Elisabeth, and the ferrymen Jeff and Richard, the latter just back that day from the Bahamas with a tan to prove it.

It was midnight by the time I made my way home, and there was a message from Marianne on the answer-phone. Would I ring her immediately about tomorrow?

Six pints to the good, I had no qualms about ringing her when she might be in bed.

In the event, she answered the call with disconcerting alacrity. "Yes?"

"Dan here," I said. "I got the message."

"It's about Lucy. I wouldn't bother coming tomorrow. She came down with something. She'll be in bed for a couple of days."

"What's wrong?" I asked, fear gripping me by the throat.

"It's nothing serious. The doctor came, said something about a virus."

"I'll come anyway," I said. "I want to see her."

"Don't bother," Marianne said. "I really don't want to have you over here if it isn't absolutely necessary."

"I couldn't give a damn about what you want!" I said. "I want to see Lucy. I'm coming over."

But she had slammed down the receiver, leaving me talking to myself.

I considered phoning back, but stopped myself. It would only show her how angry I was. I'd go over in the morning anyway, whether she liked it or not.

A blizzard began just as I set off, and the road over the moors to Hockton was treacherous. It took me almost an hour to reach the village, and it was after eleven by the time I pulled up outside Marianne's cottage.

I fully expected her not to answer the door, but to my surprise she pulled it open after the first knock. "Oh," she said. "It's you."

I stepped past her. "Where's Lucy?"

She indicated the stairs with a plastic beaker full of juice. I climbed to Lucy's room, Marianne following.

"Daddy!" Lucy called out when I entered. She was sitting up in bed, a colouring book on her lap. She looked thin and pale.

I sat on the bed and took her hand. Marianne passed her the beaker of juice. I looked up at her. "What did the doctor say?"

She shrugged. She was hugging herself, and looked pinched and mean, resentful of my presence. "He just said it was just a virus that's going round. Nothing to worry about."

"What about medication?"

"He suggested Calpol if her temperature rose."

She retreated to the door, watching me. I turned to Lucy and squeezed her hand. "How are you feeling, poppet?"

Her head against the pillow, she smiled bravely. "Bit sick," she said.

I looked up. Marianne was still watching me. "If you'd give us a few minutes alone..."

Reluctantly she withdrew.

I winked at Lucy. "You'll be better in no time," I said.

"Will I have to have more tests, Daddy?"

"I don't know. What did the doctor say when he came?"

She shook her head. "He didn't come here. Mummy took me to the hospital."

"Hospital?"

She nodded. "A doctor needled me and took some blood."

A hollow sensation opened up in my stomach. I smiled inanely. "What did the doctor say, Lucy? Can you remember what the doctor told Mummy?"

She pulled a face in concentration. "They said something about my blood. It wasn't good enough. I think they said they might have to take it all out and put some new blood in. Then another doctor said something about my bones. I might need an operation on my bones."

My vision swam. My heart hammered.

"Was this at the hospital in Bradley?" I asked her.

She shook her head. "Mummy took me to Leeds."

"Can you remember which hospital?"

She made her concentrating face. "It was a hospital for army people," she said.

I blinked. "What?"

"I think the sign said General," she said.

"Leeds General," I said. "Was that it?"

She nodded. I squeezed her hand. My first impulse was to go downstairs and confront Marianne, ask her just what the hell was going on.

Lucy had something wrong with her blood, and might need an operation on her bones. A bone marrow transplant, for Chrissake?

I tried not to jump to the obvious conclusion.

I remained with Lucy a further thirty minutes, read her a book and then chatted about nothing in particular for a while, all the time my mind racing.

By noon, I had decided what to do. I leaned forward and kissed her. "I've got to go now, Lucy. I'll pop in and see you tomorrow, okay?"

I hurried from the room and down the stairs. I paused before the living room door, but didn't trust myself to confront Marianne just yet. I hurried from the cottage and drove home through the snowstorm.

For the next half-hour I ransacked the house for the photocopy of Lucy's birth certificate, and my passport for identification purposes. Then I set off again, heading towards Leeds.

It was almost three before I pulled into the bleak car park in the shadow of the towerblock buildings. At reception I explained the situation and requested to see someone in charge. The head registrar examined my documents and spoke in hushed tones to someone in a black suit.

Thirty minutes later I was shown into the waiting room of a Mr Chandler, and told by his secretary that he would try to fit me in within the hour.

At four-thirty the secretary called my name and, heart thumping, I stepped into the consulting room.

Mr Chandler was a thin-faced, grey-haired man in his late fifties. The bulge of an implant showed at his left temple.

He was examining a computer flat-screen on his desk, and looked up when I entered. We shook hands.

"Mr Chester," he said. "According to my secretary, you haven't been informed of your daughter's condition?"

"I'm separated from my wife. We're not exactly on speaking terms."

"This is highly irregular," he muttered to himself.

I resisted the urge to tell him that Marianne was a highly irregular woman. "Can you tell me what's wrong with my daughter, Mr Chandler?"

He consulted his files, lips pursed.

"Lucy was diagnosed one month ago with leukaemia . . . " He went on, and I heard him say that the type she was suffering from was pernicious and incurable, but it was as if I had suddenly been plucked from this reality, as if I were experiencing the events in the consulting room at a remove of miles. I seemed to have possession of my body only by remote control.

"Incurable?" I echoed.

"I'm sorry. Of course, if your daughter were implanted . . . "

I stared at him. "Don't you think I know that?" I said. "Why the hell do you think my damned wife kept her condition quiet?"

He looked away. "I'm sorry."

"Is there nothing you can do? I mean, surely under the Hippocratic oath . . . ?"

He was shaking his head. "Unfortunately I've been in this situation before, Mr Chester. It requires the consent of *both* legal guardians to allow the implantation process to be undertaken in the case of minors. I'm quite powerless to intervene, as much as I sympathise with your predicament."

I worked to calm myself, regulate my breathing. "How long might Lucy . . . ?" I began.

He said, "As things stand, perhaps one month. You see, since the arrival of the

Kéthani, the funding once spent on research into terminal diseases has been drastically cut back."

I listened, but heard nothing. Ten minutes later I thanked him and moved from the room in a daze.

I have no recollection of leaving the hospital and driving away from Leeds. I recall isolated incidents: a traffic jam on the York road, passing a nasty accident on the road to Bradley, and almost skidding from the lane a mile outside Hockton.

Then I was parked outside Marianne's cottage, gripping the wheel and going over and over the words I would use in an attempt to make her agree to save our daughter's life.

At last I left the Rover and hurried up the path. I had the curious sensation of being an actor on stage, and that, if I fluffed my lines now, the consequences would be dire.

I didn't bother knocking, but opened the front door and moved down the hall.

Marianne was in the living room. She sat in her armchair, legs drawn up beneath her. She was hugging herself as if cold. The TV was on, the sound switched off.

"I've been to the hospital," I said. "I talked with Chandler."

She looked up, showing no surprise.

Heart thumping, I dropped into the armchair opposite and stared at her. "We've got to talk about this," I said. "There's more at stake than our principles or beliefs."

She looked away. She was fingering her damned crucifix. "You mean, you want me to sacrifice my principles and beliefs in order to satisfy your own?"

I leaned forward, almost insensible with rage. "I mean," I said, resisting the urge to launch myself at her, "that if we do nothing, then Lucy will be dead. Does that mean anything to you? She'll be bloody well dead!"

"Don't you think I know that? This isn't easy for me, you know."

I shook my head. "I don't see how you can have a moment's hesitation. The simple fact is, if you don't agree to the implantation, then Lucy will die. We won't have any second chances. She'll be dead."

"And if I agree, I'll be damning her in the eyes of God."

I closed my eyes and worked to control my breathing. I looked at her. I could not help myself, but I was crying. "Please, Marianne, for Lucy's sake."

She stared at me.

I said, "At least, let her have the implant. Then when she's eighteen she can make up her own mind, have it removed if she wants."

She shook her head. "I don't know . . . I need time to think about it."

I gave a panicky nod at the thought that she might be relenting. "Chandler said she had a month, but who knows? We need to make a decision pretty damned quickly."

She stared at me, her face ashen. "I need time to think, Dan. You can't pressure me into this."

I wiped away the tears. "Lucy is all we have left, Marianne. We don't have each other any more. Lucy is everything."

This, so far as I recall, was the gist of the exchange; I have a feeling it went on for longer, with clichés from both sides bandied back and forth, to no definite conclusion. The last thing I did before leaving the house was to climb the stairs to Lucy's bedroom, kneel beside the bed and watch my daughter as she slept.

I arrived home around midnight and, unable to sleep, stared at a succession of meaningless images passing before me on the TV screen.

I slept on the settee until ten o'clock the next morning, then showered and tried to force down some breakfast. Between ten-thirty and midday I must have phoned Marianne a dozen times. She was either out or not answering.

At one o'clock, the phone rang, startling me. Shaking, I lifted the receiver. "Hello?"

"Daniel?"

"Marianne?"

A silence, then, "Daniel. I have a form you need to sign."

"My God, you mean—?"

"I'll be in all afternoon," she said, and replaced the receiver.

I drove to Hockton, crying all the way. I pulled up before the cottage and dried my eyes, at once grateful for the decision Marianne had come to, and yet resentful that she had made me so pathetically indebted to her.

I hurried up the path, knocked, and entered. Marianne was in her usual armchair. A slip of paper sat on the coffee table before her. I sat down and read through the release form. She had already appended her signature on the dotted line at the foot of the page. Fumbling, I pulled a pen from my pocket and signed my name below hers.

I looked up. Marianne was watching me. "You won't regret this, Marianne," I said.

"I've made an appointment for the implant," she said. "I'm taking her in at one tomorrow."

"I'll drop by to see her after work, okay?"

"Whatever . . . "

I made my way upstairs. Lucy was sitting up in bed. Intoxicated, I hugged her to me, smothering her in kisses. I stayed an hour, talking, reading her books, laughing . . .

When I made my way downstairs, Marianne was still in her armchair in the lounge. The room was in darkness.

I said goodbye before I left, but she did not respond.

It was six by the time I arrived home, and I dropped into the Fleece for a celebratory meal and a pint or three.

Khalid was there, along with Richard and Ben, and three pints turned to six as I told them the news: first, Lucy was going to be implanted, and second, she was suffering from a terminal illness. My friends were a little unsure how to respond, then took my line and decided to celebrate.

It was well past one when I staggered home, and I had a raging headache next day at work. Fortunately, with Richard back from the Bahamas the workload was not intense, and I was finished by four.

I returned home, showered and changed, and then made my way over the moors to Hockton.

The cottage door was locked, and I thought at first that perhaps they had not returned. Then it struck me that, perhaps, Marianne had gone back on her word, decided not to take Lucy to the hospital . . .

Then the door opened.

"How is she?" I asked, pushing past Marianne and making my way upstairs.

She followed me upstairs. Lucy was lying in bed, staring at the ceiling. She looked exhausted.

She beamed when she saw me. "Daddy, look. Look what I've got!"

Her small fingers traced the implant at her temple. I looked up; Marianne pushed herself away from the door and went downstairs.

I pulled Lucy to me—she seemed no more than a bundle of skin and bone—and could not stop myself from crying. "I love you," I whispered.

"Love you, too," Lucy replied, then said, "Now that I have the implant, Daddy, will God love me as well?"

I lay her down, gently, and smiled. "I'm sure he will, poppet," I said.

Later, as she slept, I stroked her hair and listened to the words of the rhyme in my head: *Monday's child is fair of face, Tuesday's child is full of grace, Wednesday's child is full of woe, Thursday's child has far to go . . .*

254

I made my way downstairs. Marianne was in the kitchen, washing dishes. I leaned against the jamb.

"You've made the right decision, Marianne." I said. "Thank you."

She turned and stared at me. "You don't know how difficult it was," she said, without meeting my eyes, and turned back to the dishes.

I said goodbye, left the cottage, and drove home.

Lucy went downhill rapidly after that.

The next time she stayed with me, she spent most of the entire two days in bed, listless and apathetic, and too drugged up even to talk much or play games. I told her that she was ill but that in time she would recover, and she gave a brave smile and squeezed my fingers.

During the course of the last two weeks, Marianne and I took time off work and nursed Lucy at home, looking after her for alternating periods of two days.

At one point, Lucy lowered the book she was reading and stared at me from the sofa. "If I die," she said, "will the aliens take me away and make me better again?"

I nodded. "If that happens, you mustn't be frightened, okay? The Kéthani will take good care of you, and in six months you'll come back home to Mum and me."

She smiled to herself. "I wonder what the aliens look like?"

Two days before Lucy died, she was admitted to Bradley General, and I was with her until the end.

She was unconscious, and dosed with painkillers. She had lost a lot of weight and looked pitifully thin beneath the crisp hospital sheets.

I held her hand during the first day and well into the night, falling asleep in my chair and waking at dawn with cramps and multiple aches. Marianne arrived shortly after that and sat with Lucy. I took the opportunity to grab a bite to eat.

On the evening of the second day, Lucy's breathing became uneven. A doctor murmured to Marianne and me that she had only a matter of hours to live.

Marianne sat across the bed from me, gripping her daughter's hand and weeping.

After an hour, she could take no more.

She stood and made for the door.

"Marianne...?" I said.

"I'm sorry. This is too much. I'm going."

"This is just the start," I said. "She isn't truly dying, Marianne."

She looked at me. "I'm sorry Dan," she said, and hurried out.

I returned to my vigil. I stared at my daughter, and thought of the time, six months away, when she would be returned to me, remade. Glorious years stretched ahead.

I thought of Marianne, and her inability to see it through to the end . . .

I was struck, then, by an idea so terrible I was ashamed that it had occurred to me.

I told myself that I was being paranoid, that even Marianne could not do such a thing. But once the seed of doubt had been planted, it would not be eradicated.

What if I were right, I asked myself? I had to be sure. I had to know for certain.

Beside myself with panic, I fumbled with my mobile and found Khalid's number. The dial tone purred for an age. I swore at him to reply, and at last he did.

"Hello?"

"Khalid, thank God! Where are you?"

"Dan? I'm just leaving the hospital."

"Khalid, I need your help." I explained the situation, my fear. "Please, will you come over?"

There was no hesitation. "I'm on my way." He cut the connection.

He seemed to take aeons to arrive, but only two minutes elapsed before his neat, suited figure appeared at the door. He hurried over, concern etched on his face.

"I need to be sure, Khalid. It might be okay, but I need to know."

"You don't need to explain yourself, Dan. I understand."

He moved around the bed, and I watched in silent desperation. He pulled something from his inside pocket, a device like a miniature mobile phone, and stabbed a code into the keypad.

Then he glanced at me, stepped towards Lucy, and applied the device to the implant at her temple.

He read something from the tiny screen, and shock invaded his expression. He slumped into the seat which minutes before my wife had occupied, and he said something, rapidly, in Urdu.

"Khalid?" I almost wept.

He was shaking his head. "Dan, it's a fake."

I felt very cold. I pressed my hands to my cheeks and stared at him. I wanted to throw up, but I hadn't eaten anything for half a day. Bile rose in my throat. I swallowed it with difficulty.

"Khalid," I said. "You've got to help me."

"Dan..." It was a plea to make me understand the impossibility of what I was asking him.

"How long does an implantation take?" I asked. "Thirty minutes? We have time. If you can get an implant, make the cut..." I realised, as I was speaking, that I was weeping, pleading with him through my tears.

"Dan, we need the signatures of both parents. If anyone found out..."

I recalled, then, the consent form which I had signed two weeks ago. My heart skipped at the sudden thought that there existed a form bearing both our signatures. But it would take more than half an hour to drive to Marianne's house, locate the form, and return... And the chances were that she would have destroyed it anyway.

My mobile rang, and I snatched it from my pocket. "What?"

"Mr Daniel Chester?"

"What do you want? Who is it?"

The woman gave her name. I can't recall it now, but she explained that she was a police officer. "If you could make your way to Hockton police station..." she was saying.

I laughed at the absurdity of the situation. "Listen, I'm at Bradley hospital with my daughter. She's dying, and if you think for a second that I'm leaving her—"

"I'm sorry, Mr Chester. We'll be over right away." She cut the connection. It was evidence of my agitated state that I managed to push the call from my mind.

I sat down and gripped Lucy's hand. I looked up, across the bed at Khalid. I said, "What's more important? Your job or Lucy's life?"

He shook his head, staring at me. "You can't blackmail me, Dan. Marianne doesn't want this. I'm not saying that what she did was right, but you've got to understand that there are laws to obey."

"Sod the fucking laws!" I yelled. "We're talking about the life of my daughter, for Chrissake."

He stared down at his clasped hands.

I went on, "If this were your daughter, in this situation, what would you do? All it would take is a quick cut. Replace the implant with a genuine one."

He was shaking his head, tears tracking down his cheeks.

"For Chrissake," I hissed. "We're alone. No one would see."

"Dan, I'd need to do paperwork, make a requisition order for an implant. They're all numbered, accounted for. If one went missing..."

I stared at him. I am not proud of what I said then, but I was driven by desperation. "You could replace the genuine implant with this fake."

He stared at me in shock, and only then did I realise what I'd asked him to do.
He stood up quickly, strode to the window, and stared out into the night.

I sat by the bed, gripping Lucy's hot hand and quietly sobbing. Minutes passed like seconds.

"Mr Chester?"

The interruption was unwelcome. A small, Asian WPC stood by the door. A constable, who appeared about half my age, accompanied her.

"What...?" I began.

"Mr Chester, it's about your wife, Marianne Chester."

"Marianne?" I said, my stomach turning.

"If you'd kindly step out here."

In a daze I left my seat and accompanied the police officers into the corridor. They escorted me to a side room, where we could be alone.

I sat down, and the WPC sat opposite me. The juvenile constable remained by the door, avoiding my eyes.

"Mr Chester," the woman said, "I'm sorry to inform you that your wife was found dead a little under one hour ago. A neighbour noticed the front door open. I'm so sorry. It appears that she took her own life."

I stared at her. "What?" I said, though I had heard her clearly enough.

I've since learned that police officers are prepared to repeat bad news to people in shock. Patiently, kindly, she told me again.

Marianne was dead. What she had done to my daughter, what she had done to me, had been too much of a burden to bear. She had taken her own life. I understood the words, but not the actuality of what she had done.

I stood and crossed the corridor. I returned to Lucy's room. Khalid was still there, seated beside the bed, clutching my daughter's hand and quietly crying.

I sat down and told him what had happened.

The joy of being a father comes not only from the wonder of the moment, the love one feels for one's child every minute of every day, but also from the contemplation of the future. How long had I spent daydreaming about the girl Lucy would be at the age of thirteen, and then at eighteen, on the verge of womanhood? I saw myself with her when she was twenty, and thirty, sharing her life, loving her. Such pre-emptive "memories," as it were, are one of the delights of fatherhood.

—·—

Two hours later, Lucy died.

I was holding her hand, listening to her stertorous breathing and to the regular pulse of the cardiogram. Then her breathing hiccupped, rattled, and a second later the cardiogram flat-lined, maintaining an even, continuous note.

I looked across at Khalid, and he nodded.

I reached out and touched the implant at her temple, the implant which Khalid had installed an hour ago when, as Lucy's sole remaining parent, I had signed the consent form. The implant worked its alien magic, restoring my daughter to life.

Presently a ferryman arrived and, between us, we lifted Lucy into the container, which we do not call coffins. Before she was taken away, I kissed her forehead and told her that I would be there to welcome her back in six months. She would leave for the Kéthani starship tonight.

Later, I left the hospital and drove to Hockton, where I called in at the police station and read the note which Marianne had left. It was sealed in a cellophane folder, and I could not take it away with me.

Dan, I read, *Please forgive me. You will never understand. I know I have done the right thing by saving Lucy from the Kéthani, even though what I have done to you is unforgivable. Also, what I am about to do to myself. It's enough to know that Lucy is saved, even if I am damned by my actions.*

Marianne.

I left the police station and drove onto the moors overlooking the towering obelisk of the Onward Station. It rose in the moonlight like a pinnacle of ice, promising eternity. As I climbed from the Rover and watched, the first of that evening's energy beams pulsed from its summit and arced through the stratosphere.

Thus the dead of Earth were transmitted to the Kéthani starship waiting high above.

Thursday's child has far to go...

LIFE BEYOND

I've been reading and enjoying the work of Clifford D. Simak for as long as I can remember reading science fiction. His best novels and short stories speak to me on an emotional level that few other writers are able to reach. When other SF writers wrote of aliens as a threat, Simak wrote tales about aliens as neighbours, about tolerance and inclusiveness—a salutary lesson for our time, I think. Among my favourites of his work are his novels Way Station, All Flesh is Grass, *and* Why Call Them Back From Heaven?. *His wonderful short story "A Death in the House" is a classic. The following tale is my affectionate homage to the grand master.*

LIFE BEYOND...

I WAS SITTING ON MY OLD BEAT-UP SOFA—WHICH ELLIE MY GRANDDAUGHTER calls Feral on account of its looking wild. I was reading Thoreau, of course, and looking up from his wise words from time to time and smiling to myself, that complicit smile acknowledging the privilege of being addressed by the dead, personally, through the depths of space and time.

My house sits on the edge of the bluff with a fine sweeping view across the pine covered valley; from the big window in my study-cum-lounge I can see the distant Mississippi winding through the lush Wisconsin meadowland.

The sun was setting on another hot summer's day and the sky was cloudless. You could see everything there was to see in that sky, distant birds and the contrails of the domestic jetliners from O'Hare, and whatever else that might drop from the heavens, a-visiting.

On the sofa beside me was the small booklet that Ellie had written on her laptop. She had presented it to me after dinner, a little shyly, eyes downcast, before slipping off to bed. She had always said she wanted to be a writer, like me. I had assumed that it was another of her short stories, and wondered at her skittishness.

So I'd laid aside Thoreau and began reading Ellie's booklet, and soon *Excursions* was forgotten, and the impending visit of the interfering social worker too.

Oh, Ellie, Ellie... If words were the currency of our humanity, then my granddaughter was rich beyond compare.

I wept.

The piece was entitled *My Life*, and began: *One month ago my Mom was killed in an automobile smash, and since then I've lived with Grampa in his big, old book-filled place on the hill, and I love Grampa more than anything in the world but I miss my Mom so much it's like a pain inside me...*

It went on, for over ten thousand words, describing her life before the accident, her life since, and the incomprehensible tragedy of her loss.

I finished reading the booklet, and then climbed the stairs and stood in the doorway of Ellie's room. She was asleep face down on the bed, still dressed: too-small tee shirt and too-small jeans stretched tight on her spurting adolescent frame.

I was glad she was asleep: I could have offered only hugs and kisses and tears in consolation, in lieu of any explanation.

I returned to the lounge and considered the imminent meeting. I wanted to be sharp when the social worker came to try to take Ellie away from me.

She'd called earlier, a young woman with a posh Boston accent, ringing from a gas station off Highway 94 to apologize. She was running late; my place was hard to find; she'd miscalculated how much gasoline she would need.

I found myself reassuring her, friendly-like, telling her not to worry: this stranger out to wreck my life.

She'd said she would find a motel for the night, and see me in the morning, but I assured her that tonight would be fine. I wanted to get the meeting over and done with.

Now I heard movement above my head. Evidently Ellie had awoken. I heard the window of her room swing open and the window-seat creak. No doubt she was hugging her knees, staring out at the night and the stars, as she had made it her habit to do over the weeks.

I smiled and continued reading.

Then there was all-hell of a din as Ellie jumped from the window seat and thumped across the bare boards and raced down the stairs and arrived, breathless, in the doorway to the lounge, gasping at me.

"What's spooking you, girl?" I said, amused.

"Gramps! Look! Look in the sky over Wilson's Forest! I saw it coming down from way up! There, see it?"

She ran into the room and vaulted over the back of the sofa, landing beside me and hugging me to her, pointing through the window.

It took some while for my old eyes to adjust, then I saw what had excited her so.

It was a silver thing, all twinkling and scintillating in the light of the setting sun. It was hard to tell how big it was—maybe the size of a light aircraft—but it was stubby, torpedo-shaped and wingless, and was angling down steeply over the treetops. I caught a five second glimpse of Ellie's mysterious object before it dropped into the forest and vanished.

We looked at each other. My granddaughter's eyes were wide.

"What was it, Gramps?"

Common sense took hold of me. "Either a bit of some old satellite, El, or a weather balloon, most like."

"Bor-ing! Not a UFO or a time machine?"

"You've got a lively imagination!"

She glanced at her booklet, then at my book. "What you reading, Gramps?"

"Thoreau."

"Did you read...?"

I pulled her to me and kissed her mussed-up blonde curls. She was eleven years old and gawky, with nascent beauty in the lineaments of her face, just waiting to explode. I could see a lot of Sam, my daughter, in her.

"We'll talk in the morning," I said. "Now off to bed, and sleep, okay?"

She gave me another tight squeeze, then slipped from the sofa and hurried back upstairs.

I might have let her stay up a while, and talked to her some, but I had seen, way away on the winding track that led to my house and nowhere else, the beetling shape of a Buick.

I poured myself a stiff bourbon; I wanted to have my wits about me when I faced Miss-whatever-her-name-was, but also I wanted something to take the edge off my anger.

In due course the Buick rounded the last bend and drew to a halt. The driver climbed from the car and walked the rest of the way up the pot-holed track, pausing to peer at the house with a hand fitted to her brow.

She was tall and smartly dressed, with long dark hair and a strong, intelligent, city-wise face.

She was carrying something, as well as her valise. I hoped it wasn't what I thought it was.

I left the lounge and hauled open the front door before she had time to ring the chime.

"Mr Robertshaw, I'm so sorry."

"Call me Ed. Don't worry, I keep elastic hours." It wasn't what I had meant to say, but I always find it hard to cold-shoulder folk, even social workers.

"I'm Elizabeth Kovac. We spoke at length last week."

And she *was* clutching, in her beautifully manicured right hand, what I'd feared. I winced as I led her through the house to the lounge.

She sat in an armchair and I collapsed into the sofa.

"Mr Robertshaw, Ed—it's a pleasure to meet you."

"I only wish the circumstances were a little more conducive to bonhomie," I said.

I could see her glancing around the room, at the disorderly piles of books, then at my somewhat disheveled appearance.

I was not what she was expecting a grand old man of letters to be.

She placed my latest novel on the arm of the chair and patted it, somewhat primly.

"Ed, I've been reading your books for years. I can't tell you how much I enjoy them."

I shrugged. I always find praise embarrassing.

"I was wondering if you might sign it?"

I hesitated, then dragged it to me and found a pen. I scribbled my name and closed the book.

Her glance alighted on the ream of quarto on my desk. Her eyes widened. "Your latest?"

I refrained from saying, "And probably my last." I'd finished the third draft of what I considered my finest novel shortly before my daughter's death, and the accident had knocked me sideways and pushed from my mind all thoughts of ever writing again.

"I take it you and your team read my letter and the adoption papers," I said.

She sighed. "Mr Robertshaw—Ed. As I said on the phone, this is an exceptional case, and in any other circumstance we might have considered your application."

"Ellie's happy here," I said, despising myself for the note of desperation in my voice. "She wants to stay with me."

"To be perfectly frank, Ed, the child's desire in cases like this is not our paramount concern."

"Then what is?"

"The long-term welfare of your granddaughter."

"I too have that in mind."

She looked at me. She said, pointedly, "The *long-term* welfare, Ed?"

Touché.

"I'm as fit and healthy now as I was at the age of forty," I blustered.

She smiled. "How old are you, Ed?"

I stared at her. She was, I guessed, around thirty, a mere child.

"Seventy-five last fall," I said.

She was smiling at me, patronizing. She no longer saw me as the patriarchal novelist; now I was some crusty backwoods hermit bordering on senility.

"Ed, please try to see the situation from my point of view. Ellie needs care for the next six, seven years. With all due respect, you might not be able to provide that care."

"I don't want El in a home," I said.

"Let me assure you that Ellie will be fostered by a caring family in the short-term, while a suitable long-term adoptive family is located."

"But my granddaughter is happy with me!" I began.

She leafed through some papers and then looked up at me. "Ed, I discovered that last fall you suffered a minor coronary."

I stared at her, gestured helplessly. "Minor..." I echoed.

"You didn't inform us."

"Didn't think it mattered that much," I said.

Kovac became business-like. "Ed, we'll do everything within our powers to keep Ellie nearby. We recognize the mutual need for continued contact..." Kovac went on, but she was spouting text-book stuff at me now, and I turned off.

I thought through the best way to tell Kovac that I wasn't giving in, that I wouldn't give up Ellie without a fight.

From her valise she withdrew a sheaf of forms and laid them on the coffee table between us. "If you could complete the relevant details and get them back to me..."

"And if I refuse?"

"Ed, that wouldn't be advisable. We'd have to take the matter to court, and that would only prolong the entire procedure."

"And I'd have Ellie for a little bit longer."

She stared at me. She clearly thought me an old fool—which I probably was. "Ed, Ellie would be taken from you and placed in a care home for the duration of the litigation. It would only prove even more upsetting for her."

I gave her my fiercest stare. "So in effect what you're saying is that I have no say in the matter? Even though I love my granddaughter and want her to stay, and Ellie wants to stay too, there's absolutely no way you're going to listen to what *we* want?"

"Ed, as I've tried to explain, we have the best interests of Ellie in mind. If only you could see that."

We bickered back and forth for a time, getting nowhere. I succeeded only in increasing my blood pressure some.

At last I stood and indicated the door. "I think we each know where the other stands on the matter," I said in my most formal and pompous manner.

She rose to leave. "I was hoping that this could be settled amicably," she began.

I saw her to the door—almost tossing her copy of my novel after her—and watched her drive away down the track and out of sight.

I made my way up to El's room and stood in the doorway. She was asleep, under the sheets this time, her clothes folded neatly at the foot of the bed.

I stood there for perhaps fifteen minutes, my head full of images of Ellie as a baby, a toddler, a feisty, independent nine year-old...

I was seventy-five, but I was good for another ten years. I would fight Kovac and the system with every means available to me. Maybe I was an old fool, but since Sam's death Ellie had become more precious to me than anything else.

She was my life.

I made my way downstairs and, almost without realizing what I was doing, I picked up the bottle of bourbon, took a long swallow, and stared out through the window.

I had told Ellie that the thing had been an old satellite, or a weather balloon...

Perhaps, looking back, I was drawn to leave the house. Or perhaps it never happened. Perhaps my memory of the following events is false, the result of too much alcohol on top of so much pent-up anger.

Whatever, I recall leaving the house and making my way along the track toward Wilson's Forest.

I was still clutching the bottle of bourbon.

It was that time of night when coons are abroad, moving cautiously through the undergrowth, and the first owls are tuning up. A full moon climbed high above the pines, and the last of the sunlight was reddening like a hemorrhage in the west.

I was *drawn*. Looking back, that's how it seems. I was an old fool to be out with a bottle of bourbon and my regrets when the sun was almost down, but it didn't seem that way.

The night air was resinous, and I recall the sense of excitement, apropos of nothing, as I left the track and took the footpath toward the forest.

I climbed through the pines, the twilight suddenly deepening, and out of the last light of the sun a sudden chill came upon me. I think I even stopped and wondered why I'd left Ellie all alone back there—not that she was in any danger, being that the nearest human habitation was nigh on twenty-five miles away.

I pressed on. I stopped once to take a chug of bourbon and then continued my climbing. I was heading toward where I judged the *thing* had come down, though quite how I might have judged that I do not know.

Then I saw a glint of silver through the trees and increased my pace.

Whatever it was, it had shaved down a good dozen sturdy pines on its entry into the forest. Now it stood on the lip of a bluff, its nose projecting out over the edge, with a fantail of pulverized matchwood in its wake.

I stopped dead in my tracks, and pushed my hand through my thinning hair; I might even have said *God dang it.*

It was a blunt torpedo, perhaps twenty feet long, and silver. At its nose was a wrap-around viewscreen kind of thing, and halfway down its length a cartoon mouse hole–shaped opening.

A short ramp led down from the opening.

I don't mind allowing that I took a good few swallows of bourbon at the sight of it, then stepped forward and approached the craft. Courage had nothing to do with my advance; like I said, I was drawn.

The vessel's occupant had taken advantage of a fallen log and was admiring the view beyond the drop. Half the county was bathed in the light of the sun, all faded green and hazy gold.

The creature was humanoid and very thin, almost skeletal, with very white skin, the regulation number of eyes, a nose and a mouth; but its features were curiously flattened and expressionless. I gained the impression that it was male, though of course I might have been mistaken.

It wore a little gray suit consisting of knee-length trousers and a short-sleeved shirt.

"You live," it said, "in a beautiful part of the world."

"I like to think so," I replied.

"I think it's important to take the time to appreciate natural beauty," it went on.

"There is nothing like," I said, "Wisconsin at sundown in summer."

The being gestured to the log. "Won't you join me?"

You think it strange, I guess, that I am so matter of fact in reporting the first recorded instance of human contact with an extraterrestrial being. In my defense let me state that although a part of me was aware of the significance of the event, it was as if my intellect had been tranquilized. I am sure that the alien was responsible for this, and not the bourbon.

Perhaps, without its feat of telepathic tranquilization, I might have been a gibbering wreck.

I sat down on the log next to the creature.

I found myself saying, "Have you come a long way?"

Of all the questions to ask a traveler from the stars!

"Since my last stop," it said, "not that far. A matter of a hundred light years or so."

"Is that all?" I said. "And before that?"

"I have traveled through the inhabited system for almost fifty of your years," it said. "Some hundred thousand light years."

Now let me say that, although it communicated to me in good old American English, its words were not synchronized to the movement of its lips, and the effect was similar to that of watching a badly dubbed foreign film.

I fidgeted. My old bones were a little uncomfortable without a backrest. I sat down on the mossy floor of the clearing and lodged my back against the log.

My alien companion did likewise.

"A good idea," it said.

I took a swallow of bourbon and, remembering my manners, offered the bottle to my guest.

It regarded the bottle. "Go on," I said. "We call it bourbon. Has quite a kick. Try it."

With seeming caution it reached out, took the bottle, and raised it experimentally to its lips. A good tumblerful of alcohol slid down its long gullet, without ill effect.

It returned the bottle. "Interesting."

I gestured to the ship beside us. "Quite a vessel you have yourself there," I said conversationally.

"You would think, wouldn't you, that after fifty years of star travel I would have perfected the landing maneuver?"

I shrugged, not knowing much about that line of thing.

"I feared my ship would be damaged, but after a thorough inspection I am happy to report that it needs but minor repairs."

"That's good to hear." I hesitated. "Perhaps I might be able to help."

"That's very kind of you, but it won't take me long."

"And then you'll be on your way?"

"I will, though I had hoped to have time to do what I came to this planet to do."

I took another swig of bourbon, and passed the bottle. My friend drank too. For an alien, it liked its liquor.

"And what," I asked, "did you come to Earth to do?"

I can hear you asking: the annihilation of the entire human race? The reconnaissance of all military establishments preparatory to an alien invasion?

I thought nothing of the sort. I kind of trusted the little alien by then. But I was curious.

"I make it my duty," it said, "to collect from every planet I visit an example of its literature. In short, I collect books."

I stared at the critter beside me. I hadn't taken it for a bookworm.

"Books," I said. "I mean, other planets possess books? I thought maybe Earth was unique in having them. I would have thought that other planets had... well, other means of recording things." I realized I was babbling and shut up.

Listen to me! Other planets? Until that time I hadn't given much thought to the possibility that other, inhabited worlds might exist beyond planet Earth.

"Oh, all sentient races the galaxy over have had, at some point in their history, objects known as books in one form or another."

"And you collect them?"

He turned his bland, flat face to me and essayed, for the first time, a smile. It failed to work fully—the effect resembled a stretched elastic band—but I appreciated the effort.

"I pick up three items from every planet I visit."

"Only three?"

"Inhabited planets are multifarious, and my ship is only small."

"And when you return to your homeworld, will you sell these books?"

"I am not a businessman," it said. "I donate the books to the Library of Lithia. My planet stands at a junction in the spaceway. Many races come to Lithia to study at the Library."

I stared in open-mouthed wonder at my informant.

I recalled what it had said, earlier. "But you fear that you don't have enough time to collect your quota of books?"

The alien stared out over the bluff, into the deepening night. I honestly think that it was quite taken with the landscape.

"That is so. The repair will take a little while. Then I will have to depart. I am expected back at Lithia in one month, Earth-time."

Something like vast melancholy opened up inside me. I thought of the Library of Lithia, and the fact that it would be without any examples of human books.

Impulsively I asked, "How long will your repairs take?"

"Perhaps one of your hours," it replied.

271

"In that case," I said, scrambling to my feet, "I'll bring you three books before you leave. For the Library. A present from the people of Earth!" I stopped and stared at the alien, who was looking up at me with large eyes. Did I see gratitude in those great milky orbs, or was that wishful thinking on my part?

"But which three books?" I asked.

"Allow your heart to make that choice," said the alien. "But I will state that I require books which reflect what it is to be a human being, books written with emotion, and not text books or scientific treatises."

"I'll return within the hour with three suitable volumes," I promised.

The alien stood also and, briefly halting my progress from the clearing, said, "And I will give you something in return, Ed."

"You will?" I said, and then hurried from the clearing. It was not until I was well down the incline, the starship hidden from view, that I wondered how the alien had known my name.

I made my way home at a shambling jog, having to stop from time to time to ease my ageing legs and lungs. Only when the house came into sight, lighted against the darkness that loomed behind the bluff, did I realize what a responsibility the alien had charged me with: my imminent choice would dictate to countless alien scholars their knowledge and understanding of planet Earth...

I rushed into the house and stood in the middle of my study, surrounded by shelves of books from floor to ceiling, books piled tottering on the floor, books spilling from chairs and boxes; thousands of books, millions, perhaps billions, of words; the concentrated thoughts of legion of thinkers from humankind's vast history.

And my alien friend wanted me to choose just three!

I paced my study. I pulled down volume after volume, made a primary pile, and a secondary pile, keeping the alien's dicta uppermost in my mind. Books written with emotion, which told what it was to be human...

When I looked up I saw that almost an hour had elapsed, and I panicked. What if the alien had departed in his silver starship without three human books for Lithia?

Minutes later I was near to making my choice.

I looked across the room, and saw upon the desk the manuscript of my latest novel, the novel which I thought summed up so many years of fictive endeavor.

If I were to slip it into a binder, present it to the alien as the third book...

To think of it, my words read by creatures from far stars!

Then my gaze fell on the booklet Ellie had given me earlier that evening.

Trembling, I crossed the room and picked up her heartfelt outpouring of loss and love and hope.

In my other hand I hefted my weighty manuscript, and then, after careful consideration, laid it aside.

I carried Ellie's *My Life* back to the pile I had made on the floor, selected two further books, and hurried from the house.

My heart was thudding with the knowledge of the choice I had made, and the thought of these three volumes residing in the distant stellar library. What a gift to the stars—what an honor for the human race!

I turned from the track and took the path into the pines. I climbed, my heartbeat banging. I searched desperately for the glimpse of silver between the trees, insane with the thought that the alien had departed already—or that I had hallucinated the entire meeting.

But there it was.

I stumbled, exhausted, into the clearing and approached the starship.

The alien emerged from the opening in the ship's flank and came down the ramp toward me.

It paused, and again that strange smile played upon its unpracticed lips as I held out the books.

It took them from me one by one.

"This one?" it asked, and I explained that it was a revered philosophical book.

"And this?"

I gave a brief synopsis, hardly doing justice to the author's genius.

"And the third?" it asked.

"This," I said, my voice trembling, "this is the true account of a young girl's grief at losing the person she loved the most, but it is also a...a testament to the power of hope for the future that lives in the heart of every human being."

The alien tucked the three books under its arm.

"The only thing I can give you in return, Ed," said the alien being, "is advice."

"Advice?" I echoed.

"Sometimes, Ed, we must relinquish that which we treasure the most. You see," it went on, before I could say a word, "I have learned this from experience. For many of your years I have garnered from around the galaxy the most fabulous items from the most fabulous planets. I refer to books, of course. Then, on my way back to Lithia, a device I have aboard the ship translates the books into my own language, and I have time to read them, and the many wonders they contain—

273

and by the time of my arrival I have grown fond of the books in my possession, so fond that I am loathe to give them up to the library."

"But you do?" I said.

"I do. Books need to be read in order to grow, Ed. I could not selfishly keep them for myself. They belong in the world beyond."

And, before I could move or say another word, with its free hand the alien reached out to me.

"One must accept, Ed."

It touched my face, in a gesture I might have found disconcerting had it been made by another man. But his touch, on my cheek, filled me with peace and joy—and acceptance.

I backed away, toward the edge of the clearing, as the alien climbed the ramp into its ship.

At the top, the creature turned and lifted a hand in a farewell gesture.

The opening vanished, and seconds later the starship lifted without a sound and moved slowly out over the bluff. It accelerated into the night sky and in an instant was lost among the stars.

I stared up at the massed constellations, my head filled with the wonder of far stars and alien cities and civilizations. Then I made my slow way home to where a young girl, at the very start of her life, was sleeping the sleep of the innocent, and maybe dreaming.

And as I went it came to me what a pig-headed, cussed, ornery old fool I'd been.

Back home, I climbed the stairs and stood by Ellie's bedroom door for a long time, wondering how to tell her that, for her own good, she would have to leave me.

All that happened ten years ago, and I survived. I even wrote more novels, inspired perhaps by my memory of the alien.

Ellie left and lived with kind adoptive parents over Millville way, and I do believe they were the very best thing for her. A professor and his librarian wife, they broadened her mind in a way I doubt I could have done.

I visited Ellie every month—but I never told her of my strange encounter with the bibliophile alien that night.

She is sleeping in her old bed above my head as I write this, returned from university for the summer break. Tomorrow is her twenty-first birthday. I have never been back to the clearing in Wilson's Forest, perhaps fearing that there will be no evidence to corroborate my memories...

And the gaps in my shelves, from where I took the books? And the fact that, on the morning after Ellie gave me her booklet, it was nowhere to be found in the house?

Tomorrow, after breakfast, as a birthday present, I will take my granddaughter over to Wilson's Forest. I will tell her of that miraculous night ten years ago, the night she saw the starship fall to earth; I will show her the trees scattered like jackstraws, and tell her that she is the author of a work read by all manner of alien beings across the vast expanse of the galaxy, a work of pain, and grief—and of boundless love and hope rewarded.

SALVAGE RITES

I wrote the following tale as a one-off for Peter Crowther's AI anthology, We Think, Therefore We Are. *Then, as is the way with some stories, the characters and setting worked themselves further into my head and I realised there was a lot more to write about Salvageman Ed, his AI pilot Ella, his engineer Karrie, and their starship* A Long Way From Home. *Over the course of the next few years I wrote another ten stories with the same characters, which appeared in venues like Asimov's, Clarkesworld, Conflicts, and others. Then I rewrote the stories and assembled them in the fix-up novel* Salvage *in 2013.*

SALVAGE RITES

THE STARSHIP EMERGED FROM VOIDSPACE ONE PARSEC BEYOND ALTAIR. Ella found it during the graveyard shift. She was jacked into the sensors of the salvage tug and buzzed me a second after locating the drifting hulk. I jerked awake in my sling, ripped from dreams I'd rather not talk about.

"Something's come up," Ella said, and cut the link.

I stumbled from my berth, found the ladder to the observation nacelle and climbed. My heart was pounding, and not only from the exertion. The thought of being alone with Ella had that effect on me.

I entered the nacelle feet-first, stopped dead and stared through the blister.

She had found the monastery starship...

All starships are beautiful. They are colossal and totally silent and they *drift*. But the *St. Benedictus* was something special. She was twenty-five kilometres long from her nose cone to the flaring bells of her ion boosters. Her carapace was excoriated from five centuries in voidspace. Stained-glass viewscreens lined the length of the starboard flank.

Ella slid me a casual glance. "This what you been looking for half your life, Ed?"

"More than half," I murmured. "Call it thirty years."

Shaking, I collapsed into a sling and stared out at the wallowing starship. All of us have dreams, but most of them remain just that—fantasies that can never be realised. Here, before me, was my dream made real, the culmination of so much longing, so much hopeless yearning, that part of me disbelieved the search was at an end.

Though, perhaps, it was only just beginning.

"Oh, Christ," I said, near to tears.

She just looked at me. "You humans amaze me," she said at last.

I glanced across at Ella, slouched in her sling. She wore ripped shorts and something strapped around her chest in order to cover her non-existent breasts. She was slick with sweat, and her slim limbs highlighted the glare from the nearby sun.

I'd fallen in love before, but never with a non-human entity.

"Why's that?" I asked.

Staring out at the monastery, she smiled to herself. "I *know* what obsession is," she said. "I *know* what piety is. I just can't *feel* them."

"I don't know if that's your loss or not." I smiled at her, smitten by her beauty. Her template was Venezuelan Indian, her somaform that of a twenty-year-old female.

I'd found her in a bar on a backwater world of Sinclair's Landfall, Procyon, all her cash spent and without the funds to upgrade. Sitting alone, she'd seemed small and childlike and utterly vulnerable. I'd hired her on the spot, bought her a pilot addendum and introduced her to my tug, *A Long Way From Home*.

I think I looked upon her, then, as my salvage project.

"I monitored for signs of life," she said. "Nothing."

"Try hailing them, all frequencies."

"Already done that. No response."

Something felt very cold within me. "Can't all be dead," I whispered.

Ella was watching me.

"It isn't the salvage rights," I began.

"I know." She smiled. "I've seen you praying nights, after your shift."

I shrugged. "So . . . maybe they *did* find God."

She tipped her head to one side, then transferred her sceptical gaze from me to the becalmed behemoth.

I gave Ella the history lesson that was missing from her memory cache.

The *St. Benedictus* was launched with the blessing of the Vatican five hundred years ago when Earth received the coded tachyon vectors out of a star in the Lesser Magellanic Cloud. The decoded message spoke of God-like beings who'd seeded the galaxy with life, but the Catholic Church was sceptical and decided to send its own investigative party. Sub-lightspeed, the *St. Benedictus* headed off to the Cloud with a thousand monks in cold sleep—a state they called suspended prayer—and calculated they'd take around two hundred and fifty Earth years to reach their destination.

"And now they're back," Ella said. "But how did you calculate where they'd emerge, Ed?"

I shrugged. "Simple. They launched from Altair III. Made sense they'd emerge around here at some point."

"And you've been scouring the vicinity for thirty years?" she said in a tone halfway between wonder and ridicule.

I nodded and stared out at the drifting colossus, a sensation like epiphany welling in my diaphragm.

"Something I don't get, Ed. What makes you, a good Catholic boy, think these frozen monks've found God? The Vatican was sceptical, right?"

"The Pope back then was fallible, Ella. Look at her turnabout on the issue of AI sentience."

She tapped her head. "I wasn't programmed with such historical trivia." She smiled at me, as if to sweeten her acerbity. "So you been dreaming that they've found all the answers? Even found God?"

Unbidden, tears filled my eyes. "Ella, I haven't told anyone this for fifty years."

She looked at me, her expression blank. "What?"

"Back when I was a boy, just fourteen, my kid sister and me... we lived near the sea, a place called Sydney, Earth. We spent a lot of time just messing around, exploring the rock pools."

She tipped her head to one side. "And?

"And one day, a storm blew up. Maria was standing on the edge of the headland, taunting the waves... She always was a tom-boy."

"She died, right? The sea got her?"

"A wave swept up and took her away."

Ella said nothing, just tipped her head to the other side and stared at me.

"I watched as she was swept away. There wasn't a thing I could have done. I raised the alarm, then went straight to Church and prayed that she'd be rescued... and the next day, when they found her body, I went right back and prayed for the salvation of her mortal soul." I shrugged. "Guess I've been praying, on and off, ever since."

Ella just looked at me with those massive brown, non-human eyes. Did I read pity there, or were they merely empty?

I sat in the co-pilot's sling on the flight deck while Ella nuzzled us up close to the flank of the monastery ship.

Karrie, our engineer, stood before the viewscreen, her mouth open as she stared out at the great cliff-face of the starship. She turned to me and touched my hand, her eyes diffident. We were close—I'd worked with Karrie almost ten years, so of course we were close—but never *that* close.

It was not the ideal situation, the three of us cooped up in the confines of *A Long Way From Home*. I'd thought of firing Ella, two weeks after hiring her, when I began to realise what I felt for her. But by then it was too late.

"That's about as near as I dare go," Ella said.

"Near enough," I said.

Karrie swept greying tresses from her face and glanced at me, worried. "We need to talk it through," she said. "Let's not rush into this."

Ella said, "Ed's made up his mind, Karrie, as soon as he saw that thing out there."

Karrie shot Ella a venomous glare.

"Hey," I said. "I know what I'm doing. Don't worry. I might have waited years for this day, but that doesn't mean I'm rushing into anything. I've had plenty of time to plan this, get it right."

Karrie tried a smile. "Just wondering how we'll manage the business if you don't come back, Ed."

"I'll be back. I'll suit up and take the bell across. I'll be in there an hour, in com-contact all the time. After an hour, I'm outta there. Then we'll talk over what I found and take it from there." I looked from Karrie to Ella. "That sound sensible?"

Ella stared at me, calculating.

Karrie still looked worried. "Take care, Ed, okay?"

I slipped from my sling and made for the bay.

Karrie readied the bell, and I was suiting up when Ella's soft drawl sounded through my earpiece. "Ed, I'm getting something from the monastery ship."

"I'll be right up."

I left Karrie to finish off preparations and, heart pounding, climbed to the flight deck. Ella sat in her sling, her skull jacked into a com-line.

Her eyes were turned up to show their whites, eerily, and for second I was worried. Then she jerked, reached up and yanked the com-jack from her occipital augmentation. Her eyes were glazed when she turned to me.

"What?" I asked.

She shook her head. "Coded. Gigabytes of the stuff. Didn't make the slightest sense. Look, I need a couple of hours to work on what I cached."

"So there's someone alive in there?"

"Or the ship's AIs are running the show. I'll be able to tell you that in an hour or two."

I stared across at the ship, excitement pulling at my innards.

"Ed, I'd hold off going over there till I make sense of what they sent."

"I can't do that, Ella. I'll be in com-contact. Fill me in as soon as you've worked it out, okay?"

She reached out a small hand, touched my arm. The gesture could have been interpreted as caring, but I knew better.

"Ed, Karrie was right, you know? We shouldn't rush into this. It'd make sense to wait till we have as much knowledge as possible."

"So why didn't you back Karrie up earlier?" I asked.

"We didn't have the communiqué from the ship back then," she said. "And anyway, my agreeing with Karrie wouldn't make her hate me any less."

I looked at her hand, then touched her slim wrist with my fat, blunted fingers. "It'd be nice to think you cared."

"I care that you might be getting yourself into danger, Ed."

"Yeah. Who'd employ you, then?"

"That's cruel."

"It's true."

She stared at me and said, "I can empathise with you enough to realise when you're putting yourself in danger because of something irrational."

"Don't you ever feel anything other than the rational?" I asked her. "Christ, how sterile your existence must be!"

She shook her head. "Do you think I relish this emptiness, Ed? Don't you think I'd love to feel..." she gestured towards the monastery ship, "feel what you're feeling now? I can appreciate the philosophy of religion, understand its origins, but all I feel is its emptiness."

"I'm sorry, Ella."

"I'd love to experience rapture, to have faith, the knowledge that there is more to existence than the sheer mechanistic rote of birth and death, more than the existential certitude of entropy. But I'm not human, Ed, and never will be."

I chose to read self-pity into her words. I looked upon her, slight and apparently female and pathetic, and something moved me to stroke her arm and say, "Ella, ever since I first saw you, back in the bar on Sinclair's Landfall, something in here"—I thumped my chest—"went haywire. It's been growing ever since. I know, I'm old enough to know better. I don't want to call it love, but, Jesus, what else can I call it?"

"Ed." She tried to pull away.

"And the hell of it is, you can't feel a thing."

I stared at her. She returned my gaze. "When we get back, if you like, we can do sex."

I laughed at that. "You can't even call it making love, Ella."

"I have the physical urges that correlate to sexual arousal," she began.

"And you'd do it with anyone or anything that came along. Well, listen, with me . . . call me old-fashioned if you like, but when I 'do sex' I like it to mean something."

She looked away; I'd like to think that my outburst had in some way affected her, but the fact was that her console was flashing: another communiqué was incoming. She jacked herself into the com-line and showed me the whites of her eyes, and I fled the flight deck and joined Karrie in the bay.

I finished suiting up and inserted myself into the bell. Minutes later I was drifting through space, navigating my way from the tug and across to the curved flank of the starship. I eased the bell between two stained-glass viewscreens and it latched onto the deuterium panels like a limpet.

I activated the device I called the can opener, and ten minutes later the console signalled I was through. I initialled entry procedure from my wrist control panel and wriggled feet-first through the lock.

"Ed?" Karrie's voice was tinny in my helmet. I activated my wrist-screen and stared at her.

"I'm okay. I'm inside."

The perfect circle of metal from the ship's flank lay at my feet, its pitted surface contrasting with the stone-slabbed floor of a lateral corridor. A remote sensor detected my presence and obligingly activated the lighting.

"What's it like, Ed?"

I stared around me, and whistled. "Like . . . You ever been to Earth, Karrie? You ever seen a monastery?" I panned my wrist-screen around to give Karrie a virtual tour.

"Me, I'm a fully paid-up atheist, Ed."

I wasn't in a starship, but in the cloisters of a monastery. The curved walls were adorned with religious imagery: crucifixes, icons, effigies of saints . . . And the illumination wasn't your usual starship strip-halogens, but simulated candles in wax-encrusted sconces.

I swore I could smell incense, but that was my brain, playing tricks. My suit was sealed.

I'd pored over the schematics of the *St. Benedictus* for hours during my off-shifts, preparing myself for this moment. I turned right and headed off down the lateral, towards the cryogenic chamber where I hoped to find the sleeping monks. If, that was, they were still alive. I recalled Ella telling me she'd monitored for life, without success, and I wondered what I'd find.

I walked a kilometre. The ship was programmed for Earth-norm gravity, perhaps a little lighter, which made the hike easier. My movements alerted the sensors, so I progressed the length of the lateral in a constantly moving bubble of illumination. It gave me the eerie feeling of being observed.

"Ed?" Karrie said, all concern.

I glanced at her headpiece on my screen. "I'm fine. Making my way to the cold sleep chamber."

"Keep talking. I'm uneasy when you're silent."

I laughed. "There's nothing to be concerned about, Karrie."

"You don't know that. The ship's been away five hundred years. The monks might've..."

"What?" I said. A part of me was touched at her concern; another part felt guilty at wishing the concern was coming from Ella.

"I don't know. What might they have seen, Ed? What if what they found sent them mad?"

"You been watching too many holo-vees," I laughed.

"Just be careful, okay?"

I came to a junction, watched over by an effigy of the Madonna. I turned right. Ahead was darkness, banished as I walked.

"Where's Ella?" I asked.

"Right here on the flight deck. She's...not with us. Jacked in. Calculating something—like machines do."

"Working out what the monastery sent us, Karrie."

"She gives me the creeps, eyes turned up like that and spasming."

"Spasming?" I couldn't keep the concern from my voice.

"Yeah," Karrie said. "Jitter-bugging like she's taking a thousand volts." She turned her wrist-screen to show me Ella, writhing in her sling.

"Routine procedure," I said, more to reassure myself.

A beat, then Karrie said, "What do you see now, Ed?"

I looked around me. "Corridor, a long corridor. I should be coming to the chamber soon."

Karrie said, "You've been gone twenty minutes, Ed. You gave yourself an hour, right? Then you're outta there."

"Right, boss," I said.

I stopped walking. Up ahead I made out an arched entrance. "I'm there," I said. "The cryo chamber."

I approached the entrance and slowed. I remembered entering a cathedral, the last time I was on Earth. St Paul's, London, I think it was. Now I experienced the same charge, increased a hundredfold.

I crossed the threshold and a faux chandelier came on, filling the circular chamber with light.

The cryo-pods were catafalques... except, these tombs were empty.

"Ed?"

I crossed to the nearest bank of pods. The crystal lids were lifted, revealing vacant containers with masses of redundant leads and subcutaneous needles.

"Ed, for Chrissake!"

I panned my wrist-screen to shut her up. "It's okay. I'm in the cryo-chamber, but it's empty."

"Where are they?" Karrie asked.

"If they're alive, then..."

"What?"

"Think about it. What would you do at journey's end, but give thanks? They're in the chapel, Karrie. Stands to reason." If they're still alive, I reminded myself.

After a short silence, she said, "You've been gone almost thirty minutes, Ed. You'd better be thinking about making your way back pretty soon."

"Will do," I lied.

I quit the cryogenic chamber and headed into the heart of the ship.

I heard the chant of plainsong well before I reached the chapel.

A thousand voices sang, supernal; the sound crescendoed, filling my chest with a nameless emotion. I felt like weeping. I thought about Maria, drowning all those years ago. I thought of Ella, who would never experience anything like this.

"Ed? What's that?" Karrie asked.

"Kyrie eleison," I told her.

"It's—"

"Beautiful," I finished for her.

I closed my eyes, and I was young again, and Maria was by my side; we entered the church, and she knelt and prayed, and later I asked her and she told me that she had prayed for my eternal happiness. I was eight, and sentiments like that meant all the world to me, then.

I could never explain that to Karrie, or to Ella, for fear of ridicule.

I opened my eyes and approached the great double doors of the chapel, pushed them open and stepped inside.

The pews were filled with kneeling monks, and the sound hit me in a wave. Heads bowed, cowls hiding their faces, their voices soared to heaven.

Ahead, raised in the pulpit, I made out the small figure of the Abbot, arms spread wide as if in welcome so that he resembled the great crucifix that hung behind him on the bulkhead.

I progressed down the aisle.

Heads turned, faces stared at me.

I felt real fear, then. I must have made a sound of alarm.

"Ed?" Karrie said.

"They're ... " was all I could bring myself to say.

"Ed!"

To a man, the monks wore cranial addenda, matte-black augmentations embedded in their skulls. Some had receptors instead of eyes; others, as if in some perverted rite of mortification, had replaced all their facial features with embedded sensors, silver panels etched with arcane sigils of alien design.

"They're cyborgs ... " I whispered.

"Ed, get yourself out of there!"

Instead of obeying her frantic command, I continued walking towards the altar, and as I went I made a sickening observation.

The closer to the altar, the more augmented—I should say ravaged—the rows of monks became. Not for these pious devotees the simple sensory implants of their fellows further back. I made out naked monks enmeshed in silver webworks, their etiolated flesh pressing between cheese-wire filaments of God-knew-what provenance. Others were encased in exoskeletons, the interface between machine and flesh weeping blood like some unholy stigmata.

I was at the altar now, and staring up at the Abbot, or rather what remained of him. He was naked, and wore his augmentations like some chitinous carapace, and the only part of his face still human was a mouth twisted into a demented smile.

"Kneel," he said, and like a lamb I knelt before him.

Karrie was screaming now for me to get the hell out.

The Abbot made the sign of the cross above my head, and intoned, "We have beheld the work of the Lord, and have returned to spread the word."

The chanting ceased suddenly, and in the following silence the Abbot spoke to me.

They had found the race that, he said, had moved throughout the galaxy aeons ago and seeded worlds with the stuff of proto-life, and then returned to their homeworld and settled into what they called a state of blessed Uplift.

The Seeders, as the Abbot called them, had undergone a radical surgical procedure and melded with their inventions, AIs that bequeathed them insights into the nature of being not granted to puny biological intelligences.

Then the Seeders had offered the Abbot and his monks the opportunity to join the blessed. "You might say they wished to *salvage* us," said the Abbot.

He gazed across his flock, and his smile became beatific. "We accepted their offer, and were Uplifted, and oh...the joy! We looked upon the truth, and marvelled. We realised how blessed we were, and how cursed we had been, purblind with our limited senses, our nascent minds incapable of grasping the true nature of reality."

I managed to ask, "But did you find God?"

Before the Abbot could reply, a voice yelled in my earpiece. "Ed, she's gone—" It was Karrie, and in the sensory overload of the moment her words made no sense.

"Ed, are you there? Ella's left the tug! She's in the second bell and making for the ship. She took something from stores. I followed her but I couldn't make out what she'd taken. Ed, if you can hear me, get back to the bell and get yourself over here!"

I moved my lips to say something, but meaningful words were beyond me.

The Abbot was saying, "We are like children come to adulthood, granted awareness—"

Another voice intruded upon my consciousness. It was Ella, shouting at me, "Ed, I'm coming for you. Get back to the bell. I'll see you there."

"Ella?" I intoned, incredulous. She was coming for me. Did that mean she perceived some danger? Did that mean she *cared*? Was it possible, I wondered.

"Ella?"

"Ed, I decoded their communiqué. I understood only a part of what they said, but that was enough." Her voice broke up, chopped by static.

The Abbot smiled down at me. "Yes, child, we did find God."

He was beatific as he declaimed to me. He spoke of abstruse philosophies that my tug-captain's mind had no hope of grasping; he spoke of intellectual destiny, of the manifest truth hardwired into the universe at the level of quantum strings. "We beheld the genome of God, and were blessed."

I reached out to him, as if for help. "But did you learn . . . did God tell you . . . ? Is there . . . " I sobbed, "is there an afterlife?"

The Abbot laughed, a sound less human than mechanical, and cried aloud, "There is but one destiny for those of piety, and that is life everlasting when the state of Uplifted grace is achieved."

"But?" I pressed. "For mortals like myself?"

He turned silver sensors upon me, and I interpreted his blind gaze as one of great pity. "There is but one road to salvation," he said, "and that is to enjoin us in blessed Uplift."

"Maria," I wept. Into my head flashed the last image I had ever had of Maria, alive: a tiny girl in a red dress, screaming as the wave took her . . . and then, later, laid to rest before the altar of the church.

"Ed!" Ella's voice cut through my grief. "I told you to meet me at the bell!"

"Where are you?" I said.

"I'm coming for you!"

"Ella . . . "

"Ed, listen to me. When I monitored for life earlier, and didn't find any—that's because they're *dead*. Get out of there, Ed!"

"Dead?"

"Biologically dead!" Ella shouted at me.

"But they said they'd found God—"

Ella said, softly, "How can the dead find anything, Ed?"

Static cut off her words, and above me the Abbot smiled.

I fled him and his accursed acolytes. Their renewed chanting followed me all the way from the chapel and down the corridor as I ran like a man possessed, haunted by visions of Maria. I cried two names as I went, those of the only people who had ever meant anything to me.

At a sound from behind me, I turned.

The first of the monks were hurrying along the corridor towards me. As I stared, incredulous, those in front raised weapons and fired. Hot vectors missed me by centimetres and turned the walls to slag.

I sprinted.

———.———

Ella collided with me at the corner of the junction, with the Blessed Virgin Mary smiling down at us. "Ed!" she cried with relief.

I don't know what I replied, if anything. I did not want to ask if she really cared; I was content enough to interpret her actions as solicitous.

She looked up, past me, towards where a phalanx of monks rounded a corner, chanting.

Only then did I see what she had taken from stores. The fusion-bazooka was lodged on her hip, as ugly as she was beautiful. She pushed me behind her, roughly, then knelt and fired. The leading monks exploded in beautiful flame, like votive candles.

Then she half-dragged, half-carried me along the corridor, turning from time to time to lay down covering fire. The monks loosed vectors after us, and Ella screamed with what sounded like human fury and pulled me along after her.

Long minutes later we came to the holes in the skin of the ship where our bells had cut through.

Then she took me by the shoulders and shook me. "Ed! Listen to me. These people—they're dangerous. You can't imagine their power, and their commitment. They think they have the monopoly on the truth."

"Ella, I simply wanted to know—"

She stared at me, and I saw compassion in her eyes. "I know, Ed. I'm sorry." She pushed me towards the bell. "Get back to the tug."

"And you?" I resisted her pressure.

She stared at me, as if calculating something. "They want to convert you, Ed. They want to convert the human race to . . . to what they have become. And they have the means to do it. They've got to be stopped."

She pushed me, and I resisted, terrified of what she planned. "Ella!"

"Please forgive me, Ed," she said, and reached up and inserted something into the input socket of my suit. Electric pain lanced through my body, and consciousness dwindled.

The last I knew, Ella was bundling me into the confines of the bell. I heard the hatch hiss shut and passed out.

Karrie helped me out at the other end and hauled me up to the flight deck. I recall little of those long minutes. My head was full of Maria's futile death, and whatever Ella planned across the vacuum in the monastery starship.

Karrie eased me into the sling and opened a communication link with Ella.

The screen before us wavered, then resolved itself. I stared into Ella's magnified features. She was staring into her wrist-screen and talking to us. Karrie located the audio channel and Ella's words flooded the flight deck.

"Listen to me. Get the tug out of here, okay? And purge the smartware core—I wiped what I could, but I might have left something."

"Ella?" Karrie said.

"They beamed codes across, blueprints," she said. "They call it the Uplift Bible. If that stuff got into the wrong hands..."

I leaned forward, desperate. "Ella, what the hell are you doing?"

In reply, she panned her wrist-screen. She was in the engine room, dwarfed by the monstrous forms of the fission reactors.

"Ella...?"

She stared into her wrist-screen and smiled at me, and I thought she mouthed, *I love you.*

But I was wrong, of course. I was delirious, and mistaken, for Ella was not human, was not capable of such sentiments.

I stared at Ella's beautiful Venezuelan face as she smiled out at me. "They must be stopped," she murmured, and adjusted the setting on her fusion-bazooka.

"Ed?" Karrie cried beside me.

"They're coming for me, Ed. This is the only way."

Ella's face disappeared from the screen, and the picture became a crazy blur as she swung her weapon and aimed at the reactors.

"Ella!" I cried.

A roar, followed by an actinic explosion. The screen went blank, and I transferred my gaze to the outer viewscreen and stared at the bulk of the *St. Benedictus.*

The starship bucked. It seemed to heave once as the reactors detonated deep within its innards. In places, as multiple explosions ripped through the ship, outer panels glowed red hot; in others, where the carapace could not hold, the stained-glass viewscreens exploded outwards and scattered through the vacuum like confetti, scintillating in the light of Altair.

Then the ship slumped and listed to starboard, truly becalmed now, and I whispered, "Ella..."

——·——

Much later I manoeuvred the tug towards the *St. Benedictus*, and Karrie activated the grapples. Together we obeyed Ella's final instruction and purged the smartware core.

I wondered if what I had told Ella, before I left for the starship, had somehow instigated her actions. Had my avowal of love made her see the sterility of mechanistic existence, and the fate wished upon us by the monks of the *St. Benedictus?*

I wondered, as I set course and boosted the maindrive, if my words had damned Ella to eternal oblivion.

Karrie smiled sadly, reached out and took my hand. I squeezed.

We towed the monastery starship towards Altair III in silence.

LAYING THE GHOST

I've assembled the stories in this volume in the order in which I wrote them, to give some indication of how my writing has changed—for the better, I hope!—over the years. Although I wrote the previous Salvageman Ed tale before the following story, chronologically "Laying the Ghost" comes before "Salvage Rites" (which explains why Ella is alive again in the following tale—I'm glad we've got that clear). I enjoyed writing about Ed and Ella and Karrie, and one day I'd like to write more about them. "Laying the Ghost" first appeared in Clarkesworld 49, 2010.

Laying the Ghost

WE WERE WINDING DOWN AFTER COMING IN FROM ALDEBARAN WITH A haul of starship wreckage. I'd sold the scrap en route and left it in geo-sync orbit above Constance, Altair III, for the merchant to collect. The funds were already in my account and I was treating Ella and Karrie to a meal and a few drinks.

A pianist was improvising Lyran mood-music and the ceiling pulsed with images of Jovian superstorms. Across the spaceport, starships were phasing into and out of the void in eerie silence.

While Ella was at the bar, Karrie said, "For an AI, you know, she's almost . . . well, human."

"She's running on a self-aware paradigm, Karrie. That paradigm is human. She has all the emotional capacity of you and me. As far as I'm concerned, she's our equal."

Karrie just looked at me.

"What?" I said.

"Talking about emotional capacity, Ed . . . Have you ever considered your own?

I stared at her. "*Mine?*"

"Have you heard of the expression 'a cold fish'?"

You can know someone for years—in this case almost ten—and still be amazed at how they view you. "Me? What on earth makes you think that?"

She enumerated her argument with calloused fingers. "One, you never talk. I mean about things that matter, your feelings, your emotions. You never allow people into your head."

I said, "You wouldn't want to go there. It's full of day-to-day rubbish. Nothing deep going on in there."

"You see—there you go again. Trivialising what is important. Two," she went on before I could protest, "you never talk about your past, what's affected you. Three, you rarely speak about the future, what you want—other than the next big haul."

"And what's wrong with talking about the next big haul?" I said dismissively.

Karrie snorted.

I was glad to see that Ella was returning with a tray of drinks. As she slinked through the crowd, I noticed a few men and women covertly eyeing her slim body. She slipped into the booth, smiling at me.

"What do you think, Ella?" Karrie said, taking her drink.

Oh, God . . . I thought.

"About what, Karrie?"

"About Ed. Do you think he has deficient emotional capacity?"

Ella looked from Karrie to me, her expression serious. She said, "I think his emotional capacity is far from deficient, Karrie. What is deficient is his ability to express, to *show*, those emotions. I suspect some past trauma is inhibiting him in this respect." She looked at me. "Maybe you will tell us about it, one day?"

Karrie was smirking at this turn in the conversation.

I said, "Well, thanks. Here I was, enjoying a quiet drink with my crewmates, when everything gets suddenly psychoanalytical. Listen, there's nothing wrong with me, emotionally or otherwise. I have no hang-ups, no inhibitions. I'm happy Ed, the salvageman."

I raised my glass. "Anyway, here's to many another successful haul."

Around then I noticed the figure in the Orion warware spacesuit. It was moving from group to group of drinkers, talking to them briefly and then moving on. From the dismissive gestures of the people spoken to, I received the impression that whoever was in the suit was asking for something, and being turned down.

A minute later the figure perched itself on a stool at the opening of the booth and stared at us.

I say 'stared', but I only assumed that. The oval faceplate in its sleek, silver helmet was as milky as opal. Its silver suit was streamlined and body-hugging, the surface swarming with millions of nanoware-bots like iron-filings in oil.

From its shape, I guessed there was a woman in there.

"What do you want?" Karrie asked brusquely.

"I find myself in a difficult situation," it said. Its voice was feminine, but transistorised. For all I knew, the inhabitant of the suit might not even be human.

She went on, "I need to leave Constance, but I cannot locate a ship heading in the direction I require."

Before Karrie could jump in with some sarcastic comment, I asked, "And where's that?"

A hesitation, then, "The Chandrasakar Stardrift."

I whistled. "That's quite a way away."

"Five thousand three hundred light years, give or take."

Karrie shook her head, derisive, and took a long swallow of beer.

"Where specifically in the Stardrift?" I said.

"A planet called Serimion, Kharran II."

"Serimion..." I said. "Now where have I heard the name before?"

Ella said, quick as a flash, "Serimion: site of the war between human colonists and the native inhabitants of the Kharran system. It was a particularly brutal and bloody conflict. The alien race known as the Kha, from the fifth planet of the system, invaded without provocation. Approximately three million humans lost their lives on Serimion."

The person in the suit said, "Precisely three million, two hundred thousand and ninety. Let no lost soul go unmourned."

I asked the obvious question. "But why do you want to go to Serimion?"

The being hesitated again, before saying, "I have my reasons."

"But won't it be dangerous? I mean, won't the Kha be hostile to human arrivals?"

"They allow a certain number of mourners and war historians to visit the shrines of Serimion every year," she said.

I wondered which category she fell into.

I considered for a minute, then said, "Well, it's a long way, and not where we were heading. The fare would be hefty."

A silence. The opalescent faceplate turned to me, and the soft, feminine, transistorised voice said, "That is the other slight problem. I am without the funds to finance the journey."

Karrie snorted and shuffled from the booth. "I'll be back at the ship, Ed." She stood and hurried from the bar.

The milky oval of the faceplate, behind which anything might be lurking, was still regarding me.

I said, "A lack of funds is certainly a problem. I don't see how..."

The figure pointed to my flight-suit. "I see you bear the sigil of a salvage captain. There is a small starship, a strike vessel, drifting in orbit around Serimion. It belongs to me. You may take it in recompense, if you agree to transport me there."

I looked at Ella, who said, "What kind of strike vessel, exactly?"

"A Corinthian, Class II."

Ella said to me, "Even badly damaged, it would fetch approximately twenty-five thousand Altairian units on the open market."

Which would more than cover the cost of the return journey to the Chandra-sakar Stardrift.

Of course, there was no way of telling if the being in the suit was telling the truth.

I said, "Show me your face."

After a moment, on some internal command, the faceplate cleared.

"You're human?" I stared at the pretty, impish face revealed; dark, short hair, high cheekbones, a snub nose. She looked no older than twenty.

"But why the suit?" I asked.

She shrugged, twisted her lips uncomfortably. "I... I have a certain condition. My immune system is dysfunctional." And she left it at that.

She looked at me, hope evident in her big brown eyes. "Well?"

I said, "What's your name?"

"Katerina," she replied. "Katerina Reverte."

"Well, Katerina... Why don't you give me five minutes to discuss things with my co-pilot here?"

Katerina rose and strode across to the floor-to-ceiling viewscreen that looked out over the expanse of the spaceport. Reduced in the perspective, she looked tiny, vulnerable.

"Well," I said. "What do you think?"

"I think the situation is certainly odd. She is wearing an Orion warware suit, which is even more expensive than a Corinthian. She could sell the suit, which would more than pay for her medical treatment. It would also pay for her return to Serimion."

"You think she's lying about her condition?"

"That is certainly a possibility."

"And about the Corinthian, too?"

"Impossible to ascertain."

I said, "It'd be a risk."

"I would like to know the reason she wishes to return to Serimion."

"My guess is she fought in the war. She wishes to return to lay ghosts, to revisit old battlefields."

"Maybe."

"Well, perhaps we'll find out along the way."

Ella fixed me with one of her impassive stares. "You will agree to take her?"

I nodded, and looked across the lounge to the suited figure. Katerina had turned and was watching us. I signalled her over.

She came hesitantly, almost wincing. I held out my hand. "We phase out in five hours," I told her.

Her expression, behind the faceplate, was joyous.

Karrie took a while to simmer down, even when I told her about the Corinthian.

"But you know nothing about her! Who she is, what she is! She's striding around here in that damned war suit... You realise how powerful those things are?"

I shrugged. We were a day out of Altair III, sailing through the marmoreal realm of void-space, two days away from the Chandrasakar Stardrift.

Karrie went on, "Why did you agree, Ed?"

I shrugged again. "She's young, vulnerable. Everyone else back there had turned her down."

She stared at me. "I just don't believe you."

I smiled at her. "What did you say back at the port, that I didn't show my emotions? Well, I'm showing them now. I feel sorry for the kid and I want to help her—"

Karrie pointed at me. "This has nothing to do with your emotions, Ed, and all to do with your male biology."

"Bullshit, Karrie!"

Ella chose that moment to slip through the hatch and cross the flight deck. She eased into her sling with a smile at me. "For two people who have been in each other's company for almost ten years," she said, softly, "you spend a lot of time in altercations."

"That's what ten years of being banged up with a sarcastic, sour-faced cynic like Karrie does to you."

"And fuck you, too," Karrie spat.

"Anyway," Ella said, "the drives are functioning at ninety-eight per cent efficiency, the smartcore reports no problems, and mechanically all aboard the ship is running smoothly." Did I discern the stress she put on the word *mechanically*?

Under her breath, Karrie muttered, "And you'd know about that, girl," but if Ella heard her, she chose to turn the other cheek.

"Have you had a chance to talk to Katerina?" I asked.

Ella nodded. "I took her on a tour of the ship."

"Learn anything?"

"Very little. She said she was born and brought up on Serimion, but when I asked about the war, and whether she fought in it, she clammed up."

"Do you know much about Serimion?"

"My cache has an extensive file on the planet: settled by humans over two centuries ago, a pastoral place of vast agricultural concerns, a million villages, considered by the rest of the Expansion to be technologically backward. It was settled by a breakaway faction of the Amish community of Mars. The attack by the neighbouring Kha came out of the blue."

"And no one has ever found out why the aliens invaded?"

Ella shrugged. "A motive was never discovered. That's what rankles with the survivors to this day."

She fell silent and stared through the viewscreen at the grey void.

"I think I'll go talk to Katerina," I said.

As I slipped from my sling and approached the hatch, Karrie said, "You'll have difficulty getting that suit off her, if that's what you're thinking about. Seems she's welded to the damned thing."

I bit my tongue and pulled myself through the hatch, wondering what Karrie's problem was.

As I descended the ladder, I heard Ella saying, "You should cease your criticism of Ed. He is, after all, biologically impelled by male drives."

And I'd thought Ella was on my side . . .

I found Katerina in the observation lounge. She was seated before the great curving viewscreen, staring into the void. She had the cowed aspect of a devotee at a temple, a worshipper in a cathedral of the infinite.

"Do you mind?" I asked, gesturing at the foamform beside her.

She looked up. "No, please. Be my guest."

I sat down beside her and saw that her faceplate was once again blank.

"Ella told me she'd shown you around the ship."

I stared at her sleek silver suit, wondering at its power.

"She gave me a guided tour." She paused, then went on, "She is an AI, isn't she?"

"Yes, but one running on a self-aware paradigm."

She turned her faceless faceplate to me and said, "Does that make her human, Ed?"

I smiled and shrugged. "I honestly don't know, Katerina. It does make her a sentient being. And my equal. That's what matters to me."

"Will you apologise to Ella for me, Ed?"

"What for?"

"For my inability to... to talk to her openly. She wanted to talk, I sensed, but I was unable to respond."

"Because she wasn't human?" I asked.

Instead of replying, she retuned her gaze to the infinite. A little later she said, "Do you believe in vitalism, Ed? The idea that—"

I smiled. "I know what vitalism means."

"Well?"

"I don't know. Perhaps, once, I did. It's a nice idea, after all, to think that humans are imbued with a special, God-given light of fire, vitality, soul..."

"Perhaps once?" she said. "But no longer?"

I smiled. "Then I met Ella and I had to rearrange my thinking a little."

"So you think that life can exist without that vitality?"

"Look at Ella," I said.

She turned to look at me. "Yes," she said, "but is Ella truly alive?"

I shrugged, and let out a long sigh, out of my depth and uncomfortable. I said, "What about you? Do you believe in vitalism?"

She turned her head to me and said, "Oh, I know vitalism is real."

I nodded. Ella had informed me that the Serimion colony had been religious.

She went on, in her own time, "I was brought up believing in a just God, a God who punished the bad and rewarded the good. We were a peaceful people. We practised non-violence, living within our means, at one and in harmony with our environment, our world. We knew how lucky, how God-blessed we were in settling on Serimion, and we gave thanks."

Beyond the viewscreen, the grey void swirled. There were times when I thought I discerned patterns in the marmoreal streaks in the infinite, and others when I knew that the void was purely random and chaotic.

Katerina went on, softly, "I was brought up on a big farm, run by my parents. I had four older brothers... They treated me like a princess." I'm sure, had I been able to see her face, I would have witnessed her smiling. "We worked hard and worshipped daily, and life was bountiful and good. We knew our neighbours and trusted them. They were like us. I never really apprehended that there was an outside world, and other ways of doing things. Even when I graduated from school and attended college ... all the world was one, one belief, one way of doing things. And then ... "

And then, I thought, the Kha attacked.

"I was on holiday with friends at the time. We were in a resort on an island far to the south. This saved my life. We were aware that something terrible had happened ... the firestorms in the atmosphere, the explosions. We saw their attack ships in the distance. And when we returned to the mainland ... "

She fell silent. I reached out and laid my big hand over her small, cold silver mitt.

She went on, "Devastation. Destruction. All the cities, every one of them, all the small towns ... destroyed. Firebombed, and worse. They'd used weapons we didn't even understand. Reducing people and places to dust ... We never stood a chance. We didn't even ... didn't even have an army." She fell silent. Then: "I returned home, or to what was left of it. I found my parents, my four brothers. They were dust, Ed, with just scraps of clothing here and there to identify them."

I let a respectful interval elapse, then said, "How did you get off-planet?"

"A Federation ship had monitored the attack and sent rescue rafts. All told, just seven thousand of us survived. We—well, a few thousand of us—decided to fight back. Our rage, our grief, overcame our pacific instincts, our long-held beliefs. We had assets lodged in banks across the Expansion, and we bought attack ships and ... " she raised her hand, "and state-of-the-art warware. And we returned to Serimion and fought the Kha."

I said, "What happened?"

She turned her helmet towards me. "We lost."

Minutes elapsed. We were alone with our separate thoughts as we stared into the void.

I said, "And vitalism, Katerina? Your certainty ... ?"

She turned to look at me. "I know it's real, Ed, because of what happened to me in orbit around my homeplanet." And she left it at that and hung her helmeted head.

I hesitated, then asked, "What happened, Katerina?"

She just shook her head in silence.

I squeezed her gloved hand, and thought it wise to leave her to her memories.

I returned to the flight deck and was relieved to see that Karrie was not there.

Ella hung in her sling, her head flung back and the whites of her eyes showing.

She sensed my presence and came back from whichever cyber-realm she'd been inhabiting. "I was integrating with the ship's smartware core, Ed," she said matter-of-factly.

I smiled to myself, wondering at the process which allowed her to commune with my ship's logic matrix.

"I've been talking to Katerina," I said. "She told me about what happened on Serimion." I told Ella what Katerina had said about the attack, her return to fight the Kha. Her defeat.

"Which makes me all the more curious why she wishes to return there, Ed."

I shook my head, and then found myself reaching out and taking Ella's hand. It was small, warm, and very human. I held it tight and said, "Ella, when I was young... my sister died. That's another story. I don't want to talk about it now."

She stared at me with her big brown eyes. "What do you want to talk about?"

I took a breath. "After what happened, I found myself drawn back to the place where Maria died. I was compelled. I couldn't explain why. It was the place where she'd last been alive; perhaps that was it. Perhaps I thought I might commune with whatever of her remained. Silly, I know. But anyway, I had to go back. And you know something? When I did, when I went back and stood on that spot, and thought of my sister and the tragic accident that robbed her of her life, and when I cried... Well, I felt a lot better for doing so." I squeezed Ella's hand. "Perhaps that's why Katerina's going back? Can you understand that, Ella?"

She returned my gaze with her lustrous eyes. "Yes, Ed," she said. "Yes, I understand perfectly."

One thousand Kha sentinels, grey and monolithic and as vast as ten city blocks, hung in space around the defeated planet of Serimion.

My ship's smartware core spoke in its soothing, feminine contralto. "Kha AIs have established contact, Ed. They wish to know the purpose of our visit."

"Tell them that we're here to pay our respects to the human dead," I said, "and we seek clearance to land on Serimion."

We eased to a halt beside one of the sheer grey monoliths, and waited.

Framed within the girdle of sentinels, the planet tilted ten degrees off its polar axis, blue and white and twice the size of Earth.

Ella said, "It's beautiful."

"I'm not looking forward to finding out what might be down there," I said. "If the Kha let us through, that is."

Karrie joined us on the flight deck and eased herself into her sling.

I said, "So, our passenger proved the security risk you mentioned, Karrie?" I couldn't help the jibe.

She looked at me. "No, but there's something seriously wrong with the girl."

"What?" Ella asked.

"Have you noticed she doesn't eat? It's been three days since leaving Constance, and I've taken six trays of food to her berth. She hasn't touched a thing."

I shrugged. "So . . . the girl wasn't hungry. She's returning to the place where her family, her people, were massacred, after all."

Ella turned in her sling. "Ed," she said, almost reluctantly. "There is something else that doesn't quite ring true. Physically, Katerina appears to be twenty, twenty-five years old."

"Go on."

"I've been double-checking the records. The Kha attacked Serimion twenty-five years ago."

I stared down at the slowly rotating planet. I recalled Katerina's youthful, elfish face within her helmet.

Karrie said, "Seems to me like the girl's been lying to us, Ed."

I was about to ask Ella why Katerina might have lied when the smartcore said, "Clearance granted. The Kha have issued a two-day pass. We must be out of Serimion airspace within forty-eight hours."

Katerina joined us on the flight deck. She stood between my sling and Ella's and stared through the viewscreen at her homeplanet.

She had cleared her faceplate, and her youthful face stared out, her eyes wide in wonder.

"I have the coordinates for the Corinthian," she said, and reeled off a series of numbers to Ella.

We eased past the sentinel. I was glad to leave the cold, inhuman monolith in our wake. Ten minutes later, Ella pointed. Through the viewscreen we made out the becalmed wreck of the Corinthian, nose down in relation to the planet, ragged holes puncturing its fuselage.

Karrie said, "And you survived that?"

"I wish I hadn't," Katerina said, softly.

I said, "Okay, Ella. Stow those coordinates and we'll tractor beam the Corinthian on the way out." I turned to Katerina. "Now, where do you want us to land?"

—.—

"No one has ever seen the Kha," Katerina told us. "They have had no contact with the Human Expansion, and do not allow visitors to their homeplanet. When they struck Serimion, they did so from altitude. Later, when we returned and engaged them in battle, we saw their ships but never the Kha themselves. The few Kha vessels we managed to destroy exploded in space, so no alien remains were ever discovered." She paused, then went on, "Some say the Kha resemble devils, others maintain they are insectoid. To me, it does not matter. The very sound of their name conjures absolute evil."

We were drifting slowly over the planet's vast southern continent. Ruined villages and townships punctuated the green continuity of the veldt. Roads and rivers threaded the landscape, but nothing moved down there. Absolute stillness greeted our gaze, and I could not help but think of the planet as a cemetery without gravestones.

We floated towards the planet's equator, where Katerina's family had farmed the land. Veldt turned to rainforest, a vast tangle of alien vines and great gnarled, crimson trees, and then the rainforest gave way to a range of purple mountains that ran parallel to a great rift valley. Between these geographic features stretched a plain of fertile land that was Katerina's birthplace.

Ella touched my arm. "Look. Down there."

Something squatted on the plain. I said, "Bring us down, slowly."

Ella eased the ship to within a hundred metres of the thing.

Katerina said in a tiny voice, "Could it be a Kha?"

We hung in the air, observing.

I could not tell whether it was mechanical or biological. Twenty metres long, perhaps ten high, it was armour plated with what looked like matte black chitin, domed and segmented and squatting on the ground as if devouring prey.

From what I guessed was its head section, or what might have been its control centre, a long proboscis—or drill—punctured the soil.

Whether a Kha, or one of their creations, its act was symbolic of the rape of the planet.

As we watched, it seemed to shiver with ecstasy, or maybe just mechanical vibration.

I glanced at Ella. "Sound?"

She passed her hand over her controls and a deep ululation filled the flight deck. It reminded me of the chanting of a thousand monks, resonant and dolorous.

I asked Ella, "Do you know whether it's alive, or...?"

She went rigid in her sling; her eyeballs rolled to show only their whites as she attempted to communicate with the thing.

She shook her head. "It's hard to tell. I sense a biological core, surrounded by extensive technological addenda."

I looked at Ella, saying nothing.

In a tiny voice, Katerina said, "We revered our planet, Ed. We loved the earth. This... this *thing* is robbing its vitality."

I reached out to take her gloved hand, but she pulled away. "Get us away from here! I don't want to..." She turned from the viewscreen, holding her helmeted head in her hands.

Ella sped us from the thing, towards the continental rift valley.

We came down on a plain of lush grassland beside the escarpment.

A hundred metres before the ship was the outline of farm buildings, and beyond them the geometric pattern of fields, their crops gone wild long ago.

Katerina said, "I would like a few minutes by myself, Ed. Then, would you come and join me? I have a lot I must explain."

"Of course," I said.

She left the flight deck. Minutes later her tiny figure emerged from the shadow of the ship, moving past the ruins of the farmhouse towards the edge of the escarpment.

She stood with her arms on her hips and stared about her.

In silence, we watched.

After a minute she moved towards a lone tree that grew at an angle, leaning out over the rift valley. It was similar to those I had seen in the rainforest, crimson and contorted, with a vast, spreading leaf canopy.

She found a place in its gnarled root system and sat down, staring out across the abyss.

Like this, very still, she remained for perhaps fifteen minutes.

At length she turned and raised a hand, and I took this as a summons.

Ella and Karrie said nothing as I left the flight deck and climbed down to the air lock. I cycled myself through and stepped out onto the soil of Serimion. The first thing I noticed was the scent, a heady, spicy mix of soil and flower blooms. The grass, I saw, was embroidered with a spread of tiny yellow flowers, which gave off an almost overpowering perfume as I strode from the ship towards where Katerina sat.

At one point I paused and looked back. Ella and Karrie stood before the viewscreen, gazing down at me like figures in an aquarium.

I passed into the shade of the great leaning tree and picked my way through the knuckled roots until I came to the girl. I sat down beside her. "It's a beautiful world, Katerina."

She turned to me. Her youthful face showed behind her faceplate, and she smiled. "It was even more beautiful, Ed, before they attacked."

I looked away, and then saw, standing among the raised roots on the edge of the escarpment, six simple wooden crosses.

She saw the direction of my gaze and said, "We had a custom on Serimion, Ed. We buried our dead beside trees, and this was my parent's favourite place on all the planet. At sunset they would come out here with a drink and just sit and admire the view."

The silence stretched. A warm wind picked up the scent of the flowers and swamped us.

She said, "After the attack, I drove back here from the southern coast, passing devastated towns and knowing what I would find. The farm was destroyed, looking much as it does now. I found no personal possession, no mementos . . . Perhaps that was a good thing. To have found objects that belonged to Mother and Father and my brothers, that would have been too much. Now, I would like something to remind me . . ." She turned and smiled at me. "Is that silly?"

I returned her smile. "Not at all, Katerina."

"I found what was left of my family . . . or perhaps I was kidding myself. I found scraps of clothing, and dust, and scooped it up and carried it over here and buried it beside the tree, then planted wooden crosses I made from what remained of the farmhouse. I even said prayers, and then vowed to get my revenge.

"I don't know whether it was hours or days before I was found by a rescue ferry and taken to the nearest human colony world." She waved. "Anyway, two years later I did come back, in this suit, in the Corinthian, and I did exact a futile, limited form of revenge. I destroyed two Kha craft and then, and then . . ."

She gathered herself, then went on, "And then a Kha fighter struck, and disabled the Corinthian, and left me for dead. A rescue vessel picked me up, took me back to the colony world . . ."

She gazed down at the forlorn row of crosses. From this angle, I could not see her face.

"I said I had a lot to explain, Ed."

"The attack happened twenty-five years ago," I said, "and yet your face is that of a woman of twenty. You never eat, never open your suit . . ."

307

She turned her helmet and looked at me. Behind the faceplate I could see silver tears tracking down her cheeks. She raised a gloved hand and stared at it. "These suits were the latest Orion warware. They were made to help a fighter fight, augmented with an integrated AI to boost physical reaction time, mental acuity." She stopped, and her next words surprised me, "Do you know why I came here, Ed?"

I said, "To pay respects, to lay the ghost?"

She laughed, briefly. "That's good. I like that. Yes, to lay the ghost." She stared at me. "I came to this grave site to bury myself."

I stared at her, and watched as she lifted her gloves to her helmet and touched a control at the neck. The helmet opened slowly, folding out in sections, blooming like a flower. At some point in the process the hologram showing her youthful face flickered off. And I stared, unable to believe what I was seeing.

A skull sat askew on the notched column of her vertebrae, grinning out at me.

It was all I could do not to back away in shock. I almost retched.

Her voice, her soft, feminine voice, continued, "These are fighting suits, Ed. And they go on fighting when the fighter within them is technically dead. Shrapnel punctured an elbow seal in the suit when my Corinthian was attacked, and I died of asphyxiation. I was cerebrally integrated with the suit's AI, and it uploaded my memories into its operating system... and I would have gone on fighting, if the Corinthian had been capable."

"Oh, Christ, Katerina."

"For two days after the attack, when I was rescued and taken back to the colony world, I thought I'd managed somehow to survive. And then a medic broke it to me, and opened my suit, and..."

Her gloved hand lifted, indicated the grinning skull.

"You cannot begin to imagine the shock, Ed, the terror."

I could only shake my head and bite my lips in an effort to stem my tears. I stared at the lopsided skull, and it stared back at me, its orbits huge and shadowy. I wanted to get to my feet and run, but my legs felt weak and bile rose, acid, in my throat.

She said, "I told you that I believe in vitalism, in the soul, because of what had happened to me. I am less than human, now, a mere mechanical set of stored memories and emotions."

She reached up, took her skull in her gloved hands and lifted it from her spine. She lowered the skull to her lap, where it sat gazing blindly out across the abyss.

"The terrible, terrible thing is, Ed, that in my heart... or whatever passes for my heart now... I know that vitalism is a fact. Because now I am *reduced.*" She touched the chest of her suit, and slowly its torso opened, two flanges hinging outwards to reveal a chaotic jackstraw assemblage of bones within.

She leaned forward, over the skull in her lap, and with both hands scooped a hollow in the fine earth before the closest cross. I watched, appalled yet fascinated, as she placed her skull in the grave, then reached into the cavity of her chest and one by one withdrew her bones.

She raised her right arm and her ulna and radius, then her smaller metacarpal bones, rattled into the suit's torso. She did the same with her left arm, and collected the bones and laid them, reverently, in the grave. Next she split a seam in her legs and withdrew the femur and tibia from her right leg, along with the smaller bones, and then the left, and I closed my eyes and wept.

When I looked again she was covering the bones with soil to create a small, compact mound.

She turned her suit to face me, and her disembodied voice said, "Humans, Ed, are far more than mechanistic machines. I know this because of what I am now. Although I have the memories of what happened, I do not have the ability to feel real emotion, to grieve."

I wanted to tell her that she could be upgraded, that AIs had developed so much over the past twenty-five years. I wanted to tell her that she could be *made* human.

"I had a lover, a young man who fought alongside me and survived. While I was in hospital, he came to see me. I had just been told what I had become, and I showed him..." She paused, then went on, "Ed, the look on his face, the horror, before he fled..." She turned her opened helmet to me. "But for all I could intellectually appreciate what he might be feeling, I could not find it within me to empathise. And I felt... *nothing.*"

The silence stretched, and I could find not one word to comfort her.

The sun was setting behind the far horizon, laying down gorgeous laminates of tangerines and pinks. Far below us, shadows turned the abyss into a dark, inky pit.

At last she said, "I came here to bury myself, and I came here also to die."

And she reached into the cavity of her chest and pulled out two slim columns. She held them up before me. "The suit's energy system, Ed. Without them the suit will run down in hours."

"Katerina..."

"It's what I want. Peace at last. I can't feel grief. I can't feel sadness or pain. Or joy, or happiness, or love... All I have is the memories of these emotions. Now is the time I have dreamed of for so long. To die, here."

She took the silver columns, drew back her arm and flung them into the rift. I watched them sail through the air, end over end, catching the dying sunlight as they fell.

She hunched forward, hands upturned in her lap, her open helmet bowed as if in supplication.

She said, softly, "I can feel myself slowing down already, Ed, and it is wonderful."

"Katerina, I'll stay."

"No, please go. And say to Ella . . . tell her that I'm sorry, so sorry."

"Goodbye, Katerina."

She failed to respond, and I reached out and took her gloved hand for one last time, then stood and made my way through the root system of the great tree towards the ship. I stopped, once, and looked back, but the woman who had been Katerina Reverte was now no more than an empty Orion warware suit, head bowed, seated on the edge of an abyss.

I heard the hatch of the ship hiss open, and Karrie stepped out and faced me. Her eyes were hard, questioning, and I knew I could not bring myself to describe what had happened, yet.

"Ed?"

I hurried past her, and stopped before the hatch. Ella had appeared, and was watching me. Her expression was unreadable. She said, "I listened, Ed. I heard what Katerina told you." She reached out her arms towards me. "And I just want to say that I understand your pain."

At the sight of her standing there, so slight and vital and *human*, something broke within me.

I stepped forward, and took her in my arms, and wept.

ZARLA'S WORLD

One of my favourite sub-genres of science fiction is that about life on other worlds, and I particularly enjoy stories about human colonies on far-flung planets. When life on those planets is hard, and survival not guaranteed . . . well, all the better. A previous tale in this collection, "The Children of Winter", was set on a world that suffered brief, blistering summers and long, cold winters. Here's another one, about a brave young woman, an enigmatic alien race, and what happened when their failing colony was recontacted by a mission from Earth.

Zarla's World

ZARLA WAS GATHERING KALTBERRIES ON THE HILLSIDE ABOVE THE ICE plain when the starship appeared.

"Look!" a fellow gatherer called out.

Zarla and the other girls looked up into the night sky. The vessel moved slowly over the ice plain and hovered above the settlement far below. For three nights, the starship's winking lights had appeared high overhead, tracking west, and her uncle had announced that, at last, a starship from Earth had arrived.

As she watched, the ship landed a hundred metres from the settlement with a roar of multiple engines like a deep-winter thunderstorm, turning the ice first to meltwater and then to steam.

Her people emerged from the longhouses, bearing flaming torches, a group of five hundred men and women led by her uncle, Gregor.

She glanced over her shoulder to see how the hek were reacting to the starship's arrival. The dozen tiny aliens lined the ridge above her, protecting the kaltberry gatherers from attack by the ice wolves; though ten times smaller than the wolves, the hek exerted a strange power over the predators that Zarla had never understood.

Her fellow gatherers were shouldering their panniers and making their way down to the settlement and the starship.

Zarla stood and lifted her own pannier. A hek approached her, scurrying down the hillside.

"No," the hek said. "Come, this way."

Cuhm, vis wah... It had taken Zarla months to attune her ear to the sounds the hek made. At first she had been reluctant to believe that the noises meant anything at all, but as the hek had repeated the sounds, and accompanied them by gestures

313

that could not be mistaken, she had understood: the hek were sentient and could speak her language, after a fashion. She had asked them how, time after time, but they never answered her questions.

"But . . ." she began.

"Queen, talk with you."

Kwhe, tah wi yuh . . .

She made sure that none of the other gatherers were looking her way, then hurried up the hillside with the hek and joined the others. The tiny creatures led the way along the slope to the ravines and Zarla followed, singing a poem-song composed by her grandfather soon after arriving on Hadamar seventy-five years ago. "Clans of flesh and blood, in a land of ice and fire, we live through evil winter, and greet the rising sun . . ."

She avoided the first ravine, even though it was the fastest route to the alien's lair, and walked an extra half-kilometre to the next rill in the gently sloping hillside.

One Terran year ago her father and uncle had set off on a hunt up the first ravine, but only her uncle had returned. Stricken, Gregor had recounted how her father had fallen from the cliff at the head of the ravine, attempting to escape from an ice wolf. When a party of hunters had ventured out, later, to retrieve his body, they discovered not a trace of his remains—taken, they said, by the very creatures her father had been hunting.

His death had frozen Zarla's heart, and every time she passed the ravine, the ice in her chest expanded painfully.

The dozen hek flowed across the ice, climbing a defile to their lair. It was almost dawn; the light of the giant sun was turning the sky above the flat horizon to the orange hue of embers. Hadamar was moving ever closer to its primary, and the long winter was drawing to a close. Next came the short, bountiful spring, when edible plants bloomed all across the land, followed by the even shorter, searing summer, when her people rarely ventured out. Autumn was a welcome relief, gone all too quickly—a prelude to the return of the punishing five year winter.

Many people did not survive the depredations of winter; always fewer emerged from the longhouses than had entered five years earlier.

She hurried up the slope, picking her way carefully through the thinning ice and scree. Ahead, one by one, the hek poured themselves into the inky cutting slashed into the hillside. Exhausted from the climb, Zarla swung the pannier from her back and dropped to her knees before the entrance.

She glanced over her shoulder to ensure that no inquisitive gatherer had followed her. She had been very careful over the past year, ever since the hek had contacted her, to keep her secret to herself.

"What does the queen want?" she asked.

The last hek turned and stared up from the mouth of the cave, its huge brown eyes glistening in the starlight.

"Come," it said, and vanished into the darkness.

The giant hek that dwelled in the depths of the lair, and never saw the light of day, was not called the queen, of course—but that was how Zarla had interpreted the aliens' word for the creature.

She bent double, squeezed herself through the opening, and followed the hek down the pitch-black tunnel, dragging the pannier after her and careful not to bang her head on the rock. After a hundred metres the natural corridor opened out, and she could walk upright, though still in absolute darkness.

The tunnel descended for another half-kilometre and dimly, ahead, she made out a faint light. The green glow intensified, and at last she came to the lair of the hek. She had forgotten how vast the chamber was. Far bigger than her people's largest longhouse, its walls were coated with a layer of phosphorescent algae which emitted a dim, verdant light. In hollows that pocked the walls of the chamber, hek snuggled in families of a dozen or more.

In a larger hollow beside the entrance, the queen reposed.

Before his death five years ago, her grandfather had told Zarla of the time when the newly arrived colonists had hunted any creature that moved. They had even hunted the hek, which he called bushbabies—which meant nothing to Zarla—as they resembled the Terran creatures of that name. The only reason they had stopped hunting the hek, he said, and concentrated their attention to ice wolves and the blubbery summer worms, was that the hek had been fast and hard to catch, their meat stringy and lacking in nutrition.

A year ago Zarla had been collecting kaltberries when twenty hek swarmed up to her, rubbed a pungent juice across her face, and dragged her semiconscious across the ice and down into their subterranean lair.

On coming to her senses, she had had her first audience with the hek queen.

She had trembled with fear, expecting the ugly, bloated creature to kill and consume her—perhaps in retaliation for the deaths her people had inflicted on the hek, many years earlier.

But the queen had spoken to Zarla in an approximation of her own language, astounding her; and astounding her again with the content of its speech.

The queen had said that her people were called the hek, and that they had been studying the humans ever since their arrival. Zarla, the queen told her, would work for the hek now: she would deliver kaltberries to the lair. The fruit were a delicacy enjoyed by her people, but were too large for the hek to handle in great numbers. Every second day she would divide the content of her pannier and share her harvest.

And in return, the hek would protect her and her fellow kaltberry gatherers from the ice wolves that roamed the plains and accounted for half a dozen gatherers every spring and autumn.

"You? Protect us?" she had asked, bemused. The hek were tiny, compared to the fearsome wolves.

"We have powers over them that you would not understand," the queen had told her.

Then the queen had dismissed Zarla, but not before warning her that she was to tell no one about her relationship with the hek.

"But why? Why don't you want anyone else to know?"

But the queen had not replied, and Zarla returned to the settlement wanting nothing more than to tell her father what had happened, but at the same time feeling privileged that she had knowledge that was all her own.

And a few days later her father had died while out hunting. An orphan, as her mother had succumbed to illness six years earlier, when Zarla was ten, she moved in with her uncle and aunt and their three teenage boys, all hunters.

Her life, never easy, was even harder then, with long hours of kaltberry gathering in sub-zero temperatures, scant rations with which to fuel her labour, and little affection from her new family. But she had the hek, who now protected the gatherers from the predatory ice wolves. The harvest increased, despite the hek tithe, and she managed even to gain grudging respect from her taciturn uncle.

Now she approached the queen, lifted the pannier, and tipped half of the kaltberries onto the ground before the creature.

The queen reached out a stick-thin arm, grasped a berry in its claws, and lifted the fruit to its mouth. Zarla watched, hiding her disgust. The queen was twenty times the size of the other hek, its bloated body coated with grey fur. It had a dozen thin arms, a tiny head with huge protuberant eyes, and a pointed muzzle full of sharp, ugly teeth which stuck out at angles. At the opposite end, a long pink ovipositor squeezed out a succession of translucent eggs.

The queen gnawed messily on the fruit, spilling juice down its fur.

Zarla had forgotten how repulsive the creature was.

She had forgotten, too, how the queen's words soothed her.

"My little human friend..."

"You wished to see me?"

"Your people have arrived, at last."

Zarla sat down on the rocky ground and stared up at the queen. "They came in a great ship, as my grandfather, my father, and my uncle said they would."

"Do you know why they come?"

"My uncle says they'll bring supplies, food, seed, and machinery—things which will make our lives here much easier."

"Your uncle is wrong."

Zarla blinked.

The queen regarded her with its vast brown eyes. Thin membranous lids closed across them, almost lazily.

"Wrong? I don't understand. Surely—"

"The ship from Earth has come to take you away from here. Your colony is failing, little by little. Every winter, more of you die. The people in the starship will offer you salvation."

Zarla shook her head, dumbfounded. "But how do you know this?"

But the hek rarely answered her questions, and the queen merely said, "Your people are divided. When the people from the starship make their offer, some of you will choose to remain, others to go."

"I don't understand! How do you know this?"

The queen said, "I summoned you here, my little human, to issue you a warning: you must not mention the hek to the crew of the Starship. They must not find out about my people."

"Because you fear they will hunt you?"

"The people of Earth will take us, examine us, and perhaps even exploit us—as they have with other extraterrestrials they have found among the stars."

Zarla stared at the queen, wide-eyed. "They have?"

The queen blinked at her, unspeaking.

She does not know, Zarla thought. That was it. The queen did not know, but she feared what the humans in the ship might do. She feared that they had found, and mistreated, other alien races, basing those fears on the actions of human hunters all those summers ago.

The queen said, "Go now. The sun rises. You will burn on your way home."

She hesitated, staring at the queen. She had asked this question before, and never received an answer, but nevertheless she asked it again. "Why me? Why did you contact me, a year ago, and not one of the others?"

The queen blinked at her. The silence stretched.

Then, to her surprise, the queen replied.

"Because we trust you, my little human."

She waited, but the queen only said, "Go now. And remember, tell no one about my people."

Zarla picked up the half-full pannier, slung it over her shoulder, and made her way to the tunnel leading from the lair.

The sun was up when she emerged.

It was the largest thing she had ever seen, and straddled half the horizon. Her world was passing so close to the primary that she could see spouts of fire writhing up from its circumference, and the heat was searing. The ice turned to slush beneath her feet, and within a minute she was baking inside her animal skins.

She made a wide detour of the starship and hurried across the melting ice to the settlement.

Her people were no longer standing outside with torches; she wondered if they had boarded the starship to speak with the people of Earth.

She moved to the longhouse, where she lived with her uncle and twenty others, and opened the door. The dwelling was empty.

She felt a sudden panic. What if the queen had been right, and the humans of Earth had offered to leave with her people? What if they had boarded the ship and would soon take off, leaving her?

Then she heard voices coming from the communal longhouse, where important meetings were held, and a wave of relief swept through her. She hurried across to the building and hauled open the door.

Over five hundred people were gathered inside, seated around a central area of packed earth; flaming torches lit the gloom, and the stench of summer worm fat and unwashed bodies filled the air. The sound of voices boomed; faces turned to stare at her late arrival. She squeezed through the press of bodies to her aunt and sat beside her.

Her uncle stood tall, staring around at his people. He wore the traditional silver ice-wolf pelt of the clan leader, and carried a great hunting sword at his waist, fashioned from the tailfin of the original colony ship. The weapon hung to his knees, its blade dented from a thousand encounters with the wild beasts of Hadamar.

Gregor held his arms aloft, gesturing for silence.

"They took me into their ship and I spoke briefly with the captain. She and her team will join us in less than an hour."

"They've brought us food, medicines, supplies?" someone called out.

Gregor spread his hands. "She did not say. We'll find out soon enough. They have to run checks, analyses, before they can venture from the ship. She counselled me, just as I counsel you, to be patient."

Beside Zarla, her aunt hissed at her, "Where have you been?"

"Harvesting."

"You took your time."

"I brought back half a pannier."

"Well done, but soon we'll be eating food from Earth. Imagine that!"

Zarla recalled the words of the queen, that the people from Earth had not brought supplies.

Her uncle moved to the far end of the chamber and seated himself in the timber seat he called his throne. Before his death, as leader of her people, Zarla's father had sat upon the seat and made decisions, given orders, and presided over squabbles and differences of opinion. Zarla recalled sitting on his lap, once, when the longhouse had been empty, and recalled how proud she had been of her huge, bearded, powerful father.

Gregor faced the door in impressive silence, awaiting the coming of the people from Earth, and all around Zarla her clansfolk chattered excitedly, shouting about the things the Earthers would bring, their gifts and devices and drugs which would make life on Hadamar so much easier.

The door at the far end of the longhouse opened, admitting a shaft of bloody sunlight, and the hubbub of conversation ceased instantly. Three tall figures ducked into the chamber and walked across to the seated Gregor.

Gasps went up, and Zarla found herself staring at the trio in awe.

They were tall, a good two heads taller than the tallest clansman, and broad. They wore brilliant white suits of a material Zarla had never seen before, and

319

facemasks which were transparent so that she could see their faces inside. As she watched, one by one they removed their helmets, the tall woman shaking out her long black hair. The other two were men, pale-faced and clean-shaven and thus unlike any grown man she had ever seen.

She experienced a strange sensation, then. She knew, somehow, that these people were better than her. No—that wasn't it . . . It was that these people *thought* they were better than the clansfolk garbed in animal skins, their faces smeared with dirt and animal fat. She could tell from the startled gazes of the trio: they think we're savages, she thought; and then, despising herself for the treacherous notion: perhaps we are.

The woman inclined her head to Gregor, and then addressed the gathering. "I'll start by introducing myself and my colleagues. I'm Captain Gina Caspari of the European Space Agency ship *Orpheus*." Her speech differed from that of Zarla's people; clearer, more precise. Zarla wondered if she were speaking especially carefully, as if to children.

"My first officer is Lieutenant David Hathaway, and my head of security Captain Edward El Haq. The *Orpheus* is a recontact ship, and as that title suggests, our mission is to contact the many colonies founded on the frontier worlds of the Human Expansion, to assess the viability of each colony, and to assist where we're able."

Someone called out that the colony needed drugs, but Gregor stared the man down, then climbed to his feet and faced Captain Caspari.

"We would welcome aid, I admit that, Captain. Existence on Hadamar is not easy. My ancestors, on landing over seventy-five years ago, endured various setbacks. We lost the hydroponics lab in a storm soon after touchdown, then suffered a catastrophic computer malfunction. Also, the consignment of machines . . . I think they were called New Vanman machines . . . proved dysfunctional. It didn't help that we lost more than fifty specialists to disease in the first dozen years. Since then, every winter, we lose more people. Conditions are harsh." He smiled across at the captain. "It is a miracle that we have survived as well as we have," he finished, as if beseeching her agreement.

Lieutenant Hathaway spoke. "I'd say it's an understatement that conditions are harsh. It's a miracle that you've managed to survive this long. We've made contact with several colonies that have failed under conditions more favourable than those you've experienced here. A blistering six month summer, with temperatures reaching sixty Celsius, and a five year long winter plummeting to minus twenty . . ." He shook his head. "It speaks volumes of your tenacity, plus your intrepid leadership, that you've managed to eke out any kind of existence from year to year." Zarla saw that her uncle puffed out his chest at this, and looked around at his people.

Lieutenant Hathaway smiled across at Gregor, then went on, "You began with three thousand colonists; you now number a little over five hundred. You have no medicines, and thus succumb to diseases and pathogens which anywhere else in the Expansion would be curable. You have no manufacturing capability, and endure a hunter-gatherer lifestyle comparable to humankind of thirty thousand years ago..."

He fell silent. Zarla looked around at the cowed gathering. She wanted to call out, "Yes, but what about our stories, our poems, our songs? What about our games, and what about our spring treks to the upland lakes to run races and swim? Our life might not be like yours back on Earth, but it is rich, even if it is hard..." But she said nothing; she sat in silence, and could not help but—despite her unvoiced sentiments—share a little in her people's sense of collective inferiority.

"All that," Captain Caspari said, "is preparatory to saying that we think, after orbital analysis of the situation here, and on the empirical evidence on the ground, it would not be in our best interests, nor in yours, to offer you humanitarian aid in the form of technology, medicines, and suchlike."

Gregor stepped forward, barely controlling his anger. "You mean...you're saying that you'll give us nothing? That you'll leave us here to starve like animals?" The expression of rage on his face reminded Zarla of the arguments he'd had with her father over how best to run the colony.

"I am saying nothing of the kind," Captain Caspari said. "Instead of offering aid which would, in our assessment, prove futile in the long run, we offer you the chance to evacuate your colony and return with us to Earth, where you will be retrained, relocated, to set up a new, prosperous existence. Our smartcore nexus has estimated that, if you do elect to remain on Hadamar, your colony will fail within a hundred years, Terran."

Zarla stared at the captain, shocked. How had the hek queen known? How could she possibly have known?

She saw the ambiguous expression on her uncle's face: he welcomed the opportunity of a new, easier life, but at the same time he had doubts about the power he would be relinquishing.

Captain Caspari said, "We will leave you to discuss the situation for a while. There is much you must consider, and much you'll want to ask on our return. It is likely that some of you may wish to remain here, and we will not coerce you into leaving. It will be your choice, and yours alone, and rest assured that we would leave you certain supplies and medicines."

She nodded to Gregor, then gestured to her colleagues, and they made their way from the longhouse.

When the people from Earth had departed, Gregor turned a full circle and stared at the gathered faces. A silence settled over the assembly, as every member of the colony, man, woman and child, contemplated the future.

"You heard what Captain Caspari had to say," Gregor said at last. "Our colony is unsustainable. Due to a series of misfortunes and accidents in the early days, we are now paying the price. The fault is not ours. This is a hostile world. It would be no shame if, when we have questioned the captain about the details of our return, we decided to leave."

He was silent for a few seconds, and then went on, "My brother Gunter and I argued about everything." Zarla, watching her uncle, felt her chest tighten at the sound of her father's name. "We argued about how best to run the colony. We argued about how to hunt, and what to hunt, and even when to hunt. However, we were in agreement about what we should do in the event of a starship coming from Earth and offering to take us away..."

"Gunter agreed with me that we had tried our best to sustain the colony, but that we were failing; and that, should a starship come from Earth and offer to take us home, then we should swallow our pride and admit that events worked against us and take up that offer."

Zarla stared at her uncle. More than anything she wanted to shout, "No! You're lying! My father told me that one day a starship would come and offer aid, but that we would stay here on Hadamar, the only world we know..."

But she remained silent, tears gathering in her eyes.

Gregor's fierce brown eyes took in the staring faces. "When Captain Caspari returns, we will ask her in detail about leaving Hadamar: how long might the journey take, and where exactly we will be relocated, and what conditions await us on Earth or elsewhere. Not," he went on, "that conditions anywhere can be any worse than they are here. But first I would like a show of hands. Those of you who, if we like what we hear from the captain, would choose to leave..."

A murmur spread through the gathering as families conferred. Tentatively at first, and then with more confidence, hands went up in ones and twos, and then in a wave around the longhouse. Zarla kept her hand in her lap, but she gasped as she saw that the great majority, more than four hundred of her people, agreed with Gregor that they should return to Earth.

He nodded. "So be it. You heard what the captain said, that those who wish to remain will not be left bereft. You will have supplies, and medicines, and our heartfelt best wishes. Very well, I suggest we go back to our dwellings and await the captain's return."

In a daze, Zarla followed the crowd outside, into the blistering heat of the sun, and hurried across to her uncle's longhouse.

She was moving to her sleeping cupboard, at the far end of the dwelling, when her uncle and aunt, and three cousins, entered after her.

Gregor said, "You did not raise your hand, Zarla."

She met his gaze. "That's because I wish to stay here."

"As a child, and in my charge, you will do as I say and come with us to Earth."

She stared at him, her anger building. "My life is here, among those who wish to remain, and with the hek."

"You and those ... *animals*," her uncle said with contempt. "We know how much time you spend with them. Time which would be more profitably spent with teachers and craftsmen."

"The hek are good and kind and ..." And she almost did what the queen had proscribed her not to do, then, and told her uncle about their sentience. She stopped herself, her face hot.

"You will gather your possessions," Gregor said, "and your spare clothing, so that when the time arrives you are ready to leave with the rest of us."

She faced her uncle, knowing that she could back down, collect her belongings and sneak out later. But she knew what her father would have done in this situation.

"I am not leaving with you!" she said, racing past her aunt and uncle and hauling open the door.

"As stubborn as her father," she heard Gregor say as she ran out into the sunlight.

In the punishing heat of the red giant, Zarla ran up the ravine to the lair of the hek, tearful that her uncle had pushed her to such defiance, but at the same time proud at the thought that her father would have approved.

She slipped through the opening and hurried blindly through the pitch-black tunnel.

She was met halfway by a hek; she felt its tiny claws on her legs as it climbed into her arms. She hugged the creature, comforted by its warmth.

Minutes later she came to the dimly lit cavern and halted before the queen.

"The starship came," she said.

"Their captain offered you the sanctuary of Earth," the queen replied. "And more than four hundred of your people elected to leave."

"You know, just as you knew why the starship came."

"Your minds, my little human, are open to us."

"You can...?"

"Read your every thought—though many we fail to comprehend."

Zarla shook her head, unsettled by the fact of her mind being open to the hek.

She was about to say that she chose to remain, but the queen said, "You are brave, my little human. You made the right decision, you and the others. We can help you."

She stared at the bloated figure of the queen, with its sharp muzzle and huge eyes. "You can?"

The hek in her arms struggled from her grasp and slipped to the ground, then held out a stick-thin hand and said, "Come with me."

Zarla looked at the queen.

"Go," said the queen.

Puzzled, she followed the hek across the chamber—not towards the exit but deeper into the cave. At the very far end, where the rock tapered so that she had to duck, she made out a narrow opening. The hek slipped through and disappeared. On hands and knees, Zarla followed.

She crept along in pitch darkness, fearing that if the rock above her should drop now she would be crushed, but knowing that her fear was unfounded. She trusted the hek.

She made out dim green light up ahead as the tunnel opened out. She could walk doubled-up, and then upright, and at last she stepped into a vast cavern at least ten times the size of the one she had left behind.

She gasped in amazement. The same glowing green algae covered the walls, and she heard the tinkle of flowing water. Great rafts of flesh-coloured fungi grew like brackets from the rock walls, swollen examples of the edible mushrooms she had found growing in crevices at springtime and autumn.

The hek turned and blinked up at her. "You and your people will live here in the depth of winter, and at the height of summer. There is water, and food. You will survive, and prosper. Life will be hard, but not as hard as it has been for you until now. And there are other, similar caverns, beyond this one, my little human."

She stared at the hek. "You call me what your queen calls me."

The creature said something she did not fully understand, then: "That is because we are one."

Then the hek led her from the great chamber and back through the snaking black tunnel, her head full of what the hek had told her.

She crossed the cavern and stood before the queen. "You will share your world with us? But why?" She gestured vaguely. "Why are you helping us?"

The queen blinked, and then replied, "Because, my little human, you are a fascinating people. We think we have come to understand you and your kind. You are ingenious, and adaptable, and we can learn from you. Also, we think, you might learn from us."

Zarla nodded, taking this in. "And why now? Why not before, in the early years when it was obvious that our colony was failing?"

"Because we did not know you, then. We mistrusted you. You are a race that thinks nothing of killing to survive, but also thinks nothing of killing each other if it might benefit you."

"Killing...each other?" she repeated.

The queen was silent for a time, and then said, "Show her."

The hek that had taken her to the great cavern now reached up and grasped her hand. "Come, this way," it said.

Once again she was taken from the chamber, but upwards this time, back out into the sunlight.

The hek scurried away from the opening and down the ravine. Zarla followed, her shadow fleeing before her. The hek turned west at the end of the ravine, moving away from the human settlement and the starship.

She was about to ask where they were going, but it anticipated her question. The hek turned and said, "To the valley where your father met his end."

Her heart hammered. "But...but that was back that way, in the ravine close to the settlement."

"It was not, my little human."

"But my uncle said..."

"Your uncle lied."

"Lied? But why?"

"This way," said the hek.

She followed the hek up a valley far from the settlement, a cutting so deep that a layer of ice still filled its bottom, where the rays of the sun had not yet reached. The hek scrambled over rocks, then paused and looked down.

Zarla joined it.

She saw something embedded in the ice far below, the shape of a man.

Sobbing, she followed the hek as it picked its way over the rocks and into the crevice.

The ice was thin now, where it covered the body of her father. It cracked with a sudden snap as she stepped upon it and moved cautiously towards the corpse.

Her father lay face down, his arms spread. An attempt had been made to cover the body with kaltberry leaves and plant stems. Zarla knelt, reached out, and broke the pane of ice with her fist.

She wept when she saw the cleft that split the back of her father's head, the clean, straight wound that could only have been made by the blade of a hunting sword.

"Come now," said the hek, "back to our lair. The starship leaves in two days, and your uncle is searching for you. With us, you will be safe."

Hours before the starship was due to leave Hadamar, Zarla emerged from the hek's lair and hurried through the starlit darkness to the ravine where her father's body lay.

Assisted by a dozen hek, she wove a bier from kaltberry canes; it was flimsy, but would suffice to transport the body on the short journey back to the settlement.

She broke the ice around the body and, with the help of the hek, dragged the corpse from the crevice and rolled it onto the bier. The hek stood side by side, watching her like mourners, then one by one they turned and scurried back to their lair.

She dragged the bier like a sledge down the ravine. The ice had melted here, revealing bare rock and making her progress with the heavy bier all the more difficult.

She came to the hillside above the settlement and stared down.

A long line of her people, five abreast, emerged from the communal longhouse and crossed to the starship, lighting the way with flaming torches. A figure stood at the foot of the ship's ramp—not the captain, she saw, but her uncle. As she watched, he addressed his people.

A smaller group of clansfolk, perhaps just twenty, remained before the settlement, watching the majority.

Zarla felt despair in her heart: even more people, no doubt coerced by her uncle's hard words, had elected to leave Hadamar.

She dragged the bier down the hillside towards the starship, sick at the thought of the imminent confrontation. The ship's spotlights burned in the night, far brighter than the torches carried by her people.

At last she approached the rear of the gathering, her uncle's words reaching her over the massed heads. "A new world awaits us, a new life, without sacrifice and hardship."

The crowd parted to allow her through, and fighting back her tears she hauled her father's body through the press, her passage arousing gasps and exclamations.

She came to the foot of the starship's ramp, and she felt both rage and fear as she halted before her uncle.

If he was shocked to see his brother's corpse, and what this meant, he showed no reaction. He stared at Zarla with ill-disguised contempt.

She said in a tremulous voice, "You said my father fell from a cliff."

All around, the clansfolk looked on in silence.

"And so he did," Gregor said.

Controlling her trembling, she knelt and eased her father's body over onto his stomach so that everyone could look upon the gaping wound.

Men and women approached, looked down at the body, and then turned to Gregor.

Zarla said, "You killed him with a single blow of your sword."

"You little fool! He fell from the cliff, just as I said—"

"And this?" she said, pointing to the gaping wound.

"He hit a rock. And what do you expect when a head hits a rock? It splits like a ripe kaltberry."

To Zarla's consternation, a ripple of agreement passed through the crowd, and even one or two jeering laughs.

Controlling her anger, she said, "You're lying! A head would smash open if it hit a rock. This," she went on, indicating the gaping wound, "was caused by a sword, your sword . . ."

Gregor looked away from her and addressed his people. "Enough of this. The girl is deranged. A new life awaits us."

"Wait!" Zarla cried out. "If you claim you didn't inflict my father's injury, then let me see your sword!"

"Go and play with your verminous hek!" he spat.

"What do you fear, if you're telling the truth?" Zarla reached out a hand. "Show me your sword."

He laughed at her, and turned to lead his people into the starship, but he was stopped by a voice from the crowd.

Gregor's second-in-command, a man by the name of Franz, a squat brute whose face displayed the claw-marks of an ice wolf, called out, "Let's get this over with, Gregor. Show her your sword and then we can be away from here."

Gregor stared down at her, defiant, a hand on the hilt of his sword.

A kaltberry gatherer, a friend of Zarla's, said, "What do you fear? Show her your sword!"

Her voice was joined by others, then more and more, until Gregor growled and drew the weapon from his waist-band and flung it at Zarla's feet.

Her heart thumping, she bent and picked it up, then approached her father's body.

The crowd moved closer, staring in silence as she held out the sword and laid its long, curving blade upon her father's cloven skull.

Gasps went up from the watchers. Zarla felt suddenly dizzy. The line of the blade matched the sliced edge of bone; where the metal was misshapen from encounters with the skulls of ice wolves, so her father's skull showed identical indentations.

The crowd pressed forward, impatient, and one by one the clansfolk looked upon the evidence.

Gregor licked his lips, his gaze darting around the gathering. "We argued. We fought. He attacked me—"

"And you struck the killing blow while his back was turned?" Zarla said. "You craved his power, his authority over the clan. You wanted things done your way."

"Power?" he spat. "Over this failing colony?"

She held his gaze. "But his power was all you could dream of, a year ago, before the starship came."

Gregor looked around at the clansfolk, his gaze seeking the reassurance of his fellow hunters. "Who do you believe?" he asked. "The word of your leader, or that of this simple kaltberry gatherer?"

Franz stepped forward, looking from the body to Gregor. "The evidence is plain to see. Your sword struck the killing blow, and while his back was turned, at that."

"But he attacked me," he said pathetically.

Zarla turned to the crowd and called out, "Gregor lied about murdering my father, and he lied also—back in the longhouse—about my father agreeing with him. They did not agree about leaving Hadamar if a starship should arrive. My father was braver than that. He was not a coward, to flee into the arms of Earth at the first opportunity. He told me, many a time, that our destiny was here, on Hadamar..."

A voice called from the crowd, "He did, at that. I recall him saying that our destiny was here."

"That's true," Franz said. "What the girl says is true."

A murmur of agreement went up from the gathering, provoking a surge of hope in Zarla's heart. She leapt up onto the lip of the ramp and faced her people. She raised her hand, realising only then that she was still clutching Gregor's sword.

"How can you follow this man, this liar, from a world we know, to a world we have only ever heard stories about? How can you trust a man who has lied not once, but twice, to lead you into an unknown future? We should remain, and prove to ourselves that not only can we survive, but that we can prosper too..."

"Words are all very well," someone called out, "but life is hard on Hadamar."

She felt a sudden surge of hope. "Life is hard, yes, but it will get easier." She paused, took a breath, and then went on, "For I have discovered something, far below the ice planes. Where do you think I have been, when my uncle accused me of playing with the verminous hek? I have been exploring, and I have discovered vast underground caverns with flowing water and fungi a hundred times the size of those we harvest in spring." She stared out at the staring faces, her heart surging. "And those of you who are brave enough to remain here, with me, I will lead to a new, easier life in these miraculous caverns."

She made a sudden decision and, without a backward glance at her uncle, jumped from the ramp and strode across the rocky plain towards the settlement. She halted outside the communal longhouse, her heart pounding. She counted to thirty, unable to bring herself to turn around and look upon her people.

Then, fearing what she might see, she did turn.

Her heart leapt. First a couple of clansfolk moved away from the starship towards the settlement, and then others, in family groups of five or six, and then more and more, walking away from the ship and joining Zarla.

She stared through her tears as a hundred clansfolk massed before the settlement, and then two hundred. Within minutes, the balance had been tipped, and three hundred, then four hundred, had elected to remain on Hadamar.

Soon, only a ragged band of twenty hunters loyal to their disgraced leader stood before the ramp, and she watched as Gregor turned and led the way into the ship.

An old woman approached her.

"Come, Zarla, and we will build a cairn," the woman said.

They dragged the bier across to the burial ground, gathered a hundred rounded stones, and worked steadily to inter her father. An hour later the job was almost done, but for the placement of a final stone atop the cairn.

"Look," the woman said, pointing.

Zarla turned as the starship powered up and rose slowly. As she watched, the ship diminished into the night, growing smaller and smaller, until its winking lights were just another constellation in the firmament high above.

The woman left Zarla and moved back to the longhouse.

She placed the final stone on top of the cairn, then looked up at the ridge high above the settlement. A line of hek, hundreds of the tiny aliens, had gathered and were staring down at her.

Zarla lifted an arm into the air, and waved.

Now she would call a gathering of the clansfolk, and tell them all about the hek, and in time, when summer came and the sun swelled and burned everything on the surface of the world, she would lead the way underground to the sanctuary of the caverns.

Zarla left her father's cairn and, under the watchful gaze of the aliens, made her way across the rocky plain to the settlement and her people.

Acknowledgements

"The Time-Lapsed Man" first appeared in *Interzone 24*, 1988.

"The Disciples of Apollo" first appeared in *Other Edens III*, 1989, edited by Christopher Evans and Robert Holdstock.

"The Death of Cassandra Quebec" first appeared in *Zenith II*, 1990, edited by David S. Garnett.

"Dark Calvary" first appeared in *SF Age*, 1999.

"Hunting the Slarque" first appeared in *Interzone 141*, 1999.

"Steps Along the Way" first appeared in *Moon Shots*, 1999, edited by Peter Crowther.

"The Miracle at Kallithéa" first appeared in *Spectrum SF 3*, 2000.

"The Children of Winter" first appeared in *Interzone 163*, 2001.

"The Kéthani Inheritance" first appeared in *Spectrum SF 7*, 2001.

"Ulla, Ulla" first appeared in *The Mammoth Book of Science Fiction*, 2002, edited by Mike Ashley.

"Thursday's Child" first appeared in *Spectrum 9*, 2002.

"Life Beyond..." first appeared in *Postscripts 4*, 2005.

"Salvage Rites" first appeared in *We Think, Therefore We Are*, 2009, edited by Peter Crowther.

"Laying the Ghost" first appeared in *Clarkesworld 49*, 2010, edited by Neil Clarke.

"Zarla's World" is original to this collection.